Grabbed my attention on the first page and kept me mesmerized to the end

"The book was mystical story-telling from Page One through the Epilogue. Between 1849 and 1861, I time- traveled from Baltimore, through New Orleans, San Francisco, and a quick moment in Paris. Through the exquisite detail, I experienced the sounds, sights, smells, tastes, and the feel of each scene. I knew how Brianna and Edward looked, and felt, their strengths and weaknesses. It was an enthralling story from beginning to end. Looking forward to Gini Grossenbacher's next book."

—Loy Holder, Author of *Dancing Up the Ladder*

Finely-crafted

"Such a fascinating story, which is made even more intriguing by the fact that the characters are loosely based on a true historical couple who lived in the 1800s. I loved the settings of New Orleans filled with French, Creole and Southern culture with its hints of voodoo, plus bawdy San Francisco with its saloons, gambling and sporting parlors. It was evident the author did a considerable amount of research to make these settings alive and vital. The writing is finely crafted and the descriptions are worth slowing down to savor. This book kept me turning pages, wondering how the main character, Brianna, and her lover, Edward Spina, would resolve their ongoing situations. The ending is so powerful, it gave me goose bumps."

—Carolyn Radmanovich, Author of *The Shape-Shifter's Wife*

REVIEWS

Madam in Silk

Portrait of Resilience and Fortitude

My knowledge of mid 19th century San Francisco and the gold rush, etc. is not vast. *Madam In Silk* is more than a story-it's an education. I highly respect all of the research that the author obviously poured into this book. It's well done without being too heavy. The heroine, Ah Toy, and her lifelong servant, Chen, arrive in San Francisco, after a tragic sea voyage, destitute and a stranger in a strange land, Ah Toy has no wish to return home. How, then, to survive in this bustling unforgiving landscape? She does what women have done since time immemorial-uses her body. In her Lookee Shop, men may look but not touch. Her exotic beauty is a desirable commodity, and business is good. Ah Toy and Chen face many challenges together. Failure was not an option. This story is a portrait of the resilience and fortitude necessary for survival. Determined to make a life for herself, Ah Toy exhibits intelligence, persistent and a grasp of human nature. She was an extraordinary woman who overcame so much and never gave up when others would have. Although scandouls, I found her inspiring. Chen' s devotion to Ah Toy was quite admirable as well. Compelling, unique and informative, this story is, in some ways, a testament to the quite unshakable strength of a woman.

—Jypsy Lynn, Historical Fiction Virtual Tours

PRAISE FOR

Gini Grossenbacher

This year's exciting addition to historical fiction

"Readers were effusive in their praise of Gini Grossenbacher's dynamic debut novel *Madam of My Heart,* based on the life of the infamous brothel owner Belle Cora. This, the prequel to her American Madams Series, is inspired by the life of a beautiful young Chinese woman of high birth brought to California against her will. She was able—and willing—to do whatever it took to find security, love and fortune in Gold Rush San Francisco. *Madam in Silk* is this year's exciting addition to historical fiction."

—Cheryl Anne Stapp, Author of *Disaster & Triumph: Sacramento Women, Gold Rush Through the Civil War*

Madam of My Heart: For everyone who likes well-deployed language and intense stories

"A debut historical novel that chronicles the struggles, loves, and joys of an exceptional madam in 19th-century America. Grossenbacher's book, the first in a planned series, dramatizes the early life and busy career of a woman named Brianna Baird. Raised in Baltimore in the decades before the Civil War, Brianna dreams of one day growing up to own a seamstress shop and marry a sweet man of virtue. But her plans unravel after she meets young Spenser Brown, a sweet-talking violinist who leaves her pregnant and betrays the promises he made. Alone and knowing little of the world, she travels to New Orleans and finds work at the notorious parlor house of Madam DeSalle. There, she earns her keep first as a seamstress and later as the exclusive courtesan of gambler Edward Spina.

"Grossenbacher's prose is both graceful and inventive. She absorbingly limns the various cities Brianna inhabits, from New Orleans and its 'web of Creole cottages, chaotic marketplaces, and secretive balconies, simmering outside her window,' to the rowdy atmosphere of frontier-era San Francisco. The occasional marvelous metaphor will surprise readers, as when 'the truth hit Brianna like a badly aimed bowling pin.'

"This isn't just a novel for lovers of history's more prurient corners; it's for everyone who likes well-deployed language and intense stories. A seamier side of American history, engagingly told through one woman's unexpected adventures."

—Kirkus Reviews, A "Recommended" Book

Brilliantly written novel of love and loss

"Every now and then you come across a new author who was born to write historical romantic fiction. Her talents include exquisite prose, exceptional historical research, and marvelous storytelling. I was immediately pulled into Brianna Baird's character, her father's alcoholic abuse and her life in Baltimore, Maryland in 1849, and subsequently in New Orleans in early 1850. If you ever wondered what life was like in those historical periods, Gini details every interaction and observation so acutely that the reader lives and breathes the sights, aromas and sounds as if one were peering through a window glass watching the story unfold. Often, I read paragraphs and then went back and re-read them because they were poignant and touching."

—Sherry Joyce, Author of *Dangerous Duplicity* and *The Dordogne Deception*

Well-Researched View

Another beautiful work of historical fiction from author Gini Grossenbacher. The second in her series based on the lives of actual madams, Madam in Silk is a well-researched view of Gold Rush San Francisco and the tough, hard-scrabble life for Chinese immigrants, particularly young women.

—Dorothy Rice, Author, *Gray is the New Black*

A Captivating Read

A fascinating tapestry of real historical events, people, and settings woven and made richer with the author's imagination. Her attention to detail brings alive a time long past in a city many of us love still today. The sights, the smells, and the sounds. A creaking harness on the horse, the smell of whiskey and cigars on the men, the vivid detail of the Chinese furnishings. From start to finish, a captivating read.

—Cherie O'Boyle, Author, *On Scent*

Readers Will Cheer for Ah Toy

Readers of historical fiction will revel in this compelling story about a celestial beauty from China who forges her own path in the rowdy world of uncivilized miners during the Gold Rush era of the mid-1800's. Madam in Silk is based on the historic character of Ah Toy, a notorious foot-bound beauty who desires a life of her own beyond the oppression of her native China. Ah Toy must navigate the brutal conditions of an emerging frontier town and also find the love of her life who is always just beyond her reach. The story illuminates rich details that illuminate China's dehumanizing constraints against women and the gutsy strategies Ah Toy used to secure her place in a new world. Grossenbacher deftly handles the topic of the 1850's sex trade with accuracy and a compassion that takes readers into the human side of this otherwise tawdry enterprise. An interesting read from start to finish, readers will cheer for Ah Toy as she perseveres in her pursuit of freedom and love.

—Lisa D, Amazon Review

ALSO BY

Gini Grossenbacher

Madam in Silk

Madam of My Heart

Madam in Lace

GINI GROSSENBACHER

JGKS Press
the past comes to life

JGKS
Press
the past comes to life

WWW.JKGS PRESS.COM

Cover design by Karen Phillips at Phillips Covers
Book design by Maureen Cutajar at Go Published

Publisher's Cataloging-in-Publication Data
provided by Five Rainbows Cataloging Services

Names: Grossenbacher, Gini, author.
Title: Madam in lace / Gini Grossenbacher.
Description: Elk Grove, CA : JGKS Press, 2021. | Series: American madams, vol. 2. | Includes bibliographical references.
Identifiers: LCCN 2021920241 (print) | ISBN 978-1-7358427-6-9 (paperback) | ISBN 978-1-7358427-6-9 (ebook) | ISBN 978-1-7358427-7-6 (audiobook)
Subjects: LCSH: Women--Fiction. | Napoleon III, Emperor of the French, 1808-1873--Fiction. | France--Fiction. | Love--Fiction. | Revolutionaries--Fiction. | Historical fiction. | BISAC: FICTION / Historical. | GSAFD: Historical fiction.
Classification: LCC PS3607.R66 M31 2021 (print) | LCC PS3607.R66 (ebook) | DDC 813/.6--dc23.

To Karl,
whose help and encouragement keep me writing each day.

To Elizabeth,
whose enthusiasm for life inspires my stories and
fuels the women in my books.

In Memoriam
To my journalist mother, Frances Marie Kahler,
my first writing teacher.
(1908-1993)

One

With Her Lace Gloves

Montmartre
Outskirts of Paris, France
October 1857

An autumn glow covered central Paris, and vineyards bloomed purple and red on the steep hillsides of the Montmartre butte. As the coach lurched up the hill, the horses struggling against the rocky soil, Celeste found her quaint remembrance of the village was an illusion. Chaotic streets overlooked Paris; the ensemble formed a tattered beret that clung to a bald man's head.

Celeste counted on her gloved fingers—at least six years since she was here. She gripped the side of the jostling hackney carriage. After Papa died, her mother Maman, whom people called Madeleine Bazin, battled constant sadness. When the gendarmerie put Maman in handcuffs, she had called out, "Do as Tante Faucon tells you. Go to America. Do not stay here; you will starve to death." Following her mother's arrest, Tante Faucon arranged her ship's passage to New Orleans. She sent her to cousin Madame De Salle, the brothel-keeper of a fine parlor house on Chartres Street.

Tante Faucon's claws had gripped her arm, set a ship's boarding pass into her hand, and thrust her into the carriage at Place du Tertre. She recalled the twisted smile the aunt gave her as she waved her on to America. The old aunt lived somewhere in the village, but Celeste had never heard from her. She never bothered to learn her address or write from San Francisco.

The horses' uneven *clip-clop* slowed, and a horseman flashed by, wearing a gold-braided red jacket. Out of nowhere, a hurdy-gurdy man dipped past her carriage. He lifted his monkey, then hooted in the window. The monkey nearly grabbed her nose with its tiny paws. She drew back, shivered, then shook her head. Luckily, her carriage hurtled away, and the pair vanished around a corner.

She sat back against the seat, her heartbeat slowing. Such a funny apparition—but no wonder. Paris under Emperor Louis-Napoléon Bonaparte III was home to strange creatures and bizarre events. She untied the strings of her reticule and eased out a brown and beige daguerreotype of her mother. The once-stiff printing paper had softened, its edges folded over because Celeste tucked it under her pillow every night.

Once in New Orleans, she and Brianna had looked at the picture. Brianna noted Celeste's high cheekbones and heart-shaped lips in her mother's face. She said, "I haven't ever seen a coat designed that way," referring to Maman's favorite wool coat with a black braid, the style *à la mode* in Paris.

The white Percheron horses slowed, churning over the bumpy, semi-cobbled road. Her thoughts ground along with their hoofbeats.

After she slid Maman's picture back into her reticule, she tried to picture the dilapidated condition of the brothel. Maman's place was called

Maison de L'Étoile, the House of the Star. Full of people—women with painted lips, men with wanton eyes. The question burned as to why Maman had sent her so far away. Her life could not progress if she never knew whether she was alive or dead. She hung suspended in the limbo of uncertainty, a winding sheet threaded through her dreams and waking hours. Other people had a family; other people gathered at holidays and festivities looking into faces that resembled theirs. Someone had locked her out; that reliable source of warmth and acceptance lay forever beyond her reach.

After Maman's arrest, Celeste suspected the woman could not bear to see her daughter become a prostitute in her own house. So Maman and Tante Faucon had decided. Better send Celeste—only fourteen—to another madam far away who would wipe her tears and scold her when she offended before she had learned to please men for money. And that was before she joined Brianna and Edward on their grand journey to San Francisco.

Then she had been poor; now she was wealthy; the California Gold Rush had set her up for life. At times men made offers of love and marriage. Poor men, wealthy men. Men who wanted her; men who deceived her. At times she yearned for the kind of true love that Brianna and Edward had, their hands touching, their glances deep and full.

Yet men's offers could not sway her from the niggling promise she made to herself—nothing would make her happy until she found Maman and their old house on Rue de L'Abbaye. *Nothing.* A bee buzzed through the carriage window, and she swept it away from her ear, then watched the twisty lanes and high walls transform the landscape into a village.

She fingered the francs in her pocket. When a California prospector saw gold among the river rock in his cradle, he called it "a flash in the pan." Such prospectors frequented her at Brianna and Edward's fancy parlor house in San Francisco. She dropped her petticoats; they dropped their gold dust. She had her treasury, but she wanted the love and companionship of her mother, secreted somewhere behind these poor and crumbling structures they called Montmartre, the Hill of Martyrs.

Tante Faucon told her the martyr story when she was a child. A 9th-century legend said enemies beheaded Saint Denis on that hill, and afterward, he walked across Paris, holding his decapitated head, to found a Benedictine Abbey. When she asked Maman how poor Denis could walk without his head, her mother scolded. "A miracle," she said.

Maman believed in miracles. Despite her lowly life, she was faithful to God. Celeste remembered that day at the window, the day of her arrest—the tilt of Maman's head, the clarity of her blue eyes. The sunbeams highlighting the angles of her cheeks. A belief in the creator. A rare gift. Celeste had not thought of miracles since she was a little girl.

But she was no longer young, and time rushed past. If only she could catch the seconds and hold them in her hands; instead, they sprinkled through her fingers like powdered sugar on a beignet. Brianna and Edward said she must return to San Francisco early next year to tend to the parlor house they left after Edward escaped the vigilante hanging.

Even though she had ample funds, food, and shelter, Celeste burned with resolve. Brianna and Edward said she should go to the police—maybe they had a record of her mother's imprisonment. She balked—better to start on foot in Montmartre. Police were worse than the criminals because they would lie, demand information payment, lead her astray.

Better to start in Montmartre, where she had last seen Maman. She bit her lower lip. She *would* find her mother and bring her back to America. Tante Faucon, wherever she might be, would help her. She swallowed hard. Only then would she feel whole again. Only then would she be free to love another.

Two

WINDMILLS

The horses' reins jingled, startling chickens who fled to the roadside. A dog lying next to a doorstep raised his head in dreamy indolence. A woman in wooden shoes appeared at an ivy-covered doorway, and Celeste gazed with interest at the naked baby resting on the mother's hip. The coach groaned past ochre buildings, their plaster shredding, their sloping rooftops faltering. A yeasty aroma met her nose; someone was baking bread behind those windows.

In the distance, the giant windmill's sails rotated—at least that had not changed. There had been many more windmills during Celeste's childhood—now she could count maybe ten to twelve. The windmills, called *moulins à vent,* added grace notes to Montmartre's landscape. Their twirling paddles fixed against the blue sky streaked with scudding white clouds.

The coach bumped around corners, brushing past cafés on the winding street until it reached a tree-filled square called Place de L'Abbaye, a jumble of clothing shops, bakeries, and wine bars. The noisy midday marketplace triangulated on ancient cobblestones surrounding a fountain dribbling spring water. She knew that fountain; she sampled its fresh water as a child.

The so-called *brocantes* or junk vendors displayed every conceivable item for sale: she used to stroll past nude statues of embracing men and women, porcelain plates with garish red geraniums, and leather-bound books, their pages yellow and torn. The scent of old leather permeated the air.

Sunlight filtered through the plane trees. The square's bazaar looked so much smaller than in her memory; then, she loved sneaking from one food table to another, sometimes pinching an apple or stalk of celery to help Maman fill out their meager dinner plates.

After skirting the crowd, steering the horses around the corner onto Rue de L'Abbaye, the driver eased into the *porte-cochère* of the post office, jumped down, and tended his animals. Since no footman came, she unlatched the door, slid down, and set her feet firmly onto the cobblestones. As in New Orleans, she must make her way by herself.

After dragging down her valise from inside the coach, she dropped it at her feet, missing her toes. The driver peered through dusty eyebrows. "Ten francs." His weather-beaten face spoke of Parisian life, sometimes desperate, other times joyful, depending on the emperor's whims.

She drew open her reticule's drawstrings and fingered her coins. She passed ten francs to the driver. "Take them."

He caressed the money glinting in his palm, then twisted his lip. *No gratuity.*

And rightly so. After all, no footman came to help her; no kindly gentleman prevented her from slipping in the muddy street.

The driver picked at an eyebrow. *Pfft!* was all he could say. The coach rolled away.

Now she must decide what to do. Her insides jangled. She gazed at the façade of the post office, then at the customers. Stiff-looking men clutching envelopes skipped up the stairs, and teary-eyed, empty-handed women shuffled out of the building. No news. Never a good sign. Their husbands probably served in Napoléon's army in the Chinese Opium War. Such women had difficulty making ends meet; husbands forgot to send home their combat pay.

Two soldiers with bayonets guarded the *entrée* to the post office, and they stared as she crept past them with her luggage. She had a sudden instinct to turn her face away. The guards would see her, a stranger in this neighborhood; no need to provoke their interest. When her stomach growled, she headed past them toward Place de L'Abbaye. Maybe she could find something to eat.

A coal fire burned at a central marketplace stand. Through bursts of smoke, Celeste made out two bearded men in long aprons tending roast meats. A line of men and women in hats and jackets formed in front. Before leaving the Paris house that morning, Brianna insisted Celeste have a croissant with jam, but she had only nibbled it. Suppressing her hunger pangs, she joined the queue, then looked around.

Men in top hats stood chatting; young women strolled arm-in-arm around the market, clutching baskets and bags. A village atmosphere relaxed the place. Away from the bustle of Paris, from Brianna's house in Le Marais.

In front of her, a little boy in a sailor's top and short pants held his mother's fingers. "I love roast meats. Which shall I have, Maman?" The mother scrutinized the chalkboard, which displayed the simple items—*Porc, Poulet, Boeuf*—pork, chicken, beef.

"Well, small Jacques. We have only a few *sous* today, so we will share the chicken *en brochette*. The beef is way too expensive." She reached down and straightened the collar of his shirt with her white lace gloves.

"And after that, may we have a sweet?" He pointed toward the corner of the square. A jolly woman tended rows of hard candies and chocolates; she adorned her stand with pink satin ribbons.

The mother nodded; a blue feather waved on her bonnet. "Of course, but only this once. We cannot do this every time we come to market."

He tugged at her sleeve. "But *Grand-mère* always gets a sweet." He bent down and pulled up the white sock that gathered around his ankle.

"Grand-mère spoils you." She ruffled strands of his blond hair.

Celeste stepped closer, her French coming quickly. "*Pardonnez-moi,* but I could not help overhear."

The mother flushed, pulling her son closer. "Do I know you, mademoiselle?"

"I grew up in Paris and Montmartre, and I have returned from California. I see you are blessed to have a lovely child."

"California?" The mother drew back, her son clinging to her side. Celeste thought they saw her as an exotic being from another world by the way she said the name. Indeed, small Jacques' eyes seemed to bore into her own. If she did not reassure them, they might turn away.

Celeste gazed into the boy's hazel eyes. "I was a child once here in this very marketplace, holding my mother's hand, asking for meats on skewers, cooked over charcoal. Or, in winter, the roasted chestnuts. And the fish . . . always the fish." A prickly tear stung her eye, and she brushed it away.

The mother loosened her grip. "Do you live now in Montmartre? I see your suitcases, so are you moving here?" Her voice warmed, though her eyes narrowed.

"No, I am here to find my mother. I have not seen her in five years. At times I wonder if she is still alive, you see, and well—." She bit her lower lip, then drew Maman's picture from her reticule. "You do not know her by chance?"

Nancy's voice softened. "Lovely. But no, I have not seen her. You see, we recently came here from Normandy, so we are getting used to the crowds. My husband works at the gypsum quarry."

Celeste tucked the Daguerre into her sleeve. Maybe she would show it to other residents.

Nancy cast a glance at a white-haired woman sitting on a stone bench at the edge of the square. Celeste followed her gaze. The lady wore mourning black, and a small prayer book rested open on her lap. She must be their relation.

Since the line moved a few steps toward the concession, Celeste had no time to consider. Odors of sweat and fresh basil wafted around her. The red satin tablecloth on a chocolate vendor's table caught her eye. "I would like to buy your little boy his treat today–perhaps a bit of *chocolat*?"

"Perhaps." Nancy looked at her little boy.

He hopped up and down. "Please, Maman?" His loose sock traveled back down his ankle. "Can we buy one for Grand-mère?" He looked over at the white-haired woman on the bench who waved.

Celeste said, "Most happy to buy an extra piece for her."

Nancy sighed. "Very well, Jacques." She eyed Celeste. "*Très gentille.* So kind." A wariness underlined her words.

Celeste paused. "But first, I must know your names. *You* are Jacques." The little boy's eyes widened. His mother slid his forelock away from his eye.

"And you?" Celeste asked.

"*Je m'appelle Nancy.*" Her bonnet feather trembled.

"*Plaisir,*" she nodded. "I am called Celeste."

A friendly silence fell between them. Celeste sniffed, inhaling the aromatic blends. Garlic. Rosemary. Smoking charcoal. Burning fat. The smells carried her earliest sensations of Faubourg Saint Germain and her mother in those joyful days before Papa died. Soon after, she and Maman fled their Paris house for Montmartre to escape his creditors, men who raided the home, taking their possessions, even her mother's inherited ormolu clock.

While Nancy and little Jacques spoke their orders to the food vendor, Celeste observed other customers. A young, slouch-capped man bearing a guarded expression shoved his hands in his pockets. He avoided her eyes. Wary. She had seen such men, gamblers, or miners like him in San Francisco. Such a man wore secrets next to his heart.

She cast him a half-smile. The cut of his sideburns was longer than the French style; he might be Spanish. She took in his dress. By his jacket's body-hugging cut, he was most likely Italian.

His face brightened. Though he was roughly dressed, his smooth facial contours piqued Celeste's interest, and she could not resist another sideways look. If only she could decipher his unreadable features. Maybe sensing the awkward silence, he peered at her intently, revealing deep chestnut eyes surrounded by feathery lashes.

Something pounded in her chest. She lost her bearings for a moment—or maybe hunger made her weak. The stranger stepped away and surveyed the corner hat sellers. Probably better. Her pulse resumed its regular beats, so she adjusted her cloak and straightened the baggage next to her. Those Italians. *Pfft.* No time for a male encounter.

Having received their orders of brochettes in butcher paper wrappings, Nancy and small Jacques lingered booth side, steam rising from their handheld skewers. Nancy called to Celeste, "We will be over there with my *belle-mère*, my mother-in-law." She pointed to the stone bench and the white-haired woman.

Someone rapped on wood. Grimy hands smoothed a greasy apron. "Mademoiselle, your order?" Celeste shook her head—she had become so sleepy she almost missed her turn.

The chef's *toque* or white hat perched off-center on his furry head. "*Dépêchez-vous!*" He pointed behind her. Customers glared, shifting their feet.

Celeste shouted. "Chicken with onions, *s'il vous plaît*." She stood on tiptoe, gazing at him through whiffs of steam. Drops of sweat bubbled on his forehead. He passed the skewers to her, along with the standard paper wrapping.

She dropped several coins on the counter; they vanished into his chubby hands. Maybe her fatigue from the day's journey—surely not that Italian man—caused her distraction. No, not the man with the feathery eyelashes. Her stomach rumbled.

After obtaining the chocolates and meats, Celeste joined Nancy, small Jacques, and the white-haired woman on the stone bench. Somehow the family's ease with one another and their gentle patter eased Celeste's nerves, and she ate, dabbing her mouth with her handkerchief to catch the grease dribbling down her chin.

Earthly delights, Maman had called these brochettes. Celeste had missed them, though New Orleans cuisine proved a distraction from the mix of spices in French food. Shrimp Remoulade. Gator Sausage. Seafood Gumbo.

But she had longed for the subtle power of French cuisine, the ability to smoothly blend spices and olive oil to give her palate tranquility and balance. She gave a private laugh. No wonder she loved it. This food made up her childhood memories.

While savoring the dark chocolates alongside Nancy and her son, Celeste could not resist. "Does Grand-mère live in Montmartre?"

As she spoke, Grand-mère fetched a lacy white handkerchief from her reticule, licked the edge, and applied it to a spot of chocolate on Jacques' cheek. He tolerated her, then pulled away and hopped from one leg to another.

Nancy swallowed. "Yes, but she is my *belle-mère*, mother-in-law. I lost my mother to a painful affliction last year."

"At least I have one grand-mère left," Jacques nibbled his candy.

"You are fortunate, Jacques. My grand-mères are in heaven. I have only one mother, and I must find her whereabouts here in the village, and if I can't locate her, I need to find my Tante Faucon. I can't move on with my life until I find Maman. She is the reason for my journey."

Small Jacques frowned. "I don't want to go yet. I like you, Celeste."

She warmed. Children could be so direct, so intuitive when it came to expressing themselves. Adults lacked that quality.

Nancy faced him. "You like our new friend but remember Grand-mère is taking us shopping. Your short pants are getting tight, and it is time you started wearing long pants to church."

Maybe their grand-mère would know her mother, or at least how to find her house along Rue de L'Abbaye. Celeste leaned over and addressed the older woman. "Madame, *pardonnez-moi.*" She spoke in a low tone, not wishing to startle her.

"What do you desire, mademoiselle?" A mosaic of wrinkles creased her upturned face.

"I am searching for my mother, whom I have not seen in many years. The last I knew, she lived in Montmartre, but I have long since forgotten my way around here."

"How old were you when you last saw her?"

"Fourteen."

"So . . . five years ago or maybe six? That is a long time at your age. Everyone needs their mother, but why search for her now?"

"Every year that passes, my longing for her grows worse until I seem unable to go on. I must find out what's happened to her. She is a part of me, and the mystery of what happened—where she is—well, it has begun to torture me. She said she would join me in New Orleans, but she never came or wrote back. Maman said she would always protect me, but then, the gendarmes arrested her. In New Orleans, I never heard more."

"You have experienced a loss, *ma chérie*, like my grief after my daughter's death. But I see a difference. I know where my daughter lies in the graveyard at Père Lachaise Cemetery in Paris. I can go there, lay flowers at her resting place, talk to her. You, on the other hand, suffer from invisible grief since you do not know what happened, whether she lives or dies."

"Some people look at me like I'm crazy since all I do is talk about finding her. They do not understand my sadness."

"How unfortunate, *ma chérie.* A girl needs her mother. Alas, my daughter died in a typhoid epidemic last year. I would also say that a mother needs her child. She must be missing you." She paused, her watery eyes softening. "Perhaps I could help in some way."

Celeste's gaze flickered over Nancy and small Jacques, who nibbled the edges of their chocolate, their grins reflecting their enjoyment. She returned her gaze to the grand-mère and spent a moment lost in the dark circles pooling under the woman's eyes. Maybe she could trust her.

She drew her mother's Daguerre from her sleeve and passed it to the older woman. "Her name is Madeleine Bazin. I went to *L'Amérique*, and after I left, I had no news. She was always reliable. Fierce. Always involved in political activities, and so I am sure the worst has happened."

"You say politics?" The grand-mère tucked the remains of a chocolate packet into her reticule. "Indeed, many citizens dread the future in France these days." She lowered her voice. "We are under the thumb of an emperor whose selfish whims cost our people dearly." A shadow crossed her face. "Of course, *ma chérie*, have you considered—?"

Nancy, appearing to sense a dark turn in the conversation, put an arm around small Jacques' shoulders and pulled him toward her.

Celeste drew back, heat traveling in ribbons up her spine. "What? I am not sure what I might have considered, madame."

The web of lines deepened on the grand-mère's cheeks. "There is always the possibility that your mother fell ill in prison or went to God. Many political prisoners are never heard from again."

Although the grand-mère seemed sympathetic, Celeste dug her front teeth into her lower lip. She wondered why the woman brought up such dark possibilities. But then, she trusted this stranger; she had no other choice. Shaking it off, she pressed on. "I am thankful for your help, madame. Even if something did happen to her, I must find the truth."

"Grand-mère," small Jacques said, "I think you are scaring our new friend."

The woman glanced over at Jacques, then Celeste. "Please do not let my words upset you. You look so like my daughter—your white-blond hair, sparkling blue eyes, youthful vigor." Her lower lip trembled. "I would do anything to have her back."

"I feel the same about my mother because I am so desperate. By the way, I am Celeste. Your name?"

"Geneviève. What is the address you are looking for? Though I come to this square for market day, I do not go alone down Rue de L'Abbaye. Some questionable houses there."

Celeste said, "98 Rue de L'Abbaye, the address from 1851 where we lived before she sent me away."

Geneviève leaned over to Nancy. "I want to help this young woman. I know the address she seeks. The very least I can do is take her there."

Nancy reddened. "Sure? Dangerous to go wandering down those lanes by yourself."

Geneviève turned and patted small Jacques' hand, then faced her daughter-in-law. "What if you were seeking my whereabouts? Wouldn't you want someone like me to guide you there? Besides, I have my cane. I can whack anyone who comes near." She grinned.

Nancy said, "Well yes, but—"

Small Jacques leaned on his mother's knee. "I think Grand-mère should help our new friend."

Nancy's jaw slackened. "Very well. But you must meet us at our house in one hour. Remember we are going shopping. I need to buy short pants for Jacques. He is growing out of everything in his closet."

Geneviève rose, leaned down, and kissed Nancy and Jacques on both cheeks.

Nancy picked up their lunch trash and dropped it in a nearby bin.

The grand-mère turned to Celeste. "*Très bien, suivez-moi.*" Geneviève led her through the busy square and out into the crowded street.

Three

NUMBER 98

On either side, two-story pale-gray buildings dominated the street: some worn, some tidy, some with red geranium flowerboxes, and some with boarded-up windows. In certain spots, the cobblestones gave way to scrabbled dirt, and Celeste picked her way along the path behind Geneviève, who kept up a steady pace with her cane. Shoppers with cloth bags elbowed her—men sporting grubby jackets, women swishing broad skirts, the crowd heading to the brocantes at Place de L'Abbaye. She tried to keep up with Geneviève's lithe steps, but the going was brutal against the swarm.

Appearing to sense Celeste's frustration, Geneviève slowed her steps, drew back, then matched her pace. "I apologize for leaving you behind at such a busy time of day. My husband said convent houses of the nuns from L'Abbaye de Montmartre used to populate this street."

Upon instinct, Celeste made the sign of the cross.

"But the Abbaye was destroyed during the Revolution, and all the nuns fled."

While passing a streetside café, Celeste glanced over at a tart in a low-cut red gown who bent over a glass of red wine. Across from her, a bearded man licked his lips. He appeared to savor her as if she were as sweet as chocolate.

Somewhere a church bell pealed the hour.

Geneviève said, "Many of the women we see at the bars and cafés nowadays are hardly the type who go to Mass. People come to live in Montmartre since they do not have to pay the high taxes in Paris."

"I remember Tante Faucon mentioning that reason when she helped Maman found her brothel. That is why we came up here to live after Paris." Celeste read the blue ceramic address tiles beside the door frames. "This one says 78. We must be close." A passing cart hit a dip in the road, and mud splashed on her traveling dress. She bent down and lifted her skirt. Dirt penetrated the lower petticoat ruffles. What a pity—no time to get it laundered.

Ignoring the dampness seeping into her stockings, she followed Geneviève, who dodged groups of men gathered on corners around makeshift chess tables. The houses leered through bent window frames and gaping doorways. The street transformed into near squalor, piles of paper mixed with dried leaves and horse droppings.

Strolling men ogled her through a smoky haze, and she avoided their eyes. Experience taught her that when she made eye contact, trouble followed. A day seldom passed when she did not sense a man's superior power. A flick of a stranger's wrist and she was flung into a doorway, raped, then pushed out onto the street, cautioned to keep her mouth shut. It happened more than once in New Orleans.

"We must be getting close." Geneviève tapped her cane.

Celeste's heart pounded. She might be close to finding Maman. After all this time, to hold her near, to gaze into her crystalline blue eyes, to unload her problems. But there was not time to contemplate such joy. She must concentrate.

Four shabby structures rose cheek-by-jowl on her right. The first house featured an open window yawning onto the street. An infant's cry burst through the second floor's open window. A drunk reeking of urine curled up in the doorway of the second house.

She held her nose while she examined the third doorway. "Where is the address tile?"

Geneviève touched her left arm. "There—do you see?" She pointed to the left of the lintel above the door. White numbers gleamed against a blue background. The third house was number 98. A chipped red door tile read "*Maison de L'Étoile*," House of the Star. Geneviève stepped back and appeared to survey the structure.

Oh no. Part of the roof had caved in over the second story, its timbers exposed to the open sky. The façade peeled away, revealing the brick-and-mortar underneath. Loose boards sagged above the doorsill, and angry winds and rains clawed out the door's paint and left bare, worm-eaten wood.

"Bad shape," Geneviève said.

"No house I remember ever looked like this. But it is number 98." Celeste's words fell, dirty raindrops clinging to a web of lost reflections.

Someone touched her—Geneviève's arm tightened around her shoulders. "Courage," she whispered.

After a moment's pause, Geneviève drew her arm away, and Celeste pushed open the squeaky door and stepped over the threshold. She turned back. The grand-mère would surely follow her inside. Instead, Geneviève set her lips in a straight line. "I would not go. You do not know what lurks inside—vermin, dogs, men. Your mother would not be here, of all places. Montmartre is a haven for the dispossessed. Be careful."

"I know, but this was my childhood home." She pressed a fist against her chest.

Geneviève bit her lip. "Listen, child. I have lived in Montmartre for thirty years, and I never go near Maison de L'Étoile or any other brothels. I did not mention it earlier, but you do not look like the type to frequent such haunts. "See that?" A shredded piece of yellow curtain caught on the third-story window casement.

Something rose inside of Celeste. She aimed a sharp glance at Geneviève. "But now that I am here, I must go in. Maybe I can find some idea of what happened. Besides, Maman might have left something for me."

Geneviève shrugged. "Suit yourself. Vandals comb through houses like these, and someone may be inside." She tugged at the watchchain around her neck. "I will wait only thirty minutes; then, I must rejoin Nancy and Jacques." Her eyes narrowed to a taut line. "I will call out and let you know when half the time has passed, but when those minutes are up, I will leave with or without you." Geneviève gave a shiver. *"Cet endroit me donne la chair de poule."* She had the creeps.

Celeste nodded. "Not long—a quick look." She stepped around fallen timbers in the hallway, then turned left into a formal parlor featuring a patchwork of broken windows whose light shone on red velvet chairs. Something smelled funny—maybe wet wool socks. Perhaps rain penetrated the window cracks. Mildew spotted the once-deluxe scarlet drapery.

Toile wall coverings in red and white patterns hung in strips. She wondered what was on the decoration, so she stretched her hand to the wall, lifting a shred of cloth, then held it up to the sunbeam. Lords and ladies frolicked at a woodland picnic. Even in decay, the rich reds contrasted with the white background.

She let the strip fall back against the wall and took a moment to stare. That covering had been in place when she gave her music recital for Maman's male guests. She wondered how old she was—probably age seven. Maman seemed proud that day; her mouth turned up in that sad-happy expression she often wore when regarding her.

Celeste surveyed the room more thoroughly. Though much of the furniture lay under sheeting, there must be a melodeon somewhere. When she lifted one of the coverings over a fainting couch and a lamp, she spied the oblong form, its hardwood brilliant despite its age. She and Maman used to polish the instrument themselves, using a mix of linseed oil, vinegar, and lemon juice.

After casting off the sheet, Celeste sat on the bench and raised the keyboard cover. Did it continue to work? The ivory keys were in place, gleaming as if new.

Maman would dress her up in blue velvet, braid her hair, and ask her to play simple Mozart tunes. Male guests would gather around her listening, canting their heads, swaying slightly to the harmony. If she sat very still, she could almost hear their murmurs.

She would feel an unfamiliar tap on her shoulder. *"Quelle petite princesse!"* What a little princess, one overweight man would say, twisting the ends of his mustache between thumb and forefinger.

"Elle est destinée pour le theatre." Another patron's slicked hair caught the light from the flickering candles. Celeste would be suitable for the stage. On those occasions when a man leered intently, Maman tugged her arm, led her upstairs, gave her cocoa, and told her to lock her door from the inside.

At the time, Celeste had never thought there was anything different about their lives compared to everyday people. She never wondered about the semi-nude women who lounged on the laps of the hungry-looking men in their salon. She never questioned why Maman sometimes vanished at night from the bed they shared, only to emerge the following day from a room down the hall.

Maman would trail a heavily bearded merchant from a bedroom. He would tug on his greatcoat, and she would hand him his hat and cane. A bag of francs would dangle around her wrist. Celeste never wondered why—it all seemed to be natural, for it was Maman's work, her way to make money after Papa left.

Separating the tangle of memories, she pressed the melodeon's ivory key, middle C. No sound. She held down the F key. No sound. Another, and another, until she had exhausted the keyboard.

She got up and lifted the board covering the instrument's inner workings. It was bare. No wonder. Someone had stolen all the reeds. She wondered why someone would do that. Maybe to punish Maman. Or perhaps to command a fair price at the brocantes at Place de L'Abbaye.

At any rate, it was a cheap move, and she took it personally. Her melodeon, her house, her Maman, even her gentlemen. All were part of the semi-glorious pastiche that imitated France's finest homes, which made up her past, present, and what she might become in this world.

With a tug of irritation, she brushed away a spider's web dangling overhead. She wondered where that time had vanished. And along with it, her precious Maman. *Unfair.* She closed the glossy wooden cover over the melodeon's keyboard. The hollow echoes of the room's former music, voices, and harmonies faded, and she could hear Geneviève's voice filtering into the hallway.

"*Mademoiselle? Attention, s'il vous plaît! Quinze minutes!*"

Celeste posed, transfixed in the shadowy remnants of her past, and for a moment, she could not understand Geneviève's words. "Ah! Oui! Fifteen minutes!" she called out, then heard a shuffling and the front door closing. For a moment, she balked.

Geneviève reminded her of the peril in this abandoned haunt where who knows what came to spend the night. If only she could wrap herself in the comforting musical notes she played as a child. That was a time she witnessed the truth but did not know its bite. There was peace in ignorance.

On this day in the firm contours of adulthood, she saw through the façade of Maison de L'Étoile. The faux-elegance, the champagne, the candelabra—all concealed a bitter truth that here young girls and women sold their bodies to men not once but many times a day. With each surrender, the girls lost part of themselves, the exchange of bodily fluids draining the essence of their personalities, leaving them as lifeless as discarded tissue paper.

If she were to find something of her mother's, it would be upstairs. Celeste took quick steps out of the room and gained the banistered staircase leading to the second floor. Faint window light in the hallway painted the walls taupe. The right-hand door was her mother's bedroom. She inhaled deeply, turned the knob, and the door creaked open.

A bundle of rags and a feather-poked pillow lay on her mother's bed where Maman would rest her head—usually with some man or another. Rats gnawed chunks of the mattress that popped through the holes in the covering. Other vermin and insects found a home here—the tight knot of a spider's web enfolded the curled-up carcass of a dead moth. Most likely, the roving predator expected this dessert.

Next, she pried open the door to what had been her room. Ignoring the stale odor of dusty neglect, Celeste entered the drift of her past life. After the men had paid and left, her mother would knock, Celeste would unlock her door, and Maman would join her on that same mattress to finish the night's rest. There she had lain in the crook of her mother's arm from childhood to adolescence, listening to Madeleine's calm and even breathing, the steady clop of horses' hooves passing outside.

If only she could remain longer, gathering ghostly images in the ether. Though Maman appeared as a vivid flash, she was no longer real, and her mother's form faded as if an artist's brush swept her away. *Merde!* She could only keep her mother's face in her head for a moment or two, and then it became a strain. She ran a shaky hand across the bumpy mattress. Even though she kissed Maman's faded daguerreotype every night, she wondered if her hollow cheeks had deepened. Her once-brilliant blue eyes would be sunken by now.

She shivered. The gendarmes had arrested Maman. Tante Faucon had sent Celeste off without even telling her when she could come back home. How dare she. But then—Maman might have wanted to get rid of her. Tante Faucon could have lied when telling her it was for her safety. Too many complications. Her corset itched, and her palms grew sweaty.

Maybe Maman was not worth finding. She wondered what kind of woman would do that to a child. Maybe she deserved to get arrested. Perhaps she was not even worth the search. She might find her, only to discover Maman did not want to see her. But once again—no time for bitter recollection or even the doubts she had. Maybe here she could find some remnant, some clue that might lead her to Maman.

No hints remained in what used to be her room. Cobwebs hung in lacy strips, emphasizing the neglect she saw both in the house and herself. Back in her mother's room, she eased open the door of a wardrobe where a spangled black gown hung from a hook on the back wall. Odd. Maman would never have left such a gown—it looked valuable—unless she had to hurry away. It might mean that after her arrest, the police never let her return to the brothel. She shifted to the mirrored table where Maman would braid her hair. Maybe she would find something there.

She slid open the right-hand drawer.

A tin of tooth powder rested alone; all other contents emptied. Come on—there had to be more. "Please, Maman, leave me a clue, even if you are below the ground, moldering in a grave."

She glanced at her apparition in the wavy mirror. She hardly recognized herself. Instead of the usual carefree expression, black smudges framed her eyes, and she wiped away a tear. Thinking she might find some sign in the left-hand drawer, she opened it.

Next to a small used bar of lavender soap, an envelope appeared, its cover stamped with fancy lettering. It read, *"Pour le Gentilhomme,"* for the gentleman. The portrait of a smartly dressed man in a top hat stared at her. Strange. From inside, she pulled out a *capotes anglaise,* referred to as an English Overcoat. She held up a long thin pouch made of sheep's gut with ribbons attached.

Though the packaging was unfamiliar, she recognized its contents. Madame De Salle's brothel in New Orleans had required their patrons to wear one. This item had been laundered and folded neatly; the sheath was ready to slip onto the man when he visited their brothel.

Undoubtedly Maman demanded her customers wear them since many courtesans she knew had died or gone mad from syphilis. A sheath was not something Maman would carry away in a hurry. There had to be something more; Celeste would settle for anything.

She stuffed the pouch back into the envelope and pulled the drawer out further. She reached into the back end, praying she would not be bit by a spider or roach. In the darkness, her fingers rustled what must have been small slips of paper. She pulled out one or two; they looked like store receipts. One last try. Nothing but paper. As she made one final swipe of the back of the drawer, her fingertips grasped something cold and metallic, and she held her breath.

Four

Le Consulat Café

Within the strands of dim light, Celeste held up a round holy medal; she resisted the shaking of her hands, pressed the object to her lips for a moment, then looked at it. The golden oval dangled at the end of a small chain, its disk a replica of the Miraculous Medal of St. Catherine Labouré that her mother used to wear night and day. The Virgin Mary's image was stamped on the medal's surface; she radiated benevolence, her open arms granting help to those who prayed. Celeste had played with the medal as a tiny girl in this same room.

"What does it say, Maman?" she would ask.

"*Ma petite*, the meaning is too difficult for you. You are too young to understand."

"No, I am not. I am eight years old, and at school, I am receiving top marks. Please, Maman, tell me what it says."

"Very well, *mon enfant*. It says, 'O Mary, who conceived without sin, pray for us who ask for your help.'" Celeste heard her mother's voice the way it sounded when she would dress her. Maman's face was soft and kind like the Virgin's, her arms held open, ready to help.

"Mademoiselle Celeste!" A sharp voice broke into her reverie, and she swallowed hard, then put the medal around her neck for safekeeping. Right now, she did not have time to think about it. She had to go, and Geneviève would be pacing back and forth on the sidewalk. Did new memories erase the old? She hoped not. If only she could linger a bit longer.

After one last check around the room, she rejoined Geneviève outside. The woman glanced at her pocket watch, then advanced a step. "You have dust on your cloak." Removing her gray glove, she brushed what must have been lint off Celeste's shoulder. "Did you find what you were looking for?"

"Sad to say, only this small thing stuffed in a drawer. I did find the melodeon I used to play. But it no longer works." She held the medal against the darkening sky, puffy clouds gathering overhead.

"Memories trick us—best left undisturbed, my child."

A few feet away, a young man not more than twenty vomited onto the street, then collapsed face-down in a mess.

Geneviève pressed up her jacket collar, covering her mouth and nose. "Not a good area for you to linger alone. Even together, we are at risk. Have you no one to go to in Paris?"

"My friends Edward and Brianna will always give me a home, but I cannot rest. And though there is little trace of Maman here, I will continue to search. And if I do not find her, I will locate Tante Faucon."

"What did your aunt do? Did she have a family? Was she a seamstress or married to wealth?"

"Uh, no. She had a brothel, too. Somewhere up here in Montmartre village. But I am unsure where."

Geneviève leaned against her cane. "Very well. You will have more searching to do. But it grows late, and the sky darkens with cold. I must go, yet I would like to take you somewhere safe, away from Rue de L'Abbaye. I would never forgive myself if something were to happen to you here."

"Where should I go?" she asked.

"A café at the corner of Rue Saint Rustique, not far from my home at Place du Tertre. I am on my way there anyway to meet Nancy and small Jacques. The place is well-populated, and you will be safe until you decide further what to do."

Celeste trailed Geneviève through the empty Place de L'Abbaye, the marketplace filled with pigeons pecking at the chunks of bread and cheese lying amidst the cobblestones.

After a short trek through winding streets, she paused next to Geneviève outside a red-painted corner café, its red and green awning bearing the words "Le Consulat." The cobblestones ended, and Geneviève led her to the patio populated with young and old chatting over bowls of mussels and glasses of wine. A waiter wearing a grease-soiled white apron carried coffee trays to the customers.

Geneviève gazed at the menu. *Omelets, Crêpes, Plats, Desserts.* Celeste spotted several customers through the windows, their small plates heaping with fruit tarts and cakes.

Someone tapped her arm, and she regarded Geneviève's hazel eyes. The woman said, "Très bien. You are safe here."

"Merci, madame."

Geneviève reached out and rested a hand on Celeste's forearm. "But I would not advise you to linger in Montmartre, and as for your Tante Faucon—a brothel? Is putting yourself in danger worth your life? Your mother's place sounds mild compared to most. My husband, the magistrate, talks endlessly of the murder cases he saw cross his desk, most originating from brothels. The victims were inevitably women."

A knot formed in Celeste's throat.

"Have a nice meal here at Le Consulat. Then find a carriage back to your friends in Paris. Do you need some francs for a meal?" She held up her reticule.

Celeste shook her head. "No, I have plenty of money today."

"I do wish I could stay here with you. One of the café's specialties, the Croque Monsieur, is crisp like no other, especially when the cheese melts over the ham and bread. I come here often since I live close by because I like the light up here. Many artists say it is good for painting. They call themselves impressionists. But now, I must go." Geneviève passed her a calling card. It read:

Mme. Geneviève Le Brun
48 Place du Tertre,
Montmartre

"As I said before, my husband is a retired magistrate. He knows many influential people in Paris. If you are ever in need of help, please contact me, dear girl. Promise me that." She drew Celeste close, then planted a firm kiss on each cheek. "Oh, by the way—the carriages to Paris leave from in front of my house at Place du Tertre. You will see them in the middle of the square. I believe the last one leaves at seven o'clock in the evening, so you have time to eat before going back to Paris."

"Oui, Geneviève. Most grateful. *Au revoir.*" Celeste saw the white-haired woman evaporate into the street crowd. The aroma of coffee blending with caramel cream swirled around her in the warm air, and she stepped inside Le Consulat Café.

Celeste made her way through the narrow restaurant aisle, her full skirts brushing tables on each side. Her thoughts meshed with the busy atmosphere. Parisian-style cafés were like this—often crowded, abuzz with people carrying on business as well as love affairs. She passed a young couple, their hands laced together, forming an arch over their table. A pair of snowy-haired women shared reminiscences along with sips of ruby port.

A mother and child drank from the same cup of hot cocoa, the mother wiping her child's face from time to time. Celeste drew back, deciding where to sit. Four men huddled around a table in the back. Only one free chair formed an endcap.

Merde. She would have to put up with men. She glanced around the place. On either side, people clung to their tables and chairs like scabs on a mangy dog. No way she could get any other seat. She advanced to the table, her steps halting. Maybe the men would be kind. She rested her hand on the chair and looked at them.

Luckily, they did not break their conversation. No one looked up in greeting; no one nodded their permission. She sighed. Deep in the world of men, she was a mere speck on the periphery. Maybe they would pay her no mind. That would be the safest place to be.

She pulled out the chair, settled her reticule in her lap, and peeled off her cloak, letting it drape over the chairback. A waiter appeared, drying his hand on a dirty apron. "*Quest-ce que vous voulez, mademoiselle?* What would you like?"

"Citron pressé, croque monsieur."

"*Merci bien.*" He flashed a grin and stepped toward the kitchen. Around her, the restaurant echoed intense conversations. She settled into the Parisian-style atmosphere she knew as a child. Matters of the day were baked, broiled, and fried under the watchful eye of its citizens. Dissatisfaction and unrest peppered the air.

Broadsheets littered the tables, their front-page sketches featuring Napoléon III, a man with a distinctive, horizontal mustache sticking out in waxy lines like piano wire. Parisians discussed the emperor in corners such as these. He demolished the city's narrow lanes and replaced them with three-story Haussmann buildings, displacing thousands of Parisians who wandered the streets begging for food. The emperor claimed to rid the city of its disease; the populace said he wished to rid the city of its poor.

She turned back to the table, the men bent together, intent on a conversation. She fluffed strands of blond hair gathering at the nape of her neck, pulled her hair over her shoulder, and brushed the dust off her jacket. She wondered how people minded their own business when they heard men say words like *emperor*, *traitor*, *plot*, *injustice*, *tyranny.*

Injustice and tyranny resonated with her. Americans shared the French values of liberty and fraternity. Their talk reminded her of Maman's political discussions with revolutionary activists around their dinner table at Maison de L'Étoile. Maybe if she took a side-glance at each man, he would not notice her staring.

The full-bearded man closest to her on the left looked to be in his forties. He had deep-set brown eyes and spoke French with an Italian accent. At first, she thought it might be French with Spanish, but she figured he was Italian after listening.

Next to him on the left–yes–it was *him*—the man from the brochettes line at Place de L'Abbaye. Long eyelashes swept his cheeks from time to time. Luxurious sideburns, wavy brown hair. Her breath caught in her throat. Maybe if she looked down, he would not see her savor his striking features. He also spoke Italian-accented French.

To the right sat a more formally dressed man, and she heard some French mixed with English words. He had a bush of red hair and a full red beard. He chewed his fingernails from time to time, stopping to think. She guessed he was English.

The fourth man hunched over the table in the right-hand corner, a ball pipe clenched in his teeth. He penciled lines and words on a piece of butcher paper. Though they kept their conversation muted, she spied the scrawled word "Opéra." They could be building designers.

After the waiter delivered her meal, she sipped her lemonade and forked her hot dish, glancing over as their drawing appeared under the careful hands of the sketch artist. Maybe if she ate quietly and avoided spilling her drink, they would continue their intriguing discussion. She continued to wonder if they were architects. Maybe people having to do with the opera. They could even be artists or actors planning a performance.

She jostled the edge of the table, sending a tremor through the wood frame. The men looked up, and a moment of silence ensued. The man from the marketplace in the far corner glanced at her and then flashed a grin.

She tried to suppress a smile, but he had disarmed her. His smile was as intimate as a kiss, and a glow consumed her. The man in the full beard caught his smile, looked over at her, perhaps noticing her for the first time. He elbowed the smiling man, reaching across him and pointing at the map.

The waiter brought her more lemonade, and she continued her quiet observations, sipping and watching, pretending not to be interested as the man's paper filled with small street maps of Paris. Then she heard mention of Normandy; they must have doings there. She scolded herself—none of her business. If she bothered herself with these men, she would end up in trouble.

She drained the lemonade, ate the last morsels of melted cheese on her plate, and raised the cloak from the back of her chair. The café emptied, its patrons having better things to do mid-afternoon. The shops opened, children hurried out of school, and mothers headed home to scrub floors and launder petticoats. Young girls met their beaus in secret angles of nearby parks.

Maybe she should catch the coach back to Paris, as Geneviève had mentioned. She could regroup, study her memories, think of another clue to her mother's whereabouts. Figure out a way to find Tante Faucon. Geneviève knew this village and its lack of safety. She should probably listen to her advice.

Yet Maison de L'Étoile anchored her to the past. If only she could stay in Montmartre. Another day or maybe two. She might unearth more information, meet others who might know Madeleine, locate Tante Faucon.

But about a lodging—she hadn't reserved a room in a boarding house or hostel. She kicked herself for not having researched her plans more thoroughly. Even if she had a list of places to stay, she looked suspicious reserving a room without a husband or companion. People would wonder why she lingered in Montmartre. If she meandered about at night, she would be caught up in a kidnap or worse, a murder, like girls from the demi-monde. When the gendarmes fished their white mackerel bodies out of the river Seine, gruesome descriptions filled columns in the broadsheets. They were usually suffocated or had their throats slit, according to the reports.

But then—before they left the café—maybe someone in this group could tell her where a lodging might be. The men relaxed their tight circle. The full-bearded gent to her right slackened his pose, leaning back in his chair. He downed the remains of red wine in his glass, then stood. The others followed his lead, and they headed toward the entrance, their legs grazing her skirts as they left the table. She would have to get up and follow them. She dropped two francs on the table for her meal and gathered her cloak and blue-ribboned bonnet.

The man she recognized from the brochettes lingered behind the group, leaned down to her, and said, "I remember you. Weren't you at Place de L'Abbaye?" His French carried an Italian accent.

She set her cloak about her shoulders. "Yes, in fact, we were next to each other in the line."

"I remember your telling the young mother that you were from Paris."

She nodded. "Yes, but I have lived in America, too. I come to Montmartre—"

"I know—to find your mother."

"Perceptive, monsieur."

"My friends tell me I am a good listener. May I walk you to your destination, Mademoiselle—er?"

Instead of giving him her name, she aimed her feet toward the door. If she dared ask him about a lodging, he might think she wanted to go to bed with him.

"By the way, I am Carlo." His smile brightened his face, erasing all shadows. So much like her father. Papa used to toss her up into the air while she giggled, his smile the expression she remembered long after he put her to bed at night.

"Are you Italian? I wondered by your accent."

"Yes. I work in Paris. The pay is better here than in Italy."

She followed his broad back through the last clutch of diners hunched over their glasses of wine and plates of cheese, through the patio where men and women caught the cool breezes, into the narrow streets of Montmartre. She set her bonnet on her head, tucked her fly-away hair under the back of the hat, and tied the blue ribbons under her chin.

He wrinkled his nose. "So, where are you going?"

"Ummm. It may seem inappropriate since I am alone, but I need to find lodging here in Montmartre. It is getting late. Probably too late to find a room. Maybe I should get on the coach back to Paris." She looked around at the sun's rays lengthening across the cobblestones. "Must be nearing four o'clock."

"There are coaches round the corner in Place du Tertre." He pointed left. "Pity—even though I only met you this morning, I feel I have known you for a long time."

"Do all Italians say that?"

He laughed. "Perhaps. Yet I would like to get to know you better. And I know you would like to find your mother here on Montmartre. If you go back to Paris, you will have to return another time. Instead, if you stay here, you may begin your search afresh tomorrow."

She paused, absorbing his features. His head tilted to the side; a jovial grin played about his mouth; a cap perched jauntily on his head. She could not trust this strange man. Yet her heart fluttered wildly. She had bedded many strangers. Coins had thudded on her table, day after day in San Francisco. All the same, she could not remember a man like him. When she spoke, he seemed to give her his full attention.

She said, "Perhaps you know of an inn, a safe place for me to stay the night?"

He said, "The house where I–that is we–stay is nearby. You are more than welcome to come there. I assure you the men are honest, and you will feel at home in our company."

"It is not quite proper. Are there ladies at the house?"

His eyes widened. "My younger sister, Liliana. She came with me after our parents got into political trouble in Venice. She will like another female companion if you come to stay. But in our community, no one thinks about propriety. We only think about justice."

Those were lofty words. Celeste hesitated. In San Francisco, she would not have dared follow him. The miners were beasts. Brianna and Edward never let anyone in who could be a danger to the girls. And he mentioned his sister. That could be a ploy to get her there.

But then, he extended an arm, his touch on her elbow sending her a jolt of energy. This man might like her for herself, not just to ride her like a spent pony.

"Come, then. I will lead the way." His grin returned—there was her father again. Papa used to lead her by the hand into the alleys of Montmartre, shielding her from leering drunks and hardened women.

"Very well. But I will have to leave in the morning to continue my search." She set her chin.

"As you wish." He relaxed his hand on her arm. "Through here." He lifted a low-lying branch, and she ducked under it.

She followed him into a narrow street that verged on the café's wall. The dark gray buildings were set so closely that if she reached out both arms, she would touch their façades. She gazed at the sliver of darkening sky and the wrought-iron lamplights hanging from the sides of the buildings.

Though she wondered if Carlo was taking advantage of her youth and trust, she knew one thing. Maman waited for her in France, somewhere behind one of these solid doorways.

Five

REVOLUTIONARIES

A few minutes later, Celeste followed Carlo into a two-story building. The passage opened onto an enclosed, trumpet vine-covered courtyard, and to the right, steps led up to a second-floor flat. Her heart thudded. Maybe she had made a mistake coming here. From her place at the threshold, she recognized the same group of men from Le Consulat Café; only this time, they did not huddle around a map.

The full-bearded man boiled water on the cookstove, and the taller man with an English accent piled wood into the oven, fanning the flames to keep them lit. The bearded sketch artist lounged on a settee covered with a shredded drape. He puffed on a ball pipe and petted a black cat.

Carlo tapped Celeste's arm, then pointed toward the full-bearded man at the stove. "Felice loves his pasta. He makes it from scratch, and cooks it perfectly, *al dente*." He grabbed half a loaf of bread. "Like some?"

Celeste fanned her hand in front of her face. "No, I had plenty at Le Consulat."

Carlo shrugged. "You haven't eaten real food until you've tasted what Felice makes."

The man called Felice lifted his stirring spoon and dripped water on the floor. "Who might this lovely apparition be?"

Carlo beamed as if he had caught a prize pheasant. "Her name is Celeste."

"And you are?" Celeste loosened the satin ribbons under her chin and let her bonnet rest against her back.

"Felice Orsini, mademoiselle. And what is your name?"

Celeste drew closer, sensing his curiosity. "Celeste Bazin."

"And how do you spell that last name? B-a-z-a-n?"

"No, monsieur. B-a-z-i-n."

He gave Carlo a playful swat. "You always did know how to find great women." They exchanged a knowing glance.

The taller gent with the English accent approached and gave a half-bow. "Welcome to our humble dwelling. My name is Thomas Allsop."

She nodded, captivated by the scents of olive oil, tomatoes, and oregano floating in the air. "Who makes the sauce?" Celeste asked.

Felice's skin reddened under his beard. "I do! I come from Roma. That is where the best sauces are made."

"Nonsense!" Carlo chomped on a heel of bread. "I come from Venice, the home of the best cooking. We call it *cucina veneziana*."

Felice faced them, his cap askew, his beard curled from the steam. "This, *signorina*, is why Italy needs to be united. We are all stuck in such divided states. We don't even speak the same language. Do you know that a person from Brindisi has trouble understanding a person from Florence?"

Carlo held her elbow. "Never mind him. Let us get you settled." He beckoned her deeper into the flat, which revealed a great room populated with couches, pillows, tables, and all manner of books and papers. They passed a side hallway having two other bedrooms.

"Where should I put my things?" Celeste asked. She surveyed the great room. Manuscripts covered tabletops; maps and boxes spread over the floor space. "Here?" she pointed to a bare spot.

The sketch artist on the couch grunted. "Eh, no, mademoiselle. I think that is Diavolo's space to sleep. In Italian, his name means devil."

She swept her gaze around the room. "Have I met Diavolo?"

Carlo pointed to the black cat, now snuggled on the sketch artist's lap. "Meet Diavolo and Odéon. Soulmates."

She bounced lightly on her toes. "I'll bet your cat spends most of the night sleeping on laps, doesn't he?"

Thomas chimed in where he stood in the kitchen. "Diavolo won't tolerate anyone but Odéon. Must be Odéon's evil nature that attracts him."

"Ha! I give him scraps instead of kicking him aside as you do." Odéon's grin faded into a flat line. "Carlo, what are you doing here with this mademoiselle?"

"I am helping her for a few days while she searches for her mother."

"Not sure that's wise." Odéon frowned. "Always up to something, aren't you?" The cat nosed into the crook of his arm, curled up, and closed his eyes.

Carlo pointed to the corner. "You can sleep over there on my cot, Celeste. It has a warm blanket. And Diavolo might join you."

She flinched. She wouldn't mind Diavolo but certainly hoped Carlo did not intend to creep into her bed—neither he nor anyone of the rest of them.

He must have read her dagger-filled gaze. "Do not worry. I'll sleep on the couch."

"Where does Odéon sleep?" She stopped mid-step. A wave of tension passed through her and out the ends of her fingers.

"I sleep over there." Odéon gestured with his pipe stem to a pallet in the opposite corner, then drew a blanket over himself, and turned away toward the wall, Diavolo assuming a regal pose on top of his hip.

She set her cloak on the end of the cot. "You mentioned your sister. When will I meet her?"

Carlo said, "Liliana should be back any minute now."

Felice stirred the sauce. "I sent her out to the bakery for more *pain ordinaire*. We were running out of bread. And now that we have an extra guest, I am glad I did."

Assuming there was a sister, maybe she would be safe here after all. She dropped her bags next to Carlo's cot, pulled up the duvet, and turned the pillows over. There might be the usual bedbugs. Finding none, she fluffed the pillows and glanced around. Someone had installed heavy drapes over the windows, and it could be night rather than the afternoon. She turned to Carlo, "Why have you darkened the windows?"

"Nosy neighbors. Streets are narrow, and people peer into each other's windows."

"All neighbors are that way, even in Paris. In Le Marais, they sit by the windows for hours. Kind of like vultures."

"Even more so here in Montmartre. In this village, word gets around fast. People gossip in the churches, the post office, the marketplace. And false news spreads faster than the pox."

"Maybe I can find someone who knows my Tante Faucon."

"Perhaps." He crossed the room, rejoining Felice in the kitchen.

After hanging her hat on a wall hook, she curled on the bed, wrapped in her cloak, envisioning curious eyes watching her through the windows. Drowsiness enveloped her, along with the conversation that flowed among the men in the kitchen. She found herself lulled by the warmth of the apartment and the snores of Odéon reclining with Diavolo on the couch.

A while later, someone jolted her, and she looked up into Carlo's deep, Italian eyes. She could not place her whereabouts. She could not figure what this man was doing by her cot. After a moment, the aromas of basil and olive oil brought her to the present. She must have fallen asleep; hunger ranged in her stomach like a rabid dog. On the other side of the room, murmuring voices blended with the steam rising from the stove. A young girl's words rose in conversation with the men.

"What time is it?" She sat up, swinging her feet to the ground. She rubbed her dry eyes and blinked away the blurriness.

Carlo peered at his pocket watch. "Nearly seven o'clock. We are going to eat now. Want a plate?" A tender flash illuminated his face.

A sudden shyness overtook her, and she grew breathless. "I do not want to disturb you."

"Felice would be sad if you did not sample his cooking. He is very proud of his sauces. Come, you must meet my sister Liliana."

After crossing the room, Celeste got a close look at the young girl. Liliana put down her fork and raised her hand. "*Piacere,*" pleased to meet you. She resembled her brother Carlo, her eyes deep-set, her gaze intense and penetrating. Young with a slim waist, maybe aged fourteen or so, her medium-length brown hair parted in the middle, a cascade of ringlets crowning her shoulders. A young beauty dressed in humble brown cotton.

"*Mon plaisir,*" Celeste said. "Do not let me disturb you while you eat." She assessed her situation. Carlo might lie about other things, as did most men, but he did have a sister. And those glamorous curls framed his forehead.

Two hours later, after consuming bowls of pasta, trays of cheese, and plates of sausages, Celeste sat among the group, their tongues loosened by bottles of red wine. She glanced at Carlo on her left as he bantered with the men. He was a blend of fire and calculation. The substantial profile, the shape of his hands, the wavy tendrils of dark hair tucked behind his ear. It could be the heat from the boiling pot, or maybe his nearness stirred up some latent flame. She hadn't felt such a rising desire in a very long time, a longing she could ill afford at the moment. To distract herself, she dropped into a stream of thought about the group.

Carlo represented the men's freedom that she never had. Growing up in brothels in Montmartre and New Orleans, she was never free to speak her mind. Celeste had to listen to men, take in their confidences, keep her mouth shut. If she aired her political views publicly, she risked losing her business since her clientele was one of the most egalitarian of all venues. A prince could lie down with a courtesan in one room, but next door's client could be a common laborer. A soiled dove provided her services to anyone willing to pay.

Liliana kept up a steady chatter, her voice chiming in the way a young mockingbird trills at the break of day. She spoke of Venetian holidays and her love of Carnivale when the town transformed with revels and masked balls.

Their joviality emboldened Celeste. "Where do you work? I know there is a gypsum quarry nearby. I learned this from a woman at the marketplace this morning."

Felice poured himself another glass of wine and sat back, regarding her. "We travel from place to place, mademoiselle."

She leaned back in her chair, listening. "Are you *Romani*? *Gitanes?*"

He chuckled. "Our life involves traveling, but we are not gypsies. We work at enough odd jobs to get by. Our reason is to ensure justice and peace in each town where we rest our heads. Not many can say they do what we do." His voice lulled her like a child's song, a musical variation of French with Italian notes.

She sighed. "So, you are bohemians. What a pleasant life. I have traveled much as well—from Paris to New Orleans, then to California, and back again."

Carlo speared a green olive from a bowl in the center, then popped it into his mouth. "Why did you leave California? The entire world is going there, isn't it? People say the streets are lined with gold."

"Not exactly. Just as many young men are poor as they are wealthy.

Prospectors struck it rich in the early days, but most of the wealth now belongs to the men who built businesses serving the miners—bricklayers, mining suppliers, and bankers, of course."

"And why are you back in France? A girl as lovely as yourself wandering alone. Are you not concerned for your safety?"

"I am on a mission to find my mother, whom I have not seen for six years. When I left France, I was a mere girl. Tante Faucon told me I would have a better life in New Orleans." She filled him in with details about her life in America and her current search.

Felice wiped his mouth with his sleeve. "And did you? Find a better life that is?"

"New Orleans was where Madame De Salle introduced me to Brianna and Edward. After a terrible fire, we escaped with freed slaves to San Francisco."

Carlo set his hand on the back of her chair. He sat so close she could sense his heat. "And how did you end up returning to France? Did you come alone?"

She took a sip of red Barolo wine. "When Brianna and Edward found themselves in trouble, they told me they wanted to come to Paris and that I should come and help them get established. And I did. But of course, I told them that I would not be happy unless I found my mother."

"Does your mother have a name?" Felice licked his finger, then put out the central candle on the table. The wick made a fizzing sound, and a small column of smoke spiraled up.

"Madeleine Bazin. Have you heard of her, or do you know anyone who might have known her?"

Thomas, previously quiet, spoke up. "What does she look like?"

"Around sixty, her hair white-blond, pulled back in a bun. She is thin—wears a pair of gold drop earrings my Papa gave her in the early days before he died."

Felice shook his head. "Sadly, I have not met such a woman."

"Then have you heard of Madame Giselle Faucon? My aunt?"

"Does not ring a bell." Felice bit into a crust of bread.

She heard a creak from the direction of the wooden door, then footsteps entering. Odéon came into view, shuffled toward the table, and flopped into a chair. He reached for a crust of bread and tore off a piece.

Carlo said, "About time you came to dinner. I thought you were going to sleep through it."

"Wait a minute." Odéon held up his hand. "I need this." He poured himself a glass of wine and downed it in one gulp. After he swallowed a chunk of bread, he aimed a narrow-eyed glance at Celeste. "What is she doing here? But more importantly, what are you talking about?"

Thomas rose from the table and helped himself to Felice's pasta and sauce in the kitchen. He sat down, knife and fork in hand. "Yes, what are we talking about? I want to hear this."

Carlo glanced at Odéon. "Very well." He pressed his lips together, regarding Odéon. "Your grandparents lived here, and you have been to Montmartre before our stay here. You might remember a brothel. What was the address again, Mademoiselle Celeste?"

"Rue de L'Abbaye—number 98, to be exact," she said.

"Do you know her—this Madeleine Bazin?" Carlo asked.

Odéon shook his head, but his gaze remained thoughtful. "Not personally, though I do know the street. When I was a child, my grandparents had an apartment here. They told me to be careful going down that block. But mademoiselle, I think you need to find Madame Faucon. I learned about her when visiting as a curious teenager. She has been in the streets of Montmartre since her birth. She makes it her business to know everyone in this village. And she is in the—em—trade you speak of."

"She is my aunt. I need to locate her." Sweat prickled on her forehead.

Carlo smirked. "Odéon, time for a confession. Did you use this Madame Faucon's services? How else would you know her?"

Odéon reddened. "Though I am no angel, I did not meet her for the reasons you are thinking."

Felice rose and collected some dishes. "Why else would you know her, my son?"

Odéon straightened in his chair. "She helped me find this flat for our group. To be exact, she was in a liaison with the owner of the building."

All this signaled a stroke of luck. Celeste said, "Could you give me her address? I will go seek her out tomorrow." If only she could figure out the puzzle of Tante Faucon's whereabouts. Any lead would help.

Odéon said, "Better yet, I will take you."

"I do not think you should do that." Felice broke in.

The two men exchanged dark glances.

Odéon's voice lowered. "Well, then, maybe Carlo could."

Carlo blanched. "No, I have told you before that we must keep to ourselves as much as possible, especially during these early days. It is one thing to host a lovely girl like Celeste who knows little trouble, but another to put ourselves in the knowledge of the town crier like Madame Faucon."

A brief silence ensued. Celeste paused, brushing aside any misgivings. These men were kind and idealistic; there was a gentleness about them. She had little option other than to feel safe in their company. She put both elbows on the table and leaned forward. "I can go by myself to see Madame Faucon. My mother ran a brothel, so I am not afraid of such places or the people who keep them." She paused; maybe she said too much.

Carlo raised an eyebrow. "So…have you been…er…*un petit bateau de pêche*? A little fishing boat?"

Celeste hesitated whether she should tell the truth or plaster it over like the new walls the emperor was building in Paris.

The men drew back in their seats. She glanced from face to face. They were looking at her the way people examined corpses in the street; maybe they thought she was an exciting specimen or pathetic like

Diavolo, the alley cat. She took a deep breath. Well, she was more than a stray cat, and anyway, she had a mission.

Liliana lifted her fork and toyed with a spaghetti string on her plate.

Celeste shifted in her chair, then looked at the men, meeting their wide-eyed stares.

"I have already told you I grew up in a brothel. And yes, I have been a little fishing boat. Something I am not necessarily proud of, but there you have it—my past life."

Carlo gave a shaky laugh. "I am glad you were honest with us. There is no shame in being a *fille*."

She could have hugged the man.

Odéon nodded. "Many times, our friends and families have fallen into desperate circumstances. Our emperor has created this." His voice hardened. "Look at what he is doing to them. Entire families curl up on street corners in Paris, their children starving. You did what you must to survive."

She looked heavenward. What a relief they were not judging her—at least not now. The whore's code ran in her bloodstream: a prostitute's repression was complete since not only could she not speak freely to her clientele, but she also had to watch her back around her fellow courtesans. It was a tentative sisterhood. In some ways, the women were all in the same situation, degraded, subject to the whims of their madams; in other ways, they competed with one another to attract a favored john.

Though these people espoused a revolutionary cause, they could not easily understand what her life as a little fishing boat was like; in truth, she hardly knew herself the extent of a woman's physical bondage.

Felice wiped his hands on his apron. He said, "This calls for a bottle of Vin Santo."

Odéon said, "I thought you were saving that for a special occasion."

Felice tilted his head. "This is very special. We have a petit bateau, a little boat of the night, floating among us. She has survived a life which destroys most women." He searched a cupboard in the kitchen, found the bottle, uncorked it, and poured them a round.

"Raise your glasses with me," he said. His beard gleamed in the candlelight. "To Celeste, who has endured the street life. *Salute!*"

Their musical voices cheered the drab gray walls. "Salute!"

She raised her glass, the distant candle flaming through the swirling altar wine. Maybe she had survived but had her mother? She took a sip, letting the warm sweetness drift down her throat. After glancing at Carlo, she looked over at Odéon. Two different men. If Carlo were a dancing spark, Odéon would be the slow-burning ember. Each offered excitement but in opposite ways. In contrast with Carlo's passionate outbursts, Odéon's subtle movements and facial expressions showed he was thinking. Yet no one doubted each man's dedication to their mission, the details of which remained fuzzy.

She waved away a drift of Odéon's pipe smoke and took another sip of Vin Santo. Here was a moment to reflect. The village of Montmartre held many secrets within its shadowy streets. These men took up a severe cause, and they had deadly aims in mind. At least she could hope for one thing: maybe Tante Faucon would show her the right path toward Maman. She tapped the holy medal around her neck.

Six

Le Beauvoir

The following day, clutching a crude map in her hand, Celeste headed out to find Tante Faucon. Odéon warned her to be wary but firm since Faucon could be a good ally, though she made it her business to report on the community's inhabitants so close to Paris, yet in some ways so far from it.

A slight breeze ruffled the brim of her bonnet when she rounded the corner onto Rue de L'Abreuvoir, to the left a set of two-story houses, some with windows shuttered, some half-timbered, some beige, some light pink, but all facing an ivy-covered wall across the street. A sweep of ivy cascaded from the high wall's battlements, and a robin sat on one of the twigs, regarding her. He would know Tante Faucon and see all the comings and goings at the brothel. If he could talk, what stories he could tell.

Crossing away from the wall, she made her way across the cobbled street, then mounted the steps leading to the front door. Two girls came to the open French window on the second floor, maybe hearing her footsteps echoing on the cobbles. Celeste peered at them. The nymphs were naked from the waist up, their breasts crushed against the grillwork of the balcony that stretched across the lower part of the tall window. She heard a giggle from above. “Madame! Someone at the door!”

Celeste held her bonnet against the crown of her head and gazed. Theirs was a balancing act, one that required skill. One false move and the girl attracted too much attention, became suspect, then ridiculed, then ejected from the house. The girls curried favor with the madam, often willing to perform the most degrading acts to increase their income and privileges, such as one day off a week. There was always one in the bunch who drew ire. Always one scapegoat among the women. The role seemed to rotate. And it was precarious.

A grim-faced matron pushed between the girls, leaned over the balcony, and stared at Celeste. A nest of iron-gray hair perched atop her head, and a hairpin of fake brilliants caught the light. “What do you want, child? If it is soaps, we bought some yesterday. If you bring us muffins, we have enough from the patisseries.” A mesh of frown lines splayed across her lips.

Celeste called out. “I am seeking someone you might know. Someone dear to me.”

The matron cupped her ear, then yelled down. “I cannot hear you. I will come down.” She drew back inside and disappeared.

Meantime, the two topless girls reemerged, their faces reflecting their curiosity. They pointed at her and resumed their giggling, their breasts bobbing. Celeste recognized that type of hilarity that verged on hysteria. Brothel girls had a certain kind of laugh. On the surface, it sounded carefree, but underneath, the smirks carried the sharp edge of a steel blade.

Such girls sported knives in their corsets; such girls strangled customers who got too rough; such girls shot a bullet through a man’s head if their lives depended on it. The gendarmes at Place Pigalle encountered dead men in gutters between two and five in the morning. “Casualties of debauchery,” they would say to one another, shaking their heads.

Widows would visit the morgues, then weep over the corpses. "How did this happen?" They would cry out. The gendarmerie would shake their heads. "Evil companionship," they would say. "Who was it this time?" Again the gendarme would shrug his shoulders. "He deserved it. No evidence to speak of." An unfortunate but necessary part of Parisian life—no names were ever exchanged.

Tromping footsteps advanced toward Celeste from behind the front door. The latch clicked, the door swung inward, and the iron-haired matron beckoned her inside. Celeste found herself in a dark hallway illuminated by a desktop oil lamp that lit a stairway snaking to an upstairs landing. An odd smell permeated the place—perhaps the sweet, strange perfume masked the odor of smoked opium. Hard to tell. She could not see the matron very well, so she stepped away when someone brushed her arm.

The matron cast her a lip-wrinkled grin. "Do not be afraid, mademoiselle. What we have here in the brothel is not—catching." She sat down at the entry desk with a whale-oil lantern that sputtered black smoke. No wonder the walls were grimy, the once-happy figures of dancing lords and ladies suffocated beneath layers of gritty toile.

"Please sit down." She pointed to the chair on the other side of the table.

Celeste settled into the seat and eyed a large black lacquered box. She recognized its type from Maman's house, for that held the cash. Though she could not see the other side, she knew the box would feature various drawers, some full of room keys, some full of change. Not only did her mother own one of those, but also Madame De Salle in New Orleans. Since the men paid mostly in gold shavings or nuggets in San Francisco, Brianna and Edward collected their money in pouches.

For a moment, she paused, remembering her mother's brothel on Rue de L'Abbaye. A madam or her matron would make sure the desk was the first stop of the night for a gentleman seeking companionship. A customer would have to pay before the prostitute rendered her services; otherwise, he could fly out the kitchen door, running with his pants in his hands. It happened more than once, and the police were not sympathetic to the brothel owner. But any ill will could be smoothed over in the arms of a soiled dove, and all would be forgiven.

The candlelight flickered mysteriously over the woman's high cheekbones. "What may I help you with, mademoiselle? Employment?" Her gaze roved over Celeste's figure. "We are looking for a new girl. We lost Clotilde last week from typhus, you see, so we do have an empty bed. By your looks, I think we would be able to use your—eh—talents. Of course, I would have to see you naked first." Gravel layered the madam's voice, hardened with the cement that buried the young victims of her trade.

A thought resonated. If Tante Faucon carried on an affair, or liaison as Odéon had said, she was rather old for this business. This matron must be in her seventies, based on her wrinkles and gnarled, arthritic hands.

The woman's sharp eyes and long nose gave her a bird-like appearance, and Celeste pictured her pecking at her young charges, bullying them into submission, readying them to follow the wishes of the heavy-handed men who waited every night for them. Her wrinkled lips parted. "How did you know to come here?"

Celeste leaned forward. "The tavern-keeper in Place Pigalle told me that you ran Le Beauvoir, a prominent brothel and that you might be able to help me." How handily her lie rose to her lips; early training at her mother's knee proved helpful.

The woman's fingernails scratched idly at the surface of the table. "So, you are not interested in—shall we say—employment, mademoiselle?"

"No, I have come on other business. I am seeking the whereabouts of my dear aunt. Madame Faucon resides here, does she not?"

The woman's beady eyes widened. "So, you have come seeking Madame Faucon, spilling out your stories, not even knowing whether or not she lives here?"

"She is my aunt." Celeste's cheeks grew warm.

The raspy voice continued, "Who are you? And more importantly, what are you looking for? We get all sorts of stories, claims of long-lost relations—girls will say anything to have a job. I have a mind to cast you out the door right now." Two small red cherries centered on the woman's sallow cheeks.

Voilà—Celeste's poorly aimed dart had hit the bullseye. She had made an inroad. Now, she must get to Faucon. "My name is Celeste, and I am searching for my mother, one Madeleine Bazin, the sister of Madame Faucon. She owned a brothel on Rue de L'Abbaye, and the last time I heard from her was eight years past."

"Do you have any proof that you are the niece of Madame Faucon? Any papers? Locks of your mother's hair?"

"I have a holy medal belonging to my mother. Maman always wore it around her neck."

"Show it to me."

Celeste drew the medal from her reticule and held it up before the sputtering lamp.

"Catherine Labouré." The woman's bony claws darted toward the medal.

Quick. Celeste drew back and slid her medal into the reticule for safekeeping.

The matron ran her blackened tongue over her jagged lower lip. "If I help you see Madame Faucon, I will need the proper—eh—compensation?" She opened a bony hand and slid it, palm up, toward her.

Celeste knew the gesture. One paid for information in Montmartre—all the while not knowing if the informant was ever telling the truth. But that was the risk she would have to take. She opened her reticule and dropped two francs into the woman's cupped hand.

The woman's fingers clamped shut like a vise, and the arm controlling that hand disappeared under the table. She could hear the muffled clinking of coins when the woman dropped them in a hidden pocket of her skirt.

"Who are you?" Celeste asked.

The matron's hand reappeared, her nails resuming a *scritch-scratch* on the table's surface. "In this house, we do not have names. But come back tomorrow at this hour, and I will have news for you, good or bad."

Celeste peered at the wall clock through the smoky darkness. Eleven o'clock. "Very well. I will be here."

She rose and gathered her skirts about her, settling her bonnet on her head. As the woman opened the door, a shaft of light fell onto her face. Celeste drew back, fixed on the woman's jagged lower lip where drops of saliva seemed to cling to save their lives.

Maman said that people grew to look like what they had become. As she stepped away from the house, she wondered. Had the woman told so many lies that her mouth became distorted after each telling? What a grotesque human being.

The robin continued its perch on the hanging bushes across the street. She looked up at him. "I should stop lying, *mon petit*," she said. "I never want to become like her." She pulled down her lower lip. The robin turned his left eye toward her, then inclined his beak. He seemed to approve of her resolution, yet another branch rustled somewhere above, and his brown wings flashed away into the greenery beyond.

Seven

Yankee Doodle

After making her way through the ramshackle streets of Montmartre, some buildings windowless, others finely painted, Celeste wondered what to do next. Maybe she would find Carlo at home. She tingled—his nearness was both disturbing and exciting. Odéon greeted her at the door. He cupped his ball pipe in one hand and made a sweeping gesture. "No one's here but me at the moment."

She sank into a chair at the kitchen table. Diavolo rubbed against her legs, and she reached down to pet him. Odéon set out an additional cup for her and poured an Italian coffee into the tiny cup. "Sugar?" he asked. His gentle voice surprised her. Though his features were peaceful, they were work-hardened.

"No, black is fine. Merci," she said, then reached for a loaf of bread Odéon had set earlier in the middle of the table. She put a chunk of bread near her teacup, avoiding table crumbs from last night's dinner. A dirty spoon lay on top of a French newspaper called *Le Bulletin des Halles.* Faded red spots of pasta sauce embellished some of the pages.

Odéon separated some loose sections from the newspaper and appeared to scan them.

She swallowed a gulp of café. "So, I see by your choice of newspapers, you follow politics?"

"A hobby of mine, or better yet, a passion." His eyes blazed like summer fire, and he poured himself a cup of coffee.

Celeste said, "One must be passionate about things these days—daily life for the people is so difficult. I have seen a change since I came back from San Francisco. The streets of Paris are blowing up to make room for these new buildings the emperor favors. He aims to rid the streets of vermin and diseases."

Odéon measured her, his look cool and appraising while he sipped from his cup.

"We know that is code for getting rid of the poorest among us who have no means of escaping their lot. Now, where are they to go?" She marveled at her forcefulness and ease with this stranger.

He remained silent, seemingly lost in thought. Yet his silence was not forced or awkward; he was companionable, and she was conscious of his nearness. She even wondered how it would feel to rest her head against his broad chest.

Memories swirled inside her dark spaces. Maman used to talk about politics; even though Celeste had been too young, she had noticed. Diavolo curled up on her lap and tucked his head under her hand. She scratched his ears. Brianna and Edward had been at war with the vigilantes in San Francisco, but she preferred to stay inside the parlor house, learning about the violence secondhand.

Yet here in Paris, on the hunt for her mother, new social ideas were beginning to matter to her. Maybe people like Felice, Odéon, and Carlo could make a change in the world. The way her mother yearned for more rights and freedoms, not just for herself and her brothel girls, but for everyone in France.

Odéon cleared his throat. "I wanted to ask how your visit went—

did you meet Madame Faucon?" His gold-brown eyes lit up, reminding her of lanterns at a winter carnival.

"No, but I did talk to a strange, bird-like matron with a scarred lower lip."

"Did her lip go down like this?" Odéon demonstrated, pulling his lower lip between his thumb and index finger.

She strained to see his lips through his bushy beard, then held back a laugh. "How did you know?"

He tore a slice off the bread loaf on the table and folded it in his hand. "She is Hortense Montreux. To understand Hortense, you must know more about Madame Faucon."

"I am growing weary of trying to see my aunt. Why is she so important? So hard to meet?"

He took a bite of bread. "The woman acts as patrol and control of the streets, alerting all its inhabitants of the presence or absence of the police whom we call *les fliques*. From your description, the person you met was Hortense Montreux. A smarmy woman, but in terms of social justice, also a victim.

"Her career in the flesh trade left her scarred, broken, and poor. The story says a john cut her lower lip out of spite when she was young. In the old days, the residents used to feed Hortense scraps, and one shop owner allowed her to sleep in the back of his place like a watchdog."

"And then Faucon took her in?"

"You might say she put her to work." His eyebrows formed a steeple over his nose. "Have you ever looked down into a deep well, wondering where the water came from?"

"Yes, of course."

He shrugged. "Well, that is Faucon. She is an eternal source, a spring of evil that never fails to surprise us. And her league includes the mayor and city officials who protect her. She knows too much about their doings, in and out of the brothel. And over the years, her power has grown, such that no official dares to cross her."

Somehow his nearness gave her comfort. As if he knew the edgy milieu where she had grown up. Celeste risked bothering him with more questions. "I do not understand. If she is a source of evil, why does she protect its victims, someone like Hortense Montreux?"

"That, of course, is the paradox of the underworld. They must trade in filth to have power over it. And sometimes that results in untold kindness." He took another bite of bread, then washed it down with coffee.

She shook her head. "Poor Hortense. What an unfortunate creature."

Odéon clucked his tongue. "She is hardly poor but an associate of an evildoer, like the devil's familiar. I hope you did not tell her too much."

Celeste swallowed hard and bit back tears. She hoped so, too. Then it was her turn to silence. She thought back to her days in Madame De Salle's brothel in New Orleans. De Salle traded in sin, but she did so in the glow of candlelit dinners and moonlit assignations.

Later that afternoon, their conversation exhausted, Odéon left the flat to run an errand. The sweet tang of his tobacco smoke lingered. She found herself missing him—he conveyed such gentle understanding—an old soul who knew her profoundly and could see into her being.

Celeste found the lodging growing stuffy in his absence, the closed-up windows and dark curtains contributing to its suffocation. She had enough of that claustrophobia on the ship from New York to Calais. She fought off the memory that wrapped itself around her, but the vision persisted.

Down in the hold, she had sat squashed between two other women on a cot. During the voyage, they took turns stretching out on the bed, the whale oil lamps sputtering above them in the semi-darkness, her stomach tossing and turning as the ship rose and fell within the peaks and valleys of the Atlantic Ocean.

She peered at Diavolo, the cat who snored softly on her lap. "I would like a glass of absinthe, mon chéri."

The cat yawned up at her, plainly sleepy from the heat.

Celeste caressed the black fur along his back. "I agree, too hot to think in here. I will go out and find a breeze on Montmartre. This hill has got to be cooler than down in Paris." She rose, grabbed her white parasol, and headed to the door. The cat mewed behind her. When she opened the door, the feline stretched, lifted its tail, then promenaded past her out onto the street. If only she could be as calm as Diavolo when it came to finding Tante Faucon. Easier said than done.

She headed in the direction of Place du Tertre. Late afternoon shoppers were out in abundance. Women clutching market baskets strode from shop to shop, and girls and boys in pinafores and short pants stood on tiptoe, peering through the corner candy shop window. A group of grimy workmen in overalls was smoking together on the corner. She veered from the walkway into the muddy lane to avoid them.

A white handkerchief flashed in the distance. Maybe someone was gesturing at her. She wondered where she was anyway. After she turned back to see Le Consulat Café at the other end of the block, she figured she was around the corner from the flat. The handkerchief approached, and Carlo was waving it.

He skip-ran in her direction then caught her forearm. "Where are you headed?"

Her pulse skittered. "To a bar to drink absinthe. Are you back from your search?"

He pulled a watch from his waistcoat pocket. "See, it is four o'clock. Rather than absinthe, could I interest you in a glass of wine?"

He was hard to resist. Celeste asked, "Where to?"

"Let us have a stroll to the Clos Montmartre. I know the owner, and he always lets me sample his new vintage. Come along?"

She hooked her arm under his elbow. After a few moments' stroll, they lingered on the hill, looking down at a steeply terraced vineyard.

The breeze ruffled russet grape leaves on their posts; yellow grasses clung to the late autumn hillsides. Beyond lay the smokestacks of Paris, hazy in the bronze afternoon light. Amid the terraced rooftops and tree-lined parks rose the twin bell towers and the soaring spire of Notre Dame de Paris. Soot on buildings made it hard to see the details, but she squinted, trying to make out its distant silhouette.

"Well, are you going to tell me what you're looking at?"

"Wait!" She tented her right hand over her eyebrows. "I can see Notre Dame from up here."

"That would be a marvel on a day like today . . . well, yes, if you angle your eyes just so—maybe to the left."

She tilted her head, and out of somewhere, Carlo's arm swept her into his embrace, and he gave her a long, tender kiss. What might have been a surprise melted into a surrender. His tongue probed the soft chamber of her mouth, and she responded, her mouth meeting his in mutual pleasure. She let his tongue explore the outlines of her lips. Blood surged from her fingertips to her toes. She let herself stay in his arms for a moment, and his heart thudded against her chest.

"Celeste," he whispered, his voice flowing into the flush of air around them.

No one said her name very often, not even Brianna.

He nuzzled his face in her hair. "I have wanted to do this since the moment you sat at the edge of that stupid table at Le Consulat, pretending to mind your own business."

She inhaled sharply. "I was minding my affairs—I am not a snoop."

A scarlet stain spread across his cheeks. "So the political world does not interest you?"

"Only so much as it affects my personal rights."

"Did you have freedom in America?" he asked. "The songs the barman plays on his accordion seem to say so. 'Yankee Doodle came to town, riding on his pony.'" He threw his head back and laughed.

Startled at his response, she dug deeper. "American men have liberty, women a little, but there is a movement I hear to give women more rights. A woman named Elizabeth Cady Stanton writes articles about it in the news sheets. They've even had a convention for women's rights. They are even talking about allowing women to divorce their husbands—imagine that?"

"Divorce? That would never happen here. Besides, in France, women have many rights. They come and go freely, do they not?"

"No. Certain places in Paris are so dangerous a good woman will not go alone. And consider women who live proper lives with children and husbands; people do not consider it correct for them to go out on the streets without chaperones." She cast him a wary glance. "But you already knew that, Carlo. Why ask me?" She stepped away—a man like him might not have room for her among his crowded political affections.

"To prove to you that you *are* interested in politics. Your freedom means a great deal to you."

"Honestly, I wish I had even more freedom."

"Though I am not a woman, I also wish for more liberties, not only here in France but in my Italy—throughout Europe." He swept his arms wide.

Footsteps approached from behind them, where they stood on the terraced steps. A voice chimed. "The vineyard is closing. Did you want to buy a bottle of wine?" A bearded winemaker in beige overalls and a black beret made long strides toward them. "Is that you, Carlo?"

"It is, indeed, Raoul." Carlo grinned.

The vintner clapped him on the back and extended a hand. "Mademoiselle?"

"This is my friend, Celeste." Carlo tapped her shoulder, and she stepped forward.

The vintner embraced her as if she were a precious pearl within an oyster. "*Enchantée*, mademoiselle." Her parasol clattered to the ground; he bent down and picked it up. His manner was pleasant; he treated her as an equal.

Raoul turned to Carlo. "Now, let us go into the cellars. I have some new rosé I would like you to try. If it has gone bad, you will be the first to pour it out; if it is good, you will be the first to get drunk on it!" His cheeks flamed, and he drew out a handkerchief and patted his sweat-lined brow. At the entrance to the cellar, he grabbed a torch that flickered against a wall. He held it up, lighting the way into the dark passage ahead.

The musky smell of wine pervaded the cool, damp cellars. Rows of oaken casks, side-by-side, three barrels high, lined the rooms. Carlo extended a hand to Celeste, and she folded up her parasol, using it as a walking stick to steady herself on the damp ground of the wine cave. After following Raoul deeper into the dark passage, down one tunnel, then another, she said, "This is a maze." She caught herself in a stumble but steadied herself on the handle of the parasol. The aroma of grape musk enveloped her, along with a giddy sensation.

Carlo reached out for her arm, then squeezed her hand. "Wait until you taste his wine."

From either the musk or his touch, she grew lightheaded.

After walking a few minutes, Raoul stopped and fixed the torch on a post above the barrels. He drew a tasting glass from a rack on the side. He twisted the spigot, and the pale pink wine trickled into the goblet. He swished the wine around, then held it up to the light of the torch. "I am looking for sediment—it usually settles at the bottom."

Celeste examined the wine. "I see a tiny bit of purple, but not very much. The rosé looks clear to me."

"*Bien*!" Raoul took a sip of the wine, narrowed his eyes, then downed the rest. His eyes sparkled. "Good enough to share." He drew out two more glasses from the side of the barrel and held them under the spigot until they were half full. After passing them their drinks, Raoul poured his own and swirled the contents.

Celeste held up her glass and measured her fill against Carlo's goblet. "Equals," she said.

Carlo winked, "Just like you and me."

Raoul raised his glass in a toast. "To young lovers!"

Carlo added, "To young wine!"

Celeste could not help herself. "To Montmartre!"

Their glasses clinked together, their musical notes echoing through the tunnel beyond.

After downing the wine, she followed the men upstairs. The men exchanged laughter and unfamiliar names of wines. Though they were mere footsteps in front of her, Celeste had a moment to consider her situation. Carlo moved too fast, and she had little experience with men outside a brothel. Celeste had trouble judging whether men were after her for her looks or her authentic self, flaws and all.

She stepped around a small table with a barrel stave resting on it. *Bang!* She stiffened. Some worker must have dropped something heavy—probably a tool—and the sharp sound echoed through the tunnel. She ground her teeth and returned to her thoughts. Though she found herself captivated by Carlo's fire, she needed to filter his advances against her limited experience. If only she did not tend to fall first, think second.

With time, he could prove to be either a true friend or a passing fancy. She would call him a flame, but the heated distraction was the last thing she wanted. A dalliance would pull her away from the most important reason for her being—to find Maman.

Eight

Nothing But Whores

The following day, Celeste approached the brothel called Le Beauvoir for the second time. The skies had darkened. Maybe a summer rain would fall that afternoon. She held her bonnet strings tightly against the breezes that ruffled the brim of her hat. The robin from the previous day was away from his perch, probably taking shelter from the impending storm. The clouds hovered, somber and threatening over Montmartre and the streets of Paris. She needed to hurry, lest she get caught in a downpour on the way home.

As in the day before, several bare-breasted women, not all young, lingered against the window railings, some stark naked. A curtain moved inside an upper window of Le Beauvoir, and a moment later, Hortense Montreux joined her outside on the front steps. Hortense glared at the women. "Get back inside and get some clothes on." Her voice grated like a stone on metal.

A flurry of swear words, some of them in dialect, poured out of the older soiled doves.

Hortense pounded the heel of her hand on her forehead. "Not my idea to take in these *filles,* if that is what they call them at their age." She shook her head, plainly disgusted. "A brothel on Rue de L'Abbaye closed some years ago, and unfortunately, Madame Faucon took in some that were definitely past their prime."

Celeste's eyes widened. "What about the younger girls? I saw some hanging over the balcony."

Hortense picked at a broken side tooth with a gray fingernail. "Ah, those other, newer additions were former dancers and performers in Paris who fell from grace in the city and have fled to our village where they hope to be incognito in their new profession."

Celeste flinched at the mention of Rue de L'Abbaye. Hortense must not suspect what she was after. She would not want word to get out. "I think it is sad they still have to work at this trade, even later in life."

Hortense's bent lip turned down in a sneer. "Pah! Nothing but whores. They gave their souls away long before they came here."

"In truth, I have never seen naked older women dressed in such theater paint before." There had been older dames at Maison de L'Étoile—she enjoyed telling this lie.

Hortense sucked in her broken lip. "You are a fortunate one, *ma chérie.* You are on this side of the threshold, not the other. After you see such sights, you know they matter little. If a woman gives up her life to please men, she will suffer the consequences. And what if she never learns but thinks she is still young and lovely into older age? It is only her delusion, nothing more." She shook her head, grinding her toe into the space between two cobblestones.

Celeste said, "Madame, I came when you told me I might be able to see Madame Faucon. Do you not remember?"

Hortense pounded her forehead. "Yes, how could I forget? She agreed to see you, and she arrives any moment. Come and follow me into the parlor. Juliette will bring us some tea while we wait."

Not long after, Celeste sat next to Hortense on the parlor couch. After watching the toothless maid Juliette serve the tea in unmatched cups and saucers, Celeste lifted the flowered cup to her mouth. The warm brew slid down her parched throat.

She stared at the bevy of porcelain statues that lined the surrounding walls. Men and women in erotic poses, in various stages of undress. She knew their purpose, to stimulate the clientele, to speed up the process so they would choose the less savory girls on exhibition and turn the sessions around more speedily—more francs to make, more coffers to fill.

After a series of sliding footsteps sounded from the hall, a large, peacock feather-hatted woman dominated the doorway. She wore a long chemise of white lace cascades that bowed out over a buoyant black skirt. After surveying the room, she floated in like a midsummer breeze. With each step, she pulled a finger out of her black kid gloves.

Her feathers bobbed in all directions, and she glided over to Celeste and extended a multi-ringed hand. Prominent among the rings was a large diamond that reflected light from the doorway. Also prominent among the rings were the woman's arthritic knuckles. This madam was older than she wanted anyone to know.

Hortense rose to her feet and curtsied in Faucon's direction. Her teacup rattled against the saucer in her hand.

Though she kissed Faucon's hand, Celeste stayed seated, her mind full of wonder, awe, or a mixture of both. Hortense, the matron, acted so familiar with Faucon's guests. Madame De Salle would never have tolerated that behavior. Of course, that was New Orleans, and this was Paris. Such customs may have changed since she was a child; these attitudes were more common, less refined.

"Hortense, put down your teacup." Madame Faucon rasped. "See to the girls. I want them dressed by now—it is nearly noonday, not a time for them to lollygag about the windows. That comes later when the usual traffic passes by in the street. If we advertise their wares too early in the day, they will no longer be unique to the passersby. More like wilted flowers." She sniffed audibly.

"Oui, Madame," Hortense gave another broken curtsy, then bustled out of the room, leaving the door open into the hallway.

Faucon shrugged. "What is one to do these days, mademoiselle? Help is tough to find."

Celeste nodded, considering. This madam was very hard to please.

Faucon tilted her head, looking at Celeste with a rare intensity. She might have recognized her, or perhaps that was another illusion.

Celeste knew the "once-over" typical of brothel keepers. First, a madam would examine the woman's bosom to assess the fullness of the breasts, then the hips to see if there was enough heft to please a demanding customer. The process would finish while the girl was clothed.

If the young girl passed the test, the madam would invite her to undress, and no orifices were spared while the madam fingered her wares. How well she knew. How well she remembered. But this was her aunt. A shudder passed through her, yet she pressed onward.

"I am your niece, Celeste Bazin. Madeleine's girl. You shipped me to L'Amérique six years ago."

"I have little memory of that occasion."

"I was fourteen at the time. You sent me to Madame De Salle in New Orleans."

"If you are telling the truth, I was probably trying to help my sister. Hortense said you have Madeleine's miraculous medal. Show it to me." Her voice was flat and lifeless as a wagon rim left in the road.

If only Celeste's hands would stop their trembling. She dug in her reticule, found the medal, and set it into Faucon's outstretched palm. She dared not breathe.

A cryptic expression deepened the lines in Faucon's face. She rose, crossed the room, and closed the hallway door.

Nine

A Soulless Leader

After several breathless moments, Celeste took stock. Tante Faucon would not embrace her nor even greet her as a relative. She nevertheless persisted in steering the conversation into deeper waters. Since Faucon had closed the hallway door, she might be prepared to divulge something she wanted only Celeste to hear. She could only hope. "I am searching for Maman. Do you know her whereabouts?"

Faucon stiffened, then she poured herself a cup of tea, maybe to put some distance between herself and Celeste's prying question. "If you must know—which in truth I wonder why, given that you are a lovely girl and have promise outside walls like these—" She cast her eyes around at the figures, narrowing her eyes at one pose of a man entering a woman from behind.

"Your mother operated the brothel until six years ago; at least that's my recollection. She got into trouble with the local guards, and they arrested her. She asked me to arrange your passage to New Orleans. Mind you, I don't have the details since to pry into the matter might lead me also into suspicion, and I keep my head down and keep my business running."

"What sort of trouble was she in, Madame?"

Faucon set down her teacup and scratched her cheek. "I'm trying to remember—ah yes—it had to do with some political group. Your mother was very outspoken in those later years, and she seemed not to care that by speaking her anti-Napoléonic beliefs in public, someone might brand her a traitor."

"That makes sense. Political causes captivated Maman, but I was young and bored by the discussions she had with people who came over at night."

"I never went back to the house. She and I shared the deed, but I never sold it. For one thing, I did not want to draw attention to myself or the fact that since she was a felon, the government could confiscate her property. I figured in time no one would remember her arrest, and that way, we could keep the house until she returned."

"I visited the old house, and it looked as if she might have left in a hurry. The house is showing signs of abandonment. As you say, no one sold the house—some of her belongings are still there. That was where I found the medal."

Faucon leaned over, running her hand over the shining disk. "Your mother was odd. She seemed drawn to this religious nonsense. Pretty rare in a madam since we trade in sin. We are lost, and no kind of God—real or imaginary—would ever take pity on us. Knowing Madeleine, though, it makes sense that she would have a medal like that, but why on earth would she leave it behind?"

"I wondered the same thing," Celeste said. "She might have forgotten it."

"What circumstances would make her forget it?" Faucon leaned back on the settee and fondled the tiers of lace on her bodice.

Celeste tucked the medal back into her reticule. "I thought you might at least hazard a guess that would lead me in some direction. I do want to find her, no matter the trouble. She was impulsive and passionate."

Faucon's hands balled into tight fists. "Mademoiselle, I would like to help—but—." Her glance slid sideways toward the open window.

"If it's money you want, I can offer you 500 francs for the information. I'm quite willing to get it to you as early as tomorrow. But please—I must find Maman. You are the only one who can give me any clue."

"It is not that—I do not need your dollars from America. I worry about my safety and my business. You see, the imperial guards and their agents are everywhere, even up here in Montmartre. Ours is a nervous emperor. Louis Napoléon fears his people. He sent us to fight Russia in the Crimean War, and we lost over 95,000 troops. Now that he and that dreadful architect Haussmann chop our Paris into parts and redesign it, he has sent his populace out begging in the streets. His citizens are hungry, simmering with anger. Do you understand?"

"Well, if my mother is fighting this evil, I want to find her more strongly. She may be in some serious trouble, jailed in some secret place. You must help me—tell me what you know."

"Mademoiselle, you should go back to America where you earned your gold. That is the new world, not this old one that you see falling apart under France's emperor who cares only for his Spanish wife and son. We know of his luxury. He lives in splendor, changing palaces every season so he can hunt the local animals and hold festivals and balls to please himself and his courtiers." Faucon drew herself up in her chair. Her beak-like nose presided over purple lips, which opened and shut indecisively.

"One last time, Tante. I beg you. Madeleine is my mother, the one I have lost. She is all I have in this world. Think of yourself—how you would feel in my *sabots* or in the slippers you wear on your feet."

"You are young, silly, naïve." Her upper lip rose in a sneer. "Did you ever consider that your searching for your mother, bandying her name about, may put her in greater danger?"

Celeste shook her head. "No, that would not happen. Not to Maman."

"Child, listen to me. I wish to help you, but you must know this. If she faced arrest, it was for an excellent reason. People said her name linked to a group that wanted to overthrow the emperor. Your wild idea of finding her is just that—crazy. *Folle!*"

"It may be risky, but I am determined. I will take every precaution and be careful to only speak her name to those I can trust."

"*Bah!* What are you at your age to know or trust? You have not lived your mother's life to see whom she trusted and whom she betrayed. Consider every person you meet your adversary, especially those who seem so friendly, so willing to help. Listen to me—" Faucon leaned toward Celeste and enfolded her hands in a claw-like grip. "Promise me you will be more than careful. Swear to me that you will trust no one."

Celeste's throat constricted. She wondered why her cold aunt seemed concerned. But at this point, she had no other alternative. She had to give in or lose this precious lead to her mother's whereabouts. "I promise. That is, I swear I will trust no one."

"Very well. But if you tell anyone you heard it from me, I will deny ever knowing you and denounce you as a traitor to the emperor. *Comprenez vous?*"

Celeste's throat constricted. "I understand."

"Very well. The word is that Madeleine was convicted, but her sentence required her to serve at an orphanage in Compiègne, not far from the emperor's autumn hunting palace. Funny thing, those orphanages."

"What makes you say that?"

"They're run by the Daughters of Charity, the same religious order founded by the nun depicted on your medal, Saint Catherine Labouré. I only know this because I, too, was raised Catholic in the same era as your mother. I am the eldest by two years."

Celeste eyed the strands of gray hair gathering around Tante Faucon's temples. She wondered how her mother would look. Maybe her angel-blond hair would be turned white, bleached by a hard life under men's bony knees.

Tante Faucon accompanied Celeste to the front door of the brothel. "Here is your medal. Do not come again." Her frigid hands pressed the disk into Celeste's open palm. As the door closed, Celeste heard her whisper. "Remember, you will be in great danger alone. *À Dieu vit!* Godspeed."

Faucon's prayer lingered in the air like a curse.

Celeste gazed across the street at the ivy vines cascading down the side of the wall. No robin graced its leaves. Maybe something happened to him. Perhaps her fortunes spiraled on the same downward path. If only someone could help her.

Unearthly giggling pierced the air. Two naked girls gyrated on the balcony to some hell-born silent music.

Later that afternoon, Celeste reached the vineyard. If only she could talk to Carlo, he might be able to help her. Raoul hunched over his account books in the great hall of the vineyard house. He looked up as she entered, his eyebrows pinched together. "If you're looking for Carlo, he is down in the cellar."

"Merci." She hastened down the cellar steps where a hammer pounded on wood. Sure enough, she found Carlo, his back facing her, hewing wine casks. He lined barrel staves inside the circular pattern of an iron rim.

Dispensing with the usual greeting, she skirted the barrel and spoke across to him. "I knew I would find you here. Felice was at the flat, but he was not sure where you might be."

Carlo had unbuttoned his white shirt front, and sweat misted his chest. He wore a yellow bandana around his forehead.

She ached to reach over and touch him. "You look like a brigand or a pirate."

"My true calling." He grinned and put down a set of barrel staves. "What brings you here?" Maybe she was mistaken, but she thought he blushed.

"I have something to tell you." She pulled off her heavy cape and tucked it under her arm. "Is anyone else about? I need you in private."

"Raoul is up at the main house. I can tell by the worry lines between your eyes that this is important. Does it concern my—well—kissing you? Did I take unwanted liberty?" His cheeks darkened, their red flush growing scarlet. "If so, I apologize."

"Oh, that—no." She snuck a hand to her throat.

He took a step closer. "I am glad of that, then. So, what is the matter?"

The flood of words rose to her lips in no order. "I need to find Maman—now. I must leave right away. She is in Compiègne. I do not even know where that is—or how far."

"Wait a second. How did you find this out? Is your source trustworthy?"

"I think so. The person swore me to secrecy, so I can't reveal who they are, no matter what. But I am sure as I can be that they are telling the truth."

Carlo pulled the scarf off his head and rubbed the back of his neck with it, avoiding eye contact. "Do go on," he said.

"She was arrested for her political activities. Maman would speak her mind, you see, even back in the old days. Groups of people would meet in the back kitchen at our house. They held protests—planned disruptions. I used to admire her for that, but now I am afraid it led to her jailing."

He tapped his index finger against his lip. "Do you know where your mother is in Compiègne?"

"Yes, she works at an orphanage, and I want to go there tonight, or at least tomorrow. As soon as I can, I will hire a wagon to get there."

"An orphanage? Hard to believe they would give her such a lenient sentence."

"Maybe they figured she was of little threat to the empire. I cannot speculate."

"Have you given any thought as to what will happen if you find your mother?"

"I plan to bring her back with me to Paris, then San Francisco to end her days with me in America."

"I see. But have you thought about the dangers of traveling alone? A young woman such as yourself on the roads with brigands and mercenaries, to say nothing of the emperor's guards? How old are you? You look so young, just a girl."

She gathered the blue ribbons of her bonnet, scrunched them, then let them go. "I am no girl, monsieur. Though I am but twenty, I have lived twice the life of many women my age. I have known bitterness and sorrow and loneliness in spades. In California, I even learned how to shoot a gun."

He gave a slight cough. "That may be so, but no matter your Wild West past, you'll still be in danger in France."

"I will find my mother, no matter what I have to do. And now that I know where she probably is, I'm going. I don't need your approval or anyone else's, for that matter." She turned away for a moment, swallowing hard. A long-tailed rat scuttled between the barrels. Maybe Carlo told some truth, but she should not trust him. Faucon's words rang in her head. She had probably already said too much.

His hand grasped her arm. The touch unnerved her, and she turned back. "Look, I'm sorry," he said. "I sense your frustration, so maybe we can find a driver. I'll see what I can do."

"I have no one else—my mother's brothel is a shambles. I need to find her, and you know people."

He put down his gloves and drew her close. His muscles enfolded her like a leaf sheltering a small bird. "Calm yourself. My friends and I will get you to Compiègne. We know it well. In return, we may ask a favor of you."

"What sort?" Her legs went numb.

"Say nothing to anyone."

"Is that the favor?" Her bottom lip trembled.

"I must ask Felice . . . he may want you to do something."

"What exactly is something?" Sexual positions from the New Orleans brothel life flashed before her.

"I won't know until I get his direction." His lips brushed her cheek.

She heard nothing for a moment save the drip of water in the wine cave, followed by the swish of a rat's tail when it must have brushed past a wine barrel. She relaxed against Carlo's chest, lulled by rhythmic breathing, pounding heartbeats, and whispering echoes.

The next morning's dawn lay tucked under clouds layered over Montmartre and extended across Paris down below. Carlo's torch lit up the inside of the stable yard, spreading flashes of orange and crimson and white across wooden timbers, restless horses, glimmering haybales. The serge cloak itched Celeste's skin: the place reeked of horse urine. She blinked away the watery tears rising to confront the stench. Whatever she had gotten herself into, it better be worth it.

Carlo drew her into his broad chest and kissed her lips softly, slowly. "I shall miss you—please do not take any unnecessary chances." The Italian lilt in Carlo's voice intensified, deepened.

She softened, but a part of her would not yield. Her life was on hold until she could finish the puzzle of Maman's whereabouts.

Carlo helped her up onto the jockey box, where she took an uneasy seat next to Odéon, whose posture magnified his hefty build, thick beard, and black beret. After exchanging greetings, she glanced behind at the white canopy forming an O shape over the wagon bed. Through the opening, she glimpsed their journey's provisions: gray blankets, thick bedrolls, some bottles of wine, and straw baskets that must hold food.

If only she had more sense. Maybe she had lost her wits—if this was Carlo's scheme, she needed to rethink their relationship. A spark between them grew hot at times, and it scared her a little. She never really understood him because there was a side that he never shared, and she suspected that could become a source of frustration as they grew closer.

She glanced behind at her leatherette suitcase resting on a blanket in the wagon bed. She patted the sides of the carpetbag sitting at her feet. Inside, her American passport lay folded next to her pistol.

No one could travel through imperial France without a *passe-port*. And she must not forget her gold pieces to be used only in emergencies. They nested with an envelope in a hidden pocket of her chemise while French francs jingled in the reticule resting on her lap. She would either threaten or bribe or entice her way into Compiègne's good graces.

"Are you sure I should not wear the gun on my person?" she asked.

Carlo drew her gloved hands into his open palms, then folded her fingers in his grasp. "Odéon will keep you safe. Remember Felice's instructions. You have agreed to be his courier, to say no more than is necessary. Once inside the palace, go directly to the secretary. Speak to no one else, save for to ask directions. Tell me again, rehearsing. What are you to do when you find him?"

"I am to say 14 January, Paris." She touched the base of her throat, where her blood pulsed.

"He will give you a message and further directions for Odéon."

"Then I am free to find my mother?"

"Yes, and Odéon will assist you."

Odéon pulled up on the reins as if commanded, and his horses snorted, chomping on their bits. His voice rang out. "Look smart, Carlo. We must away! Felice wants us out of Paris before sunrise—see the horizon?—the land is getting lighter."

"Au revoir," Carlo said, the words catching in his throat. He reached up and pulled her toward him, his arms cradling her shoulders.

His soft curls brushed her cheek, and his lips captured hers. She lost all sense of time for a moment, but then, a thought crossed her mind. She drew back. "But when will I see you again?" Celeste sent a whisper into the shadowy space that trapped them.

"You will know." The torch flamed, the whip cracked, and Carlo vanished down the road.

Ten

The Picardy Route

The horses stomped, appearing anxious to leave the stables and dance on the open road. As the muddy lanes of Paris flew by and they reached the country roads heading northeast toward the Picardy region, Celeste grew accustomed to the jostle, sway, and bump of the wagon. The byways were ill-kept, at specific points non-existent, and she curled her knuckles around the handrail in front and to the side to avoid tumbling out.

They made slow progress, for they had to stop and wait while other carriages and horse-drawn vans passed in the opposite direction along the narrow route. About five miles outside Paris, they gained the Picardy Road at midday. The highroad snaked along autumn wooded areas filled with birdsong, bubbling streams, and through narrow village lanes where passing women carried market baskets, and men smoked pipes, their eyes glancing up as their wagon passed.

After an uneventful afternoon's journey with occasional stops to water the horses, Celeste peered out into the gathering darkness. A clearing appeared down a one-track country lane to their right. Pinpricked lights shone in a farmhouse far away, their tiny yellow dots punctuating the landscape. A small stream meandered alongside a flat inlet sheltered by almost bare trees and low-lying bushes. "What about over there?" She pointed.

Odéon set his teeth around his ball pipe and steered the horses into the secluded space. After he unhitched the horses, he led them to a stream to drink and later to an unscythed area along the bank where they munched on wild grasses.

He showed Celeste how to build a fire from pieces of stick wood lying about, in addition to a fallen oak log. "What about that one?" She strolled over to a stubby oak branch, probably hewn by the landowner.

He joined her, knelt, and rose, turning the log vertically to gaze at its core. "See that?"

"What?" She peered at multiple rings fanning out from the center of the cut wood.

"Put your hand right there—in the middle of the core."

She rested her hand across it. "Like this?"

"No—more like this." His fingers wrapped around her hand and lifted it, extending her index and third finger and guiding her hand back and forth across the core."

"It's damp—now I can feel it. So, this wood is—"

"Too green, mademoiselle. Or damp from recent rains. Not usable for our fire." Somehow his hand lingered around hers long enough to feel his warmth, pulse, something stirring. As though her touch became unbearable, he released her hand. "I think we have enough wood, though. At least for tonight."

She released her breath, letting it flow into the space between them. Odéon rose and said, "We must make proper camp now."

The nearby stream sped by, full of water from recent rains. Its bubbling laughter drowned out any other sound save the overhead swoop of a Eurasian Eagle Owl whose swishing wings heralded the evening's hunt for small farmland prey. With night's creeping darkness, the air grew colder, and she resisted the urge to explore their surroundings, drawing closer to the source of heat.

After checking the horses, he returned to their fire and lingered, warming his hands. Even though she had conversed with him plenty at the house in Montmartre, here was her chance to get a good look at him up close. Though average height, he had a muscular bearing; though weather-beaten, he was not too old, probably in his late twenties. She removed her bonnet and set it next to her on a makeshift log table.

"Is it safe here?" she asked, more to fill the space between them than to find out the answer. "I do not know where we are. To be frank, I do not read maps very well. I feel helpless out in the wild, and I am not sure I like it."

"We have found a sheltering spot, but we must be ever vigilant at night. Thugs and brigands abound on the Picardy route."

She shivered and peered out toward the road.

"But let us not think of that now." The pistol on his waistband caught her eye. He had sidestepped her question—but perhaps he could only guess as to their safety. She stole a glimpse at the wagon, imagining her gun nestled inside her carpetbag.

After he brought out a block of cheese and a loaf of bread from the wagon, along with an unlabeled bottle of wine and two upholstered footstools that served as seats, the two of them sat in comfortable silence, the fire's crackle accenting the stream's harmonies. Odéon popped the bottle's cork, and the *glug-glug* of wine splashed the interior of the glasses and echoed into the woods beyond. He set the bottle on the log and did not try to hide that he was gazing at her. Light smoldered in his gold-flecked eyes.

Though his eyes held a sensuous flame, some instinct rose within Celeste, a tight weaving of her childhood encounters with men and the johns in the New Orleans brothel. Rough hands, groping hands. Money exchanging hands. A twig snapped in the fire's heat. A winged creature rustled the branches overhead.

Though she enjoyed the easy-going nature of his quiet companionship, she stopped herself. This Odéon was a stranger. His beard turned auburn, its golden strands brightening against the kindling sparks. The way he sat apart, the way he regarded her, not as a toy but as a flesh and blood being—those ways told her much about him, but they also left her with more questions.

A man of his age and experience—she paused—maybe he was married. Perhaps he had children left at home. Only God knew in what dark labyrinth his past lay hidden.

She wondered about his loyalty. If someone attacked them, he might run off, or he might stay and protect her. But she could defend herself with her gun—she knew how to level and shoot it, having practiced with Edward in a field above San Francisco harbor.

"*A votre santé!*" He raised his glass to hers, and their flutes clinked together.

"To your health!" She sipped the sugary young wine.

"How long have you known Carlo?" she asked.

He gathered his jacket about him and leaned toward the flames. "Long enough to know he is a good man, full of principle."

"A friend?"

"You might say that."

"Where is your home?" she asked, casting him a sidelong glance. A breeze caught a couple of strands of her hair and brushed them across her face.

"Normandie. Near the coast. Do you know the region?"

She tucked some stray hair behind her ears. "No, but our ship landed at Le Havre last year. I did not see much of the port since our coach went directly to Paris."

"I see you are French, but you do not know much of your own country."

"Sad but true. You see, I was born in Paris and raised on Montmartre. We were too poor to travel. The farthest we ever went was Paris for shopping, but that was more than enough. I think Paris encompasses many cities."

"Not me. I was a farm boy, brought up helping my father plow the land and plant apple orchards. I like to be out in this—" He swept his hand across the landscape around them. "A quiet life."

"How did you end up in Paris with Carlo and Felice? Nothing quiet about that—though parts of Montmartre can be miles away from everything." She scooted a bit closer to hear his reply.

"I guess I wanted more, especially after the Crimean War. After I came home from the fighting in Sebastopol, I was quite unsettled. Some say soldiers experience this—how do you say it? Inquietude, restlessness, unhappiness. I still have nightmares of the fighting. Mademoiselle Celeste, I saw things no one should ever have to see. I did things to men that no one should expect. Afterward, my parents' farm hemmed me in, and I needed to live my life away from them. I could not see harvesting crops for the rest of my life."

"And you never married? With a wife, you might wish to live on the land."

"Too busy fighting. There were a few ladies, but nothing permanent."

"And so do you have more—now—with this—with Carlo and his men?"

"I believe in their cause."

"What motivates that?"

"Justice for the poor, the downgraded, the people of this country who cannot speak for themselves. The emperor does not mete out justice—he only takes for himself." She wondered if that red flame in his eyes reflected the dancing firelight or his rising passion.

The air grew still between them. Celeste had no answer for Odéon's fervent words. Her ignorance of the situation in France had been compounded by her leaving the country at fourteen. Sure, there had always been the emperor, a man who claimed the throne for himself. Now six years after the war that even she had read about in America, she had jumped into a *pot au feu*, a French political stew filled with beef and hot peppers.

She struggled to match the zeal of his words. "Are you part of a movement?"

He answered in a more measured tone, maybe wondering if he had said too much. "Many uprisings are happening in Britain, France. Italy, too. Much unrest. One cannot help but get involved, especially in Montmartre where people are freethinkers."

"Ah, I suspected as much, but I have limited experience. But then—now that I think about it—in San Francisco, there was an uprising called the Committee of Vigilance. They believed in hanging suspects without a fair trial."

"You witnessed that?"

"Edward, Brianna's husband, nearly was hanged at the hands of one such committee. Convicted by a secret trial. That is why I came to France—we escaped their grasp."

A gentle gaze replaced the hard glint in his eye, and she read admiration in the soft wrinkles around his eyes. She went on. "You see, Odéon, I believe that we know little of the people we encounter, the stories they have lived, the secrets they keep close. When we scratch someone's skin, we rarely see the blood running underneath."

"Again, how old are you, mademoiselle?"

"Twenty."

"You have the wisdom of someone thrice your age." He placed his index finger against his lips, maybe pondering the truth of what he had just said.

A bat sliced the air in the beech stand above, and crickets chirped their nightly chorus in the near pasture. Celeste cocked her head, listening. "Strange—aren't those field crickets? It's late fall—seems they would have stopped chirping by now."

"I agree. Nature holds many surprises and exceptions." Odéon shifted his gaze. "You wear a holy medal around your neck. Are you religious?"

"No, but I believe there is a spiritual path. I found this when I looked for Maman at the brothel in Montmartre where I grew up. She might have forgotten it in a drawer. I do not understand why she would leave it. She wore it next to her heart. After Papa died, she wore the medal during good times and bad when employing young girls as prostitutes. Odd, of course—a madam wearing a holy symbol."

"A badge of honor." He shrugged and looked into the dark canopy of branches.

"More than that, the medal testified to her belief in God, the true faith. She also believed in aiding the oppressed girls who worked for her." She unclasped the medal, removed the chain around her neck, and passed it over. "Here. Take a look."

He fingered the disk, turning it from back to front, then dangled it between himself and the firelight. A golden luminescence flared: a burst of sparks illuminated the oval whose surface featured the Virgin Mary, her arms at her sides, her palms open. His lips parted. "I have seen people wearing this medallion in the past ten years, but I never knew what it stood for. My father was an atheist, you see, and my mother died when I was eight, so I never learned such things."

"This medal inspires service to others, Maman told me."

"Service? What kind?" He squinted.

"Catherine Labouré, who founded this order of nuns, believed in dedication to the service of abandoned children. This order builds and manages orphanages. You may have seen the nuns—they wear black and white habits with white coifs on their heads that look like angel wings." She shot her arms up and angled her hands in opposite directions.

"I see. I have seen those nuns. Exactly where I am not sure." His tone was level, seeming to accept her words. He passed the medal back to her, his hands gentle, his manner respectful. After suppressing a burp, he said, "Eh, bien. Time for bed." He rose, then set out his bedroll next to the fire.

Sweat gathered under her arms. Though she rested in the tranquil arms of Mother Nature, nothing about this moment was serene—the *zzzz* of a mosquito hummed in her ear. She hardly knew Odéon, and trust was growing between them, but she knew many other men who intended to harm her. This stranger-companion might not be any different. Most men only wanted what was between her legs, not what was between her ears.

A silence crept between them like a bothersome tick between the bedsheets. The silence was more provocative when an owl double-hooted in the trees and a fish splashed in the nearby stream. Men's *zing-zang* intentions toward her flared in the bedside candlelight of New Orleans and San Francisco. When presented with a maiden like her, an average Frenchman would take his fill. If only Carlo were here with them. He would never let that happen. She needed her gun—here beside her.

Odéon laid out a gray serge blanket over his bedroll, unfurled the top, and laid a second bedroll as a pillow. She stood watching his agile form move about the space. Since he was used to the road life, his practices were fluid and expert. She had to admit she was mesmerized by his deft hands drifting back and forth against the firelight. Despite his self-contained manner, she sensed a delicate thread growing between them. Maybe his vulnerability was real, or perhaps she had imagined it.

If he expected her to join him, he would be sorely disappointed. She would bite his face, kick his groin, knee him in places that he did not imagine existed. Then she would grab his gun, cock it, and pull the trigger, same as any man. When Edward had taught her how to shoot, he said every western girl needed the skill.

Odéon sat cross-legged on the serge blanket and relit his extinguished pipe. He puffed the tobacco to life, pointed toward the wagon, and blew out a cloud of smoke. "There, mademoiselle, you have the bed of the wagon all to yourself. I am quite content here."

She slid from her upholstered footstool, picked it up, and blinked down at him. There had to be something else this man wanted. They always pretended they were not interested–at first. And she was ready. She would smash the footstool over his head if he tried something.

He pulled a flask from his jacket pocket and took a swig. "You waiting for something?" He pointed to the flask. "If it is brandy you seek, I have but little left to sip with my cigar. Otherwise, I would share it."

"No, I do not need a drink." Her muscles tensed, and she made ready for his sudden movement.

Instead, he directed his gaze toward the fire and yawned. "We leave at dawn to make Morienval before noon."

A horse turned his head and snorted as if hearing his words.

She took a step backward, then swept her long skirts around and made haste for the wagon. When she peeked over her shoulder, he was tucking himself into his bedroll, a swirl of smoke lingering over his head.

She dared to think she was safe from him or any man. After climbing up into the wagon bed, she unfastened the second bedroll that Carlo had left for her. *Carlo.* She touched her lips, reliving his deep kisses from the morning. But Carlo—a puzzlement. Just when he might reveal part of himself to her, he would withdraw and busy himself with the furtherance of the cause.

She wedged herself under the blanket, pulled it over her knees, then sat up, taking in her surroundings. The horses snuffled nearby, the light breeze gave a *whish-whish* among the beech trees, and the wagon bed creaked when she moved slightly. She reached up to her chest and flattened the holy medal against her skin, sensing its calm surface.

Through the opening in the canvas at the rear of the wagon, a panorama of stars studded the frosty night sky, framed by bare willow branches bobbing and shifting against the breeze. The constellation's bright pinpoints flared, appearing close enough to touch. Those stars could see her—down here. And they knew where her mother was. If only they could talk to her.

The breeze ruffled something outside the wagon. Maybe footsteps. For a moment, she listened—hard—for another footfall. Her pulse thudded in her ears, and she stifled her breathing. Gently she pulled her pistol from the carpetbag and cocked the trigger. Several seconds passed, though they seemed like hours. Her grip hand moistened around the gun.

But no sound came, only the peaceful gurgle of the flowing stream. Her heartbeats slowed. She curled into the bedroll, tightened it around her, stretched out, then reached for the gun. Once in her grasp, she pointed it away from herself but kept it within easy reach.

She turned onto her side, fixing her eyes on her weapon. Her lids grew heavy; sleep crept in, weaving its web of dreams, capturing her in its spell.

During the next day's journey, when the wagon gained a vantage point on the road, Celeste saw the road sign for the medieval village of Morienval, its ninth-century church spires dominating the countryside. Before entering the town, members of the departmental gendarmerie halted them. Those were local police who kept a post on one side of the road. Since there was no room to pull off onto a byway, Odéon had no choice but to reign in the horses.

Two gendarmes in red jackets, blue trousers, and bearskin hats approached the wagon, one on each side. Each carried a long rifle, topped by a bayonet so finely polished that it mirrored its surroundings. Odéon eased the sweating horses to a stop. Obviously of some rank, the older officer peered up at Odéon and reached out a gloved hand. "Your transport papers, please? And identity card? We want to know what you carry and where you head."

Odéon seemed well-used to these exchanges since he drew out his papers from a box at his feet and handed them down to the guard without comment.

Celeste watched them out of the corner of her eye. She must not draw attention to herself, even though her knees trembled, and the tips of her fingers tingled. She sank deeper into the shelter of her itchy hood.

The capitaine regarded him, then pushed up the visor of his hat. He took his time scanning the documents. "These papers say your name is Odéon Delamare? Hmmm. Related to the famous archeologist, Adolphe Delamare?"

Celeste had heard the name—and yes, she remembered the man. News of him had reached New Orleans. Madame De Salle had even mentioned him. He traveled, sketched, and wrote about the Roman ruins in Algeria.

"He is my uncle." Odéon squared his shoulders as if proud of the association.

The capitaine's eyebrows arched, disappearing under his visor. "A famous man, an explorer, eh? His drawings and excavations were written about in all the papers, *non*?"

"Yes. Sadly, I do not see my uncle often since he is traveling."

"As are you, I see. *Bon.* Very good. And what are you are carrying?"

"Go and see for yourselves. Merely my friend's suitcase and my valise, along with our bedrolls. We are on an errand since my friend wishes to see her *Tante Marie* in Compiègne.

"Your Aunt Marie, you say?"

"Oui," Celeste told her lie without enthusiasm.

"*Très bien*, I will go and check your wagon's contents. Meanwhile, the lieutenant will examine the lady's—er—papers." He gave his companion a wink.

Celeste's heartbeat quickened. She wondered what she would do if he found the gun in her carpetbag.

"Passe-port, s'il vous plaît, mademoiselle."

She drew her passport papers out of her reticule and handed them to the lieutenant. He unfolded them with a smirk, a corner of his lip rolled up, and he glanced upward through bloodshot eyes. Disgusting man. If only they could make a break for it. The farther away from such men, the better. She controlled a shudder.

The wagon bowed slightly as the capitaine climbed up into the bed behind them. Celeste heard a series of creaking noises followed by the shifting of bedrolls and bags. Odéon's knuckles tightened around the horses' reins, and one of the horses strained against his harness.

The lieutenant took his sweet time—his head was down, his hand all but caressing the stamps on her passport. How annoying.

He smirked. "Capitaine, this woman is *American!*"

The wagon bowed again. The capitaine must be leaping down off the back of the vehicle. Rapid footsteps pounded the earth in her direction.

"*Alors, aha.*" The capitaine grunted, thumbing the document and pointing out the red, green, and blue country stamps from Panama to New Orleans to New York to Le Havre.

He cocked his head and narrowed his eyes. "Many women desire to travel to these places. But you are quite young. Exactly, mademoiselle, where is your home?"

"San Francisco, California."

"*L'Amérique! Californie!* Land of gold!" He drew a plug of chewing tobacco from a pocket and nested it in his cheek where it bulged. "Either you are an explorer or a woman of the night traveling with a man who is not your relative." He cast her a knowing sneer. "Or you are an actress playing a part, eh?"

Her heart thumped against the wall of her chest. In her experience, this entrée into a conversation inevitably led to dangerous territory. Besides, they were taking too long. When she leaned out the jockey box, she saw a line of piled-up vehicles waiting for the checkpoint. Transport mixed with personal vehicles snaked into a ribbon for at least a half-mile behind; she spotted a landau, some carriages, and a mule-drawn van.

Horses chuffed, and harnesses jingled. Men in shabby, patched work clothes had gotten off their vehicles and were standing around, some in conversation, others urinating by the side of the road. Feather-hatted women in small groups formed semi-circles, raising their traveling skirts to avoid the mud. Their heated glances darted in her direction. She cringed.

The truth reared its ugly head. *She* was the problem. The lieutenant leered up at her, his gaping mouth revealing a series of uneven brown teeth, incisors caked with yellow scum. Nausea rose in her belly and sat in her throat like a layer of day-old pudding. She imagined the worst. The crowd behind them would roil with anger, ease into a mob, then aim their forceful complaints against their wagon, settling their rage on her, hungry hawks upon a spring lamb.

Droplets of sweat trickled from Odéon's beret onto his sideburns, then hung suspended on the edge of his chin. His gloved hands gripped the reins as the horses grew restless, raising and lowering their heads and neighing. His sidelong gaze telegraphed his dread.

She knew what to do as any Frenchwoman knew—this was the unfortunate truth of those surviving under the reign of this emperor's thumb. They did not need much excuse to detain her further, hold her for more questions, and harass her needlessly. "Wait," she said.

Her words ignited an engine, and the lieutenant at her side of the jockey box reddened, and the capitaine gripped the handles of the jockey box. Celeste opened the drawstrings of her reticule, put her hand inside, and fingered three coins. She avoided shuffling her bag. That way, the men would not hear the multiple coins pinging against one another, a sign she had more money to offer. Instead, she took time searching the reticule as if troubling to locate her few coins in the bottom of the sack.

The capitaine set the lieutenant aside as if moving a chair in his home. He stared up at her, his eyes widened, and he reached out a gloved hand. Maybe he, too, was anxious to be done with her, and since the crowd in line was beginning to get noisy, a mere girl was not worth dealing with any longer.

She dropped one coin into his gloved hand.

He regarded it as one might look at a crumb. He frowned and shook his head.

As though her hand was heavy as a concrete block, she plumbed the depths of her reticule and squinched her cheeks into a grimace. "*Deux*," she mouthed, sneaking the second sou out of her bag and dropping it into his open palm.

"Hurry up!" A voice burst from a van behind them.

"One more, and *voilà*." The sergeant's breath wafted toward her; it smelled of digested wine, moldy cheese, and gum decay. If only she could hold a handkerchief to her nose to block the odor. But instead, she bit her lower lip, pretending to search the empty corners of her bag. She lifted out one coin. "*C'est tout*," she said. "It's all I have left."

He grunted. "*Passez-le moi*." His fingers gestured toward his open palm, where the other two francs lay. "Put it here, mademoiselle."

The coins clinked together as he closed his gloved fingers over them. A catlike smile snuck across his lips, and with his other hand, he beckoned Odéon to pass.

A few hours from Compiègne, the horses needed rest, food, and water. Odéon pulled into a small, wooded rest area off the road, leaped off the jockey box, and came around the wagon while extending his hand up to Celeste.

"I am quite fine stepping down by myself," she said, easing her right foot down onto the lower step.

A cloud passed overhead, darkening his features. His voice grew businesslike. "I will rest the horses, but then we must hasten to Compiègne where we can be safe from thieves and robbers. The sooner, the better, mademoiselle. This road is notoriously dangerous, especially as we near Compiègne." He led the horses to a small brook, where they drank and nibbled on dandelion leaves.

She glanced back and forth down the road. "How so? This area does not look threatening, but what do I know?"

"Imperial guards patrol here because this is the season when high-class society travels this route. They are guests of the emperor, particularly now when he is in residence at the autumn palace in town. He holds fall hunting parties, balls, soirées, and hiking adventures in the surrounding Forest of Compiègne."

"I am more afraid of guards than I am of thieves. Though I have plenty of money, I do not want to visit a bank for fear of causing a stir. Everywhere I go with an American passport, people notice. And if my mother is in trouble, I do not want to leave a trail behind me."

"I agree. We do not wish to call attention to ourselves, especially after the gendarmes' lengthy stop." He offered her a sudden, arresting grin. "They seemed captivated by your charms, mademoiselle."

"And my money did not hurt, did it?"

"Coin is the universal language."

After sharing water from a flask and bread and sausage, Celeste relaxed and accepted Odéon's laconic company. After all, Carlo would not set her loose on the world with a scoundrel. She had to trust him, though she knew she was gullible. And there was something about Odéon that warmed her more than any fire. But so many questions persisted, she took a risk. "What is your business at the coast?"

He drew back, his pupils round and black, reflecting the white oval of her face. "How did you know I head to the coast?"

"Carlo told me that you would take me to Compiègne, then you were going to Normandy, to the coast. I assumed you had some affairs there. Family perhaps? What is it that you do when you're not—em—taking me to Compiègne?"

He sat mute as a stone, then rose and stepped over to the horses and adjusted their harnesses.

How distressing. She hated it when people shut down and refused to cooperate, especially after asking a simple question. Maybe she had been mistaken about him. She huffed a sigh, got up, and stood by his side while he examined the horse's bits. "So, by not telling me your doings, I am sure you are up to something illegal." She set a hand on her thigh and angled toward him, keeping her gaze steady on his face.

He caressed the horse's nose, grunted, and passed a hand across his beard, allowing a forest of breadcrumbs to tumble onto his jacket. He sniffed and looked up at the trees above, stately firs who dominated them and eavesdropped on their conversation.

She suppressed a grin. "No one will hear us . . . only a horse or two," she said.

He shook his head. "One can never be sure. Besides, mademoiselle, if you have information the imperial guards want, they will torture you for it."

A cow mooed far away, and a calf bleated for its mother.

Celeste said, "This sounds then like a serious mission that you are on. You speak of imperial guards and torture. Are you sure you are not merely making this up to tease me so I will admire your exploits? Mind you, I have heard that story from every man in San Francisco."

She rested a hand against her hip. "Do you know that one man even told me he was the mayor? Then, two weeks later, the mayor himself came to have dinner at our parlor house. At first, I doubted that the second man was the real mayor until he proved his identity with a daguerreotype showing him on stage cutting the ribbon for a new bank."

"Do men lie like that in *L'Amérique*?" His gruff demeanor softened into boyish wonder.

"Of course they do. Such men come from all over the world to settle there. Even some from France."

"From the war, I know that men will do anything for gold. Their lies become a way of life."

How well he understood her: if only she could fling her arms around his neck and pull him close. She might be losing her feelings for Carlo. With a pang, she realized she was.

His tone grew businesslike. "That is why we must hitch up the wagon and head to Compiègne before thieves get wind that we are here. By now, the word of you, the American maiden, will be traveling up and down this high road. Now, mademoiselle, out of my way so I may prepare the horses."

"Very well, and soon I shall see my dear Maman."

He slung the food satchel into the wagon bed, brought the horses to the wagon, set them into their traces, and handed her the ends of the reins.

She took the reins, stepped up into the jockey box, and gathered her skirts around her.

Odéon gentled the reins from her grasp, then steered the horses into the direction of the open road. He said, "With luck, mademoiselle, you will find your mother. Nothing is certain in this world. Remember that."

"We have more than luck. We have this." She tapped the medal on her chest and tightened her hooded cloak around her. Then she gave a silent whisper. *And thank God, Odéon, I have you.*

Eleven

THE LETTER N

Had they arrived in the town of Compiègne with tremendous fanfare, Celeste figured it would not have mattered. Their humble farm wagon shrank in the early afternoon light among the multitude of carriages, landau, and barouches surging at the massive columned gates in front of the royal palace. She craned her neck, looking up at the Napoleonic structure. It loomed against the cloudless sky; its three two-story Tuffeau limestone wings embraced a central courtyard, with all traffic halted on the massive stone parade ground outside the exterior gate.

A tricolor blue, white, and red standard fluttered overhead, its surface embossed with golden bees, and in the middle, the imperial coat of arms signaled the emperor was in residence.

Celeste drew in a breath; her truth was an understatement. "We have arrived."

Odéon scanned the imperial building and stepped back. He pressed a hand against his chest. "Have you ever seen anything so grand?" He maneuvered the horses and their wagon into a queue managed by imperial guards. They engaged in checking in all guests and turning away pretenders. The line snaked along the periphery of the terrace amidst the grassy tang of horse droppings, the occasional whiff of rose perfume from a passing carriage, and a random drift of woodsmoke from a nearby chimney.

Celeste double-checked the papers Carlo had given her. One page had instructions—when soldiers motioned their wagon to the entrance, they would enter the palace through the main gate, show the imperial guard their papers with a special invitation embossed by the palace secretary.

Then she would ask to see Pietro Fargella, assistant secretary to the emperor. She rehearsed the steps in her head. Seldom had this trip's passage turned out as expected. She had to be strong enough to take this on, so she gulped and bent herself toward the task—she would do this for Carlo since it served his cause. In what way, she could not be sure. Besides, Odéon would be by her side—she admired his sound intelligence. And her discomfort was worth it—the exchange paid off in her gaining passage to the orphanage where she would find her mother. She was willing to risk a lot—though she did not know the extent of her gamble.

Not long after, the palace guard appeared at their wagon. "Documents, s'il vous plaît."

She fished her papers from her reticule and passed them to Odéon.

Instead of adding his papers, he said, "Only mademoiselle will be entering today."

Her chest tightened. She could not figure out what the hell was going on. She never considered entering the palace alone.

After the guard took her papers inside an outer guardhouse to check, Odéon said, "Mademoiselle, I will not be going in with you."

She took a quick breath. "Why not?"

"I do not have the papers, and besides, I have to mind the horses. No place to feed and water them, so I have to use the water containers

I brought in the wagon and the feedbags back there." He jerked his thumb toward the back of the wagon.

"Ah," Celeste moistened her lips. She must look a fright. Earlier, when she had contemplated going into the palace, she pictured herself alongside Odéon's scruff, and she thought to blend in at his side.

She removed her bonnet and combed her fingers through her unkempt hair. "Do I look–em–presentable? I must have grass stains and mud on my skirt from our nights on the road."

Odéon's grin revealed an uneven set of white teeth. His gruff features softened. "*Tu es très belle, ma chérie.* Most beautiful."

His flattery probably masked the truth. But she had no time to consider his sincerity, so she reset her bonnet and tied the ribbons under her chin.

The guard reappeared, "You have been approved, mademoiselle, but your time in the palace is limited. You have two hours." He lifted papers to her, and his gaze was stern. "Anyone found on the grounds with an expired pass will be detained and possibly arrested. Is that clear, mademoiselle?"

Not wishing trouble, Celeste said, "Oui, monsieur." She did not know what to call him, not familiar with the military life and their ranks. She examined the royal stamp smothering the writing of the pass, a scrawled signature from a palace official, and the words *expires at 2:20 p.m.* If only she could stop her hands from shaking.

"What time is it?" She asked the guard who reached out his hand and helped her down from the jockey box. He peered at her from under his visored cap and gave a huff. She looked at the long queue behind their wagon. Poor guard, he must be pressured. He asked another guard the time. The second guard grumbled, then pulled out a pocket watch. "12:30," he said.

They shorted her ten minutes. Of course. She was not nobility or a vital guest who would sashay in the door with much fanfare. Instead, she was grubby and smelled, unlike the waxed and perfumed ladies whose fans bobbed in front of their faces, their crinolines waltzing with their steps.

She waved back at Odéon, who sat chewing the end of his pipe. He tipped his hat.

The guard's hand pressed her back, propelling her toward the palace gates, motioning her toward an open side door facing the courtyard where another set of guards checked all who wished to enter. She waited for what seemed an eternity among an extensive line of tradesmen and women with handcarts carrying sundry items such as pots and pans or piles of tapestries. Of course, daily life continued at the palace among all its finery.

She winced at her small stature compared to the stately courtyard and imposing structure she was about to enter. A worm would not be closer to the ground than she, a brothel girl. The gates, the columns, the filigree with the letter "N" for Napoléon—all conspired to belittle her. She trembled, not from fear but from being reduced to a tiny planetary ant.

Word of her must have traveled up the line since her name was called out of turn. The purveyors ahead turned in their scruffy hats and patched breeches, and they glared and smirked as she passed.

A footman appeared in a red waistcoat, gold braid, and white breeches. His knee-length black leather boots were highly polished; they reflected light and shadow from their surroundings. "*Suivez-moi, mademoiselle*," he said, and motioned her to follow. He led her along a columnar hallway filled with marble busts of gods and heroes and up a private staircase where butlers and house cleaners scurried in both directions.

Once upstairs, the footman led her along a second columnar hallway, fronted by a series of opulent rooms: she peeked into a gold-painted ballroom where maids set out tables of fruit and violinists tuned their instruments. Imperial staff polished silverware and washed the windows. She covered her open mouth with her hand. *Quelle majesté!* Massive sprays of scarlet, yellow, and orange chrysanthemums and purple hydrangeas hung from wall sconces. She had never seen such grandeur—only in a fairytale Maman would read to her.

After the footman cleared his throat, she regained her path behind him, a bit dizzy from her opulent surroundings. She passed more marble busts, this time those whom she guessed were family members, and stopped. "Who are they?" she asked, holding on to a column for support.

The footman slowed his pace, doubled back to her, and frowned, tightening his white gloves.

Irritation sliced through her. "Am I forbidden to ask questions?" Surely underneath his powdered face, the footman had a family, too.

He paused, leaned up and down the hallway, maybe concerned to be seen. He extended a white-gloved finger toward the marble bust of the straight-mustached man with a pointy beard and marble eyes fixed straight ahead. "The emperor, of course." Next to him was a crowned woman with such sad-looking, close-set eyes. "The Empress Eugénie." Then a sculpture of a little boy with curls adorning his head. She pointed at the child's statue. "He is most cunning."

The footman paused, apparently disarmed by her directness. "Ah yes, Napoléon, Prince Impérial. A sweet child—Louis. I get to see him at times when I pass his nanny in these hallways." Celeste tapped her cheek. There was a soft side to this emperor who tore down buildings and left his people to starve.

The footman stopped at an unmarked door and knocked. Celeste could hear snatches of conversation—two men—from the other side of the door. She made out the words, "dinner party," "Versailles," "the count." She cocked her ear—a sliding sound, a patter of footsteps, then silence. Maybe they had gone. The footman remained expressionless. He knocked again.

"*Entrez.*" The door muffled the words; the voice gurgled like a stopped-up drainpipe. If only her hands would stop their twitching. The footman ushered her into a spacious book-lined study with a table set at an angle facing the room. Behind the desk sat a man Celeste assumed was the assistant secretary. He sported a fashionable knee-length gray jacket with a velvet collar, wide lapels, and a burgundy silk tie that stuck out at horizontal angles. He wore spectacles and wielded a pen on paper as if it were a knife sliding on skin. A pile of documents and folders sat to his right. The front of his desk held a lacquered sign with the imprint,

Pietro Fargella
Secrétaire Impérial Adjoint

After leaving her in a chair facing the secretary, the footman rounded the desk and whispered into Fargella's ear. Their conversation was too low to decipher. Meanwhile, she took a moment to look around. Never again would she be in such august surroundings, close to the beating heart of the empire. She glanced at the two French windows boasting bright green curtains parted in the middle, filtering light through a set of gauze panels. Despite the sunlight, two Carcel oil lamps flickered on his desk, one sizzling loudly. She focused on the assistant secretary, who wore a scowl chiseled on his features.

Fargella glanced at her, frowned, and told the footman, "Leave us—this is a private meeting."

The footman raised his right eyebrow, then reddened. "*Oui, Monsieur le Secretaire.*"

For a moment, she cringed. She had heard the words "private meetings" many times in her brothel life. The secretary might have his occasional flirtations with women such as she. God, let this not be a time she would have to fight off another advance.

"Please state your business here." His words peppered the air between them, his tone crisp, his manner aloof.

She opened her reticule and passed him the papers. The man might be in his early forties. From the name and dark olive complexion, he was Italian by birth. Many Italians worked for this emperor who was born in Corsica, as had been Napoléon the First. Though Corsica was French, it had a history as part of the kingdoms of Pisa and Genoa, so Italian sympathies lay within the population. His gaze seemed to soften—for a mere moment—then hardened.

She imagined a sliver of recognition passed between them. Perhaps, but maybe not. After all, Fargella was assistant to the secretary, the webmaster named keeper of secrets. This man spun threads around the emperor who presided in the center of the orb, a spider commanding his web, dangling truth and lies in equal measure.

Fargella glanced at Celeste's papers, then set them under the ink blotter on his desk. In one smooth movement, he rose and stepped to the left-hand bookshelf. He lifted a couple of the volumes, one marked Cicero, the other Hortensius, laid them on the desk and fingered the wood paneling on the back wall in the space. Whatever he was doing, he could be playing her for a fool. Her palms grew sweaty inside her gloves, so she drew her fingers out of them and set her bare hands on her lap.

He probed the paneling, his right-hand fingers scuttling like a spider's legs.

For a moment, she forgot to breathe. But the pause became unbearable. "Monsieur, may I ask what you are doing?"

After a moment, he turned, replaced the books on the shelf, and said, "I always check to make sure my wood caulking is in place."

"Caulking?" Maybe this man was disturbed—maybe she should let herself out.

His skin drew tight against his high cheekbones. "There were spy holes drilled in the walls during the time of Napoléon Bonaparte. Some may continue there, although His Imperial Majesty had a recent search conducted, and that one that he caulked seemed to be the only one still in use."

"What is over there?" She imagined a desk on the other side, manned by an ugly troll with a feathered quill who spied on them through a peephole, then took down furious notes.

"The passage leads to the secretary's mezzanine along with entry to Empress Eugénie's apartments." He pointed to the far end of the wall. "Do you see where the bookshelf paneling is uneven?"

She squinted at the asymmetrical surface where one of the bookshelves did not appear level with the adjoining wall. "I'll bet it's a—" For a moment, she lost her words.

He inclined his head. "It is a secret passage to the other side, and we must make sure no one is listening. The emperor's spies fill every nook and cranny. I had a terrible experience three years ago—intelligence slipped, threatening the security of the emperor's hunting party, and we had to take measures." He returned the Cicero bust to its former place and raised the ink blotter with one hand.

He paused while his eyes roved back and forth across her papers, and a twitch passed across his mouth. "Your papers are in order."

"Why are you willing to meet me here? It could be dangerous if the emperor's spies found out."

He shrugged. "On the contrary, mademoiselle. What better place to do this business? Right under the emperor's nose. His agents are out checking for spies under every rock. They are not suspicious of me, a man who has worked here as assistant secretary for thirty years."

"But what of the danger—to yourself—your family?"

He raised and lowered his shoulders. "Me? I am a bachelor. But you ask of my family? My sister and her husband died at the barricades in Paris in 1848."

Something tightened in her stomach—another victim of the barricades.

"I am true to the cause of the French, and this tyrant—" He jerked his head in the direction of the empress' apartments. "He makes life worse each day for our people. Over the years of service to the empire, I have never seen such thuggery. And I cannot be a party to it. If there is a way I can help ensure his downfall, it is what I choose to do."

"And what happens if his spies discover you?" Her jaw clenched.

"High treason." He swept his hand across his throat. "Madame La Guillotine."

Her mouth opened.

"That goes for you as well, ma-de-moi-selle." He tapped his pen on the paper, accentuating each syllable.

"For me?" Her breath came in sporadic bursts.

"*Bien sûr*. Of course. You would be labeled a co-conspirator, *n'est-ce pas*?" He put down the pen and ran his fingers back and forth across his lips. She followed the path he made, a hypnotic back-and-forth motion, a razor slicing bloodless flesh.

Several moments passed, their silence was broken by hounds baying and trumpets blaring somewhere on the grounds. The secretary said, "Your message, mademoiselle. And then you must go."

"14 January, 7:00 p.m.," she said.

"That is all?" he asked, his eyes narrowing.

"Oui."

"Very well, here is my message. Paris Opera, 12 Rue Le Peletier. Tell your people. The marquis must know."

"Which marquis? His name?"

"No need for you to know." He passed her papers back to her, tilted his head, and chewed his lower lip. "I wonder if—*bah!* It is worth it. Mademoiselle, would you like to see the gardens?"

"Monsieur, it is most unwise. Somebody could spot me—those

palace guards frowned at me on my way to your office. I certainly do not belong here—in these." She lifted the folds of her gray traveling skirt. Spots of caked mud clung to her hem.

"No problem." Fargella rounded the corner from the desk toward her. "The guards are distracted with the flurry of guests here at the Palace. I have the daily schedule, and today they are hosting many dignitaries from England, Germany, and Spain. They will only see you from afar. It is unlikely the nobles would notice a young woman like yourself. You will most likely never have the means to see a palace again."

"I am well aware of that, monsieur."

"Well then, let us proceed." He led her down the back stairs and onto the pebbled terrace, which gave a sweeping panorama of the multi-hectare property. The sight spread before her like a tableau she had only dreamed of in the brothel in Montmartre. Behind her lay the limestone façade of the palace, its walls stretching flat as if it were a giant's broad chest.

She looked up behind her at the hazy-paned windows dominating two stories where she glimpsed an occasional face peering out, followed by a swish of curtains, or maybe it was a woman's skirts. Ahead lay an enormous expanse of land, a vine-covered canopy that stretched away into the distance on her left.

"How big?" She swept her hand across the landscape much as a painter might brush his canvas.

"14,414 hectares."

"Ah, more than 35,000 acres in *L'Amérique*."

"Napoléon Bonaparte opened the center divider that you see. It splits the forest into two sides until it ends in pure woods." He pointed straight down the middle. "Voilà. On either side are woods and there at the end, a great forest."

Celeste found such vastness hard to digest. She was a city girl limited to the heights of Montmartre, the confines of New Orleans, and the piers of San Francisco. She gazed out at the beech trees that supplied a patchwork canopy of reds, yellows, dark greens. The woods appeared to be on fire at some points, the leaves blazing in their autumn finery. She had heard about such woodland places but had never explored them. In parts, the forests appeared deep blue and foreboding; in others, the sun illuminated patches of green and gold splendor, and a pair of orange butterflies danced in the air.

A group of women in white voluminous tulle skirts floated out from the tunnel of vines. Their fans flowed back and forth, and they stopped to exchange what appeared to be comments and patter. They were not here for the hunt—only the social life. A hunting party gathered to her right beyond the terraced steps, dogs yelping around a bevy of horses and riders, men and women. "What is their reason for being here?" she asked.

Fargella paled. "Their reason?"

"Yes, what do they do?"

He chuckled, clearly entertained by her naïveté. "My child, the women paint, they gossip, they change their clothes at least four times a day. After that, they play cards, hunt with their husbands, and ride in the forest. The guests eat full meals at least four to five times a day. And in the evening, the emperor holds the series—nighttime revelry including games, dancing, performances, fireworks. With drink, my dear. And always food."

"What a lazy life. Aren't they bored?" Maybe she sounded impudent—ungrateful for his help. She stepped back. "I do not have all these things—their clothes—this grandeur. Yet I would not trade their boring lives for mine."

"'Tis true, mademoiselle. Since they were born into their roles, they have little choice, or perhaps the wealthy industrialists or diplomats have made their way into this life. As far as doing something genuine, these women care nothing about tomorrow." He cocked an eyebrow. "Imagine if someone answered your every whim and satisfied all your tastes. You might become as indolent and wasteful as they are."

"In truth, I can see them here—now—and observe their lives, but I cannot understand." She bit her lower lip. "You see, I have spent the last years in L'Amérique where the quest for land and gold provides the reason for most people's daily existence, to make themselves better, to raise the level of those around them. What does the purpose of all this hunting do?"

The secretary swallowed. "Ma chérie, there is no purpose. Do you not see? It is all for show. The emperor must prove his might through frivolity, waste, and excess. The masses do not matter when one is an imperial majesty. He shows this power off to these dignitaries, his fellow royals. They come from all over the world, and he hosts them here."

"I bet the price of those dresses would pay a year's wages for a washerwoman in Paris."

"Ma chérie, you have every reason to say that. But I tell you to mind your tongue. Not only here under His Imperial Majesty's nose, but elsewhere in France. People have disappeared who have said less inflammatory things. Remember your power lies in the mask you wear, not in the unveiling of it."

Servants scurried, apparently preparing to set up a long dining table for guest luncheon. Fargella led her out into the graveled expanse that looked toward acres of forested grounds. "This is hunting season, and the emperor is in residence."

A series of horses and riders galloped away into the woods, and Celeste heard shots fired as the party disappeared. A group of finely dressed women passed before them; their necklaces and brooches reflected the sun's rays.

The secretary gave her a sidelong glance. "And what is your reason for living? Besides helping the cause."

"I am to go and find my mother. She must be here in Compiègne. My driver has the address of the orphanage where she works in community service on orders of the court."

"I have lived here many years—which orphanage?"

"The one run by the Daughters of Charity."

"That religious order has come under surveillance now and then for their revolutionary causes and philosophy of helping the poor. Nothing major, mind you, but the emperor has his eye on their goings-on." He gave a quick intake of breath. "Wait—mademoiselle—do you see her? There?"

He held a tiny spyglass to his eye, then passed it to her. A slim red-haired woman was galloping sidesaddle toward them on a white stallion, her brilliant lavender riding habit billowing as the horse cantered.

"It is—"

"The very one."

"No—I cannot be seeing her—the Empress Eugénie."

"The very same."

The empress dismounted a white mare; a hostler grabbed the reins and led the horse toward a stable at the far edge of the trees. The women from the tunnel of vines approached and gathered around Eugénie. They would be talking about food, the next ball, winter season in Paris. Even from this distance, their high-pitched, meaningless laughter rose in the air.

A sudden urgency enveloped Celeste. She had completed her errand and had seen enough of the excesses at this palace. She had viewed the empress. That would make a memory for a lifetime. But she did not belong here, any more than her shoes belonged on the marbled staircases or parquet floors. No, her shoes belonged on the pathway leading to the orphanage where she would find her mother.

"I must go. The day will wane. I have waited years and—" Thick clouds floated overhead and darkened the rear terrace and the façade of the Palace. "It may rain—"

"*Un moment, s'il vous plaît,*" Fargella said. "Let me give you a proper farewell. He leaned down and kissed the back of her hand. "Godspeed. Do your duty. This contagion, this carrion must be gone. For the sake of France, go, brave girl."

"Maybe I should explain more about Maman."

Fargella held up his gloved hand, palm toward her. "Say no more, mademoiselle. The less I know, the better. Let us return to my office at the library, and I will summon the footman to see you out."

Back in the library, he opened the door to the palace hallway. Footsteps sounded, and a footman appeared, his expression as lifeless as marble. He carried in the tray of café, whose cups and saucers rattled onto the desk.

After Fargella spoke to the footman, he gave Celeste a half-bow. "A pleasure serving you, mademoiselle." She gave a half-curtsy in return, her back foot wobbly. She followed the footman down the servant's staircase to the stone courtyard and went out alone through the iron gates.

Though the footman escorted her out with the customary delicate hand under her elbow, she tired of the cool detachment of the Imperial Palace of Compiègne. Despite her lowly occupation, her San Francisco freedom was something the royal women here would never experience. Or understand.

Never had she felt such a widening gap between herself and France, the country of her birth. She left through the same gates she had entered earlier that afternoon, but something changed. Though she was forever a daughter of France, she was no longer its subject. Instead, she looked forward to the day when she could rejoin her wild unkempt life as a free American.

Having reached the courtyard gates and passing through to the parade ground, she tented her hand and peered into the gaggle of waiting coaches. Somewhere in this crowd of horse-drawn vehicles was Odéon and the wagon.

Twelve

Hôtel-Dieu

The palace gate clanged behind her, the imperial guard unsmiling and indifferent to her departure. She regained Odéon's wagon after some minutes searching the queue of carriages that by now looked to be settled in for the late afternoon into evening, its inhabitants doffing their cloaks and setting out stools, drinking wine and chatting in the unseasonably warm November sunshine. Tobacco smoke drifted through the air.

Odéon lay stretched out on the seat of the jockey box, and she could hear his snoring as she approached their wagon. Poor man. He must have been exhausted. Or perhaps he drank a bit too much wine while waiting for her. Either way, she would have a bit of fun.

She plucked a weed growing between stones on the parade ground and ran it across her cheek. It tickled. That would do. She watched as his nostrils flared, then unflared with his breathing, his chest rising and falling within his dreamy realms. She mounted the steps to the jockey box as quietly as she could, then held the weed under his nose. When he did not respond, she passed it across his upper lip then around his nose.

"A—achoo!" His eyes startled open, and he grabbed for something—anything.

She looked down at him and burst into giggles.

He stared up into her face, his cheeks scarlet as fermented sausages. "*Mon Dieu!* You half-scared me!"

She bent down and caressed his cheek with the back of her hand. "That is what you deserve for sleeping on the job. I jest, of course, dear Odéon. But we must make for the orphanage. I hope you know how to get there." She settled into her usual seat next to him.

He blinked, jerked up, and rubbed his eyes. "Of course. My father used to bring me to Compiègne on market day. I know its streets like the back of my hands." After suppressing a yawn, he clucked the reins and guided the horses off the parade grounds. He gave her a sideways glance, and she fought the dizzying current that urged her closer to him.

Odéon stood up on the jockey box, talking the horses through the melee of visitors continuing to flock to the palace. He eased the wagon out of the burgeoning crowd, narrowly missing the fender of a black cabriolet whose reckless driver must have been in such hurry he nearly missed the evening's revels.

Celeste surveyed the passing landscape, the limestone palace fading behind the tree-lined streets of Compiègne. If anyone suspected her doings, they were clever since no one followed them. Instead, a continual procession of carriages passed them on their way. The night's palace revels would begin at dusk—another evening of excess, sloth, and drink.

She gained the realization that her pathway lay prickly with brambles, not smooth with sheltering leaves. The tree-shaded canopies bent over their wagon as they turned onto twisting, narrow lanes. She wondered where Carlo was and his current plot. And Odéon—she had no desire to back away. Though Carlo promised heart-pounding excitement, Odéon had the steady hand of loyalty, of burning sensuality. But she must never forget the purpose of her journey. She could only hope that her mother lay at the end of that lane—here—in Compiègne.

It did not take Odéon long to find the building housing the orphanage. After a few minutes' ride, he turned their wagon onto Rue Jeanne D'Arc and reined in the horses before the ancient Hôtel-Dieu Saint Nicholas. The building perched in the middle of a narrow winding street, lined with stone buildings whose windows peered down at them as if asking, *What are you doing here?*

Celeste had not counted on arriving so quickly. She pulled a comb from her reticule and arranged her stray hairs into a clip at the base of her neck; after that, she set her bonnet on her head. A Hôtel-Dieu was a sacred place founded by the church—a hospice, orphanage, school, and sanctuary for the poor and disabled in the community.

"Do you want to come in with me?" she asked. Odéon shook his head and drew the ball pipe from his pocket. "I must tend to the horses. Go on—you are going into the arms of the church. You will be fine. I hope you find what you are looking for." He patted her forearm, his touch gentle and warm.

"So do I," Celeste said, and sprang down from the jockey box, smoothed her ballooning skirts, and picked off the dust from her jacket. By now, it was not necessary to ask Odéon how she looked—she wore the day's journey on her face.

She pulled the heavy knocker, and the thick orphanage door swung open. A tall nun belonging to the Daughters of Charity appeared wearing the habit featuring a winged coif made of a white-starched fabric. After a few seconds of adjusting to the outdoor light, the nun's green eyes widened. "Bonjour, mademoiselle. If you are selling something, please note the door sign, *No Solicitations*."

"I am not selling anything—I am here to do a business with the church."

"Well, in that case, child, do come in."

Celeste swallowed and stepped forward into the foyer lit by stained glass windows somewhere above. "Bonjour, *ma soeur*. I am here from Paris, seeking someone who may be a guest of your religious order. Her name is Madeleine Bazin."

The nun stepped across a blue ray coming from the window. "Ah, bien, come with me." She waved her hand, and Celeste followed her swishing black skirts and waving white coif, which resembled a rush of birds in flight. Somewhere the smell of fresh-baked bread filled the air, and she could hear female voices singing the *Ave Maria*.

Wood paneling lined the walls along the hallway, and they passed a series of spacious rooms that served various functions: one with a long table and chairs for meetings; another a chapel with what looked to be an altar for Mass or meditation; another small room with a small couch and two chairs for intimate conferences. At the end of the hallway, a series of rickety wooden chairs leaned against the paneled walls.

"Please wait here," the nun said. She had either a frown or a smile on her face. Celeste puzzled at the nun's sphinxlike expression. Hardly surprising that the churchwomen guarded their own. They had to. France had many movements against its religious orders, resulting in a massacre of Carmelite nuns in Compiègne during the French Revolution. After the nun disappeared around the corner, Celeste heard murmuring voices, the twist of doorknobs, and the screech of a rusty door hinge. She fiddled with the medal around her neck. Something was taking too long.

Her stomach growled. She could not remember her last meal. The day's impressions lay like a collage whose images featured limestone squares, the flutter of white linen skirts, and the long expanse of Compiègne's forest.

At long last, footsteps pounded the floorboards, and the nun reappeared. "Come with me, mademoiselle," she said. She made a half-bow as if in prayer.

Celeste let out a long breath. They traced another long corridor that led into a refectory where she heard the clanging of pots and pans, along with a chorus of adult and children's voices. The steamy tang of vegetable soup triggered her earliest school memories. The nun introduced her to Sister Alphonse from Daughters of Charity, who served soup to a line of filthy children in rags, some toothless, some missing patches of hair.

"I hear you are seeking my help in finding someone. I will be with you in a moment." Sister Alphonse spoke while dipping the ladle into the bowl, then pouring the chunky broth into one bowl after another, the children's outstretched hands cupping the contents. "Be careful, child, do not spill." A little boy complied, and he steadied his bowl. So young. The child could not be more than four. And to end up here motherless and alone.

She knew a kinship with these youngsters. For she also was a motherless child. And fatherless, too. Maman had set her adrift early—too early, and the children's vacant expressions mirrored her child-like thoughts—that voyage to New Orleans, the taking-in-hand of her luggage, the schooling of Madame De Salle in the ways of men.

Yet misery had its degrees. These little ones were gaunt, nearly starving, and babies were crying while clinging to the nuns' hips. Sweat mingled with fecal odors, and Celeste grew dizzy. The nuns around her seemed habituated, for their calm gestures and soothing whispers calmed the children's anxiety, and once the youngsters sat at the long tables with their soup bowls, they supped in relative peace.

Having fed the last of her charges, Sister Alphonse prepared two more bowls and carried them to the end of a trestle table. There she and Celeste took their seats across from one another. "Now, ma chérie, let us eat." She lifted her spoon and cast Celeste a penetrating look. How smooth was the skin of the nun's face; how calm was her expression—no wrinkles around her eyes, yet the woman must be past forty based on the tones in her voice—husky, well used.

After Celeste explained the search for her mother, Sister Alphonse put down her spoon and dug her fingernail into a crack in the table. "Madeleine Bazin, the woman you seek, lodged here on court-ordered community service, working for the poor, both at the almshouse and the neighborhood shanties. She was deciding whether to become a Daughter of Charity at the time and undergoing a crisis of faith."

"My mother was thinking about becoming a nun?" Celeste drew in a breath. That was impossible. Her mother, the madam of Maison de L'Étoile, could never become a nun. She searched her mind for a reason as to what had possessed her. Such a crazy notion. Sure, she was devoted to her faith despite her sinful life, but there were many other choices besides a nunnery. Celeste fought back a feeling of disgust mixed with wonder that her mother would make such an odd decision. "Don't you find that a bit strange?"

"I know all about her background, my child. Over the time she was here, Madeleine was not shy about telling me her past flaws. Your mother was conflicted about taking vows because she also was full of hatred for Emperor Napoléon and his treatment of the citizenry. She would attend secret meetings in Compiègne—who knows what plans they cooked up? When she tried to tell me what they were doing, I would raise my hand and tell her to stop. The emperor's secret agents would stop at nothing to get such information, and I would not put the orphanage or Hôtel-Dieu in such jeopardy."

Out of the corner of her eye, Celeste saw a small child, frail and rickety, who made his way to them, then stood behind her, tugging at her shirtsleeve.

"Another bowl, please." The petite girl held out an empty bowl, and Celeste noticed faded bruises around her wrists. Someone might have tethered the child like an animal.

"Of course, my little love." Sister Alphonse put down her spoon, rounded the table, and led the child to the soup kitchen, where the cook filled her bowl again.

Celeste could have been that poor child if Maman had not kept the brothel. After Papa died, they might have ended up anywhere. Maybe in the Hôtel-Dieu in Paris, standing in a soup line, wondering if there was enough broth to fill their raging hunger.

When Sister Alphonse returned from helping the child, she gathered up their empty soup bowls, took them to the kitchen, and returned. "Come with me, mademoiselle. There is more for you."

Celeste followed Sister Alphonse to a small office. A large crucifix hung on the wall behind the desk; a faded color sketch of the Virgin Mary matched her miraculous medal. Next to the cross, a brilliant sepia portrait of Catherine Labouré peered at the world with saintly wisdom. "I know these images, *ma soeur*. I have the medal my mother left in the last place she lived." She reached below her lace collar and lifted out the disk.

Sister Alphonse took a step closer and examined it. "Yes, indeed. You have the medal of the Virgin." She made the sign of the cross.

Celeste pressed the medal once more against her chest. "I don't understand why she would leave this medal behind her at the house where she lived."

"Maison de L'Étoile? The brothel on Montmartre?" Sister Alphonse gave a half smile.

"Well, yes, although I was not sure you knew, of course. Maman did not tell anyone outside of Paris what she did for a living."

The nun gestured toward two chairs facing the streetside window. "Here, let us sit down. There is much you need to learn."

Though Celeste arranged her buoyant skirts around the chair, she hardly rested back; instead, she sat on the edge of the seat, leaning forward to hear every word.

"Your mother became a good friend, so I learned her entire story. I even knew about you, though I never expected to see you in France. Last she knew, you were in San Francisco. She read your letters, but she could not write to you. Her court sentence forbade it. I think she had given up ever expecting to see you again. But it broke her heart to think that."

Celeste choked back a sob.

The nun continued. "Around six months back, as she kept meeting with the activists in Compiègne, I noticed strange, top-hatted men from outside Compiègne. They would come alone or in pairs, lingering on the street corner near the bakery or over at the tobacco shop across the lane. I commented to my Mother Superior, asking who she thought they were. She wondered if they were surveilling our Hôtel-Dieu because Madeleine lived here.

"And then, one day, the imperial guards arrived and took charge of Madeleine and her meager belongings. We at Hôtel-Dieu were very concerned about her welfare. Mother Superior had many contacts at the magistrate's office. She did some investigating. When she returned with the news, we were stunned. Through her political activities, Madeleine had broken the conditions of her sentence. Thus, the court would impose a harsher punishment.

Celeste raised her hand then pressed it against her mouth.

The nun continued. "The Bureau of Prisons coach took her away five months ago."

"Did you hear any more from her?"

"We exchanged letters through Mother Superior, who was the only one allowed to make contact. Madeleine's faith grew stronger once faced with the mortal nature of her sentence. As time passed, she needed stronger spiritual direction than Mother Superior or I could give her. I directed Madeleine to go to my friend Father Jean, the prison chaplain, who agreed to be her spiritual advisor. I hope she might find her path more clearly. She might see that rather than counting off the days until her death, she could be marking the days until she unites with God."

"Can I go visit her?"

"I doubt it. She is a murderess, kept under the tightest restrictions. And she already violated the imperial trust; they consider her a candidate for execution, depending on the emperor's mercy."

"And where is the prison?"

The nun's gaze narrowed. "Are you sure you want to know? It will only cause you pain, my girl."

Celeste sat upright, setting her jaw in a firm line. "I would like to know anyway. What is the address, Sister?"

Drops of sweat appeared on the nun's upper lip. "The Imperial Prison, Mont St. Michel."

Thirteen

The Cider Must Be Strong

Celeste recoiled. Something shoved against her chest—hard—making it tough to breathe—*Maman*—Mont St. Michel—France's most notorious political prison. Tales abounded from former prisoners, the lucky few who survived. The authorities housed entire families in its frozen womb, high above the channel waters. Her teeth chattered; images fluttered in her mind. Maman sat among the starving prisoners; a rat gnawed on her bloody ankle.

She pounded her forehead. What a fool she had been to blame Maman for not writing to her. If only she had known. It was all she could do to stumble out the doors of Hôtel-Dieu, mount the wagon steps, and huddle against Odéon, who stretched out his arms, a giant bear enfolding her like a cub.

After a few moments embracing Celeste, Odéon freed one hand and guided the horses away from Hôtel-Dieu and out of Compiègne. He asked no questions; better since she could not talk anyway. She needed to fill her lungs with fresh air—the nun's information had smothered her.

Later that afternoon, a half an hour's drive outside of Compiègne, Odéon looked up at the horizon's lowering sun. "We must rest and regain our path tomorrow," he said. "This is a good place to stop." He pointed at a half-timbered coaching inn named *Le Jardin des Roses.*

She surveyed the place. The ancient inn was set between ramshackle buildings; its carriageway opened onto the street. There were no roses to be found—drifts of straw on the cobbles and a bowl of what she presumed to be innards for stray dogs and cats. But no roses.

After guiding their horses into the yard, Odéon handed the horses' reins to a hostler who grabbed the lines and tied them to a hitching post. The horses sweated and chuffed, their breath filling the brisk air with white puffs.

Celeste and Odéon gathered bags from the wagon, and the hostler led the horses and wagon into the stable yard behind the building. Celeste followed Odéon across the cobbled courtyard of the medieval structure to a small office housing the first-floor concierge. In tandem, they pushed open the French doors and ducked into a low-slung room.

The clerk behind the desk peered through dusty spectacles. A curious gray cat with black-tipped ears meandered over from the far end of the room, wound through Odéon's legs, then sniffed the edge of Celeste's skirts. "Two rooms under the names Monsieur Blanc and Mademoiselle Neige," Odéon announced to the clerk. The cat leaped up onto the central ledger and licked his front paw with abandon.

"Mr. White and Miss Black?" The clerk dabbed his pen tip in the inkpot and hesitated. "Are you quite sure you do not want to share a room? We have a large suite on the middle floor with a lovely view." He ran his tongue slowly across his lower lip. Celeste figured he either guessed them to be unmarried adventurers or a couple having a fling, their spouses unaware.

Odéon fumbled, dropping his beret on the floor. He took his time bending down to pick it up. His hands trembled slightly.

She hovered between pleasure and suspicion since the proprietor might concern himself with the inn's reputation. She gazed at the price sheet glued on the counter. Apparently not. The cost of the suite was a third more than the two rooms combined.

A quizzical expression, almost merry, played about Odéon's eyes. His gaze riveted on her face, then swept over her bodice and crinoline skirts. He aroused her curiosity as well as her vain impulses. That might be an invitation. Well—maybe—but she had not considered him in that way, or perhaps she had. Carlo, yes, but not solid Odéon. But she had to admit stirrings when he was near. And she trusted him, no small matter where she was concerned.

"Two single rooms," she said.

Odéon looked up at what appeared to be a crack in the ceiling plaster.

"Très bien." The clerk bumped the cat aside with his elbow and printed their fictitious names in the ledger. He did not ask for identification. "Suivez-moi, monsieur, mademoiselle." Then he led them outside across the cobbles and up an outdoor set of rickety wooden stairs to two rooms, one above the other. He unlatched the doors to the rooms and gave them each their keys.

Celeste pointed. "I'll take the top chamber, Odéon. That way, if you hear anyone coming up the stairs, you will know I am in danger." She maneuvered up the steep steps, tucking her long skirts under her arm. It felt good to release the ribbons under her chin and pull off her bonnet, letting her hair flow in white-blond waves over her back and shoulders.

Odéon stood on the landing, chewing the end of his ball pipe stem. "Excellent idea, mademoiselle. I would be devastated—er—concerned if anything were to happen to you." He hastened to add, "Carlo would not be happy." His voice was thick, as unsteady as the sloping steps under him.

The innkeeper cleared his throat and said, "We serve le dîner promptly at eight in the snug downstairs. Tonight, the chef prepares Cassoulet à la Normande, featuring apples, potatoes, and pork. Taste our local hard cider, famous throughout the land. Your head will spin, I guarantee. *Au revoir.*"

"Would you care to accompany me tonight?" Odéon asked. "I planned to dine here." His voice was intense, his tone husky.

His formality caught her off guard. After these days and nights on the open road, she had not suspected he could be such a gentleman. "Of—of course," she stammered.

"Very well." He eased a pocket watch from his coat pocket. "It is now six o'clock—may I call for you at fifteen minutes to eight? That should give you enough time to freshen up, n'est-ce pas?"

"C'est bien." She took the stairs, her hands balanced on the half-timbered railing. After skipping up the winding steps and standing on the upper floor landing, she swept her gaze over him.

He flashed her a brief grin, his teeth dazzling white against his dark beard.

After a much-needed cold sponge bath in the claw-foot tub, Celeste dressed in her tattered dingy skirts, her chemise giving off an odor that would turn a saint's flesh grey. What would Maman say to see her so grimy? Or Madame De Salle in New Orleans? She shrugged into her lace-up half-boots and strolled over to the window facing the lower courtyard. Were she not in such dire circumstances, she might believe it to be a quaint locale.

She opened the small window and looked out. Potato vines with amber and purple leaves laced the walls surrounding the intimate, cobbled courtyard. Already a chilly evening, the twinkling lamplights illuminated the ground-floor interiors. The concierge and his family sat together before their evening meal while an older woman, most likely the grand-mère, hobbled around their table, setting down loaves of bread, along with plates of sliced meats and cheeses.

Whether viewing the tranquil family eating together around the table or hearing the fictitious names Odéon had used downstairs, something caused a twinge in Celeste's stomach. Her thoughts sharpened; her questions penetrated. She wondered what the secret message she carried meant to accomplish. If only she knew what had happened to Carlo and his friends while she and Odéon had traveled to Compiègne. Carlo's smile flashed into her mind; she had almost forgotten his energy, his fire. She wondered about Liliana, tagging alongside her. Though she fit the group comfortably, she was young to be in such a difficult situation.

Carlo might face danger in his endeavors. She was disappointed that she would not be able to see him. But then, she had given up trying to understand what he and Felice were doing, yet this scheme had to be life-threatening.

She could not fathom what kind of scheme was involved. It had to do with the emperor. Maybe the group worked for the emperor or plotted against him. She wondered whose side Secretary Fargella had taken. They might have a reason not to trust him; he could lay a trap. And she mused about Odéon's role in all of this. If only she were not so ignorant about politics.

What a shame she lacked schooling. Maman should have educated her beyond the sixth grade. She had not sent her to school with all the other neighbor children in Montmartre. Each morning Celeste would peer out the front window where her old friends Marthe and Jeannette strolled arm in arm, rucksacks on their backs, and then again at noon when they returned home for lunch.

At other times, too, Celeste paused, broom in hand, and watched other schoolchildren pass Maison de L'Étoile, clutching papers filled with numbers, letters, and colored pencil drawings. And later, she would meet the adolescents in the streets, their uniforms crisped, their pants pressed, their skirts without stains. And by then, Marthe and Jeannette no longer greeted her, for they were a world apart, a world with a promise, a world with a future.

She closed the small window against the night air. On the ground floor, the family bent their heads in prayer around the dining table. She tapped the Virgin's medal lying flat against her chest. Maybe she should do the same.

Celeste supped with Odéon that evening in the downstairs snug, which functioned as a bar and hot food establishment. For some reason, when he greeted her, she noticed a change in his manner. Odéon presented as a well-dressed man who would court a woman instead of the scruffy, ill-kempt wagon driver. When he removed his beret at the threshold, his wavy hair glistened, parted in the middle, as if freshly washed. He even smelled of lavender pomade.

She giggled to herself. Odéon might be trying to court her.

He guided her to the far corner where few customers lingered since most of them hung about drinking near the crackling fireplace. After helping take off her cloak, he handed it to the same man who functioned as the day concierge. He set his chair next to hers on the same side of the table.

A pock-cheeked youngster appeared; his half-apron was stained and greasy. He aimed a glance at Celeste. "How many plates?" His question meant they might share one portion—that was intimate.

Sensing that this was a one-course establishment, she looked at Odéon. "I-I do not know. How many?"

Odéon grinned and put up two fingers.

The server nodded. "Deux cidres?" Two ciders, he asked.

"Bien sûr." Odéon reached into his pocket, brought out his ball pipe, and ran his hand lazily over the stem. Light from the corner lamps played across the pleasant angles of his face.

The waiter vanished into what must have been a kitchen behind the bar. Odéon scooted his chair closer. His nearness took her breath away, and his mood seemed lighter. "You didn't tell me what you found out about your mother's whereabouts." He brought a lit candlestick to his pipe and bent nearer, puffing until the tobacco flamed red. Then he gazed at her, his lips slightly apart.

Before his appealing smile, her defenses melted away—all but one. She stiffened. He had not appeared so interested in Maman before. In fact, in their earlier talks, he had merely listened. She wondered why this sudden shift.

He regarded her through a cloud of aromatic tobacco smoke spiraling around his head. After picking some tobacco leaves off his lower lip, he said, "I am dying to know. I was surprised when you came out of the orphanage alone, but I did not want to say anything for fear someone would overhear."

His nearness made her giddy, almost reckless. It was all she could do not to rest her head on his shoulder and entwine her arms around him. But she resisted—at least for now.

A loud tinkling of glasses bumping against one another alerted them. A serving girl with Dutch braids set down their cider glasses and a full carafe. Odéon drank as if his portion was water and poured himself another. Celeste sipped her heady, light mixture of fermented apple juice. Her mother served hard cider at the brothel, and she remembered its pungent, sweet taste as a young child.

She looked at the remaining cider in her glass, its beige color deepening to gold at the bottom. "You know, she is at Mont St. Michel."

Odéon rested his pipe on a tray. His eyes flickered for a moment, and then he rubbed his beard. Odd. He appeared to hide something. After a pause, he said, "We are headed in that direction tomorrow."

Her heart thrummed. "I plan to get a ride to Mont St. Michel from there."

"I could not reveal our plan to you earlier for fear you might spill to someone along the way. We are headed to Normandy, but I can't tell you exactly where we are going until we get there."

"Well—if we will be in Normandy, could you take me there—that is, to Mont St. Michel? To Maman?"

He scanned the room, appraising the various travelers in the bar, at neighboring tables, and around the hearth. He raised his palm toward her. "Not now, Mademoiselle Celeste. There are ears everywhere."

The serving girl appeared, steaming plates in her towel-wrapped hands. "Be careful. The dishes are scorching."

Celeste found it hard to ignore the simple elegance of the ceramic bowl set reverentially before her. She spied what appeared to be sauce-covered chunks of pork in a nest of bright orange cut carrots, aromatic brown apple bits, and sliced white onions. She bent her head and breathed in the fragrance of garlic, thyme, and onion which deepened her hunger pangs.

She set her fork into the dish, and the meat fell apart quickly. Ever since New Orleans cuisine at Madame De Salle's brothel, she had seldom sniffed such a savory profusion of flavors. After she swallowed her first bites, she said, "I taste the alcohol in this dish—the cider must be strong."

Odéon paused, the meat-piled fork inches from his mouth. "You are correct, ma chérie. Fermented Norman cider from a local orchard, no doubt. Where I come from. And this is apple-picking time, so the ingredients in our local dish are nothing but fresh." The fork disappeared into his mouth.

She recalled the chef in Maman's brothel hovering over his stewpots as though they were church offerings. "I'll wager it took much time to prepare this."

Odéon spoke through a mouthful. "Two full days, if not more."

"Ah, that gives the flavors time to blend with the meat." She swallowed bites of the heavenly mixture, along with intermittent sips of cider. If only she could eat this way every day. She thought about

Brianna and Edward's brothel she planned to take over in San Francisco's Little Canton on DuPont Street. She would include this meal and drink on the next fall season's menu for her guests. Bien sûr. Brianna and Edward would be pleased.

"Mademoiselle. As to your question about taking you to your Maman in Mont St. Michel." He sipped his cider and regarded her, a nest of tan lines highlighting his deep-set brown eyes. "For youth, that question comes easily, but with years you will understand that it is not that easy to fulfill our wishes—just like that." He flicked his tobacco-stained fingertips against his chin. He lowered his voice to a whisper. "After all, we must deliver your secretary's message to someone in Normandy."

She bristled. "He was not *my* secretary. I was only returning the favor of your taking me to the orphanage—or wherever I could find Maman." She swatted away a teardrop that clung to her eyelash. She would not—could not—let him see the extent of her disappointment at not finding Maman at Hôtel-Dieu. A deep chasm opened whenever she contemplated the possibility of never finding her at all. The only way she could fill that crevasse was with information. And so, she vowed to press Odéon—he must—he would—cough up more details.

After dinner, they stretched their legs, strolling along the darkening streets in the small surrounding neighborhood. They passed blocks of buildings housing ground-floor businesses, their lace-trimmed windows shuttered for the night, the only sound a barking dog or an occasional mangy cat mewing in the alleyways.

Beyond the local housing, she could hear the agricultural sounds—an occasional lamb's bleat or cow's lowing in a distant pasture. A stiff breeze caught her skirt, and she bundled her cloak about her. She should have brought along her neck scarf. But she would endure this chill—she needed Odéon to fill in some missing gaps.

She said, "Why are you in this group with Felice and Carlo? It seems like the son of a Norman farmer or orchardist would not need this—adventuring." She waved her hand in the air, partly to clear the haze of smoke that enveloped them as he puffed his pipe.

"I am a republican who believes in the ideals of the French Revolution. These conservative monarchists are laying waste to France." Odéon's voice took on a rhythmic lilt in Norman dialect as he narrated his family's past. "My father fought in Russia for Napoléon Bonaparte and nearly died of starvation and frostbite, and he warned me that I should never trust any member of Napoléon's family. He argued the Bonapartes were power-grubbers not interested in serving the needs of our populace." He stepped off the curb, guiding her across the muddy road and onto firmer ground.

"I remember such talk in Maman's brothel growing up. The men she served had strong views which they felt safe sharing with the prostitutes."

Odéon continued. "But that was not all that made me raise my fists against this regime. My two younger brothers died at the barricades in the Paris uprising of 1848. The cause I'm risking my life for has to do with undermining Napoléon's power at any cost. And I am not alone. Many in France would do the same, but few dare to undertake such an operation."

"Maman lost her brother at those same barricades." She took a quick breath.

He closed the step between them.

She tilted her head to one side and stole a look at him. She found herself aching for his touch.

Removing the ball pipe from his mouth, he enfolded her in a hug, the open lapels of his greatcoat enclosing her in his warmth, his body a cave sheltering her from the threatening surf whose incoming tides might engulf them both. She stretched her arms around his waist; his muscles were taut and hard. He caressed the stray tendrils of hair around her neck; his lazy fingers lingered on her bare skin.

They stood wrapped together for who knew how long, letting the warm waves pass over them. Their common grief struck a deep chord inside her. She pressed him an elbow's length away. "You and the men—this is some plot? A conspiracy?"

He released her and buttoned his greatcoat. "It gets colder, mademoiselle. Time to head back." He cleared his throat, turned abruptly, and aimed his footsteps back toward the inn.

She kept up his pace, marked by long strides.

As they passed a shuttered bakery, he spoke. "If not for the Italians who want revolution in their own country, along with their British allies, Frenchmen would not have the guts to embark on such a movement."

"That is why we see Felice and Carlo involved. They are the prime movers?" She narrowly avoided turning an ankle on a loose cobblestone.

He bit down on his pipe stem. "I cannot say too much, mademoiselle. If captured and tortured, you might tell too much."

"What would I say? Torture?" Her neck stiffened.

"It is getting late, and I have perhaps said too much. You must act as if you know nothing, ma chérie. This information could cost not only your life but the souls of many brave men and women who cheer us on. Though they would never admit to it, nor should you."

Inside the inn, she stood on the steps outside her lodging door. She looked down on Odéon, who watched her from the shadows. Her loneliness—her confusion—her yearning. All welded together in an upsurge of involuntary longing for him. Wispy smoke obscured his expression. He vanished into his room. Smoke lingered in the air long after he was gone.

Fourteen

VERGONCEY

After three days meandering on muddy country lanes winding through villages and apple orchards, Odéon and Celeste arrived one late afternoon at Château Maintenon, near the town of Vergoncey. They neared the border between Normandy and Brittany, Odéon had informed Celeste along the way. Though familiar with place names, Celeste did not know her geography. It was not her mother's fault—after Papa's death, she needed Celeste to help run the brothel. That was why she had not continued at school. Or so her mother had said.

Lulled by her memories, she scanned the autumn landscape for clues as to their whereabouts. They might be at the ends of the earth for all she knew, though this end was picturesque with its farmyards and hedgerows dotted with farmhouses. She had learned peaceful contentment by Odéon's side. A pity this might be at an end.

He steered their wagon through an open gate and onto a pebbled road that fronted an 18th-century grand château. Since he had been here before, he acted as a tour guide. "The house was torn down and rebuilt in 1763 by the former marquis. It has many rooms, most of which are quite lively and interesting. We will meet the current marquis."

She took in the two-storied grand manor house looming in the distance, its white-beige façade fronting a great expanse of lawn and a stream-fed pond with a wide bed, flowing in and around inlets with a small island on one side. A wooden footbridge led from shore to the island, where wrought-iron chairs surrounded a small table. She ran a dirty finger across her cheek, lost in considering the scene. She had seen much elegance in New Orleans and beauty in Paris, but this was a fairytale landscape.

A team of snowy ducks paraded across the lawn, and a duckling waddled into the water. A gust of wind swept the lush canopy of trees over the scene, revealing a startling leafy array of dark browns, hazel greens, and deep crimsons. Not long from now, the gorgeous panorama would be barren, gripped by ice and snow. An ancient chapel appeared on a small hilltop to the right, its limestone hues matching the house.

"What are we doing here? Is this our last stop? How long will we stay?" Celeste peppered Odéon with questions until he raised his hand. "*Arrêtez*—stop! *Patience*, ma chérie. You will see it in time. Do you not trust me?"

Celeste raised her eyebrows. "Of course not. Very few men—if any—have my trust. Especially since you never told me directly where we were going before we got here. And I am tired of you not telling the reason behind all this plotting. I have got a mind to go—somewhere else."

Odéon shook his head, surveying the road ahead. He was in no mood to humor her.

She bit a hangnail on her right index finger and entertained her thoughts. If she left Odéon, she had no idea where she would go or how many kilometers to the nearest town. She was in no condition, tired and tattered, to go out walking. Supposing she made it to town, she had no idea what she would do. Maybe find a coach for hire to take her to Mont St. Michel. They might not even have a transport service in a town as small as Vergoncey. Hardly likely. A sob rose in her throat and stuck there like an undigested piece of carrot.

The horses slowed, their breath sending chuffs of steam into the late afternoon air. After the wagon came to a stop, a Brittany spaniel with white and brown patches sped out of the house and greeted her as she eased down off the jockey box. He took an end of her skirt in his teeth and tugged. "What are you after, my little friend?" she asked. He dropped her dress and headed back to the steps of the house where an older man waited, his back slightly bent, his long white hair flowing over his shoulders.

A stable boy appeared from behind the house, and Odéon settled the wagon and the horses. She lingered near him as he calmed the sweating animals. "What am I to do now? After we meet with the marquis, where will you be?" For some reason, she would feel lost without his calming presence, the sweet tobacco fragrance of his coat.

His eyes widened in surprise, and flecks of gold sparked. "I will be working with the men, mademoiselle. We have a mission, and I have my tasks."

"Please at least give me a proper goodbye." She stood on tiptoe and kissed him on one cheek, then the other. She lingered a moment before his lips, then brushed them lightly with her own.

He flushed, holding the horse's mane with one hand, the reins with another.

"Who do I follow if you're not—well—with me?" She asked. She petted the Brittany spaniel, who returned. The friendly rascal jumped up on her and gave her licks on her cheek.

"I think you follow him," he said, a wistful smile curving his lips.

She had no choice but to follow the dog. The spaniel bounded ahead of her toward the entrance of the grand house. When she reached the older man at the top of the steps, he bent over and kissed her first on one cheek, then the other. "Welcome, my young lady. I see our dog Pierre has brought you to our door. This is Château Maintenon, my house. You are to make yourself at home here. I have heard much about you already." Crinkles papered the surface of his cheeks, and furrows encircled his eyes.

"Already? But Mon Seigneur, we have only just met." Her mouth fell open, and she clamped it shut—she did not want to appear stupid in front of such a worldly gentleman, but she had never met an aristocrat in person. The nobles were distant figures passing by in elegant carriages or viewed from a distance at Compiègne. Never this close.

After stabling the horses, Odéon mounted the steps and stood next to her, his hat in his hand. His ball pipe was visible inside his breast pocket.

The marquis regaled them with cheek kisses and escorted them into the mansion.

The doors plunged open onto a vast hallway, beyond which lay an opulent dining room painted in lime green with white crown molding. Low horizontal sunbeams filtered from windows displaying a vast landscape behind the house. Celeste wished she could take steps across the tiled floor and gawk at the giant chandelier presiding over the dining table.

The marquis cleared his throat as if reading her thoughts. "You will see more of the house and grounds during your stay here, but now, we must conduct the affair closest to our hearts, *n'est-ce pas*?" He laced his fingers together, and Celeste noticed his manicured fingernails, so different than the cracked, muck-encrusted digits of working-class men. Of course, she told herself, the marquis did not do manual labor—none of the nobles did. Others worked for him.

Her wonderings took a sudden turn. She questioned what Odéon, a self-professed republican, wanted with the marquis, a member of the noble classes. *Patience,* Odéon had said earlier. She bit her lip hard. She might not be up for this ordeal. It was one thing to gather a message from the palace; it was another to find herself at a country house populated with men. Besides, she was without the means or opportunity to get away. And a ribbon of hunger traveled through her. If only she could eat again soon. She tried not to think about that.

The marquis led them into a cozy wood-paneled study. On the far end loomed a bookshelf filled with volumes that reminded her of the palace library at Compiègne—she had never seen so many books then or now. And a great hearth whose fire sputtered, its dying embers needing more wood and an attendant to fan the flames. The marquis beckoned them to sit at two chairs facing his desk behind which clung wall paintings of the grounds and house and a daguerreotype featuring a lock of white hair. An older woman—a piece of black crepe graced the frame's exterior. That must be his wife who died, a good guess since the marquess had not come out to greet them as was the custom.

A black-jacketed servant carried in three small brandy glasses and served each of them.

Their host sipped first. "Enjoy the Calvados, our local apple liqueur." Rather than engaging in pleasantries, the marquis swept them into the business. "Let us put to rest the matter that awaits us. Odéon, you have visited the Imperial Palace at Compiègne and mademoiselle, you have received the message from the secretary?" She nodded, and her sideways glance revealed Odéon, who did the same.

The marquis continued, his accent reflecting the rolling cadence of the upper classes. "Bien, I do not write anything of importance related to these matters, so please tell me the message." He tapped his temple with his forefinger. "In here are many secrets, my dear friends."

Celeste breathed in profoundly and swept the back of her hand across her dusty forehead. "Opéra Le Peletier, 12 Rue Le Peletier, 7:00 p.m."

The marquis drew back and rubbed his hand over his mouth. "You say the Paris Opéra? I repeat to verify."

"Those were his very words." The Calvados was relaxing her bones. And now that she had passed the message, she could relax. Her eyelids grew heavy; she settled back into her chair.

The marquis said, "This news signals a shift—a most dangerous change in plans. It will take more technique than the previous idea." He exchanged glances with Odéon.

"But this is not impossible, given the English ammunition." Odéon drew out his pipe from his pocket; he stirred the small tobacco leaves within its bowl.

The marquis ran his finger around the rim of his glass. "We must wait to see what the others think."

"The others?" Celeste leaned forward, dizzy from her strong drink and an empty stomach.

A pause ensued. Each man withdrew into silence. A crow cawed outside the window, and the Brittany spaniel stirred beneath the desk. Celeste leaned down and ran her fingers along the dog's back, the touch of his soft fur comforting her. A map of France lay on the desk under the marquis' elbows. She could see dark marks and red arrows drawn on it. She leaned closer to see what the arrows showed. A strip of blue. Maybe they were pretty near the coast. If she stretched her neck, perhaps she could see Mont St. Michel on it. *Merde.* She was so ignorant of geography. What a shame. She knew America better than her native land.

The marquis broke the quiet. "But I am a terrible host." He pointed at a pre-revolutionary timepiece ticking on the fireplace mantel. "It is now four in the afternoon. Let me show you to your rooms where you may rest before dinner."

On their way up the wide stone staircase to their chambers, she turned to the marquis. "I have a question."

He rested his hand on the banister and took a moment to catch his breath. "I may not be able to answer some of your questions—it depends."

"How far is it from here to Mont St. Michel?"

"Why, only sixteen kilometers. I take many of my guests there on junkets. We lodge at a pleasant inn run by Madame Poulard on the island. Her omelets are famous throughout France."

She turned back to Odéon, who stepped behind her on the stairs.

"Did you hear that? Sixteen kilometers to get to where Maman might be?"

"Oui, bien sûr. I know."

"You know? Have you always been aware of this?" Her voice trembled.

He cleared his throat; a patch of red bloomed on each cheek.

Odéon knew, but he never told her. He was either cruel or plain stupid. Consumed by a silent burn, she rolled her ankle on the steps, and the marquis caught her before she fell. "Watch your step," he said.

She brushed off his hand. "Oui, I will be more careful." Once again, she savored the lie.

Though the dinner had been sumptuous, the mattress comfortable, and her quilt protective against the autumn chill, Celeste spent a restless night with many a toss and turn among the stiff cotton sheets. Every squeak of a mouse or trill from a night bird woke her, and her dreams filled with patchy and disconnected images. She got up and perched atop the chamber pot, relieved herself, covered it, and slid it back under the bed.

She placed one leg up on the mattress, about to climb back into bed, when she heard the crunch of wheels on the pebbled ground and the grumbling of horses against their bits. Something was going on. She put two feet on the wooden floor and tiptoed to the tall French windows facing the main carriageway fronting the house. She unlatched the wooden shutters and peered out at the dark expanse.

Torches and lamps lit the entryway. Other wagons arrived, and men unloaded giant boxes and crates, hoisted them into handcarts, then disappeared with the cargo around the left-hand corner of the house where the stables and barn were situated. A significant movement was afoot.

A coach pulled up, and through radiating light, she saw steam rise from the horses' mouths. While his servant held a flambeau high above them, the marquis, wearing a nightcap and long robe, exchanged cheek kisses with a tall, top-hatted man. There he was—Carlo in profile. She put a finger against her throat where her pulse raced.

He must be part of the operation, whatever it was. The giant boxes and crates were not carrying vegetables—that she could be sure. Most likely equipment or weapons. Odéon mixed with Carlo and Felice from Montmartre. They gathered, then broke apart, the marquis leading them into the house below. A stable hand took the horse and carriage back toward the stables. Not long after, the pebbled carriageway lay in shadowy stillness, erasing all sights of the scene that had taken place.

Celeste grabbed her shawl, flew out the door, and reached the dimly lit staircase leading to the ground floor. She stepped down the first set of winding stairs but halted before a landing where the stairs turned right, leading down to the reception hallway. If she stayed shrouded, she would be unseen. The group of men entered, doffed their top hats, and removed their cloaks. Wall sconces and lanterns lit the scene like an evening's pantomime.

Luckily, Carlo did not glance up the stairway, so she remained on the unlit marble staircase. She was dressed only in her nightgown and wrap; experience in the brothels taught her not to push her luck. Even though familiar, a group of men involved in a dangerous activity could pose a threat for a woman who got in the way. Thus, she watched and waited.

Fifteen

That Tickling Weed

The men in the entryway circled the marquis, and she could make out only a word here and there. She pressed her nose through the filigreed railing of the stairs. They took turns clapping each other on the back, and an occasional peal of laughter rang out. A butler joined them from the central dining room, carrying a tray with what appeared to be a brandy bottle and small glasses. They must be going to celebrate something—she would love to know what that was.

After filling their glasses, the men headed toward the combination library-study whose book-lined haven served as their meeting room. Carlo was the last to enter. If only he would turn around. She drew back into the shadows. No—Carlo did not see her—just as well—she would not want to draw too much attention to herself—but she would have loved to race across the hallway and grab him around the waist, startling him and the others. *Click.* The double doors closed tightly behind the men, and a shuffled murmuring faded away.

She tucked up her long nightdress and eased herself down the steps to the foyer. Hazy light from the wall sconces cast shadows across the floor. The black and white stone tile pavement chilled her bare feet, but she could tread lightly without shoes or slippers. She eased across from the stairway to the double doors of the library. Maybe she could catch a word or a phrase that would give her a clue about what they were planning. Through the large keyhole, she could spot the marquis in an armchair across from the lit fireplace, but she could only hear the others' voices—wait—if she was reticent, she might listen to their words.

"Mont St. Michel," Carlo said.

She sucked in a breath. Maybe she had imagined it. No, she heard it again; this time, Odéon spoke. "Mont St. Michel." Then—"the beach"—and other voices rose, their crosstalk and intonations making it difficult to hear specific words. *Morbleu!* If only—

Someone touched her elbow; her thoughts jangled.

"Mademoiselle?"

Her heart thudded.

The butler's black buckled shoes were shined to perfection, his knee stockings pearl white. She gazed into the lashless eyes of the white-wigged manservant, his black jacket and white gloves resembling those of a judge or magistrate. "Are you lost? Would you like me to bring you some after-dinner liqueur? Some hot milk? A bit of absinthe?" His voice rang with goodwill, but his eyes were devoid of emotion.

A burning sensation melted the tips of her toes, and flames of embarrassment licked her spine. "No, I—I—well, yes, some hot milk does sound fine."

"I shall bring it right up to your room, mademoiselle. May I suggest you wait for me there?" His familiar voice handled the errant guest who might find herself where she did not belong, yet he would never be so bold as to tell her directly.

She traveled back up the chilly stone steps to her second-floor room. Someone may block her from entering the library to hear what they said, but she could not stop wondering. Maybe Carlo would not want to tell the others that he knew her. After all, he set her up as a courier to the palace at Compiègne. Though she did recognize Pierre, Felice, and Odéon, she did not know who else was in his party and other friends of the marquis. What they were up to, she could only guess.

Someone's knuckles tapped on her door. The butler entered, flourishing a silver tray with a lace doily, a teacup, and a vase full of milk. After setting the tray on a cherrywood table by the hearth, he poured the liquid into the teacup and asked, "Sugar, mademoiselle?"

"No, merci."

She was tempted to ask him to tell her about the marquis' involvement, but she did not dare. If only she had carried more money with her from Paris, but even with a bribe, she could not be sure he would tell her the truth.

Long after the butler backed out of the room, tray in hand, and shut the door behind him, she sat on the edge of the bed staring at the white marble bust of a young girl gracing the mantelpiece of the hearth. Her identity was a mystery. Braids wound around the back of her head, ringlets around her ears, and her bustière revealed an 1830s style. Maybe she was the marquis' daughter. She looked to be eighteen or so.

Her thoughts returned to events downstairs. Carlo had sent her to Compiègne as a courier. What meaning did the message have for the marquis? She itched to know the details of this grand scheme. She crossed the room, unlatched the shutters, and peered down into the darkness. No activity took place in the front of the house, but maybe something was going on around the back and sides. The wagons had disappeared into what had to be the stable yard at the back of the property. She guessed the tall window at the end of the hallway might look out on the stable yard—worth a try.

She picked up a lamp from the same table that held the hot milk and carried the light down the hallway to her right. She must have passed ten rooms and another servant's staircase at the hall's end before reaching the tall window facing what must be the stable yard. Torches and lanterns lit up the place. More wagons continued to arrive—she counted three or four—heading around the drive into the stable yard. She bit her lower lip. Tarp covered what she guessed to be wooden boxes. If only she knew what was inside them.

Voices, muffled at first, then louder, reached her ears. The men from down below. *Morbleu!* It was all she could do to resist taking the servants' staircase down to the stable yard. She must get back to her room without being spotted as they came up the stairs. She raced down the hallway, cursing the long nightgown that made triple steps awkward, then reached her doorway.

She lingered at her door, her chest heaving, listening to the men's goodnights and the marquis' wishes for good sleep. Which room was Odéon's? He would park his fragrant pipe on the side table before setting his curly head on the pillow as she had seen him do while they were on the road.

And of course, Carlo with his sharp gaze and conquer-the-world spirit. He had to be sleeping in one of the ten rooms on this floor or perhaps the story above. She could not exactly go down the hallway knocking on doors to find either one. And yet, as she lifted herself onto the high mattress of her bed and tucked her legs under the quilt, her last thoughts were of Odéon and the day she teased him with the tickling weed. She could not resist a laugh, which eased her into the pleasant land of nod.

After a toss-and-turn night, Celeste welcomed the dawn's rays that pierced the cracks of her window shutters. She rose, stretched, and put on the clean chemise from her carpetbag. After donning her smudged day dress, she eased into the boots whose cracked leather toes displayed wear and tear. She made use of the ceramic chamber pot and tucked it back under the bed. Strands of blond hair tugged at her collar and clung lifeless to her shoulders. She pulled a brush from her bag and ran it through her locks, then fastened the hair with a barrette, letting it flow down her back.

She joined the marquis at the breakfast table in the grand dining room. As she entered, he beckoned her toward side tables replete with meat, cheese, bread, and jam. After filling her plate, she sat down at his right hand. He lifted his fork and knife and cut into a slice of smoked ham. She gazed up at the chandelier, its crystals sparkling from the morning light beaming into the window. *Mon Dieu.* She was as awkward in here as a toad in a teashop.

A maid glided in, poured her café au lait, and Celeste watched the stream of hot milk swirl around in her cup. When they were alone at last, she sipped her coffee and regarded the marquis over the rim.

He managed the contents of his plate as efficiently as accountants arranged numbers at tax time. One quadrant of his plate held meat, the other cheese, the other apple slices, and the last some pâté. He chewed and swallowed a piece of *jambon*, the local ham. "How is your room?" he asked.

"My room is lovely, Mon Seigneur. The bed is soft, and the view is sweeping."

He lifted a morsel of bread and balanced a piece of cheese on top of it. "You have the room that belonged to my daughter Solange. She drowned—a boating accident—aged eighteen."

"So that is her sculpture on the mantelpiece in my room? The girl with the braided hair and ringlets?"

His brows drew together. "Yes, Solange will forever be that young girl." His tone was wistful, full of longing.

"And your wife?" She plunged into deeper territory. Maybe he would reveal some secrets. She leaned toward him.

"Her name was Georgette. She died many years ago. You see, this house is empty now, so I busy myself with other things."

She sat back. So much was contained in the word "things"—politics. Uprisings. Underground movements. She longed to know more, but she leveled her chin and buttered her croissant, then smeared raspberry jam across it.

She could not stop wondering where the group of men had spent the night. Carlo could be staying away from everyone, or maybe he had left already. And Odéon. Perhaps the men were still asleep upstairs.

Though she was bursting to ask him of Carlo's whereabouts, she did not wish to reveal what she had seen last night. The territory was uncharted, but she knew one thing. She would continue what she had come to France to complete. Somewhere on this soil, Maman waited for her.

Her throat was parched after bits of salty ham, so she took a sip of café. "Mon Seigneur, I thank you for your generosity in allowing me to stay in such a fine house. Yet I have a pressing, urgent need."

The hard lines in his face softened; crevices deepened around his mouth. "And what could preoccupy such a pleasant young lady?"

She poured out the details about her search for her mother, Madeleine Bazin, beginning in Montmartre at Maison de L'Étoile. At the same time, he dispatched the quadrants of food on his plate. The more details she revealed, the slower he chewed. Yet, he remained an apt listener. He reached for the last morsel of bread and slathered on a burst of soft cheese. "Do go on."

Celeste said, "Mont St. Michel Prison—I must go there—it is urgent. I believe Maman resides in the care of the chaplain. The nun at Hôtel-Dieu in Compiègne said the jailor's coach took her away to serve her sentence there. I am only in France until the first of February when I have booked passage back to San Francisco from Le Havre on the ship called the *North Star*."

He set his bread and cheese down on his plate. "That is not much time."

A maid came in and set down a fresh pot of café, and he waved her away to the kitchen. He leaned toward Celeste, his eyes narrowing. "Mademoiselle, you speak of your mother, Madeleine Bazin. Though she swore me to secrecy, I must break my vow to tell you, her daughter.

"I never in my life expected to see her child—a daughter, no less.

This coincidence is indeed extraordinary, so much so that I would have doubted your identity, but for the fact, you described Maison de L'Étoile in such detail. You see, ma chérie, your mother Madeleine is in a very precarious situation—to go there will put both you, her, and her chaplain Father Jean, in great danger."

She expected his chidings about going alone or his fuss that she might borrow a necessary horse and cart, but this—she scratched her ear. "I do not understand—what situation? What danger? You sound as if you know my mother. If you do, please speak, Mon Seigneur, for I am truly puzzled."

Her voice rose with each word, but not as fast as the heat rising in her breast. "Is this a joke? That would be a mean trick indeed." She bit her lip; a knot filled her throat.

He lowered his voice. "I can tell you are upset, mademoiselle, but I owe you the truth. I know if Solange were sitting where you are, I would reveal the facts. And yes, I have known your mother for many years."

Something surged inside Celeste. "How is that?" She startled at the force of her own words.

A blush traveled from his neck to his cheeks. "Well, some years ago, after I lost my Georgette, I stayed with friends in Paris. They were widowers, too. One of them wanted to try the famous brothels of Montmartre and—so I went along. Mind you, I was lonely beyond the darkness of night. And there at Maison de L'Étoile, I met your mother who became a friend and confidante."

She covered her mouth—she would not cry out.

"Madeleine was as lonely as I, and had we been younger, perhaps something could have come of it, but with my status as a noble and her position as a madam, unfortunately, that was not to be. Mind you, to this day we continue to love each other, though not in a physical way. Nevertheless, before her sentencing, we visited each other often in addition to writing letters back and forth, and—say—I believe I have one you might like to see."

She suppressed an urge to shout. “A letter?”

He pressed his index finger against his cheek. “I think I know where the letter is. It might help you understand things a bit better. Please wait.” He crossed the dining room and disappeared in the direction of the study.

Sixteen

The Baby Slippers

Celeste heard the rustling of the maid behind her. "*Plus de café?*" The diminutive girl bent down, holding the coffee in one hand, the milk in the other. Though she guarded her look, she was plainly curious as she stared down at Celeste, who had gone numb for a moment. "Milk only," Celeste said, and the maid swirled the milk into her cup, curtseyed, and left the room.

Footsteps echoed across the terraced entryway from the study, and the breakfast room door swung open. The marquis strode across the parquet wood floor, bearing an open letter with a broken wax seal. He sat beside her, smoothing the letter with the same care he would use with a delicate rose.

Even from that distance, Celeste recognized her mother's scrawl. That same penmanship had been on grocery lists she read at the butcher shop, the vegetable markets, and the bakery when buying her mother's favorite treat, *pain au chocolat*. On occasion, her mother used to leave Celeste little love notes, calling her *ma petite chou*, my little cabbage.

She should feel joy at this discovery, a link to her mother that may lead her to where she was. Yet somehow, the letter gave her the chills. Something about it did not bode well, and she could only guess its contents. "I have a question, Mon Seigneur."

"Most certainly. What would you like to know?"

"Does the letter talk about me at all? That I had gone to *L'Amérique*? That I had left at such a young age?"

"Uh—no. Pardon me, mademoiselle, no offense, but this letter does not mention you."

"Did Maman ever speak of me?"

"I'm afraid not. In fact, in all the years I have known Madeleine, this is the first I have heard of you."

"So, you spoke of Georgette and your daughter Solange, but didn't you ask her if she ever had any children?"

The marquis could not lie, for she would know. His eyes would flicker right and left—he knew that also. She waited.

His chin leveled. "I knew—that is, I suspected Madeleine had a child because one day I found a small pair of baby slippers—you know the satin kind—in a bottom drawer of her dresser. I was not snooping as you might think; she asked me to find her a pair of stockings in there. I found the stockings, but as I lifted them, I saw a pair of baby slippers tucked in the corner."

"Did you ever ask her about them? Confront her about denying my existence?"

The marquis shook his head.

"Why not?"

The butler peeked his head through the door. No doubt he heard her loud voice. "Any assistance needed, Mon Seigneur?"

The marquis set his jaw and raised his hand. "Peace, mademoiselle. Would you please calm yourself? No, I never asked her. It seemed a prying matter. I had no idea she sent you to America. The only evidence I had was a little pair of slippers. At the time, I guessed that her baby died, and since she never talked about it, I figured she never would."

"What happened to them—the baby slippers?"

"I do not know." The color drained from his withered cheeks.

The butler ducked his head out the door. He would be thinking the worst.

"Do you have any idea how much that hurts me? That my mother would never tell anyone—even her closest lover, friend, or whatever you may be—of my existence?"

The floodgates opened, and tears swarmed down her face. All those years in New Orleans and San Francisco, she was crying for Maman, pining to hold her hand, to kiss her soft cheek, to smell her lavender perfume. And all the while, Maman denied her existence—or worse—erased her from any of her life's history.

The breakfast room grew silent but not for long. Horses' hooves clip-clopped outside the front entrance, then halted, replaced by men's harmonic voices. Clattering dishes and thumping pots and pans resounded from the kitchen on the other side of the wall.

An expanse of greenery outside the high windows, flanked on both sides by well-manicured topiary trees, stretched a long way toward the horizon. A bird flew into the windowpane, mistaking it as open. *Bang.* It bounced onto the pavement below—no time to see if it was all right. She needed to recover from this dreadful information. Some force took hold of her insides and twisted them painfully.

The marquis took careful sips of his café, her mother's letter resting next to his plate. "I will wait until you are ready, mademoiselle. You have received a shock."

She smeared the tears on her cheeks, picked up a napkin, and blew her nose. "Do go on, Mon Seigneur. I must hear the news. You say you know where she is."

"I will only read the part that pertains to what we are saying here—

the rest is—well, you can imagine—intimate between Madeleine and me."

"Go ahead."

He lifted the thin vellum and turned it over. Halfway down the page, he pointed a finger. "There. Start reading." Celeste held the paper close. So many of the flowery lines reflected her mother's lively voice and energetic personality.

I have been allowed one letter since having received my stricter sentence. I am leaving Compiègne to go into the prison at Mont St. Michel. I will be under the spiritual care of Father Jean. My purpose there is manifold: I must serve my life sentence in a holy way, yet with the intercession of Saint Catherine Labouré, I find myself fortunate. With the help of Father Jean, I will be of service to a cause that you and I share, dear Vincent. Before my arrest and trial, I worked with my friend Felice to rid this country of the viper driving our beloved France into the ground. I am working to cleanse my soul of all sin should my work lead me to a deadly fate.

She glanced at the marquis. "And who is the viper of whom she speaks?"

He lowered his voice. "I dare not speak his name in this household. His spies are everywhere, and they relish eavesdropping. If you read on, you will see."

Her heart sank. Her mother—a life sentence. Any hope she had for a simple solution took a sharp left turn. She had fallen into a bed of quicksand.

"Please read on." The marquis passed his index finger over the lower half of the paper.

My love, you may question the overwhelming desire I have to unseat this crooked man, but I will be of service to you through

Father Jean. He is allowed to receive mail, and I am not. Remember 20 November. Use the codes we have talked of in the past.

Acid from the café bubbled up in her throat. It appeared the marquis expected to rely on her mother's help from prison. Ridiculous.

"What events is she speaking of?"

"That I cannot reveal, mademoiselle. If you were captured and tortured anywhere, at any time, that could put many lives in danger, not only your own."

A soft knock sounded at the door leading to the hallway. The butler peered around the door. "Mon Seigneur, you are needed in your office."

"*Excusez-moi, ma petite.* I shall be back in a few moments."

Celeste sat in a stew of thought. Her mother was in prison for what she had done—sentenced to life at Mont St. Michel. Though the emperor's rule was draconian, this was a sentence reserved for murderers and enemies of the state. Her mother denied her very existence, sent her to America, and blithely swept her out of memory.

But one name in the letter gave her pause—*Felice.* The scent of olive oil mixed with rosemary, the steam, his roly-poly figure wrapped in a white apron—it must be the same Felice who cooked the dinner for her and the men in Montmartre. Suddenly, the parts of the floating puzzle jiggled into place, and moment by moment, she saw the pattern appear. If she was thinking correctly, she was wrapped in a grand scheme the likes of which could prove fatal not only to her mother but all of those involved.

She drew out the St. Catherine medal from her breast and went over to the tall windows facing the extensive garden stretching many hectares behind the house. A pair of doves cooed on the rooftop. Soft steps padded behind her, and she glanced at the marquis who stood by her side. She said, "So lovely."

He nodded. "Some people tell me they can see where the world ends at the horizon—out there—beyond my lands. My family traces this house to the year 1100. Our ancestors survived the French Revolution, though the *sans-culottes*, the partisans, requisitioned the house, and our family fled upstairs to live on the top fourth floor.

"Though he was an aristocrat, my father hated the excesses of King Louis the Sixteenth, and for that reason, the revolutionaries spared him and our family." A wry grin crossed his lips. "Otherwise, I would not be here today."

She tapped her medal, its cold surface causing her chest to tingle. "Our Lady protected you and your family as she does all those in jeopardy. You see, I have a family, too. Whatever you are keeping from me about my mother must be said. I see what I think is the truth, but if you are holding back something that I, by rights as her daughter, must know, you must tell me."

"I wish I could, but I cannot. I see you have a medal like the one I saw your mother wear." His eyes misted.

"Similar?" she asked. "I found this one in the drawer of her bedroom at Maison de L'Étoile when I went to the house to find her—a mere two weeks past. I thought it was hers. When did you see her wear it?"

"The medal was around her neck the last time I was with her in Compiègne."

"Wait a moment. Then—this is a different medal than the one Maman wore. I wonder if she left it, hoping I would find it."

"I do not know. As I said, Madeleine never mentioned you, so that I would have no idea."

She paused, staring out at a flock of birds forming a V in the sky above. How silly. To think that her mother would want her to find it.

He continued. "Was anything else left in the drawers? More clues? A written message, perhaps?"

"I thought she left in haste. There was a dress a fancy one in an armoire, but the house was in tatters. I grabbed my medal, knowing how precious it was to her. She might have been in jeopardy. But now—I understand she endangered herself—on purpose."

"But look, mademoiselle, hers is a higher cause, a higher calling if you will—God's work. Perhaps you should leave her to it. You cannot help her."

"God's work. Is abandoning your only daughter God's work? Not letting her get a proper education God's work? Is sending her across the ocean at fourteen, giving her to a brothel madam to become a prostitute God's work?"

His Adam's apple bobbed in his throat.

She went on. "How dare you speak to me in those terms. I sailed around the American continent and across the Atlantic Ocean to find my mother and bring her back to San Francisco. I will not stop until I find her, no matter what."

His eyes widened.

She continued. "I do not want to seem ungrateful, Mon Seigneur. You have given me your hospitality and your best information. Your words have been painful but necessary in this miserable maze."

"Cher mademoiselle. I do not know what to say." He unlatched the window. A light breeze fluttered the curtains, and the glass chandelier tinkled above the breakfast table.

If he was ignoring her, maybe she needed to be more forceful. She pressed on. "I want to go find her. Would you please send for Odéon? I must speak to him."

"Odéon? Why him? There is someone else you must see first about going."

"With no disrespect to your title, this is no time for mysteries and innuendo. I have only a certain amount of time before my ship leaves from Le Havre on the first of February. A prepaid ticket to New York and then via Panama to San Francisco. I do not have the luxury of waiting to find my mother—perhaps you do not fathom that."

"Did you notice the little sparrow that beat against the window earlier?

The bird may think she knows what she is doing, but she cannot see the truth before her eyes. If she slowed down and considered it, she might notice that she cannot penetrate glass. You, ma chérie, are that small sparrow."

She raged against the truth of his calm words, his deep-set brown eyes that gave her such fatherly counsel.

He continued. "Now, trust me for a moment. Someone very much wants to see you." He led her through the double doors, across the foyer, onto the house's front steps, and then pointed. "Go out the pathway that winds around the duck pond. Cross the little bridge. There you will find a small, secluded island with a table and two chairs. Go and wait for someone who will talk to you."

"But—?"

"No more of that." He gave her a gentle push. "Now go."

She had no choice but to follow his directions, though she cringed, not knowing whom she was meeting and for what purpose. The game was blind man's bluff. She always hated those childish activities. She despised them even more since the neighborhood children played them in the street, but they never invited her—instead, they cupped their hands and whispered about her. They all knew each other at school—she was a stranger in her neighborhood.

She huffed her way onto the pebbled walkway, over the little bridge, and plunked down in one of the chairs facing the house. Her feet nestled in a bed of bright red leaves. This mystery had better end soon, and then she would seek out Odéon. At least with him, she could find relief. Maybe she could find another tickling weed to tease him.

A white duck waddled from the pond and angled his head, seeming to cast her a penetrating look. He, too, was wondering. Carlo must know she was there but simply did not want to see her. He was no doubt complicit with the marquis who deliberately delayed her going to Mont St. Michel. A raft of ducklings, their soft downy feathers glistening with droplets of water, waddled up on the bank. They regarded her quizzically, angling their little brown heads this way and that, appearing to study her.

Celeste regarded her new audience. She leaned over and said, "Was this whole trip a wasted effort? Why did I even come here? When Edward and Brianna offered to have me stay in San Francisco and run the parlor house, I should have done it."

The ducklings tucked their webbed feet under themselves and gathered on the mossy ground. Celeste's complaints disturbed their peaceful woodland world. "Maman is in prison for life. Even if I went there, I might not even get to see her. Besides, Maman denied my very existence. But then why leave the medal in the drawer, especially if she already had one?"

A small fish jumped in the pond, sending rings across its surface. "What kind of danger will I put my mother in by making such a fuss? Maybe I should give up and let go trying to find her." A fat wood duck settled down next to the ducklings and groomed its back feathers, brilliant red, blue, and brown plumage lighting up the sandy bank.

She watched the wood duck and fumed against her helplessness. Even these lowly creatures had more power than she. From where she sat, rays of golden autumn light slashed into a small line of mist that rose from the pond; goldfinches poured out their song, the sun filtered in through the autumn leaves soon to drop from the surrounding plane trees. From now on, winter's bite would steal away the splendor only to unveil it late next spring. The same way France had stolen Maman from her. A sob rose in her throat. A crunching sound disturbed the air—maybe they were footsteps. The raft of ducks startled and fled to the pond.

Seventeen

The Rising

She would have risen, kissed him on both cheeks, and told him she was happy to see him in ordinary times. Her heart would have thumped wildly, and she might have hung on his every word. But these were not ordinary times—anything but typical. She kept her seat, anchored to what she could hold onto, a shred of truth.

Carlo grinned broadly and bent down to her. "*Enchantée*, mademoiselle Celeste." He kissed the back of her hand, then peered at her, his gaze penetrating. For a moment, she lost herself—his dark hair curled over his collar, his high cheekbones reflected the sunlight.

How easy it would be to forget it all—to relax into his arms and erase herself and her journey—but then she considered—Carlo had sent her on this wild route; now, he was hindering her efforts.

She sprang up, brushing his hand aside.

"Not even a *bonjour*?" He stepped back.

She shook her head. "By now, I should be in a carriage heading to Mont St. Michel. Instead, thanks to you, I am sitting here at some château talking to the ducks." She could not resist adding the common question heard on San Francisco streets. "What the hell?"

His hands flew up. "Now wait a moment—let me explain."

"You have a lot to answer. You never even asked for me, even though you had to know I was here at the house. You never even said my name. I asked the marquis. And now you want to kiss my hand? *Merde!*"

"Please." He pointed to the wrought-iron table. "At least give me a moment."

She perched on the edge of the closest chair while he took the seat at the other side. She set her elbows down on the surface and leaned toward him. "I have given moments to you, to my mother, to Madam De Salle in New Orleans, to Brianna and Edward in San Francisco." She swallowed hard. "I have given moments to many men in my past—traded them away. No thought of repayment except maybe an act of kindness in return—maybe even to remember my name or ask after me."

Red patches bloomed on his cheeks. "I am sorry for that, but I was busy with matters you need not know."

"Is it because I do not count? At the very least, I thought you might be different, but no—you are just like her."

"Who?"

She swept aside his question while her feet rustled the leaves on the ground below. If he refused to reveal certain truths, she could, too. Maybe this was the only game she was willing to play.

He said, "The marquis tells me you plan to go to Mont St. Michel. But that is dangerous. You cannot go there alone or even with Odéon."

"Why not? What makes it dangerous?" Nothing he said was genuine—he had ignored her before, so now he would avoid telling her the truth.

He shook his head. "It is a prison. If the emperor's spies follow you, once the tide is in, they'll trap you on the island, and they could easily kill you and dump your body in the water. It's happened before to people considered enemies of the empire."

"Wait a moment—this is fantastical. You tell me this to get rid of me—to discourage me from going. Well, if you think you can scare me, forget it. I can find Odéon, and he will take me there. I thought you might, but you have shown no more trustworthiness than a donkey's ass."

His eyes narrowed. Celeste's words hung in the air, enveloped by fog rising from the pond.

Soon after, multiple hoofbeats pounded the gravel road leading onto the château's grounds. The noise grew louder. Carlo rose and extended his hand. "Look, no one can see us here since some drivers have loose lips and spill names for money. Come with me."

She looked around at the open patches surrounding them. "Where?"

He grabbed her hand and beckoned her to stroll with him across the small footbridge leading from the island up into the trees. Beyond them lay a Norman stone chapel—its peaked roof and small empty belltower whispered of family lineage and dark crypts.

"Follow me," he said.

She crisscrossed behind him through tall weeds and grave markers until he stopped on the other side of the chapel facing the fields beyond. As she passed, her eye caught a one-piece wooden Norman cross bearing only the name ***Solange***. The young girl was buried in the flat ground below her feet. Around her, the dry grasses waved, thirsting for the rush of late November rains.

Carlo's voice rang out. "We can talk without being seen." She watched him catch his breath. He advanced, his arms outstretched. "Do come closer."

She hesitated until her heart calmed its thumping. Carlo lingered at arm's length. If he expected an embrace, he would have a long wait. It was her turn to put up her hand. "No, I cannot simply forget why I came to France and what I must find out before I see her—and despite your warnings, I will see her, with or without your support."

"Oh, you will?" He stepped back. A dark flicker crossed his eyes.

She dug her toe into the dirt mixed with the marquis' ancestral bones. "You and the others—all the shipments are coming in by carriage—the boxes, the secrecy. I do not care if you and Felice and the marquis are involved—lord knows there were many such schemes afoot in New Orleans and San Francisco where I lived.

"We harlots would simply sidestep such plots when the men we bedded attempted to involve us, but I cannot stand aside in France. I have waited too long and traveled too far. I demand to know the truth about my mother's role in your plan. And why she is in prison, sentenced to life. Whatever did she do to deserve that?"

He blinked a series of slow blinks.

She went on. "For all I know, Maman is only on a quest to save her soul, to find spiritual salvation in the arms of the Church. The Daughter of Charity in Compiègne said she was in the care of the chaplain Father Jean. The marquis said that, too. But what else is she up to? And how do you know her?"

"Father Jean? Did I hear you correctly?" He stiffened.

"Yes, the very one. And when I go there, I will find Maman in his care."

"Oh, I see. You are taking on a dangerous task. I cannot help you there."

A Percheron draft horse appeared from the neighboring field; he was chewing grasses that grew along the dry-stone wall separating the marquis' property from the neighboring farm. Carlo advanced toward the animal and clucked his tongue. The horse raised his head, his deep black eyes seeming to absorb first Carlo, then Celeste.

She could never resist petting a horse, so she went to his side. The horse's grey muzzle was slack and jowly like the old count's she would spy with his walking stick on the lanes of Montmartre. Pitiful thing—a harsh bit between his teeth had governed him all his life. His whiskers stuck out in all directions—hard and pointy to the touch. Maybe the old beast's wisdom would lead Carlo to tell her what she needed to know. She could only hope.

She softened her voice. "Why can you not help me?"

Carlo sighed. "My hands are tied. I cannot tell you any more than what I already have."

"Well, that is rich. How would you feel if we were speaking of your mother in Italy?"

He paled. "This is much larger than you and me, or you and your mother. You have no idea what you may be up against."

"Well, then, you can come with me—as long as Odéon accompanies us."

"I cannot do that." His voice rang out, his tone flat as a banker's when telling a client his account is empty.

"Whyever not?" She lifted her hand from the horse's muzzle. Seldom had her loneliness risen so acutely while in a man's presence. She anchored both hands on her hips.

"You see, I am on the emperor's watchlist." His lower lip trembled.

For a moment, she almost pitied him. "What watchlist? What have you done?"

"I cannot tell you, and you must trust me in that. You are going to Mont St. Michel—sheer madness. Four hundred imperial and prison guards man stations and checkpoints at the entrance to the rock. It is a heavily fortified prison.

"Our sources tell us that English boats land weapons on the nearby beaches. They aim to foment a revolution. The guards conduct periodic searches of the island, but so far, they have found nothing. You see, this is not a place for a woman—any woman—especially you—and your mother—well, that is another story."

"What other story? What do you know about Maman?" She set her teeth so firmly, the pain radiated through her jawline.

"She is in prison for life. You might as well accept the fact that she is not free to go anywhere with you. I doubt that you would be allowed into the prison to see her at all."

"What are you talking about? Surely they must allow family members."

"Mademoiselle, in what world are you living? Mont St. Michel is the most formidable prison in France. No one is allowed there. The farthest you can get is to the top-level guardhouse. The guards there would merely laugh at your request. And follow you anywhere in France from that point on. Maybe even arrest you on a made-up charge. More I cannot say. I wish I could, but to say more—I've already told you too much." His lips flattened into a thin line.

That was not the news she needed. Not here, not ever. She had no one to rely on if Carlo would not help her. If only she could leap on the old grizzly horse and let him carry her into a distant place where she and her mother could build a house in the woods, serene among roses and butterflies. They would no longer need the affairs of men. She turned to him and said, "I must pack my things. Regardless of your words, your threats, your scare tactics, I am going to Mont St. Michel."

"Very well. Then I bid you *adieu,* mademoiselle." Carlo planted a dry kiss on her left cheek, then her right. She fought back the tears that singed the insides of her eyelids, then brushed away those that tiptoed down her face. She heard his footsteps leading out through the dry grass.

She looked up at the horse's graying muzzle, then raised her hand and ran her palm over the animal's fur, absorbing the trust in the equine's brown eyes. The animal understood her even if Carlo did not. She had no one else to support her quest to find Maman. Though Carlo had vanished from sight, the old horse remained at the stone wall, his profile serene within autumn's ethereal glow.

After a few moments, she strode back toward the château, pausing in the graveyard next to the chapel. For the first time, she noticed another grave, this one more deeply embedded in the soil. A mixture of acorns, dry sticks, and maple leaves decorated its surface. She brushed the dust off the headstone. *Georgette.* Ah, Solange and her mother were buried side by side, in union for all eternity. Something caught in her throat. She would never have the comfort of lying next to her mother—even in death. That tender path was blocked for her, too.

In France, any prisoner who died was buried in an unmarked pauper's grave. The irony was not lost on her. She had come all this way to know Maman was alive, yet she would be no closer to seeing her than if she were standing on her mother's grave.

She turned to the more recent burial plot. "Solange, maybe you can help me. You know everything now, up in heaven. Well, you can't talk to me, but at least you can hear my voice. Pray for the soul of my dear mother and me, for we are truly lost, one from another." She gave in to her sobs and crumpled onto the forgiving ground.

Not long after, she exhausted her tears and brushed the leaves off her skirt. The château sat in reverence, reflected against the duckpond. The breeze picked up, chilling her arms. From now on, as winter approached, she would need a warmer cloak. Before leaving for the house, she peered over her shoulder at the far wall. The horse had vanished; the whispering grasses and fields stretched kilometers to the sea.

Eighteen

20 November

She aimed her footsteps through the grass and skirted the pond until she gained the gravel footpath leading into the château's central doorway. Celeste pressed open her carpetbag back in her room and snapped her well-worn crinolines and chemises off their hangers and out of drawers. She tucked her cotton nightgown into the corner of the bag. She lifted the three clean collars she alternated each day since her dress was seldom laundered. She wrapped them into a vellum tissue to protect them and folded them neatly into the bag.

Celeste weighed Carlo's information with care. No doubt she was putting her life in the balance. The penalty for traitorous behavior was death, most likely after prolonged torture. Never mind that she had an American passport. Guards would have their way with her before dispensing with her life: when Estelle disappeared from Maison de L'Étoile, her mother had whispered the woman of the night had come to a wrong end.

A policeman had entered the night before, requested Estelle's services, and she and her mother heard a scuffle ensue in an upstairs room.

The maid reported seeing a partially clad Estelle leave in the candlelit company of the policemen later that evening. Rumors abounded that Estelle had been thrown into the River Seine, though no one ever found her body. Maman seemed edgy after that, and not long after, she told Celeste she was sending her away to New Orleans.

While chasing away her past thoughts, she buckled the straps of her carpetbag. Out of the corner of her eye, Solange's bust appeared on the mantel. Every time Celeste moved, the girl's eyes seemed to follow her. Maybe she would understand. She approached the marble figure and fingered the near-perfect ringlets framing the girl's ears.

"What do you think, Solange? What if I find Maman in the care of the chaplain? Would she even consider coming away with me? Would I be putting her in danger?"

The statue's lashless eyes refused to blink.

The words from her mother's letter cut through her thoughts. *Before my arrest and trial, I worked with my friend Felice to rid this country of the viper driving our dear France into the ground.* And then *20 November*. The marquis had not told her the date of the letter. Could it have been last year? Maman had been at this dark business for far too long. And so had the marquis.

But then something clicked in her mind. *20 November.* She had assumed that had been last year since—the intensity of the message, coupled with the marquis' plans, Carlo's dire warnings. Oh no—it couldn't be.

She bent over her carpetbag, rifling through its contents for the small calendar she kept at the bottom. Today must be Friday. She ran her finger down the dates and paused on 13—indeed, this was the day. Suppose the marquis was to meet Maman on 20 November. That could only mean—an even more terrifying realization washed over her—Maman not only believed in the mission with the marquis and his men—she directed part of it.

This awakening left her reeling. She dropped the calendar back in the carpetbag. She turned once again to the bust of the young girl. "Solange, I have to find a way to convince Maman to flee with me so she will be safe for the rest of her life.

"Whatever the marquis and the men are up to, and if she is part of it, I owe her that. Whether she is doing this scheme—whatever it is—for money or love, I must take her away." She ran her hand over the girl's bare shoulders. So cold to the touch. "I must be the one now to keep her free from harm—she must come with me to San Francisco. It is the only way." After Celeste turned back to the carpetbag, she lifted it, slung a shawl over her shoulders, and gazed around the room.

There was something she had forgotten. Ah yes, her touring hat. It hung on a hook on the wall between the windows, its scarlet wool fabric and long black netting stark against the yellow-papered bedroom wall.

A knock sounded at her door. *Zut alors!* She hoped to keep her leaving a secret. After she grabbed the carpetbag, she shoved it under the bed and tucked in the bedspread around it. Another knock came, this time louder. "*J'arrive!*" She flung the door open.

The marquis stood dressed in a beige silk waistcoat with rolled-up sleeves, and his white hair swept back behind his ears. "I was looking for you," he said. "Cook wants to know if you wish soup or salad with your lunch." He glanced toward the bust of Solange for a moment, at the unmade bed, then back at her. "Maid should have completed your room tidying by now. I will go remind her."

"Very well," she said.

A frown curled his upper lip, and he turned and made off toward the staircase. Celeste closed the door behind her and leaned her hips against it. Good thing she had hidden the carpetbag. The less the marquis knew, the better. He would be a useless complication—or maybe not. The thought occurred that it might be wiser to flee in the cover of night when all were asleep, but at midday, while everyone engaged in routine tasks, her leaving would appear planned. She grabbed her reticule, her touring hat, and her carpetbag, and after leaving the bedroom door open, she hurried toward the servants' staircase at the end of the hallway.

Once at the stairwell, she paused a moment, set the touring hat squarely on her head, letting the long veil flow down her back. The staircase circled downward, and the steps were steep. What a marvel that the servants navigated it with trays and piles of laundry.

The lower door creaked open, and she found herself in the filtered noon sunlight. Men engaged in various activities in the stable yard: they loaded boxes onto carts and pulled canvas tightly over the surface. With a rope in hand, a tall worker in overalls tied down the corners onto hooks built into his cart. Another chap unloaded large crates and called to a laborer to help him. He threw his cigarette stub onto the ground, stomped on it, and joined his mate.

Maybe she could find Odéon in the barn. A man taking a break sat on a bale of hay in the sunshine, drinking from a bottle of cider. He lifted his eyebrows, looking at her. She avoided eye contact—she had to hurry. Once news of her presence in the yard got back to the marquis or Carlo, her plan would fail. "Have you seen Odéon?" she asked.

Sweat prickled the palms of her hands.

The man raised a shaky hand and pointed toward the barn.

She took a left turn into the dark barn illuminated by the sunlight radiating through cracks in the roof. After her eyes adjusted, she saw several men engaged watering the horses, and one sat on a bench, a horse's hoof in hand. Odéon bent over, tacking on a shoe. The odor of horse sweat, straw, and dust overpowered her, and she put a hand to her nose to avoid sneezing.

She took a second and watched him from a distance, letting his calm, deliberative movements wash over her. She had missed him the last few days. She had come to rely on his humor, gentleness, and steady hand on the reins during their journey. Someone was pounding what sounded like metal on the other side of the barn, creating a loud echo. Though she drew near, Odéon did not seem to hear her approach.

Sun rays brightened the auburn strands of his beard and the folds of his ears. His hat set back on his head, and his jacket bore bits of dust and straw. He wore the same dusty outfit yesterday. She missed that jacket—and him. All she wanted was to put her arms around him and hold him close.

But she lingered, letting his nearness seep into the deep fibers of her being.

Odéon finished with the horse's hoof and let it fall to the ground. After drawing a scarf from his pocket, he swept it across his forehead. The pounding ended at the far side of the barn, and a momentary silence pervaded the space.

She cleared her throat.

He looked up. A flicker of recognition passed across his face, a blush reddened his neck, and it inched up his throat, through his beard, and flecked his cheeks. For an instant, he remained thus, his expression reminding her of a naughty child found stealing a piece of fudge.

"Mademoiselle Celeste." His words carried a gentle cadence as if saying her name was the line of his favorite song.

"Odéon, I must speak to you."

He stood, placing the hammer and hoof nails on the bench behind him. His hand trembled slightly. "I have not seen you since we arrived. How are you faring?"

A breeze picked up the long netting of her hat, and she brushed it away from her face. "I do not have time for pleasantries. I need you to take me to Mont St. Michel."

He gazed into her face, open-mouthed. "We cannot speak here." He led her to a remote corner behind the haystacks where saddles and tack hung on the walls. "Now tell me what you need because I do not fully understand your haste. Oh—but mind where you stand." He pointed to a pile of horse manure buzzing with flies.

She stepped around the pile and stood so near him she saw the pulse bobbing in his throat. "We must leave now before the day wanes." She looked around the barn. "Where is the wagon? The one we came in?" Her question lingered in the air.

He lifted his pipe from his pocket and chewed thoughtfully on the stem. "I cannot take you there—I wish I could, but I need this job; besides, I would be betraying my friends—and our cause. It is as important to me as to them. They need me here. The horses need tending, and if I leave, who will do it for them?"

"I can give you an alibi—you can tell everyone that I coerced you and paid you off." Celeste dug into her reticule and waved a sheaf of francs under his nose. "You wouldn't tell a lie if you took this."

His brow furrowed, and he looked away toward the horses' stalls. "You disappoint me."

"How? I thought you were my friend. Loyal. Remember the checkpoints and our camp evenings together when we talked about—our pasts, our secrets? After all that—I thought I could count on you."

"To lie? To pretend to take your money? To ruin the trust the marquis, Felice, and Carlo have placed in me? No, no. But what is worse—you think that you must pay me off to do you a favor. The very idea wounds me."

"But there is great urgency. If I do not get to Maman and rescue her, she may die. I have no other choice."

She stepped nearer, his heady mixture of sweat, tobacco, and straw more appealing than any fragrance found in Parisian boutiques. He was a soulmate, a brother she never had, and even—yes—even a lover. Somehow within his soft shadowy presence, she felt at ease and could be herself.

The former stiffness in his bearing relaxed, and he bent toward her. She wrapped her arms around his waist and tucked her head under his chin. She heard him let out a gasp, but then little by little, he enfolded her in his arms where she belonged.

She rested in his arms where she heard the heart pounding in his chest, his steady breathing, and the clanging of hammer on metal in the distance. A sudden realization slipped in—more than anything, she wanted to remain there. "I have missed you, Odéon."

"And I have missed you, mademoiselle." He tightened his grasp around her shoulders.

"Never call me mademoiselle. Please—Celeste. That is my name. I want to hear you say it."

"Très bien, mademoiselle Ce—." He shook his head. "No—Celeste."

She drew away and looked up, allowing herself to take in his rough but gentle features as he gazed into her eyes. "I must go—since you do not wish to help, I will have to find another man who will take me there—at any price. I have sold myself before—this is the only way." She saw the hungry looks the men gave her on the way into the barn. A quick toss on a hay bale, and she would earn her ride. She knew it—she could be sure Odéon knew it as well.

He reached out and wrapped his fingers around her arm. "You do not know what you are asking—the danger. We would go there unarmed—unprotected. Mont St. Michel is a hotbed of agents, and even without proof, they could shoot us as spies simply for having a lame excuse."

Odéon forced her to consider something she had been reluctant to see. She was putting his life in danger as well as her own. "Is there someone else besides yourself who would take me then? I must go—no matter what. Though of all people, I prefer to go there—anywhere—with you." She caught herself. Had she said *anywhere*?

His eyes narrowed. "You are saying that only to get what you want. I am not sure that you understand what your Maman is doing. Or even your mission. Are you sure that you are going to rescue her? Are you merely satisfying your selfish desire to see her again?"

"I wish to save her—how could that be selfish?" A frisson spiraled through Celeste. "If we leave now, we will get to Mont St. Michel by dark, fetch Maman the next morning, and return to the château within forty-eight hours. I will take all the blame when we return. And the next stop will be Paris to arrange Maman's passage with me on the ship leaving Le Havre for America on February first."

"I must see someone about this." He ran his finger along the stem of his pipe and tamped the tobacco down into the bowl.

"Are you going to tell Carlo? God forbid." She squeezed her eyes shut.

Without an answer, he nestled the pipe in his vest pocket and left the barn.

She sat on a haybale. What a pain—in San Francisco, she had only to snap her fingers, and a wagon would take her from dusty streets into grass-laden routes. A cart would take her to the pier to sit on a lading company crate, to watch the ships unfurl their sails on their course through the Golden Gate straits. She remembered the way California's late afternoon sunlight danced like stars on white wave tips across the bay.

Not long after, footsteps padded toward her. She looked up; Odéon leaned over; he tapped her shoulder. He said, "Very well—I will do this for you."

"Why?" she asked.

He shook his head. "I do not know."

By all accounts, she and Odéon should have made it out of the stable yard in the wagon within an hour; in fact, she marveled at the speed with which he hitched up the two horses and sat upon the jockey box where she joined him.

She edged her hip closer to his. "Where did you go when you disappeared—just now? Whom did you tell of our departure?"

"You know Alphonse?" He suppressed a grin.

She shook her head.

"You've surely seen him in the stable yard. The half-drunk man who loves his cider jug."

"The one who sits on the hay bale outside the barn?"

"Yes. I told him that we had run an errand and would be back in forty-eight hours and to let the marquis know *only if asked*."

"And what was his response? Can he be trusted?"

"In his way, yes. When I gave him the information, he looked up at me, his sleep-encrusted eyes blinked, and he took another swig of cider. If he remembers where and when we have gone, it will be a miracle."

A warm infusion of happiness filled her. Odéon had more layers than first appeared, yet she must remain cautious. He could have told someone besides Alphonse. All men had the capacity for betrayal. He could be different or the same as all the rest.

Halfway down the road nearing the far-walled exit out of the grounds, Celeste drew a breath. She dared hope they could escape without delay. Odéon clucked the horses onward with his steady hand, and they had nearly crossed the outside road heading away from the château when rapid hoofbeats sounded behind them. Her temperature rose, and her heart pulsed a tune.

Carlo guided his stallion to her side of the wagon, and Odéon halted the horses. Carlo asked, "And where are you going?"

Odéon shrugged and fumbled in his pocket, apparently searching for his pipe.

When met with silence, Carlo's eyebrow arched; his brown eyes widened. He rested his hand on the pommel of his saddle. "*Molto bene,* very well. Don't tell me—Mont St. Michel. Celeste, you are a mere girl searching for your mother—I understand the idiocy of women. But you—Odéon! Why would you think to slip away during such an important operation? We need you in the stables—no one else tends the horses as you do."

Odéon did not hang his head. Instead, he gripped the reins tightly and set his jaw around the stem of his pipe. Good for him. She must remember to thank him for his strength.

Carlo pressed on. "The marquis does not yet know. What will he say when he finds out you have left? He will be furious. And Felice? *Dio mio*, my God, at such an important stage of our plan?"

Celeste all but shouted her words. "It was worth the risk, Carlo. I must do this. You may have little time for your—operation—or whatever it is. But never forget that is not why I came to France. I need to find my mother. My ship's passage home expires the first of February, and after that, I will have no more funds available."

"Pah!" He folded his arms, shook his head, and stepped back against his horse. "Italian women are useless, but you French are even worse. And to think I had feelings for you." He knocked his forehead with the heel of his hand. "Pig misery, I have been a fool."

She wagged her index finger at him. "No. You can say insulting things to me because you are angry. But look—Odéon will be with me. He got me from Paris to Compiègne to this château without harm. Trust that he will do the same again. Believe that I am far from useless. Since Odéon and I are going to be at Mont St. Michel, we can spy for you—and when we return, we can tell you what we saw."

He sneered. "This is not a simple game. You have no idea the importance of what we are doing." He jerked his head in Odéon's direction. "And what do you have to say for yourself?"

"I need to speak to you, Carlo." Odéon's voice seemed thick and unsteady.

"*Bene*, but then you must turn the wagon around and take it back to the barn."

Odéon leaped down from the jockey box and disappeared on his side of the wagon. She could hear the men whispering in harsh tones. How tired she was of hearing men say women were weak or useless. Yet a new realization came to her—she had seen Carlo for who he was—stubborn and inflexible. Maybe she had been an idiot, but only in her imagined feelings for him. He was spouting nonsense; she may be many things, but an idiot was not one of them.

She sat up, pressing her knees against her carpetbag in the jockey box. Maybe she should put the bag in the back of the wagon, but then she wondered where her pistol was. Maybe there in the bag. She had all but forgotten that she had it with her inside the château. She unlatched the carpetbag and felt for the gun and the box of ammunition. There they were—they had fallen to the bottom. She fingered her miraculous medal and breathed thanks to the Almighty.

Footsteps sounded on her side of the wagon, and Carlo appeared, something glinting in his hand. It must be a knife. He turned the point toward his chest and thrust the handle toward her. "Here. At least you can sleep with this under your pillow. You must not leave Odéon's side—he promised you would be safe."

She tucked the knife into her carpetbag alongside the gun. Their mutual silence pricked the air.

Carlo said, "I have given you what you want. Happy now? Who knows when we will meet again and under what circumstances?" He placed a gloved hand on her forearm and leaned toward her.

"You will not be here when we return?" she asked.

"No, Felice says we must go on our mission tomorrow, so we will not be at the château. The marquis is closing it up and going to Paris with his servants. He has a flat there. After the trip, you must not return here. It will be hazardous."

"Odéon will take me to Paris in that case. I will go back to Montmartre with Maman, and I will find you at the house near Café Le Consulat."

He shook his head. "That house is no longer ours; we had to flee because the imperial guards had an agent watching the house. I do not know where we will lodge once we have returned to Paris."

"Won't you be staying with the marquis?"

"His flat is quite small, and there are many of us. *Arrivederci.*" He rapped the wagon with the tip of his horsewhip; Odéon clucked the horses into motion.

Once past the walled lanes and out into the open land, she asked, "Odéon, you went back up to the château before we left. Who did you convince to let us go?"

"Felice gave us his blessing. I knew he would—he has told me more than once that he admires you and your courage in searching for your mother. I told Carlo I would complain to Felice that he was harsh and disloyal despite your pluck and honesty."

"That does not seem enough to convince Felice."

"Perhaps not, but lately, Felice has been annoyed with Carlo. Several times Carlo has ignored his wishes. He nearly sent him back to Italy last week, calling him 'a problem.'"

They headed off into the Norman countryside; apple trees were sun-burnished, their leaves drift-fallen into piles along the road. Her thoughts returned to their plans. So, after Montmartre, she and Odéon would return to Paris. Within their cocoon on the jockey box, she pictured Geneviève, Nancy's white-haired mother-in-law whom she met on her first day in Montmartre—the same woman who went with her to Maison de L'Étoile.

She unlatched her carpetbag again, feeling inside for an envelope. That had fallen to the bottom, along with the gun and the knife. She steadied her right hand on the rail of the jockey box and opened the envelope with her left. She lifted out Geneviève's card and tapped it thoughtfully against her cheek.

Nineteen

The Birthday Goose

After stabling the horses and wagon onshore, Celeste stiffened as they passed through the imperial guardpost. Carlo's threats about her danger seemed unfounded—at least for now. Their arrival followed a harrowing boat ride across the channel from shore to Mont St. Michel, nauseating high waves, high winds, then approaching land by skirting known pockets of quicksand and fear of gendarmes who glared at them from shore.

All the while, Celeste watched Odéon. He remained calm during the ordeal, even enduring her grasping of his arm and at times tendering her hand, enfolding it like a tiny kitten in his larger glove.

Safely on the island, they parted ways, agreeing that Odéon would search for lodging, and she would find food and drink. Celeste paced into the winding street, circling toward the village dominated by a church spire featuring Saint Michael the Archangel's golden statue. At a market stand, she chose pears, camembert cheese, and two baguettes, along with a bottle of local cider. Mid-afternoon shadows darkened the streets so narrow two people could hardly fit side by side. Drifts of chimney smoke gave the village a woody smell, blending with the salty freshness of the sea air.

Upon leaving the market stall, she spied a woman across the way who was looking into a meat vendor's window. The lady wore a long, aproned skirt and *sabots*, the traditional wooden shoes. Celeste gathered she was prosperous from her dress: maroon velvet strips lined the folds of her skirt; the gold braiding of her jacket matched the silk reticule dangling from her wrist.

The woman's hair was gray rather than Maman's blond hair, but her profile was similar: the nose slightly upturned, small ears visible from under her cap. Maman could have gone gray by now. She would be sixty-eight. Oh please, let her be Maman. She dared not breathe but took tentative steps toward the woman, careful not to frighten her. If this were Maman, she might not even recognize her daughter after so many years.

She stood next to the woman who scanned a headless goose hanging from a hook in the butcher's window. Maybe she would be lucky after all this searching—she could only hope. After a moment's pretending to examine the same goose, Celeste said, "Bonjour."

The woman swiveled and faced her. "Bonjour, mademoiselle. Do you need anything? Are you lost? I only ask that because we have many visitors to our prison island, and they are forever getting confused on our circular streets." She spoke mechanically—perhaps accustomed to repeating these lines to the invariable flocks of relatives seeking their loved ones.

Celeste swallowed hard. But as the woman spoke, she knew the lady was not her mother. How silly of her to imagine that. Her face was too broad; her eyes were brown, not blue. But there was yet hope. She said, "I seek my mother's whereabouts. All I know is that she is up there." She glanced at the monstrous prison dominating the mount. "I hear she is in the care of the chaplain named Father Jean."

"Father Jean? What is her name, child? Our village is small, and most of us know each other. Word of women prisoners gets around the ministry I serve."

"Madeleine Bazin."

"I do not know the name. What does she look like?" The woman's gaze fastened on the goose in the window. Another aproned customer inside the shop pointed at the same bird, apparently considering its purchase.

The bags grew heavy in Celeste's arms, so she rested them on her feet to avoid the seagull droppings on the lane. "I have not seen her in many years, but to be honest, my mother resembles you."

The woman touched her throat. "Me? What do you mean? Same age? My dress? Say it, child." She appeared impatient, apparently tearing her reluctant attention away from the goose.

"You have the same hair—blond with some gray, and you have the same kind of nose—small. You are probably close in age."

The aproned customer inside the shop was now nearing the goose, her hand outstretched, touching the feathers.

The woman passed in front of Celeste, taking steps toward the butcher shop's threshold. She turned back. "What are you after? You say this woman is my twin? Bad luck, my dear. I have no such sister. Look—I must have this goose."

"Please—I have been seeking her whereabouts for many years—at last, I think I've found where she lives. She is supposed to be in the care of Father Jean—someone said she might even be studying to be a nun. But I do not even know where to begin to look." A gust of sea air whooshed her traveling hat out of place, and she struggled to pull it back on her head.

"A postulant? Up there? Why, it is a prison, child, not a nunnery. I am sorry, mademoiselle, I cannot help you." She stood at the threshold of the butcher's shop and called to someone inside. "*J'arrive! Monsieur le Boucher,* I want that goose for my husband's birthday celebration."

The customer fondling the goose looked over her shoulder at the door; the butcher appeared at the threshold, his blood-stained apron pulled tight against his belly. He raised his hands. "What do you want, Marcelle? You cost me money—this gentlewoman wants the goose, and there is only one."

"But I have extra *sou*—my payment will top the gentlewoman's." She veered into the shop while Celeste lingered on the cobblestones outside, jostled by top-hatted men on foot, with wide-skirted ladies leaning on their arms. She gazed down at the scuffed toes of her laced half-boots and the soiled edges of her skirts. What a filthy picture she must make, and she had no perfume to cover the days-old sweaty odors that spread with her every move.

Celeste lingered outside the butcher shop—somehow, she could not find her feet. That woman named Marcelle, her sliver of hope, had evaporated in search of a goose. Maybe she should go further up the winding path fronted by shop windows and ask the vendors if they had seen Maman. Twilight darkened the street, and shopkeepers lit lamps inside display windows. A stray dog on a sniffing spree licked her ankle and bent his long legs toward the empty tables where the food market had been.

It was getting late after such a long day, and her stomach rumbled. She should probably go back to Odéon. He would be wondering where she was. The bags of produce hung like lead weights on her wrist, and the cold of the windswept cobblestones permeated her thin-soled boots. She had come all this way—something prevented her from moving even one footstep in either direction. She grew thirsty; the inside of her mouth puckered, and she labored to swallow.

Celeste took a few feeble steps leading down to the lower level where she had left Odéon, puzzled about where she would find him. If only she had the energy to get there.

Someone closed the butcher's shop door, and the *clack-clack* of wooden shoes sounded behind her. "Mademoiselle?" A woman's voice pierced the air.

Celeste took a half-step. The voice might be referring to her, telling her to wait. She debated whether to turn around, and she glanced back.

Marcelle waved; a sack of potatoes weighed down one arm.

"No goose?" Celeste asked.

Sweat drops bubbled on her forehead. "The butcher will pluck the feathers for me—it is a special occasion, and I must go prepare the house for the feast tomorrow."

"I wish you a good feast. Indeed, you do look so like Maman—at least at the age I think she would be now."

Marcelle stepped toward her, skirting a pile of dog dung. "How old is your mother?" she asked.

"Fifty-two. Her birthday was last February. Since I was fourteen, I have not seen her when she sent me to live with relatives in New Orleans."

"Mmm." The woman tipped her head back and took a glance skyward. She said, "Forgive me for what I am about to do."

"I do not understand." Celeste set the heavy bag back on the tops of her feet.

A knowing look passed across Marcelle's face. "You seem to be sincere, my child. I may be risking your mother's anger at revealing what I know, but you are so alone. My mother is long dead, and I would do anything in the world to have her back.

"There is no church parish up there on the mount. You see, the abbey was closed at the time of the revolution and converted to a prison. The church up top is a partial ruin, but the chaplain holds Mass for the prisoners each noon. I help arrange the flowers on the altar. You know I may be acquainted with the woman you describe."

Celeste's pulse quickened. "Please go on."

"A certain woman fits your description. She is a prisoner there. Since I must pass through the building, I have seen her working at the loom. I am the wife of one of the wardens, so I have permission to enter the prison. I lay flowers out in the morning, and often I stay for the Mass the chaplain says at noon. I see her praying alongside other women inmates."

Celeste bit her lower lip. "Where do you think I can find her?"

"She usually sits at the western end of the first set of pews on the left with other women. The men sit on the right-hand side. I see her there mostly every day, unlike the other detainees. From what I can tell, she is very devoted to the church. It is almost as though she were—oh, I don't know—making up for something. Maybe she's seen the error of her ways. She is probably too old to join a religious order, but she acts like a nun, to be sure."

"What do you mean—the error of her ways?" Celeste's question lingered in the air. "If your husband is the warden, you must know why she is in prison."

Marcelle fingered the braided design on her reticule. "I do not want to say anything about your mother's character. My husband would already be angry with what I have revealed to you." An angle of light crossed her forehead, and the crevices deepened under her cheekbones. "Besides, my husband is forbidden from giving out prisoner's information, though I can tell from his manner that she has done something severe."

Celeste drew a ragged breath. "Do go on."

"There is talk in the village that her case may have involved doings of some type."

"Doings?"

"Yes, something untoward. Serious, like murder. Rumor has it she is from Paris, and you know what they say about the life there."

"Do I? I am not sure what you mean."

"Well, I have never been to Paris, but people say women are bought and sold there. I do not know, but I can only imagine."

"Right," Celeste said. "What other of her *doings* do people talk about in the village?"

"They have seen her at night, backlit at her window." She pointed to the higher elevations of the granite mount, buildings reaching toward the sky, tall vertical windows facing the sea like sentinels waiting for God.

"She is not housed in the dungeons with the violent prisoners. Her prison chamber is in the Perrine Tower that looks down on the easterly beaches facing Normandy."

"I do not understand."

"Villagers have seen English shore landings late at night. People speak of torches, boats, men. My husband tells me the guards increased patrol of the east-facing chambers after a recent incident."

"What happened?"

"Not long ago, someone spotted her at her window while at the same time a boat attempted a landing along the eastern beach—down there."

Though she stood in a crowded village street, Celeste could visualize the windswept area: Odéon had told her about pockets of quicksand, shifting tides that would swamp boats, and treacherous gusts of wind that blew sailors off their ships.

"What happened to the landing boat?"

"Villagers said it nearly swamped, and several men ended up in the water. Lucky for the sailors, they were able to pull the men out of the sea before the tide went out. The guards on patrol rushed the beach, but the boat gained the sea and made off before being apprehended. Since no bodies washed up on shore, the guards figured all had escaped."

"Did they know who the boat belonged to?"

"The only thing my husband said was that a guard noticed a small white signal flag along with the flag of St. George—so it must have been English."

"And why the connection to the woman at the window?"

"When the boat floundered, her window light went out. The superstitious villagers have little to speak of, so they tell stories about her supernatural powers. Most were nonsense, I'm sure. Yet, the guards watch for communication between channel ships and the prison since many rescue attempts have been tried.

"But now I must be off. I see your tears, my child, and I cannot know the depth of your anguish. But here—" She untied the strings of her reticule and searched inside, bringing out a small pencil and a card. She wrote something on the back of it.

"You will need this to gain entrance to the prison. Tell the guards you are my friend and that you are to help me lay the altar flowers. Otherwise, they will never let you in—they only allow parents inside. Look for me inside the guardhouse. You must pretend you are assisting me. Inside the church, I will point out the woman we think is your Maman. We may remain through the Mass, and if you recognize her, I will arrange a short meeting between you. Then we must be sure to leave swiftly lest one of the guards take a fancy to you."

She pulled a card from her reticule. One printed side read

Gerard Le Pont, Warden
Mont St. Michel

On the back of the card, she scribbled,

Laisse-la passer.
Marcelle Le Pont

She passed the card to Celeste. "If you come up to the prison tomorrow morning at 11, I will meet you at the guardhouse where they will stop you. Show the guards your papers and this card; I will be waiting inside. I will escort you through to the chapel, and perhaps you would kindly help me with the altar flowers."

Celeste nodded.

The woman, self-identified as Marcelle Le Pont, said her *adieu* and strode up the hill. Celeste threaded her way down past shoppers heading to the marketplace, bumping shoulders with stout men and avoiding small children holding their mothers' hands. She wondered what waited above on the mount whose cathedral rose into the sky, a beacon for God and Saint Michael.

Twenty

Harmonies

Celeste suppressed a giggle as she approached the sleeping figure. Odéon lay full length on a low bench next to a closed fruit stand in the fading light, his greatcoat bundled tight around himself, his hands folded on his chest. His beret angled over his face while his stomach gently rose and fell in the rhythm of sleep.

After she looked around the bench for a tickling weed to stroke his chin, she realized there was none. She had loved to humor him on their earlier travels. So, she sat down against his hip and leaned over him, then tipped back the brim of his beret, moving it up above his forehead.

Careful not to wake him, she caressed his soft beard, the outline of his lips, the broad tip of his nose, and rested against his chest, avoiding the pipe that poked from his jacket pocket. She lay there, hearing the thrum of his heart, the occasional cry of a seagull overhead, the dry rustle of paper on the ground. Occasional footsteps sounded when gentry passed, but they paid her no mind. If only she could remain thus, bathed in the waning rays of light, with this man with whom she knew completeness, the sweet comfort of home.

After God knew how long, dusk gobbled up the remaining sun's crescent and cast a pall over the walkway. He stirred beneath her, and she sensed his heartbeat quicken and his arms tighten around her. "Celeste, is that you?"

She murmured. "Oui."

Her affirmation complete, he pulled her more tightly onto himself and held her close, the sinew of his muscles rippling under her, and she imagined his joy—she would return the long-held passion he felt for her. He grinned and laughed a rolling laugh, to the extent that she nearly tumbled off him.

"My love," he said and clasped her even more tightly to his chest.

Though they remained clutching one another, Celeste knew it could not last. Nothing did. The evening deepened, and they must find a place to stay. "Odéon." She sat upright and stretched her arms in the air. "We must find our rooms and lodging—I have bought food for us, and it grows late."

"Does it? Time passes so fast, and when I am with you, I hardly notice what time of day it is." He sighed and sat up, his arms encircling her shoulders. "I have found us a room—in the village above us. When I passed, you were talking to a woman in wooden shoes. You were so intent on your conversation, you did not even see me go by."

"*C'est vrai*–it is true. But I did find out some information." She cast her eyes on the now darkened street. A lamplighter passed, stopped not far up the road, climbed a ladder, then lit the street lantern. The weak light illuminated her bag of food, Odéon's boots, and the wee bits of auburn hair on his beard. "By the way, you did not wake when I lay with you here. Did you not feel me holding you?"

"Ah, yes." His smile cast burning embers between them; she sensed trembling deep inside her flesh.

It was then she knew. Though Carlo captivated her spirit with his Italian flash and stylish manners, this was the man she wanted—Odéon—whose natural French warmth and humor captured her soul.

Lamplights and shadows played hide and seek in the passageways as Odéon led Celeste to their lodging, a medieval Norman hostelry. After they picked up the key at the front desk, together they carried her carpetbag and their food bags up the curlicue wooden steps leading into the triptych of rooms. Celeste gazed at the hand-hewn doors featuring flowers and angels, massive oak beams set into the walls where the rooms recessed like niches in a darkened chapel.

They set up a table near the window inside their musty chamber. She opened one side of the pair of leaded glass windows, lit candles, then spread out the meal of cider, baguettes, Camembert cheese, and pears. The candle's glow made reflections on the small diamond-shaped panes of glass. During their dinner, she told Odéon about the information gained from the warden's wife, Marcelle Le Pont.

Odéon wiped pear juice off his mouth with the back of his hand. "What a good contact. You are very close to finding her, dear Celeste. But guard your heart. What if the woman above turns out not to be your mother? As much as you long to see her, the truth could very well destroy you."

"I had not considered that the woman she mentions might not be Maman." She bit her lower lip.

"Did she say your mother's name without your prompting her?"

"No, now that I think of it, I said my mother's name, but she did not use it."

"Ah, it would be wise to remain skeptical until you know the woman she talks of is your actual mother. Another thing you must consider—you also do not know if the warden's wife is laying a trap for you."

"A trap?" Celeste dragged her thoughts into a mire of possibilities.

"One of the reasons I like you is you are naïve, unaware, vulnerable. You are not hard like other women your age. But in this instance, you must pull all your wits together. Think of it this way—tomorrow you will enter one of the deadliest prisons in France in broad daylight. You are walking into a nest of vipers. You are affiliated with a group of revolutionaries, whether you acknowledge it or not. Imperial guards and their agents are everywhere in France, and they swarm this island. A flick of a wrist and the warden could have you thrown into a cell up there." He angled his thumb in the direction of the upper prison.

She set her hand against her tightening chest. "I need fresh air—the room is stifling." She unlatched the other side of the window and leaned out into the night air. The stiff breeze whistled through her hair. Odéon joined her, planting his elbows on the windowsill, gazing out alongside her. They sat side by side, aiming their view above the rooftops and out to the darkening channel waters.

"Somehow, the risk is worth it to me. I have come to France to find my mother, and if I leave now without her, I will live the rest of my life in regret. She must return with me to America and spend the rest of her life under my care."

"You are a stubborn woman. Have you ever thought about how you would convince the warden to let her out of prison? If what you say is true, she is in there for a capital crime."

Celeste put her index finger to her lips. "I can be persuasive when I want to be." She wetted her lips and flashed him the same look that had brought mayors and town officials to their knees at the brothel in San Francisco.

He pulled her closer—his hips moved against her leg—she experienced a jolt. Something crossed the sky outside their window. "Look—there—a shooting star." Celeste inhaled his comfortable tobacco smoke perfume, then bent, peering out at the shining waters. "A full moon," she remarked as the moonlight cast sparkling shafts of light onto the channel and spilled into the bay and fomented high tides and shimmering sands.

"You belong to those stars, that moon." Odéon ran his fingers over her hair, drew it from its pins, and let the silken strands cascade onto his fingers. He caressed her temple, then moved his fingers down her face and held it up to his. "With this blond hair, you are a precious angel, a friend of Saint

Michael on whose mountain we rest." He brushed his lips ever so lightly over her own. "God sent you to me, and I thought for so long I would never have you . . . I thought Carlo had claimed you as his."

"How could I deny what I felt?" She folded her arms around his neck and planted tiny kisses around his mouth. "It was you all along, but my romantic notions gave way to an understanding about your true nature. You are the man I seek."

"When I saw you again in the stable yard, I figured you were only there to get a horse and buggy."

"I was there for much more, Odéon. I needed—no—*wanted* you by my side."

"Show me, my love." He nuzzled kisses into her neck, and she shivered. He unbuttoned her blouse, tugged her chemise over her head, and took her breasts in his hands, licking her nipples until they were firm and hard. "This, my love, is how I show you."

She ran her hands over his back and pulled him closer until she could hear the rhythm of his breathing that grew ever more heated. He carried her over to the bed where they lay side by side, the moon their only witness.

She moaned and guided his hand up her skirt into her nether regions, where her desire surged. He moved his hand into her, his fingers taking her slowly, gently, yet pressing upward with slow and soft movements. Though she had made being in bed with a man her occupation, this was different. She had always pleasured them, not the other way around. He took his time, his gentle probing, and responses to her sighs of delight, clearly wanting her to enjoy this moment, their time, their growing bond.

"I must have you, Odéon," she said.

He came into her, thrusting his hips softly, then more firmly, with each plunge a reminder of his power and warmth, like a tide rushing into her, then out again, a mirror of the sea below whose battle with the sand continued to form the poetry of the island shore. He planted soft kisses on her neck and seemed to know where his thrusting would give her the greatest pleasure. He lifted her into a space where they hovered together, apart from the world and its people, only them, within the secret cocoon of each other's bodies.

After hours of lovemaking, Odéon asleep at her side, Celeste covered her nakedness with a blanket. She rose and padded to the open window. She leaned out and saw the lichen-covered rooftops. When the freezing air met her cheeks, her face tingled. The moon continued its vigil overhead, the tracks of light ribboned on the waves.

She peered up at the rock and the ancient abbey perched on the promontory above. Its silver spire and mottled walls testified to the eternal battle against shifting tides, relentless storms, and bracing wind. Countries fought many wars over this ancient rock, an island guarding France against invaders. The skirmish she faced might not be as large in scale, but its consequences were just as deadly.

The following day after leaving Odéon asleep in their bed, Celeste bathed in the basin of icy water provided by the innkeeper, then finished off the heel of bread and took several gulps of cider remaining in the bottle on the table. She pulled the chamber pot from beneath the bed, eased off the lid, urinated, and after sliding it under the bed, she stared up at the mount. A brilliant cerulean blue sky replaced last night's starshine; bare tree limbs thrust into the air like feet poked out of bed on a cold winter's morn.

She eased a hairbrush from her carpetbag and tugged it through the tangle of blonde strands that lay about her shoulders. She might weave it into a fashionable bun at the nape of her neck in ordinary times, but today she had not a moment's luxury. When she drew a pocket watch from her reticule—it read 9:30.

A frisson of energy surged inside of her—she must hurry—she faced

900 winding steps to the Abbey Cathedral and the prison. Early shopkeepers setting up their wares would crowd the lower steps, along with aproned homemakers searching for fresh loaves of bread and meat for midday meals. She also remembered this was the warden's birthday—Marcelle had been gracious to meet her today of all days. She must hurry—Marcelle would want to get home to set out the warden's luncheon feast.

The brisk sea air nipped at her cheeks, and each step upward toward the mount became more hazardous. She had not predicted the ice on the cobbled walkways between the shops on either side. As the route twisted and turned between patches of housing and open spaces facing the wider channel, she watched the ground to avoid slipping. It was only after some 500 steps that she stopped for a rest and looked up.

Above her loomed the clerestory windows of the church, set into the dark, forbidding prison walls whose ancient granite bulwark dated back centuries. A line of thick-cloaked women wearing knit headscarves wormed their way past carrying baskets of food. They must be bringing rations to the prisoners or the guards.

She matched their antlike pace and joined the tail end of their queue. They kept up a steady gait, avoiding icy patches. Since they seemed to know the route, she followed closely. Maybe if she blended in with their black skirts, she would enter the guardhouse without notice.

The balance of 400 steps proved arduous—each rock-carved twist led into another steep incline until, at one point, she thought she was climbing up a ladder. The women did not stop their ascent, so she kept up with them, though each breath stabbed her chest. There was no turning back. A dark muddy thought cast its shadow over her.

She wondered what she was doing there. And if her search was worth all this effort. The woman Marcelle mentioned might not even be her mother, and she would feel a fool. But the alternative was even worse. If she lingered in Paris wondering about Maman, that would have been torture. At least here she was doing something about it. *Wait a moment.*

One last turn and bright red and white jackets blazed against the grey walls. Imperial guards watched each side of the prison entrance. The street widened into a plaza, and a gothic-style portico loomed over block steps to a doorway. The line of basket-clutching women crept inside, shrinking slowly.

She kept up with their ant-like progress and avoided their curious backward glances. Rather than staring back, she absorbed the shabby magnificence of the fortress. Lichen and moss reclined in the gaps between the stones, and gothic windows glared at her through missing panes like empty eye sockets. She shivered. The mount displayed its tomb, a gray expressionless mass housing living bones, prisoners without hope, souls without salvation.

The entrance gobbled up the women's queue, and at last, she was at the front of the line. The ring of guards at the door cast rheumy eyes upon her, like so many glassy-eyed dead fish. One uniform stuck out a shriveled hand, grey like the stone walls behind him. "Documents, s'il vous plaît." She gave him her passe-port and Marcelle's card. His hand retreated, and he vanished into the dark recesses beyond. She heard whispers, then laughter, then shuffling footsteps.

Another taller man appeared, younger this time. His hands resembled furry paws, and he shuffled her documents as if they were a set of playing cards. "*C'est tout, mademoiselle?* This? Your only identification to enter the most significant prison in France?" He issued a sardonic grin. His upper lip retracted, flashing a swollen gum line that crowned a ragged set of tobacco-stained teeth.

Yet another wide-eyed guard stepped out from behind him, and that one held up an index finger and traced her body. She bristled. *How dare he*. The cur ran his purple tongue across his lips. The former two guards reappeared, their mouths open in hangdog delight. She recoiled. *Horrors*. No one said this would be easy, but she had to get past these Cerberean hellhounds.

She watched uniformed men like these fondling the younger girls at

Madame De Salle's brothel in New Orleans. If she resisted, they would take more, and if she were not careful, she would face repeated rapes among the troops, then be conveniently cast over the high walls to the rocks below. It took a guard to know an inmate, for that guard owned the same level of cunning and willingness to commit a capital crime.

She mused at the ways the empire kept its inmates inside. The same animals that ringed the prison also prowled within its walls. Maybe if she stalled, the line behind her would grow impatient. She could play this game as well as they.

She slid a hand inside her reticule and lifted out her pocket watch. The time said 10:50. "Madame Le Ponte is expecting me at 11."

The trio mocked her. "Madame Oo-la-la is expecting me for tea. Oh, what should I do?"

The line of men and women pressed behind her. A murmur rippled in the air. "What is happening?" Someone called out, "Hurry up!" Another yelled, "Let her in and get this line moving!"

The inflamed gum guard stepped out onto the platform under the portico and addressed the crowd. "Shut up! If you don't close your gizzards, you won't come in now or ever."

Waves of curses erupted amidst the crowd. Even the children took God's name in vain. Though taken aback for a moment, Celeste remembered. These were the inmates' families who visited during the short hours allowed them. Their desperation led to their beastly behavior. Even brothel madams had better manners.

A clanking came from the interior of the guardhouse, and a tall imperial guard appeared; his shining boots matched his glinting brass buttons. "What are you doing, sons of bitches?" For a moment, Celeste wondered. He must be addressing the crowd. They were already riled up—with those words, the man could incite a riot. She watched as he peered down at the guards, who shrank in his presence. When he snatched her passe-port and Marcelle's calling card from the guard's hand, he snarled. "Is this yours?"

Celeste trembled, but she held her voice steady. "Oui, monsieur."

He sniffed and held himself upright. "I am Capitaine Janvier. Who is it you wish to meet here? I see you carry the warden's wife's card. Do you seek the warden?"

The waiting crowd rumbled like distant thunder on a cloudy day. "I am to meet Madame Le Ponte." She gestured. "In there."

She looked past the pack of glassy-eyed, leering guards, avoiding their eye contact. "If you check, you will find she waits for me. The warden would not be pleased that you kept her so long."

"Go check." The capitaine barked at the inflamed gum guard who shuffled inside, then sprang back a moment later. "She is there, mon capitaine." He spoke with a crispness reserved for the higher-ranking officer.

She shook her head. What phoniness. What hypocrisy.

"*Allez, mademoiselle.*" The capitaine's arm-length leather glove all but shoved her inside; then, he extended a hand to the man waiting behind her. "Next—"

Twenty-One

ONE WAY OUT

After a moment of adjusting to the darkness that swallowed her inside the guardroom, Celeste blinked and saw Marcelle creep out from behind a massive stone pillar. "I see you survived the entrance," she said. Her wide skirt swayed and bowed as she covered the short distance between them.

"Do they grill everyone like that?" Celeste asked. Sweat had gathered under her arms during the ordeal, but inside the building, she grew cold; her teeth chattered, and she struggled to hold them still.

Marcelle proffered a weak smile. "The guards are known to give young women the worst time." She held two bouquets of fresh flowers and passed one of them to Celeste. "Here is yours. For the altar," she said. "Now, we must get out of this area before the guards change their minds about you. Come, follow me." She led Celeste down a long corridor that opened onto a vast chamber lit by four stone fireplaces. Vaulted arches fanned out over the ceiling. This room must have served for monastery meetings when the site was an abbey. Smoke and sweat lingered in the air, along with the musky dampness seeping through its granite walls.

Male prisoners pounded nails into wooden beams on one side of the room in what appeared to be a carpentry shop. On the other side, women sat at a series of looms, their hands manipulating the warp and the weft. A very young girl sat at a spinning wheel. All were thin; all could use a healthy meal. They wore grey garments with ragged holes, and many prisoners had visible sores populating their arms and faces.

Celeste could not determine whether the lesions resulted from disease or beatings, and nausea rose in her belly. She had seen the sick and dying on Paris streets before, but they were free to come and go as they pleased. These prisoners had nothing to look forward to except another day of misery. Whatever their crimes, their punishment did not merit this living death.

Guards bearing long rifles supervised the group, stationed at vantage points against pillars throughout the long chamber. Their beady eyes adjusted to the firelight that illuminated the dark room; they had no doubt lost their sense of justice.

They glared at her as she went by and bowed their heads to Marcelle, who was undoubtedly a familiar figure as the warden's wife. And her husband was their source of authority and fear—to cross her was to strike their master.

"Who are these prisoners? I am surprised to see them working." Celeste lengthened her steps to keep up with Marcelle's long stride.

"They have shown good behavior, so they are assigned workhouse duties. Of course, if they make any slipups, the guards will return them to their cells. The most violent criminals stay in the downstairs dungeons, never to see daylight. They likely die of disease or exposure before they ever meet their executioner. My warden husband often says, 'People choose many routes to Mont St. Michel, but there is only one way out—in a coffin.'"

They passed a contraption where Celeste halted her footsteps. A gigantic wooden wheel creaked and groaned against a series of thick ropes and pulleys. Prisoners wearing customary grey work suits turned the massive wheel that hoisted pallets of supplies for the prison. She watched as the men worked the ropes, a month's dirt and sweat lining their faces.

Theirs was a kind of living torture, she thought. But then, for some, laboring to death might be a happier prospect than living outside the walls in French society. Human life was expendable unless the emperor could use the person to make another endless war.

Marcelle hastened around a corner, but she returned after a moment and tugged Celeste's elbow. A frown wrinkled her mouth. "My child, do not tarry in this room. Prisoners grow restless, and we are a distraction. We are climbing upward now into the abbey." After another series of steps, this time in an open-air hallway dividing two thick stone walls, they entered the main doors of the Abbey Church of Saint Michel.

The former jewel of gothic magnificence now lay before Celeste as a near ruin. The caved-in roof only partially covered the sanctuary and the altar, and seabird droppings littered the once-glistening columns of golden stone. Yet parts of the clerestory windows remained, and even in its decay, she envisioned the glorious cathedral that beckoned pilgrims who made their journeys during the Middle Ages. These journeys heralded Saint Michael who crushed the head of Satan beneath his foot.

She followed Marcelle down the aisle to the altar. The chaplain was putting on his vestments, and he gave a brief nod to Marcelle. He pointed to two vases that adorned the altar. After smoothing the white linen altar cloth, Marcelle checked the vases for water, then set the flowers in one container.

She motioned for Celeste to do the same, and Celeste arranged her bouquet in the other vase, taking care not to spill the water inside. After situating the vase to the right side of the Holy Book, she found the bookmark and opened the page for that day's rite of the Catholic Mass.

She untangled the flower stems, avoiding the thorns; she inhaled the fragrance of lilies and red winter roses so like those in her mother's autumn garden in Montmartre. In November, she and her mother would plant bulbs under the soil—narcissus, hyacinths, and daffodils at Maison de L'Étoile. Maman always said they would make the frost bearable since they were like warm beating hearts under the snow that promised joy in the spring. *Maman*—they might meet—and soon. But then—no matter how she pictured them—none of her former dreams prepared her for what appeared next.

Rows of prisoners dressed in gray, their hair matted and stringy, filed into the pews on both sides of the church, men on the right side, women on the left. Marcelle whispered, "We must sit in this side altar behind the chapel during Mass—that way, you can have a clear view of the women's pews." She pointed to the group of women streaming down the aisle. They flowed into the pews; their downcast, shriveled faces contrasted with the mount's soaring arches and upward reaches.

"I am surprised so many prisoners come to Mass," Celeste shook her head. "Surely not all of them are believers."

Marcelle said, "Some believe, others do not, but these prisoners have one thing in common—they come to Mass to get out of their cells or away from their labors. It is their only exercise. When we started having the Mass, only a couple came; now, we fill the church. The warden sees it as a way to manage them."

"That would work for the chaplain, too. It would bring him more followers to Christ."

Celeste sharpened her attention on the rows of women, now seated listening to Father Jean's sermon. She stared at the women in the first row. Their straggled hair and dirt-lined wrinkles veiled their faces. Some were older and appeared frail, probably the result of imprisonment rather than age.

"Repent of your ways, my children. Hell is waiting for you, but there is still salvation. You sit on the rock of Saint Michael, the place where he smashed the head of Satan for all eternity. You know that Satan was once an angel even more beautiful than Michael, and he was the beloved of God. But Satan fancied himself better than God, more powerful, more intelligent, so he began to commit prideful acts using selfish cruelty that threatened all souls until God stopped him."

Among the women in the second row, one with sharp eyes and black hair seemed less weather-beaten than the others. She had worked the loom as they passed the long chamber earlier in the day. A newcomer. She must feel lost. To scan her surroundings. To know that one day she would be as listless as her seatmates. To think these endless days stretched into eternity.

The priest continued. "So, God unleashed his second angel Michael whose cleansing, humble spirit undermined Satan and drained his power until their ultimate battle when Michael crushed him and subjugated him to God's will. Yet even though bloodied, Satan was unbowed, and he crept away but now reappears in humans at certain times to remind us of man's imperfection, his vices; thus, children, we must be forever on our guard.

"Therefore humans contain both an angel and a devil, and each day we must do battle lest Satan rise from under Saint Michael's heel and devour our souls and prevent us from seeing the magnificent glory of God in eternity."

Guards stood at the end of each pew, their eyes not on heaven but on the hellish creatures sitting before them, the prisoners' faces contorted, starvation and suffering etched across their cheeks. How was she to find her mother among the twenty-five prisoners whose lifeless bodies stood, knelt, and sat during the Latin Mass? The chaplain's ritual droned on, yet at moments the noonday sun dispatched rays of streaming light, illuminating the filigreed archways, the delicate wall carvings, the occasional headless statues of saints defiled by rains and winds bent on ravaging this church.

The priest then blessed and sanctified the sacred bread for Holy Communion. The congregation knelt on the stone floor, some bowing their heads, others mumbling prayers. Some stared ahead of them. Yet among the women's pews, one knelt with an upturned face, a woman in her late forties whose gray-blond hair lay matted against her head, her cheeks once plump with the bloom of youth now cavernous, her lips now a thin, jagged line. Yet her eyes, that gentle expression, the way she gazed at the ethereal presence of the priest's hands elevating the host—the supposed transformation of the body of Christ—*that was Maman.*

An unexpected rush of tears flooded Celeste's eyes, but she wiped them away with her fingertips. This was no time to cry. After the prisoners filed to the altar rail for Holy Communion, received the sanctified bread, and flowed back to their seats, she leaned over to Marcelle. "I know which one is Maman."

"Where?" Marcelle's eyes widened, her eyebrows lifting.

"At the end of the third row—do you see her?" Celeste pointed at the woman, now seated, the prisoner's blond-gray hair shrouding her neck and shoulders.

Marcelle pried her spectacles from a side pocket. After adjusting them on her nose, she peered out toward the women. "Ah, I see. She does fit your description."

"May I talk to her?"

"Of course, my child. But we cannot remain here since somebody must guard her. We must take her to the chaplain's office—to Father Jean—out there." She jerked her thumb toward a space behind her. "But wait a moment—I must talk to someone." After tiptoeing down the side aisle, she stood face to face with the guard who minded the row of pews holding her mother. He leaned down, and they had what appeared to be a whispered conversation. He regarded her with a quizzical expression but nodded his head.

The Mass ended, and the guards herded the prisoners back to their cells or places of work. Yet one prisoner remained praying on her knees, seeming oblivious to the empty church. The sun streamed through the clerestory windows, emitting a pure white light that bathed the interior in an ethereal glow. Celeste padded down the center aisle and entered the right end of the row, while at the far left, her mother posed in prayer, rosary beads laced through her fingers. Those hands were her mother's hands . . . those same knotted hands wiped her childhood tears away and taught her to hold a fork and spoon. But something gleamed on the fourth finger of her left hand. A gold band. Maybe a wedding ring. Celeste edged down the pew, careful not to startle her.

"Bonjour, Maman," she said.

The woman crossed herself and tucked her rosary beads into her sleeve. Marcelle conferred with Father Jean and the guard, who pointed to a dark recess behind the chapel.

After casting Celeste a sidelong glance, Maman collapsed in the pew. "Who might you be who calls me mother?" she asked. "Under what pretense do you approach me?" She glanced toward the guard.

"I am Celeste, your daughter. I have come from L'Amérique to find you."

"You are too old to be my daughter, for she is only fourteen, and her hair is still in braids. You are a woman—your wild hair and your long cloak—no—you are not my child." A vein throbbed in her forehead.

"Shh—all is well, Maman. I am here, and I have much to tell you of my travels."

A look of alarm crossed her mother's face. "Guard!" she shouted and burst from her seat. "I do not know this pretender, and I wish to return to my loom. I do not know what she wants." She stepped away from Celeste and out into the aisle. The guard leaped to her side and grasped her arm.

Marcelle joined the guard. Their suspicious eyes singed her body and branded her soul. *Failure.* To have come all this way—to have finally found her—only to have her mother deny her identity. She could be that heartless.

Celeste stepped next to the trio in the aisle. "Look, I have proof of who I am."

Maman shrieked; her cries ricocheted through the empty nave. She reminded Celeste of drawings of madwomen in bedlam, clawing their faces, their eyes bulging in their sockets.

A cleaning woman straightening the altar cloth looked up in apparent alarm.

Maman had lost her senses. She might not even be able to converse with her.

Father Jean bent down. "Madeleine, come with me."

Maman gazed at him through bloodshot eyes. "With you?"

He offered her his arm and led her behind the altar. The guard and Marcelle followed, Celeste forming the tail end. She wondered what she should do now. If Maman did not recognize her, she could not go on. A life-long dream had come true, but now, it was about to be ripped from her grasp.

Twenty-Two

Mingling Voices

Instead of a tidy office, Father Jean's domain lay littered with papers and open prayer books. Bits of cheese and bread were scattered on the floor. An ornate oaken cross embellished the wall above the desk, but the Christ statue had become unglued from the wood behind it and hung precariously off the cross. Celeste caught the odor of damp rot amplified by unpatched cracks in the walls, and the single mullioned window missed a pane.

Father Jean flashed toward them in his violet chasible, and he unearthed two chairs which he set facing one another on top of piles of old newsprint. He mumbled something, probably a hurried apology for the messy surroundings.

The guard led the faltering Madeleine into the room, and she drooped into the chair. "But my work? Should I be going now?" Her limbs quivered.

Marcelle patted her hand. "Madeleine, this young woman has some news for you. You must listen to what she says."

She looked up at Father Jean, "*Père*, I do not understand." God knew her mother could not take much more. She was pulverized.

"It is well. You may talk."

The guard led Celeste to the chair. She mumbled an uneasy *merci* and settled her skirts about her. What a pair they were—she in her war-torn garments—Maman in her thin prison shift. If she had known they would end up this way as a child, she would not have bothered to live.

Madeleine rasped, her voice sharp but uneven. "But she may not be who she claims. My daughter is thinner and younger, and she does not wear such fancy clothes. She lives in New Orleans and works with my sister's friend, Madame De Salle." She narrowed her eyes and peered at Celeste. "Although—my daughter did have the same eyes—celestial blue—that is why I named her thus."

Marcelle set a hand on her hip. "Maybe you could show your mother something to convince her of your identity. A birthmark or a scar? Some feature your mother would recognize?"

"I do not have such a mark. I did have a burn scar on my hand when I was young, but it faded."

Father Jean's face shadowed. "Surely there is some way you can convince her—what about a childhood memory only you two could share?"

Celeste thought back to the bedroom she shared with her at Maison de L'Étoile. The armoire, bedstead, wooden Madonna statue in the corner, mirror over the chest of drawers where her mother kept her things—her brushes, her tooth powder, her—oh yes!—her holy medal.

And all this time, it was around her neck. Celeste plunged her fingers down into her chemise and lifted out the chain with the Holy Virgin's medal of Catherine Labouré.

"This—Maman—you know this! I found it not long ago at Maison de L'Étoile—your medal, the one you always wore around your neck."

She held out the medal, and her mother leaned over, peered at it, then set her jaw. She gazed up at Celeste who waited, daring not to breathe.

"*Ma chère, c'est tu*? My dear, is it really you?"

Celeste pulled her mother to her, closing the space between them. Her mother was skin and bones under her flimsy garment, and she could not clutch her too closely for fear of breaking a rib or preventing her from taking her next breath. This was what she had sought—this was what she had missed for six long years. She yearned to be accepted, to be known for her true self, and in her mother's embrace, she found that. She buried her face in her mother's dusty hair, ignoring the smell of mold and rot.

Her mother held her closely, whispering her name. Her words owned a distant ghostly quality as if Maman had already left this earth and was speaking from a heavenly realm. Down in bustling Paris, this netherworld would seem impossible, but it was not hard to believe on Mont St. Michel where above the world these walls spoke of the monastery it had been; its echoes and groans murmured from every corner.

Ancient whispers—voices of the builders dating back to the 8th century when the Bishop of Avranches had built the original small chapel here on the island of Mont Tombe after seeing a vision of Saint Michael. She could not fathom its age—the marquis had told her of the hallowed past. And her voice would now mingle with Maman's inside these cells.

But something disturbed Maman—at first, Celeste thought it might be more fear, but then a series of deep, cough-like sobs racked the woman's chest. Her mother choked on a series of phlegmy globs, and Marcelle grabbed a handkerchief and crossed the room.

"Is she ill?" Celeste asked. Her mother continued to wheeze, then cough periodically.

Marcelle wiped her mother's lips. "She has pneumonia—so much thinner." She frowned at Father Jean. "Has she worsened? I thought she was improving when I last saw her. Remember a couple of days ago when I changed the altar flowers? That day she had more color in her cheeks."

"What are you doing to help her—to save Maman?" Celeste kept her voice level, but inside she seethed. They did not know what the hell they were doing to her mother in this prison. They had given her a sentence, then all they did was sicken her. She cracked her neck from side to side. "Does she see a doctor? I'm assuming you have one in this place."

The guard's face whitened, and his lips formed a crooked grin. "Of course."

Marcelle's voice hit the surrounding walls with force. "Well, tell Celeste what you know about her mother's care. People call what she has the most fatal of all acute diseases. Is this some sort of joke to you? Or would you like me to summon the warden to tell her?"

The guard's lower jaw clenched; a vein bulged in his forehead.

Celeste suspected that Marcelle seldom played this high card with the guards, yet she was glad she had, and she squeezed the woman's forearm.

Father Jean stepped between Marcelle and the guard. "Last I knew, she was having a great deal of pain in the right lung."

The guard finally found his tongue. "They've been purging her innards with the everlasting pill."

Celeste said, "No wonder she is so thin and frail. If they are reusing what they call 'the little bullet,' they make her swallow and expel it repeatedly. And every time she takes it, what little food she has in her stomach is quickly vomited. You can see it is not working. Have they tried anything else? Cupping and blistering the chest?"

The guard said, "That and opium preparations."

"Those should work. She is not herself—no wonder she did not recognize me right away. She may be seeing visions. When I was ill once in San Francisco, Brianna gave me laudanum, then cocaine, and I nearly jumped off the balcony, thinking I could fly. Poor Maman. What a sorry state you are in." She covered her face for a moment. She would not have her see her distress—not now when they were reunited.

She looked up at Marcelle, Father Jean, and the guard. "Please, can you leave us?"

Father Jean and Marcelle backed out of the chamber, but the guard remained. "I cannot leave the prisoner under any circumstances. It is forbidden."

"Surely you can give us several minutes together."

"Against regulations." His eyes narrowed. "I am already pushing the limit."

"This is my mother, whom I have not seen in six years. Surely you could give us twenty minutes. Think if this were your mother—how would you feel?"

"Eh, perhaps ten, but that is all." He turned and made for the door.

Gold slept in the recesses of her reticule. She reached one hand into the purse and drew out a coin. "Wait," she said.

The guard turned, flecks of white hair salting his brown beard. He would have a family—some hungry children, a nagging wife.

"For you." She held up the coin, hoping it could attract a bit of light.

His eyes brightened. He may never have seen such pure gold before. Though he held his gaze steady, a grin played about the edges of his lips. "In that case, *vingt minutes*—twenty minutes alone." He reached his hand out for the coin.

Rather than hand him the coin, she bit the edge of it. "Solid gold from California. Impossible to find here in France. Thirty minutes."

He shrugged. "Very well—*trente minutes*—thirty—but that is all. The warden will have my hide."

Celeste doubted that were true, but she dropped the coin in his palm. He examined it in the faint light and said, "I will be right outside."

After the door closed behind him, Celeste beheld a remarkable transformation in her mother's face. Though grime lingered in the corners of her eyes and mouth, Maman's expression lightened, and Celeste recognized the same soft azure blue eyes that captivated her as a child. They clung to each other in a hug they wished would last forever, sobbing, mumbling prayers of joy. Her mother pressed her back a step.

"What a woman you have become—when last I saw you, a little flat-chested girl stared up at me in that straw hat with the red satin ribbons. Do you remember that hat? Your hair hung in plaits down your back?"

"My birthday hat. The one I almost slept in every night since it was my favorite. But I hardly remember much about that day except your being taken away in handcuffs and shoved into a jailer's wagon. And then—no word from you for six years. I thought you were dead, Maman. Or I thought you must hate me so much you refused to write to me."

"Hardly the case. The wardens forbade me any communication outside my jail. The only time I was able to get out was with the permission of the nuns at Hôtel-Dieu. And then I only had time to meet with Felice's people, no one else. I could not have mailed you a letter, even then. I did not even have your address."

"So Tante Faucon did not communicate with you?"

Madeleine drew a rattled breath. "No, she never did. I suspect she was afraid she would be implicated in my case since she was my sister. It would have meant the end of her business."

"Did you ever get my letters? I wrote to you every month for the first year, but I stopped since I thought you wanted to forget me."

"I wondered all the time what had happened to you. I worried, paced, talked to you, exhausted all my tears. And then I prayed. I put you in God's hands. I had to leave it up to the Almighty since I never knew if I would ever see you again." Her web of wrinkles softened; her expression took on a younger appearance.

"I am truly your daughter, Maman, for I did the same thing. I dreamed of your fixing my broken toys, washing my hair, and telling me about the animals. But when I woke up, you were never there. And I vowed I would find you in France, no matter the cost."

Celeste relayed the story of her life in America, her return to Paris with Brianna and Edward, and her visit to Maison de L'Étoile. She told her about Carlo, Felice, the revolutionaries, Odéon, and the marquis.

"The marquis?" Maman's face flushed, and she bounded from her chair. "Who gave my whereabouts away? No one should have discovered the nature of my work."

Celeste absorbed Maman's intense gaze; her mother gave her that same look when she stole an apple from a grocer. "What work? Maman, what have you been up to? I have a million questions about why they have imprisoned you here, but this work you speak of—please say it clearly, for we have little time."

"I worry my telling you would put your life in jeopardy. I have seen and heard torture inside these walls. We hear the screams of the political prisoners. They dangle them by their thumbs; they blind them with hot pokers—and that is mild compared to other ways they gain information, especially from women."

"My life is already in danger by coming here. Do go on, Maman. Not to know would kill me in the end anyway. I must know your truth."

"I met my friend Felice on a trip to Italy, and he convinced me to undertake this mission whose goal is to strengthen the revolutionary movements against the emperor. I began to work with him in Paris while minding the brothel Maison de L'Étoile. There I became implicated in a prostitute's murder. Her name was Estelle Fornier."

"What happened to her?"

"She was the kind of girl who had to know everything, a busybody. Estelle had not worked long in my house when I caught her going through my bedroom drawers. At first, I thought she was after money, but when I saw her listening outside the kitchen door when I was in conversation with Carlo and Felice, I knew she was unsafe, maybe acting as an informant for one of the emperor's spies. I complained to Felice about her, and he said he would take care of it. But I had to get her out of my house.

"I fired her; she packed her bags and left. I thought that was the end of it all, but then I overheard my girls saying someone found a body washed up on the bank of the Seine near Pont Neuf at low tide. One investigation led to another, and I was arrested and charged with her murder.

"Another girl, Marie, testified at trial that I had been rough with Estelle on several occasions, and I had threatened her. She told the judge that I continually harped and pestered her, showing hatred and disregard. I had no alibi for the night of her murder, only that Marie saw me throw Estelle out into the street. And so, I was convicted of homicide, and I am awaiting a sentencing trial. It will either be death or life in prison. That is why I am here."

"So, the charges were made up. Who did that?"

"After the authorities caught wind of my involvement with Felice's group, they arranged the murder, then were delighted to pin the deed on me. That way, they could silence me, close my brothel, send me to prison, and have one less troublemaker to worry about." She shrugged. "They are keen on making an example of the woman of the night. It happens all the time in our trade."

"And your ring? Are you married, Maman?"

Someone's knuckles rapped on the door. The hinges squeaked, and the guard peered in at them.

"Twenty minutes." His voice clanged like a broken church bell.

"I know. Now go away," Celeste said. If only she could bend time into eternity to hear her mother's story.

Madeleine Bazin settled down into the chair, gathering her gray skirts about her as if she were wearing a ball gown. She leaned toward Celeste. "I am the wife of the marquis. We were married in jail—during my trial. He was captivated and did not want to wait for my release. I think he truly loves me, Celeste."

"He must love you. To marry you knowing you have no future since you are here. And you will never be able to live together."

"But we have a common cause. To that end, we need weapons—specifically bomb-making devices."

"To use against whom?"

"It is complicated, but our ultimate goal is to unseat Napoléon III."

Celeste gave an involuntary shudder. "You wish to overthrow the government?"

"More than that. The government is *him.* He is a pretender to the throne. Do you know that he manufactured his election, then seized power? This man rides roughshod over his people, tearing up the streets of Paris, throwing people out of their homes in the name of ridding the city of disease. He creates a Paris of the poor, the desperate, the oppressed.

"If they sentence me to death, the emperor must die also. The plan is afoot, already in motion. In January—Paris. I cannot say more for fear for your life and the others."

"Maman, I understand your wish to overthrow this tyrant, but I do not understand the depths of your hatred. I do not remember your speaking of this when you were raising me."

"My mother's brother Claude died from wounds and disease inflicted during the Siege of Sebastopol during the Crimean War. The emperor's war. He used young men as cannon fodder, expendable, like so many animals."

She unbuttoned the top of her dirty gray work dress. Her fingers unclasped an interior pin, and she eased out a tiny wax-lined envelope which she passed to Celeste. "Here. The only thing the guards allow me to keep was this—take it." Her hand trembled slightly.

Celeste opened the tiny envelope that held short strands of black hair. "Is this your Uncle Claude's?"

Madeleine said, "After my mother died, he was my only living relative. He played horses with me as a child. I would be devastated to lose his memory, so that was why I brought it with me from Paris. But if I know you have it, I will take comfort that it is not lost."

Celeste remembered her day at Compiègne with Pietro Fargella: the buoyant white dresses of Empress Eugénie's ladies-in-waiting, the prancing royal stallion, brilliant as snow against the cerulean blue of the sky.

Then she thought of the palace hunting party—the amount of food consumed. "And how do you propose to dethrone Napoléon III? You are a convict living in the most formidable prison in France."

"That is the point. It is so hard to believe my plan works very well. I worked with Felice Orsini and the Italian uprising against the French government as a courier and a spy. From my cell window, I can spot boats coming and going from England. I report landings of designated boats carrying English ammunition supporting the cause."

"This seems farfetched," Celeste said. Her mother had gone mad. Living here would unhinge even the most stable prisoner. Her shoulders stiffened. "Carlo never told me this."

Beads of sweat popped out on Maman's forehead. "He does not know all of my movements. Besides, I do not answer to Carlo but Felice, and he only directs my actions like a great puppeteer. The leaders keep the plans from many organization members, so they will not accidentally betray one another. But there is one member who knows."

"Let me guess—Father Jean, your confessor."

"Well, yes. Jean is bound to keep my secrets through the seal of the confessional. I do not count him."

"Marcelle Le Pont."

Her mother shook her head. "She is in sympathy, but no, it is the man who shares her bed."

"The warden?"

"I would not argue with you."

Twenty-Three

THE SAILORS WILL COME

Celeste closed the gap; she reached out and held her mother close to her heart. She shut her eyes against the mélange of sweat, urine, and staleness infused in her mother's clothes and hair. "I came to France to bring you away with me to live in San Francisco. Is there any way you can escape? Maybe Marcelle and the warden could pull some strings."

Madeleine wrenched herself away. "No. The warden would risk his position, and I would surely die attempting to escape. The prisoners talk about their seeing skeletons at the bottom of *oubliettes,* deep wells. Those people who long ago tried to flee. I await my sentencing trial, and voices around me say I will be here for life. But my lungs tell me I will not be here much longer. I must complete my mission. And what is the difference if the guards caught me? It would speed up my sentencing trial.

"But my dear, death is not punishment after spending all these years in hell. I have done my penance with Father Jean, and if I must die here after serving the cause, I shall. A shipment of bomb-making material has been assembled in England and will reach the shores of Normandy tonight."

"So, it is true that you do provide a signal light to the sailors?"

"Yes. We prisoners get one candle a week. I lie in the dark in my cell, saving my candle until the night I cast the light that tells the sailors the tides are safe so they can land their goods. If they do not see my light, they know it is unsafe, and they return to England."

"But how do you know when the sailors will come?"

A knock sounded, the dreaded knuckles against the wood. This time Marcelle stuck her head in the room. "Two minutes. That is all we can give you. I am sorry."

"Maman, we have little time. You must have my medal. Your journey is harder than my own, and you need God's protection and care more than I." Celeste eased the medal and chain over her head and held it out.

Madeleine took it in hand, and tears spilled down her cheeks. She draped the medal around her neck and pressed it against her chest. "The guards took it from me when I entered Mont St. Michel. They scoffed at any religious items. I now wish to live the rest of my life in peace, and Father Jean says in confession that I must renounce my involvement in the revolutionary cause.

"He advises that my soul must be pure to meet God at my death, whenever it should come. These will be my last acts which will result in the emperor's assassination, removing the plague on France."

After Father Jean pressed open the door and stood by her side, Madeleine gave her daughter a searing look. "Promise me you will keep Uncle Claude's locket of hair for me—memories are the only things that keep me alive some days."

Life was fleeting; the final moment between her and Maman would soon evaporate into the world of dreams. Celeste pondered how this magnificent journey might end—her hopes and dreams dashed to the rocks like the channel waves at high tide.

Father Jean went to his desk and shuffled some papers. "It is nearly time—I bought you a couple more minutes." His face shadowed, his eyes downcast.

Celeste looked toward him, then back at her mother. "Is it safe to continue talking?" She whispered, leaning close.

"He is my Father Confessor. He knows everything and has vowed to keep my secrets."

"Very well. I am concerned for you. If the imperial guards discover your treason, you will be tortured and face the guillotine. Please do not pursue this path any further. I worry that Felice is using you—it is not right."

Madeleine frowned. "You do not understand, my child. For many years at Maison de L'Étoile, I joined the political activists against the emperor. The brothel brought us the income your father would have provided, but at the same time, the authorities looked the other way past the affairs of my brothel."

"So, no one suspected your role with the revolutionaries?"

"Let us say—the gendarmerie enjoyed certain benefits by treating their madams kindly."

"I guess I never really knew or even suspected that was going on. I remember people coming at night and groups drinking wine in the kitchen."

"You were too young to understand. My dream has been to make life better for our society, our people. I want to live in a free country where people have rights, even the humble among us. We have lost the spirit of the revolution, though God knows the French people simmer within their homes and cottages, full of hatred toward this government."

"So, were you coerced into helping these revolutionaries? It sounds so dangerous."

"Ah, ma chérie, it is about time you got to know your Maman. I told Felice I would help him and the cause. No one uses me."

She gripped her mother's dry, bony hands. "Come with me to San

Francisco. We can find a way out of here. I have a cabin booked on the HMS *North Star* on the first of February, and I will buy an extra ticket for your passage. I can provide through my Gold Rush earnings and make sure you live out the rest of your peaceful life in a new land."

"I do not know what life you see around you, but I see the truth. These walls remind me; my cell whispers to me; my small window facing the eastern shore tells me. My sentence is final—I simply do not know when and how I will die. There is no escaping that, my child. My life has passed; yours is just beginning. That is why I sent you to America in the first place. So that you would have a future, away from this stench, this hatred, this crumbling country."

"So . . . all this time I thought you sent me away because you no longer wanted me."

"I am sorry that you thought that. I know that in our situation—in the brothel—it must have been hard for you growing up. But I sent you away to have a bright future, to achieve the dreams I always wanted to have with your father."

"But Maman, you sent me to yet another brothel. How would that give me a bright future? It does not seem like your future worked out too well."

"I figured you would deal with your circumstances. You must have made money—otherwise, how could you have the means to return to France?"

Celeste had to admit her mother was right.

Her mother rubbed a bony hand over her face. "You see, the brothel was simply a means to an end. We planned to run it for a few years, make our money, save it, then go to Provence and live a good life with you, our darling girl.

"But after Pierre's—your father's— death, I lost that choice. Running the brothel alone was difficult, and raising you was a challenge for me. I thought that the place was too dangerous for a child, yet I could never give you up until I ran into Madame De Salle one day at your Tante Faucon's in Montmartre. They were half-sisters, you see. And

Madame De Salle said she would take you in if I sent you to her in New Orleans. I did not think they would arrest me, but when they did, I sent you there to protect you."

"Do you know she groomed me to become a woman of the night?"

Madeleine bit her lower lip. "I knew that was possible, but I wanted you to go to the New World, to know the freedom you would never have in France. Away from the emperor's grasp."

"I did not know much freedom under the thighs of those nameless men." Celeste's words grated against her throat.

Father Jean rose from his desk. "Time to return to your loom, Madeleine."

She wobbled up from her chair and held onto the back of it for support. Celeste looked into her mother's eyes. "Please, Maman, reconsider your role in this plot."

"Too late. Felice's men have contacted me, and tonight I am to give the signal."

Father Jean lifted Madeleine to her feet and tucked her arm under his elbow. "We must return her to her duties. I am sorry."

"Is this how we are to leave each other, maybe forever?" Celeste flung her arms around her mother's neck and held her so close she could hear her breathing—yet she detected a raspy rhythm to the breath, a rumbling in her mother's chest.

Her mother pulled away and patted down her daughter's hair, smoothing it around her cheeks and out of her eyes, the way she had done during Celeste's young life. "This cause is like water to someone dying of thirst. I must avenge the death of Uncle Claude and the injustices done our people in the imperial name. I beg you to understand."

Though Celeste nodded her head, her insides crumbled. She regarded the statue of Christ falling away from his cross. Her mother wished for justice and sacrificed her daughter. She loved her cause more than her freedom and her own life. Blinded by her tears, she heard Maman shuffling away and the drum beating inside her head.

Twenty-Four

THE BLACK MANTILLA

A half-hour later, Celeste stopped to rest at an overlook on the twisty path down to the village. The tide was out, and a steady stream of people strolled on the sandy reaches from shore toward the island. Fishers cast their nets in the deep tidepools. A seagull passed overhead, along with a flock of honking geese that undulated in the upper air. Groups of upward bound prison visitors jostled her on the narrow walk, and she continued her downward route, mindful of slipping on the moss-covered stones that served for sloping steps.

Odéon met her at the last reaches of the final bend nearing the village. "I hoped I would find you on your way down to me. I've missed you in the few hours you were away." He wrapped her in his arms and held her close.

The aroma of pipe smoke and thyme took her back to the night when she lay in the wagon and he at the campfire. She knew then that she loved him. At a bench near a side wall, he gestured for her to sit down. "I have a bottle of wine, apples, and some sausages. I also managed to get a baguette for us." He held the small loaf to her nose, and she inhaled its buttery aroma. "It is still warm."

He tore off a piece of bread, then cut a sliver of dried meat, along with a slice of apple. She retrieved a scarf from her reticule and spread it out on her lap. She set out the food items, and when he offered her a swig of wine from the bottle, she took a sip but then drank liberally. The wine gave her a heady feeling, connecting her to this special place, this sacred atmosphere drifting above the earth.

"I have found something for you below in a village shop." He angled his head, his tender eyes a contrast to his hard-worn features.

"*Quelle surprise*," she said.

He passed her a small brown package, tied with rough string.

She drew out a black mantilla. "It is lovely." She let the material drift against her skin; her fingertips traced the scalloped edges, the intricate lace webbing which flowed across her bare hand.

"Spanish lace. I paid many *sous* for it, but I wanted you to have it. Put it on," Odéon said.

"I have no mirror."

"I will help you," he said.

He unfolded the entire length of the mantilla, setting it gently on the crown of her head and draping it about her shoulders. He allowed his fingers time to smooth the scalloped edges above her forehead and around her cheeks. "The shopkeeper said mantillas are the fashion rage since Empress Eugénie is Spanish, and they say she wears them."

Each movement, each touch of his fingers on her face, stirred her, and she wanted this man—to take him and be taken—right here on this pathway. Together they floated high above the earth on this island that caused so much pain amidst the sea air, the birdcalls, the salty breezes that summoned them ever higher into God's realm.

He drew back, regarding her. "The black flower design sets off your blond hair."

"Ironic, isn't it?" My blond hair makes me look angelic, or so men at the brothel have said, but the black mantilla shows my sins, my humility before God."

"Your sins are only the result of life's circumstances. Poverty thrust you into the brothel life, along with so many people of your class." He pulled his pipe from his pocket and tapped it against the stone wall where they leaned. "Besides, you have made a good living at it, *n'est-ce pas*?"

"So—you don't mind that I was—am—will be—in the trade?"

Odéon opened a packet of tobacco and tamped it into his pipe. "I am a bit older than you, though by only a few years." He pointed to his beard. "You see the few gray hairs I have already growing here?"

She slid a hand over his beard and cupped his chin. "How could I miss them?"

His eyebrows arched. "They are a sign of having lived. I have known many women, both in Paris and on the road. Before joining Felice's group, I worked for my father's transport company carrying goods from Paris. I never found a woman I loved, though I liked many along the way."

She let her fingers play with the edges of the mantilla. "So, you never married?"

"Once, I came close. Yvette lived in Tours—a shop owner."

"May I ask what happened?"

"She said she loved me, but she could not picture her life with me. She longed to live in a big house with fancy things, and though I made a good living, it was not comfortable enough for her. She ended it."

"And you loved Yvette?"

"I thought I did at the time. But now, after meeting you—well, I see I did not. I was in love with the idea that did not exist."

"And am I an idea, too?"

"I think not. You are flesh and blood." He embraced her, sweeping her into their private world of desire, of dreams made real. She knew Odéon believed in her and loved her for who she was. Even as she went into the prison, he had not abandoned her, but he waited for her, as patient as the sands awaited the onrushing tides at first light.

Twenty-Five

A Lone Light

In the late afternoon's haze, she and Odéon lay tucked under an eiderdown quilt in their lodging house. Fast asleep after lovemaking, Odéon breathed steadily, his chest rising and falling in rhythmic cycles. She had opened the casement window earlier to let air into the stuffy room. A breeze blew through a crack in the pane. She padded to the window, then pulled it toward her and shut the latch.

On her return to bed, something glinted inside Odéon's open duffel bag. She debated whether to look inside. Would she betray his confidence? Oh, it would not harm him. The bag was half-open anyway. She peered in, examining the visible contents against the waning light.

Her eyes traced the outline of a pistol and a box of cartridges labeled "Lefauchaux 1854." A single-action, pinfire revolver—must have been expensive. French navy insignia was inscribed on the cartridge box. Intrigued, she plunged her hand deeper into the duffel and pushed aside Odéon's shirt and socks. He might hide something else there. She pulled out a long leather scabbard, then checked his breathing—still asleep.

Angling the scabbard toward the window's light, she grasped the knife handle and drew out the blade. She ran her fingertips along the surface—Odéon must have recently sharpened the tip, which had a deadly point. In the hands of an experienced fighter, this knife would kill.

She slid the blade back into the sheath, then nestled the scabbard deeply into the bag's interior. After setting it back in place, she rejoined Odéon in bed. She relaxed into the warm rhythms of his breathing and watched the last glimpse of the sun fade, then vanish from her window. Odéon had some explaining to do.

She was not long abed when footsteps swished outside their door, followed by a knock. Odéon stirred and rubbed his eyes. "What is going on?"

Another knock sounded.

She covered her nakedness with Odéon's greatcoat and crossed the room, her bare feet tingling against the cold tile floor.

She opened the latch and peered into Marcelle Le Pont's dark eyes. "How did you know we were staying in this room?"

"We villagers know everything, ma chérie. Ours is an intimate community, and we keep track of visitors."

She handed a bag to Celeste. "Here–your mother wishes you to have these things that authorities confiscated when she entered the prison." She browsed the room, then faced Odéon asleep on the bed. "Oh, I must be disturbing you." A flush crept across her cheeks.

"Well, yes, but not exactly." Celeste placed an index finger against her mouth.

Odéon huffed and turned his shoulders, digging deeper into the covers.

"I am sorry—this will not take long. Go ahead—open it."

Celeste unraveled the knot holding the top of the bag and removed the contents, setting them on the table. She examined the miraculous medal and a nun's habit, complete with a wimple, belonging to the Daughters of Charity. Dirt sprinkled the edges of the sleeves. "Why does she give these to me?" Celeste asked.

"Your mother says they may come in handy should you be stopped along the road to Paris. She used them as a disguise from time to time. But the medal—she says she wants you to keep it for the rest of your life in memory of her. She says it will do her no good in prison. She very much wanted you to have these things."

"Very well. Merci, madame. I do not know what to say." A thick knot formed in her throat, and she had trouble swallowing it.

"Say nothing, my child. Your mother is very much a hero to many people in France. She stands for the everyday heroism of those who fight and die at the barricades, who serve in useless wars, who die in the gutters of Paris, Marseilles, Lyon. You will not find her name mentioned anywhere in the history books or the incendiary literature published against this tyrant of ours. But she is on the lips of the people. They whisper *Madeleine,* and the mere sound of her name gives them hope. They call her *la madame en dentelle,* the madam in lace.

"France continues to carry the spirit of revolution within her breast. No matter the dictator who dominates us with his fancy wife and lavish palaces. The French people burn with disdain for this Louis Napoléon with his thin pencil mustaches and lips that tell a lie after lie."

Celeste unclenched her aching teeth. "I fear no good will come of his reign."

"If only all Frenchmen would say that. But look, I must go. I wish you Godspeed—oh, one more thing."

"Yes?"

"You may have guessed that your mother is seriously ill with complications from bouts of pneumonia. Her lungs are compromised. The doctors have bled her numerous times, but she grows weaker. I think her heart may be failing since she has less energy to do her weaving. Each day she sits at the loom staring into space."

"Well, then, what should I do? I feel so helpless—she is up there—stuck in that prison cell."

"I'm afraid there is nothing you can do since I cannot grant you any more visits. If my husband issued you more visitor passes, it would compromise his office. But I assure you this. If your mother begins to show a serious weakening that signals her end days, I will get word to you in Paris. Your mother says you know Madame Faucon?"

"I do."

"I will send my message to her house in Montmartre."

"I am grateful."

"It is the least I can do for you and your mother, who is a hero of France." She reached over and placed a kiss on each of Celeste's cheeks. "*Au revoir, ma petite.*" Marcelle wiped away a tear lingering at the edge of her left eye, then swept away down the hall, the *swish-swish* of her skirts resounding in Celeste's ears long after her departure.

Yet there was no time for in-depth explanations, or so Celeste thought, as the dusk blended into early evening, then the starlit canopy brightened the night sky over Mont St. Michel. She followed Odéon as he took the path away from the village. They wound out of the front wood-and-stone walled portico. A sentry of imperial guards formed a white, red, and silver human fence at the entrance.

"There is our boat," he pointed. A raft of various sailing craft bobbed against the pier. A man waved to them from a small vessel bouncing with the wind chop cresting at the rock base of the island. "*Allez! Vite!*" Odéon bid her hurry, and they elbowed their way through the torchlit crowd at the pier.

Thank God the tide was in; a surprising number of travelers waited in line for another boat to ferry them to shore. They must have been prison employees and workers in the village shops going to their homes in Pontorson or another small coastal village. She patted Odéon's arm. "Where are we going and why?"

He pressed his index finger to her lips and said, "Wait and see. The less you know, the better." The winds calmed; the oarsman plied their boat smoothly to shore. Their wagon waited for them when they reached the ferry dock, and a hefty unnamed man transferred the horses' reins to Odéon. He clucked the team onto the sandy road; they jostled their way to an isolated beach on the eastward side.

Once off the road, Odéon settled the horses and wagon under a weeping beech tree, lifted Celeste from the jockey box, and set her onto the ground. She held his shoulders briefly. "Please," she said. "Just give me a detail—what are we about here?" Her stomach quivered.

Rather than answer her, he drew his gun from his duffel and attached a holster to his hip. He tucked the knife into his waist belt. "Bring your pistol." His tone was even and serious.

"You know I have one?" She cocked her head.

He tightened the grip around his belt. "I know you went through my things this afternoon. But I went through your bags the first night we slept together. There. We even?"

"Maybe." She slid the loaded derringer from its safe place in her reticule. She gazed at him. "Happy now?" She tucked the pistol into a skirt pocket.

"Ready?" he asked. Celeste shivered. Maybe it was the cold, bracing air that blew her cloak and skirts, or perhaps it was the unknown. It was one thing to go into a skirmish knowing what the purpose was—but this. She had no idea why they would use the guns and knives, let alone where they would meet the supposed enemy. Her belly simmered. She couldn't figure out why the hell Odéon acted so secretive.

Though she had the presence of mind to stop from screaming out her words, she slapped him with punching phrases. "Odéon! This is madness. I do not know anything, and if we risk our lives, I must know what's going on. You think I am this stupid to follow you blindly into this—mess—or whatever it is?"

"Wait!" He stepped away from her, casting his gaze toward the island. Mont St. Michel floated like the giant hulk of a ship, a black citadel looming against a sea of stars. He raised his arm and angled his hand toward the island. "There!" He pointed to the east-facing prison walls.

Her breath stalled in her throat.

A lone light glimmered in the darkness.

Twenty-Six

UNEVEN SANDS

Soon after, Celeste heard a creak that must have been wagon wheels in the darkness of the beechy woods. Odéon pulled her behind him. "Stay back." Oh no—this moment could be their worst. The imperial guards would have spotted them leaving the island, and it would not have been difficult to trace their steps. On a clear night such as this, they would be on double duty against anti-government parties. British sympathizers crossed the channel often to cause trouble. The English channel's notorious reputation as a conveyance for smugglers, thieves, and brigands kept them on guard round the clock.

Multiple footsteps brushed against dry grass, and she questioned who they were and what they wanted. She drew her pistol from her chemise and tucked it into her skirt pocket. Then a familiar voice broke the silence and warmed the darkness. Not the police. She relaxed her shoulders.

In the dim light, Carlo appeared and crossed the beach, followed by Felice. They gave her a stern salute and headed to the far reaches of the beach. "We must follow," Odéon said. The tides licked the shore, and

Celeste found the way rough going. The ground was uneven and soft in places where the water lapped. She found herself sinking into the sandy mire which made for slow passage, but she followed Odéon. From time to time, he glanced back, probably to make sure she was there. At least he cared—Carlo had not even greeted her.

She glanced up at Mont St. Michel and searched for the window's light. There was none. The island stone reflected the weak illumination from the waning gibbous moon, the abbey church and prison buildings merging into one giant gray spire. St. Michael would be there to protect them. He who warred against Satan would surely take pity on them and their just cause.

A rush of water nearly toppled her, and she backed away from the edge. This channel was as dangerous as San Francisco Bay, but then, she had chosen this—to come to France to find Maman—but now she had lost her way. Her gloves were no match for her cold hands, and water seeped into her thin-soled boots, freezing her toes.

A sliver of movement caught Celeste's eye at the far reaches of the beach. "There!" Odéon pointed, and she followed his quick paces toward the craft. The sand featured uneven patches, and she slipped, then righted herself, pulling her foot out of the muck and approaching the boat.

She saw a medium-sized rowboat slide up onto a firm sandy reach; three men jumped out onto the beach and secured the craft in the deeper dry sand. They unloaded a handcart and rolled it up onto the sand. In the semi-darkness, she strained to see their faces. She wondered where they came from and why they were here.

One had a full beard and a hefty figure—she recognized Felice. The taller, younger one spoke, and Carlo beckoned Odéon to advance closer. She gripped the flyaway edges of her cape that wanted to fall away from her head and shoulders. Her ears stung with cold, and something dripped from the end of her nose. The dampness permeated everything, and when she ran her tongue over her dry lips, she tasted a salty tang.

She swept her hand over her nose, and at the same time, the third man leaped out of the boat. He wore an English-style serge coat; a close-knit fisherman's cap covered his ears. Though the wind whistled away from the man's words, she heard spoken English mixed with French.

As she approached them, Celeste pulled her cloak tightly against the intermittent breezes. She stepped next to the British-dressed man. "Good evening; my name is Celeste."

"Your English is quite good. But if it is my name you want, I do not give it out to strangers, Miss." His bushy sideburns stuck out in all directions.

"I see," she said. Yet the Englishman's refusal to give his name told her he was either a spy or a lawbreaker, possibly both. A guttural California Gold Rush expression rose to her lips. "Who the hell are you?"

He paused, shadows and crevices suggesting the angles of his face.

"Why won't you at least talk to me?"

His lips tightened into an even flat line, and he stepped away, busying himself on the far side of the boxes, carrying the goods to the cart. How annoying these men were. Maman had been a saint to endure their company.

Odéon stood on the shore, receiving boxes the sailors passed down to him. She tried to read the container markings. In the dim light, she caught the words *Gas Machinery*. Whatever was in those boxes? The wind numbed her face; she could barely move her lips.

She had seen other boxes at the château—were they connected to the effort? And her mother's light from Mont St. Michel. She tucked her thoughts into an envelope in her mind. Odéon would have many questions to answer. At least he talked to Celeste—no one else spared a word.

Carlo jumped into the water, pushing the sailors' boat back into the channel. The seamen plied their oars, the crests of the waves digesting them like white chewing teeth. Then darkness formed a giant yawning cavern and swallowed them whole. Beside their party, only one witness would know of their boat: the starlit canopy that stood guard over them.

She glanced again at Mont St. Michel, its dark bulk steadfast against the tidal waves crashing against its rocks. Her mother's window was opaque. She might be in her cell's damp recesses, watching their party, cheering them on. She wondered if anyone else had seen her light up there. If Maman was legendary in the community and people talked of her, there should have been a patrol boat out on the eastward waters tonight. Or guards on the beaches. So many of these puzzle pieces dangled like handkerchiefs on her imaginary clothesline.

Carlo's voice jarred her thoughts. "Celeste, we could use your hands here."

She lifted her skirts and picked her way into the midst of the activity. Felice passed her a wooden box, and she carried it to the cart. Its contents rattled, but they were not heavy. She returned for a larger container which she labored with, her footsteps sinking into the sand as she made her way to the conveyance and dropped it into the cart—*thud!* Whatever was in those boxes—they must be transporting gas machinery.

The cartons fully loaded onto the cart, Felice, Odéon, and the Englishman pulled it away and disappeared into beechy woods where Odéon had left their wagon. The dampness, the penetrating cold—if only she could stop her teeth from chattering. She had gotten entangled in a crazy plot, and it had better be worth the trouble.

Celeste struggled across the uneven sand and stood next to Carlo, who broke from the conversation with his mates when she approached. "As my friend, would you kindly tell me what is going on? That Brit will not even tell me his name. Besides, Maman explained her role in vague wording, and I saw her light from the prison, but I cannot make heads or tails of events."

"It is not safe to talk here."

"A few words from you might make it safer."

"Very well. His name is Thomas. Satisfied?"

"You think by casting me a tidbit, I will be happy. You see, it is worse because I do not know what is going on. I told Odéon earlier I might be a liability since you are not revealing to me this mission's nature and purpose."

He bit his lower lip. "I am forbidden to tell anyone. That includes you."

"So, despite our—kisses—our friendly words, you cannot even give me a hint of who you are and what you men are doing? I thought you trusted me, and for a moment—a *petit moment* to be sure—I did believe in you."

"We must walk fast—the imperial guards could spot us easily. If they spy the boat in the channel, they will be checking these shores." He took her arm, and they aimed their footsteps toward the far woods where the men had previously disappeared.

Once inside the shelter of the woods, Carlo slowed his steps. "I am active in the Risorgimento, a political uprising throughout Italy and France. The issues are complex, but let me simplify them. Our goal is the unification of Italy, but your Emperor Napoléon is against it. He would not want a strong Italy; rather, he wishes for a weak, divided one. Easier to control his neighbor that way."

"So, that is why you are working with Felice?"

"I believe in his movement. We are allied with Mazzini, a leader in the unification cause. I met Felice in Rome some time ago; he invited me to go to England, where he found sympathizers and went on the lecture circuit. Thomas is one of our supporters. As you can see, all our efforts are now bearing fruit."

She heard her mother's words as they echoed in her mind. *If they sentence me to death, the emperor must die also. The plan is afoot, already in motion. In January—Paris.* The realization wrapped about her as tightly as her cape. She was involved in a plot, the likes of which could drive them all to the guillotine.

Though Carlo hurried at her side, he could have been a million steps away.

Her anger carried a lacquer of disgust. She had a life to live—at home in San Francisco, but she managed to get involved with Carlo and this crazy cause. And what was worse, she let her mother betray her trust. She should have known.

She faced Carlo, her words arrowing into the icy wind that plastered strands of hair against her cheeks. "Your secrecy, your strange behavior. I do not see why you did not tell me. I guess I might reveal information to the imperial guards or their secret agents. What is in the boxes? Is it gas machinery? Where are you taking the boxes and why? Where is the marquis?" She twisted her foot in a sand pocket. "Ouch!" she winced.

Mired in his thoughts, he did not seem to notice her stop behind him. Instead, he ignored her outburst and plunged ahead of her into the darkness. She spotted movement and recognized the wooded landscape where they had left their wagon.

"Are you going to leave me here?"

He glanced back. "Celeste—pull yourself together. The men are waiting for us."

"Where the hell are we going?" She limped ahead, a stabbing pain shooting up her leg.

"Shhh! Lower your voice! Oh, come on, I will help you." He stepped back in her direction, put his arm around her shoulder, and helped her limp into the darker shelter of the weeping beeches. At least they might not be seen, though the woods were classic hiding places for gendarmes and guards.

They could be walking into a trap. The authorities made it their business to lie in wait for smugglers and thieves. She wondered which tree could conceal them. With each question, Celeste's temperature rose. She no longer cared about whether anyone heard or saw her. Let the guards come. How dare she be used as a pawn in this game. She thought Carlo loved her as he said, or maybe he was using her to influence her mother in some odd way. She could be seeing him for what he was—a firebrand.

Though her insides burned, she shivered. If she stood close to Carlo's flame, she would get hurt. And yet something about his look, the way his lips curved into a smile—she wanted to touch him, to feel his lips on hers, but no—no, he was not good for her. A man like him would not only lead her into danger, and instead of thanking her, he would stomp on her heart, crushing it to bits. She knew it, and he probably knew it, too. Pain radiated around her ankle. A low whistle sounded in the woods, and an owl's wings fluttered past her.

Felice stood conferring with Odéon next to their wagon. Celeste limped into their midst and tucked her arm into a notch in Odéon's elbow. He tightened his arm against hers. Felice said, "Go back to Paris with Odéon and stay out of danger." His tone was stern, his manner aloof. He meant what he said.

Odéon peered down at her, then bent down and brushed a kiss across her cheek. "Did you hear that? You will lay low at Madame Faucon's house."

"What? Why not stay with you at your house? Whyever would you set me up to stay in a brothel? Is this some ploy to get rid of me? To abandon me in a godforsaken pleasure palace while you enact a plan to destroy the emperor?"

Felice stepped close. "We have little time for discussion, Celeste. You must do as I say, or your life could end badly. Control your temper. If you believe in our cause as much as your mother, you will think of others before yourself. Follow Odéon's lead, wait for his cues, and keep your mouth shut."

"Very well," she said. "I will go back to Paris with Odéon and stay out of danger. Though I am frustrated, I have faith that you know what you are doing—maybe." She was capable of half-lies, too.

"Good. At least you are doing what you are told—for once." Carlo took a step toward Odéon. "Watch your bearings—these Norman roads are unsafe because the emperor's gendarmes are on patrol."

Felice said, "To assure your safe passage, we will load all the gas machinery boxes into our other wagon. Does that ease your fear?"

"I'm not sure. I have never felt so uneasy since I landed in New Orleans, got off the ship, and met Madame De Salle. That scared me to death—this is a close second."

"There's a good girl." She looked up at his chocolate brown eyes, remembering the day he cooked pasta for all of them in Montmartre. He had a two-chambered heart: kindness pulsed next to cruelty, each ready to spring.

Having set the last boxes into their wagon, Felice and the Englishman left under the covering darkness. Voices silenced as waves chanted night songs against the shore. Odéon helped Celeste into the jockey box. Carlo mounted his horse and said, "Odéon, take care of her on the way back to Paris. She is a pain in the ass." His horse peered at her with an equally disdainful look.

Celeste seethed. How dare he impugn her character—especially since she had confided in him. Carlo would be capable of any betrayal, and if he nailed studs into his coffin, she had no sympathy.

Twenty-Seven

RAISE YOUR EYES TO THE STARS

The channel breezes fell away as they gained their route; dense, dripping fog replaced the wind. Instead of breathing relief that they were away from the channel and its risks, Celeste tensed, less at ease as they found their route away from the coast. The fog shrouded each bend in the road and the weak rays from the lamp projected the tips of the horses' ears, nothing more. At any moment, she expected the red flash of an imperial guard to appear out of the shadows. "Where are we?" She leaned against Odéon, feeling each movement of his hip and side as he controlled the horses' reins.

"I've known these roads since I was in transport with my father's company; we are on an easterly route to Paris away from the coast. I would tell you the towns we are passing, such as Caen, but you would not be able to see them anyway." He peered into the fog, the visibility so poor she could only see the backs of the horses, their harnesses disappearing into the mist.

"Celeste, you were speaking at length with Carlo." He gathered both reins in his hand and felt in his pocket for his pipe.

"Let me help you," Celeste leaned over and drew his pipe from his pocket. "May I?" She held the pipestem toward his lips, and he nodded. Celeste secured it between his teeth.

"What did you talk about?" He peered ahead into the gloom.

"He did not reveal much, only that this dangerous mission ends in Paris."

"Look, Celeste, if you have feelings for him, I understand. I have no claim on you. But you may risk your life by going to Paris. I can take you to the port of Le Havre—even now—and you can book early passage home. You do not know the extent of the danger you face by staying here."

"I think I can guess. Maman explained enough to me so that I know the plot threatens the emperor. And that makes you, Carlo, Felice, and the rest, conspirators against the French empire. Once arrested, there is no escaping the death sentence."

"You have the gist of the plot that is afoot. We are reaching a crossroads up ahead. After we cross it, there is no turning back to Le Havre. Instead, we take the southeast route to Paris. You have a few minutes to decide, but then, once committed to your decision, you must stay with it. Do you understand?"

Celeste said, "Before I make up my mind, I must tell you something."

He glanced over at her; his tender expression melted her where she sat on the jockey box.

"I am not sure whether I should leave France—at least not alone."

"You know you cannot take your mother as you always dreamed. There is no rescuing her from the prison fortress."

"I have someone else in mind—someone I would want to take back to San Francisco with me."

"Who? Another woman of the night? Someone from Montmartre?"

"Not exactly."

She squeezed his arm, and he placed both the reins in his left-gloved hand, reached over and put his right arm around her, then drew her close.

"Might you ever consider going with me—staying with me there—in L'Amérique?"

"Pah!" His pipestem nearly fell away from his mouth, and Celeste reached over and tucked it back in the corner of his lip. He said, "I saw many Frenchmen go to seek riches in the California Gold Rush of 1849. And just as many returned heartbroken. Those who had struck it rich in the goldfields squandered their gains in the gambling houses."

"I know. Many such men frequented the brothel trade. Those kinds of losers filled New Orleans."

"But that is not all. If some did not die of cholera or typhoid, other unlucky boys went home to their mothers. They continued to struggle after they lost their youthful years to a pipedream."

"There were many diseases. I remember nursing my friend Brianna back to health at Madame De Salle's after her attack. She fell ill after the john infected her."

"You have seen much of the world, ma chérie. I think I am quite satisfied to stay in France where at least I know the language."

Something tugged at her throat. "But I am fond of you, Odéon. I will not be happy leaving you."

"Happiness—what is that? Who has time to consider such an idea when we are part of an international plot to take out a tyrant? Raise your eyes to the stars, my girl."

She peered into the fog. "Where are they? The stars, I mean."

"You must trust that they are there even when you cannot see them."

"That is fine, a romantic notion. But I prefer to have the person I fancy by my side, not far away."

He slowed the horses and leaped down from the wagon. "Wait here."

She watched after him, the fog swirling around him, then swallowing him whole.

A gloved hand reached up, grasped the handlebars of the jockey box, and Odéon emerged, the wagon's lantern catching the water droplets on his beret and beard. "Just as I thought—we are almost at the cross-roads to Le Havre. The soil on the road here changes to sandy loam, so we are nearing the coastline. I steer the horses windward toward your port with a simple lift of my rein, and you can book passage on an outgoing vessel. It would be best if you decided now, for I must make more distance before resting and watering the horses and bedding for the night. I must make Paris day after tomorrow."

"I—I have to think," she said.

He leaped off the jockey box, came around to her side, and helped her step down. "There," he said, "take a bit of time, but I cannot give you too many minutes. I will be on the other side of the wagon lighting my pipe. Call me when you have decided."

Steam issued off the horses' backs, and the animals tossed their manes, causing their halters to jingle. Celeste stepped to the edge of the road-way. The road dropped off into a ditch; running water trickled below. If she left now, she would have peace, knowing she had found her mother, along with the memories and information about her past life.

She would arrive in San Francisco and meet Mei Li, the caretaker, who would unlock the musty parlor house for her and show her into the study where the account books would lie dusty, but she would be home. Alone. And independence had its benefits. No heartbreak, no betrayals. She would grow the parlor house and fill it with French women of the night, joining the burgeoning French community in San Francisco. Charm and elegance. Alone.

If she went with Odéon to Paris, she would be in the company of would-be assassins, spies, terrorists. The emperor's secret agents roamed the country. If someone revealed their plot, she might find herself in prison alongside her mother. Or worse—executed—for the emperor had no tolerance for traitors.

Yet even now, at this short interval, she missed Odéon, the aroma of his pipe permeating the fog and signaling his presence. His arms, his naked chest, his taking her over and over, the rhythm of their breathing as one. The grin he cast along with sidelong glances, his eyes crinkling with near laughter.

And Celeste could see her mother's eyes, her haunting expression as she spoke of the plot. The dark wells of her eyes reflected her passion for justice and relief of suffering. She might have the courage to take up her mother's role in the conspiracy, or maybe she should dismiss it. Maybe her mother's plan was the folly of a failed and miserable prison inmate, her life a shambles like the bungled weaving on her loom.

"Have you decided?" Odéon's voice broke through the mist from the direction of the horses. He must be tightening their halters and checking their bits.

"Oui."

His boot steps crunched. "And?"

"Paris."

He removed the pipe from his mouth, enfolded her in his arms, and caressed her face, lingering softly, planting small, jewel-like kisses in each crevice, tickling her slightly with his beard. Then he reached her mouth, and she opened it, inviting in his tongue which tasted of fragrant tobacco.

She wanted and needed this man whose simple observations and kind aspect meant so much to her after her young life as an abandoned wretch. They remained thus, holding each other tightly, bound together in the wrap of fog.

Twenty-Eight

TIGHTEN THE LACES

Paris
January 1858

Madame Faucon's brothel Le Beauvoir possessed no flair or finery. On that cold, dreary morning, Celeste's chamber bore gray walls, chips of paint missing in spots where white stucco peered through. Her ill-washed sheets, donated by other girls, held a mixed scent of semen and vaginal fluids. A washbowl and Delft pitcher on the marble-topped dresser missed a handle. On the near wall, a painting of windmills was cracked and scratched. As she lifted her chemise over her head, she heard girls' voices raised in argument somewhere down the hallway.

She let the chemise flow down to the ground and wrapped her corset around her chest. At least someone had lit a fire in the small hearth. The place was cold outside the comforter and hot water bottle that had warmed her bed. Someone would have to tighten the corset laces behind her back. She could not do it herself; whenever she did, the stays became loose and caused her bodice to shift, scraping her breasts beneath her day dress. She tiptoed to the door. Maybe someone out there would help her. She unlatched her door and peered out.

A high-pitched voice arched above the girls' shouts down the hallway. "Stop this bickering!" Hortense's edgy words sliced the air.

A girl answered, "*Baise ta salope!*" Celeste's eyes widened. The girl said, "Fuck you, bitch!" She had not heard brothel swearing since San Francisco, and it reminded her of what she loved and hated about the trade. These girls were sometimes violent and often unpredictable.

She heard Hortense. "Put that knife away, Marie. Better yet, give it to me. Now leave poor Suzanne alone. She has done nothing to you."

Celeste stepped out into the tunnel-like hallway. Nothing unusual here. All in a day's trade. She aimed her steps toward the noisy room and peeked through the open door. "I need help," she said.

All eyes in the room turned upon her, and no one spoke. Heat crept into her body, yet experience had taught her that a timely interruption could break up many an argument. A jackknife glinted in Hortense's hand. One girl stood upright on the mattress of a corner bed. Celeste said, "Could someone help me with my laces?" She pointed to her back, then turned around and waited. Others would be afraid to turn their backs on a matron with a knife. But arguments and weapons were an everyday matter in a Maison, and she covered her mouth, suppressing a yawn.

Hortense barked. "I'll talk to you later, Marie. Meantime, leave Suzanne alone, or I shall boot your fanny into the street, and you will have no chance of achieving another brothel anywhere in Paris."

Marie said, "But—I deserve—that is I need—"

"Shut your mouth, you little devil. This is the last time I will deal with you. Once Madame Faucon hears of this latest incident, you will be at her mercy."

Hortense thumped toward Celeste, then folded the jackknife in her hand. Something clicked—it must have been the catch. She let the weapon drop into her skirt pocket.

The matron cracked her bony fingers in the air, signaling Celeste to turn her back. She looked down at her hips; Hortense set her hands there. "You must stand up straight." She peered behind her. Hortense's breath reeked of absinthe and fried eggs—how nauseating.

Then the woman set her jaw and bent to the task of tightening her laces. Her rough hands tugged at Celeste, and with each inch that Hortense grasped, Celeste lost another breath, and with each tug, Celeste saw her waistline diminish. She gulped for air. Maman had praised her tiny measurements when she was younger, but now, after San Francisco's meals of slop hash and roasted potatoes, her slim waistline took an effort to keep.

Celeste had to admit Hortense was a good house manager. A brothel needed a matron's firm hand—girls were flighty, unpredictable, and soon addicted to laudanum. When Hortense tightened all her laces, Celeste took a series of short breaths. "Merci, madame." She gave a near-gasp.

At last, someone patted her shoulder. She glanced back. Hortense stepped aside, obviously admiring her well-laced corset.

The girls quieted behind her. Marie pulled up her stockings, and Suzanne flattened the sheets on her bed. Celeste tested her breathing; her ribcage jammed up against the whalebone stays that held her like a vise. Oh well, she would have to contend with shallow breaths to look her best.

Hortense sighed. "I wish all our residents were as well-mannered as you. Come," she waved.

Out in the hallway, Celeste watched as Hortense shut the girls' door and set her trembling fingers on the doorknob. The woman's hard shell belied a soft core. The girls' behavior took its toll on her.

"Would you like a petit déjeuner?" Hortense asked.

"I am hungry. A spot of café and a brioche would make me happy," Celeste said.

"I will have cook make you an omelet, ma petite. *Suivez moi,* follow me to the kitchen."

Hortense's high bun and purple shawl led down the winding staircase past the frescoes depicting frisky nudes frolicking in various sexual activities. After the stairs ended, they turned the corner at the bottom step and veered into the large kitchen where a maid in a long apron and puffy white cap bustled between pots and pans and breakfast dishes, washing and drying the lot.

A woman appeared at the door leading to the garden, her breast flesh jiggling under a day dress with no waistline. She must be the cook. Hortense rasped. "*Un omelet, s'il vous plaît,* for our Celeste."

Celeste bristled at "our," but she let it pass. Tiny pricks of discomfort were the price for the free lodging. She sighed, recognizing the implied ownership of Hortense's assumption. Once in the brothel trade, the international language was ownership: the brothel owner possessed the prostitute; the johns possessed the prostitute; the prostitute possessed nothing, having lost her virgin treasure a long time before.

The cook rolled up her sleeves, broke several eggs into a pan, stirred the batter, folding in shredded cheeses and bits of ham. She tore off bits of parsley from an herb garden near the window, along with thyme and basil—the ingredients mixed into the mélange. The kitchen maid brought her a cup of steaming café and a jug of milk.

Celeste savored the fragrance of herbs, eggs, and butter frying in the pan.

"*Du pain*?" The maid leaned toward her. "Bread or pastry?"

"Do you have a croissant?" she asked. "I have not eaten well lately."

After reaching into a white sack on the counter, the maid pulled out a croissant which she served along with a pot of currant jam. The cook flipped the omelet onto a plate, grabbed a fork and cloth napkin, and presented it to Celeste with a flourish.

"I am very grateful, my friend." She dug into the light brown crust of the omelet, its melting Gruyère cheese rippling onto the plate. If only everyone in France could eat this well. It took selling one's body to have these luxuries—this was not a choice she had ever made, but one she would live with on the road ahead.

She took bites of her omelet and sipped her café. Odéon had briefed her of their activities once they reached Paris. She was to wait here through December and until mid-January in Montmartre with Madame Faucon. Though he would only reveal cryptic details, he told her Felice rented a set of rooms in central Paris. When Felice was ready for a meeting, he would send a carriage for her. When she pressed Odéon for more details, he told her Felice and the men coordinated the bomb construction in preparation for a night at the Opéra Peletier. Maman had taught her about the theater when she had given her music lessons on the melodeon. She stirred two lumps of sugar into her café. She had always dreamed of going to the opera.

Maybe she would see a famous singer or two: at the very least, she would spot men with top hats whose black silk plush glistened amidst the lamplights; and women in fancy dresses, their multi-layered petticoats and feathered hats that swayed and bobbed with their footsteps. The scene played out on the surface of her plate between bits of egg. Carriages would appear, disgorging their contents, famous women who would parade like so many creamy desserts, the yellow flounces of the women's skirts rising high like meringue atop a lemon tart.

Maybe the guard would allow her to peer through the vestibule doors. Even one interior glance would suffice—she would be able to say that she, Celeste Bazin, had been to the Paris opera. She swallowed her last bite of omelet, then set her fork onto her empty plate.

The faint tinkling of a bell broke the quiet of the house. Celeste heard distant voices, footsteps, the splash of water in a pot carried to the sink by the housemaid. Keys rattled; footsteps slid across the floor. "Mademoiselle Celeste," Hortense said from somewhere behind her.

Celeste brushed crumbs from her lips and cleared her throat. "Oui, madame."

"Madame Faucon desires your company."

She followed the sweep of Hortense's purple shawl down the hallway, and they entered a drawing room whose gaudy female nudes floated across the wallpaper. A giant chandelier flickered overhead, and a fern extended scrawny branches as if calling for help. Madame Faucon sat before a lit fireplace in beady-eyed silence, her feather-topped fan caressing the air between them.

Faucon waved, and Celeste sank into a soft velvet chair across from the madam whose black eyes deepened in their sockets. "I am pleased you are here, mademoiselle, and I trust your stay has been pleasant. I was fond of your mother, and I am happy to have you at our Maison Le Beauvoir."

"I am grateful to be here, madame, yet I wish to skip the pleasantries. I want to know the plan."

Madame Faucon's penciled brows arched like half-moons. "What plan? Felice told me to lodge you until you return to America on the first of February."

Celeste hesitated. So maybe Madame Faucon had not been informed of all the details. That was no matter. She would find out what she did know. "So, I am to remain here?"

"My goal is to keep you safe from harm."

"I am never safe in a brothel—you and I know the truth of the matter." She chuckled.

"Well, that is the truth." Faucon gave a rueful grin. "But Felice and Carlo do not want you to . . ."

"Finish your sentence, madame."

A large black mole blossomed on Faucon's left cheek. She set her open fan on her lap and nibbled a cuticle on her right index finger.

Celeste leaned forward. "Since you hesitate, I can finish it for you. They do not want me in the way."

"Patience, dear girl. They will send for you."

"I want to enact my mother's wishes—to be a part of this. I want to leave a part of her legacy here in France before I go back."

"A legacy?" Faucon scoffed. "In this trade, there is no legacy. Only the smeared footprints of women's dreams."

"You have a point there, but I must believe in something—anything."

"Is that why you came back to France? To find out what you believe in?"

"Maybe so. I had to locate Maman; that was all I knew. But now I understand. I had to unearth what she was—and who I am—in the grand scheme of life. And I had to discover what moved Maman, what drove her, as much as one can know another human being.

"And as you say with women, our footprints are smeared, hidden, smothered by greater forces. In most cases, no one knows or cares if we live or die. If any of us passes away, our bodies lie in a pauper's graveyard under a pile of stones marking the unknown, the shamed, the forgotten."

"Tell me, *mon enfant*, how do you think to carry on your mother's legacy? She will die alone in her prison cell. Surely you do not want to follow her. You know she was a murderess. Madeleine confided it to me shortly after it happened: she formed a conspiracy, and she may not have held the girl under the river water, but she gave the order for the men to do it."

Celeste pressed her fingers onto her breastbone. *Maman had lied to her about the murdered girl.* For a moment, all she saw was Faucon's mouth opening and closing while a noise pounded her temple. She tucked a strand of hair behind her ear. By God, she would not let Faucon see her shock. She drew herself up. "All in the past. There is nothing I can do to change that. The only direction I have is to go forward in the spirit of revolution."

Faucon pulled a dangling cuticle off her fingernail and winced. "You know the brothel life leads to madness in many of us. Take care that your devotion to this cause does not hasten your trip to the ash heap. Many a girl has found herself shot and trampled at the bottom of a barricade. Sacrificed to what? Does any cause justify giving up your life?"

Celeste paused, examining Faucon's hollow cheeks. Maman controlled the direction of her daughter's life, thrusting her into danger. Even as Madeleine languished in prison, Celeste carried out her wishes. Her mother, a murderess.

Twenty-Nine

Dancing Light

The following days at Le Beauvoir seemed endless. One late morning a housemaid appeared at Celeste's door with an envelope. After dispensing with pleasantries, Celeste tore open the note and recognized Odéon's sprawling penmanship.

I am coming for you at midi today. Odéon.

She peered at the mantel clock—it read 11:10 a.m. No time to waste. She shrugged into her substantial wool-lined day dress and added an extra layer of petticoats against the bone-penetrating Parisian cold. After flattening her lace collar, she wrapped a wool scarf around her neck and tightened it—no gaps where the frost could chill her neck. She settled a wool hat over her ears, freeing the blond hair that flowed onto her shoulders. The long strands gave her extra insulation along with the scarf.

She laced up her thin-soled boots, stood straight, and surveyed the serge cloak that hung on the door's hook. That would offer her a final layer of protection. After pinching her cheeks and adding a spot of red tint to her pale lips, she swung the cloak around her shoulders, drew it close about her, went down the stairs, out the door, and waited on the brothel steps. Luckily it was too early for passing johns to hassle her: the bare strands of ivy across the street cascaded over the gray walls, and the *chuck-chuck* of a squirrel rang out from the leafless trees above.

A cart and horse, steam rising from the horse's back, appeared around the far corner. Odéon, barely recognizable under a layer of blankets, hailed her with his whip. He pulled up the horse, hitched it to the post in front of Faucon's, then motioned her toward the cart. "Do you wish to ride like a lady or upon the jockey box with me?" Something smoldered in his eyes.

"With you, of course." She settled next to him on the driver's seat, her hip secured against his. Though layers of clothing separated her from him, she longed for his body, his touch, the way he wrapped himself around her.

Odéon guided the horses down the hill of Montmartre, past windmills, men herding goats, and into the growing crowds amidst the new four-to-six storied Haussmann buildings of Paris. The city greeted them with the chaos of buggies, carriages, and drays, the din of newsboys crying from street corners, the flash of bright flower displays alongside markets spilling their vegetables onto the sidewalks. And everywhere, crowds of people picked their way along slick city streets, avoiding icy patches and dirty snowdrifts.

They pulled up in front of a disheveled group of buildings, dingy as days-old bathwater. After Odéon secured the horse and cart to the hitching post, he steered her into a narrow hallway with a staircase that led straight to the next floor. "This is like a ladder," she said. Odéon grimaced and said, "Go first, please."

She climbed three flights, teetering on the narrow steps; two doors appeared on the third floor, and a light flickered around the edges of a transom. She glanced at Odéon. "This one?"

"Go ahead, knock," he said.

She tapped the door and waited. They would have to identify themselves. Maybe Odéon knew a code word to gain entrance.

The door edged open, and she recognized Raoul, who peered at them, wrinkling his long, hooked nose. He stepped out onto the landing, bent down, and gave the back of her hand a soft kiss. "*Quelle plaisir, mamselle.* What a pleasure."

"I have not seen you for quite a while—that day at the wine cellar."

Odéon joined her side. "Raoul has been taking care of our plans here in Paris."

"What plans?" she asked.

"Un moment, s'il vous plaît. You are about to find out." Raoul said.

The door swung open, and what she beheld might hold the answer to her question. If only.

She stepped into a dark room where murmuring voices competed for air in the stuffy space. A coal fire smoldered in a small hearth, sending occasional puffs of smoke into the room. It took a moment for her eyes to adjust to the low lighting. Sweat and whiskey blended into the swirl of gray, taupe, and beige forms.

"You are late, Odéon." Felice sat at the end of a long table, surrounded by at least fifteen men sitting on benches and chairs.

She perched on the edge of a rickety chair at the far end of the table nearest the door, Odéon by her side. After she scanned the scruffy men, whose bulky hats and coats concealed their features, Carlo raised his eyebrows in greeting. A series of maps lay on the table in between an array of lanterns. A carafe of red wine brightened the sideboard, along with a cluster of dirty glasses.

Odéon poured a glass for himself and Celeste and set it before her. She sipped from the fingerprint-covered cup, the dripping candles on the table casting a dancing light and reddening the wine she held up to her lips. The wine warmed her innards, and she relaxed back in her chair.

Odéon pointed with his pipestem to one of the maps on the table. "So, Felice, this is the Opéra Peletier. Where will we be as the emperor's coach pulls up?"

"I was just getting to that before you—er—arrived late. Now sit down and listen, Odéon."

He shrugged and settled himself down next to Celeste. The smoke from his pipe seemed thicker today, and she blinked through the haze.

Felice said, "Has everyone met Thomas Allsop?" He extended his flattened palm toward a slouch-capped man sitting to Celeste's left hand. The group murmured.

Thomas rose to his feet, removed his cap, then held it against his chest. The tall man with mutton chops spoke with authority though his English-accented French was hard to fathom. He said, "The bomb parts have arrived successfully from our English factories. With Carlo and Raoul's help along with our teammates and the marquis' grace, we have assembled them here in Paris."

The marquis. She leaned over the table, searching the clutch of thick-coated men for the elegant, coifed elder from the château. Maybe he wore the top hat at the far end of the table, a thick muffler concealing his mouth and throat.

She owed the marquis an apology for having left the château so abruptly. She recalled their conversations, his fatherly regard for her, and his counsel about her life. Maybe he was the fellow in the black beret, a cloud of cigar smoke drifting over him like a gathering storm. No, his chin was too small.

She continued her visual stroll around the table. If only she could pick out the people she knew. Wait a moment—though she had trouble seeing her at first, she was sure—by the smaller, more delicate cheekbones and narrow set of the shoulders—that could either be a boy or a teenage girl sitting next to Carlo. Oh no. They had better not be using a child in an assassination attempt. A surge of bile swam up to her throat, and she swallowed an unpalatable truth. Maybe this was a despicable mob. She had gotten herself into some pickle, some thanks for merely trying to find Maman in the first place.

A door closed inside her: it was too late to run away now. She should have let Odéon take her to Le Havre, put her on a ship, bid her adieu, and wave her westward. Be as it may, she had to accept the consequences, but *mon Dieu,* my God, they would be severe indeed. It was one thing to employ children at a workhouse but quite another to make them throw bombs.

She resumed listening to Allsop. After Thomas listed the twelve bombs, various pistols, and numerous knives, Felice unrolled a map showing the exterior of the opera house and the surrounding streets. After securing the diagram on the fireplace mantel, he showed the carriage route to the theater. "The imperial entourage, preceded by the guard troop, will turn from Boulevard des Italiens onto Rue Le Peletier. One block later, the theater's portico and awning will be here." He smacked the map with the heel of his hand, then divided the group into trios and told them to gather their chairs and meet in various corners of the room.

He assigned each trio a group leader who would give them their duties for the night in question. Carlo would be her group leader, and she was to meet with Odéon and Liliana in the corner nearest the floor-to-ceiling window. Liliana? She smacked her forehead with her palm. Of course. Liliana was a young person she had not recognized. She had overreacted to the presence of a child. At the same time, Carlo put his young teenage sister in jeopardy.

She followed Odéon, her skirts swishing across the dusty floorboards toward the window, but out of the corner of her eye, she caught the open-mouthed expression of the top-hatted man. She stepped toward him, and he rose, extending his hand.

"Mon Seigneur le Marquis?" she asked.

"The very same, Mademoiselle Celeste. What a pleasure to see you today. Your departure from the château was most abrupt—I hope you were able to find what you were seeking at Mont St. Michel."

"Yes, I found what I needed there, Mon Seigneur. And I hope I will carry forward Maman's desire—one last time before I leave for San Francisco."

"I have been concerned about her fatal illness. She must have shared that with you on your visit. Very sad, is it not?"

"Illness? She appeared to be rather frail but in good spirits. I was not aware that—" For a moment, all she could see was a drift of chimney smoke passing between them. Her eyes burned, and she blinked.

"Hmmm. I'm afraid your mother has not long, my child. Some lung infection, though she will not tell me the type. She seems unwilling to discuss it like an unpleasant houseguest that will leave of its own accord."

"Did you meet Madame Le Pont? She sends me messages regularly."

"If you write to her, she will keep you informed. Do you have her address?"

"No, I hadn't thought to ask her for it."

He fumbled for a moment in his interior jacket pocket and drew out a silver case that opened to reveal a small number of calling cards. He drew one out, closed the case, then felt in the other pocket and slid out a pencil. After moistening the tip with his tongue, he wrote:

Mme. Marcelle Le Pont,
c/o Christophe Le Pont, Warden
Prison d'État
Mont St Michel, Normandie

"If you tip the postman, he will include it with the daily imperial dispatches to the prison. Her husband, the warden, will make sure she receives it." With that, he passed the paper to her.

Felice's voice broke into her thoughts. "Mon Seigneur, you are needed with us, s'il vous plaît."

The marquis pressed her hand and said, "Mademoiselle Celeste, I wish you *bonne chance*, good luck in L'Amérique. I wish I were young enough to go with you—to escape this mire in France."

"I wish you well but wait—I have one question. Will you be at the opera? I fear for you, Mon Seigneur."

"*Pffft*, ma chérie. There is nothing to fear. A bit of confusion is all that will happen. I shall dress for the theater. My political connections in the empire are deep and longstanding. I will be there, but you will not see me."

Ahhh. Ever the enigma, the marquis. He was doing damage from behind the scenes. His moneyed connections aided Felice in funding this operation-to-come. He had only to retreat to the walls of his château, and no one would remember his involvement. If only it were that easy for her and Maman, the madam in lace.

After kissing the marquis farewell on both cheeks, she joined the group gathered near the window—Carlo, Odéon, and Liliana. "Are we to act alone? There are so few of us."

Carlo said, "Better that way. Felice gives us our directions; we act them out in small numbers, approaching our target from all directions. That way, the imperial guards find us less easy to spot, especially after we throw the hand bombs and there is chaos everywhere."

Celeste asked, "So, what are these hand bombs? I might have seen weapons among thugs in New Orleans or firecrackers in Little Canton, San Francisco, but I have never held one or been close to this type." She searched her mind, but the only thing she saw was a ball used in a slungshot. People used such weapons to crush the skull or face. She bit her lip.

"It is easy to forget your ignorance. But Felice designed these bombs. Since we all served in the first war of Italian independence in 1848, we tend to assume everyone knows about these types of projectiles. I will not draw a picture—if I were found with even a drawing of them, I would be sent to prison, given my past. We are already at risk by drawing the maps. So, I will merely describe the weapon."

"We are to throw the bombs and run away, or do we stay there?" Liliana perched on the edge of her chair. Her dark hair hung in soft ringlets framing her face.

"Sister, you are too quick for me. Relax. The bombs are four to five pounds in weight, and they are oblong, like stuffed sausages filled with an explosive called mercury fulminate which will blow up on impact. They look like a pincushion because the round surface is covered with percussion caps that protrude—like this." He pointed to different points on his palm.

Liliana leaned toward him. "I do not understand, brother. Truly. I cannot see what you are describing."

Odéon shifted his weight. "Hmmm. I think I know how to explain. He grabbed a half-eaten orange from the table around which the group had been sitting. "Look, the grenade is a bit larger than this but like an oblong orange. Do you see?"

Liliana nodded.

"What about the percussion caps?" Celeste asked.

"See here. Imagine you are preparing the mulled cider at an autumn feast. You have dried your cloves, and you will punch them into the bottom rind of this orange. You will put the cloves all around that part so that it is covered, correct? Then you will place the orange inside a bag in the cider to warm and flavor the drink, correct?"

"I see now. The cloves are like the percussion caps on the orange which resembles a bomb." She exchanged glances with Liliana.

"The bomb, like a four-pound oblong orange, will be in a black silk bag. That is what you will throw, Celeste. Understand?"

"Yes." She blinked. She would do this only for Maman.

"Good. Now let me show you where you are going." He unfolded a small piece of paper on which was a cursory drawing. "Here at the top, we see the opera house, showing the carriageway where the emperor's entourage will arrive. These boxes show you the buildings along Rue le Peletier and the cross-streets named Boulevard des Italiens, Rue de Rossini, and the rest of Rue le Peletier. Those are the routes leading to and away from the opera."

"At 7:00 p.m., you and Odéon are to arrive with Liliana. You go into the wine shop across from the theater. Have a drink at the bar; all the while, you will watch the gathering crowd."

Celeste flinched. "But why Liliana? She is so young. I do not know why you included her. She could stay at Faucon's while we are gone."

A scarlet flush crept into Carlo's cheeks. "Perhaps you do not understand. Liliana and I are all we have. Our parents are dead. She has no home other than me—these people—you—us.

"I cannot leave her at Faucon's where she will not know what happens to me—or you. What if you never return? I would never leave her with a bunch of whores. Her French is not that good. She speaks better English than French since our father's Venetian glass-blowing business did work with English importers."

"I could be sure of her safety," Celeste said. "If you let me take her to Faucon's with me, she will be safe. Nothing gets past Faucon. Maman used to say she was the toughest woman she had ever known—she has survived kings, dauphins, and this emperor. Would you please let us keep her there—secure? And of course, that way you could find her after the—"

He raised his palm toward her. "You do not understand my intention."

"Liliana is old enough to make up her mind. What age are you, child?" Celeste asked.

"Fourteen, mademoiselle."

"La! Do you see? She is the same age I was when I sailed alone to New Orleans and started to work."

He turned to Liliana. "So, ma chérie, what do you want to do—stay at Faucon's during the operation or accompany us to the opera? You will be in danger if you come with us."

"I want to come rather than stay at Faucon's alone. Please do not leave me there away from you—I would be so worried." She plunged her right fist into her left hand's open palm.

Carlo clenched his jaw. "Yes, my dear, but I need to be clear. I will be in the thick of the fight. I must throw not just one bomb as you do, Celeste. I will lead a charge with many bombs, running through the crowd, and even be close enough to take fire. I may not survive, do you understand?"

Liliana put her hand to her mouth.

Celeste said, "You want Liliana to stay with me in case we have to flee?"

"You will have no idea how serious this is until you are in the middle of it." He leaned closer. "Face facts. We are trying to assassinate the emperor, a capital crime. The guards could shoot us on sight—any one of us. You may not be able to make it back to Faucon's. There is always that possibility."

"Oh my." Celeste tore her gaze away from Carlo's. Her eyes burned as if she spent too much time staring at the sun.

"At least Liliana would be with you, Celeste, and hopefully, you will rejoin Odéon and flee to safety. Celeste, you will be at the edge of the mob. Upon my signal, you will throw your bomb at the target." He pointed to a spot on the diagram. "Aim directly at the imperial coach. Do you have your watch?"

Celeste said, "I have a pocket watch back at Faucon's house."

"Then use it. Always keep your eye on me. Again, I repeat: watch for my signal. I will raise my fist with my index finger pointing upward.

Run up and throw. Do you see?" He mimicked the gesture. "Once you do, leave Liliana at your meeting spot, and run up here." He pointed to the crude drawing of the coach at the porte-cochère of the opera house.

"You must launch the bomb directly at the horses. Like this." He grabbed a piece of scratch paper, rolled it into a ball, and threw it into the center of the room, nearly missing Raoul's head. "You must give it an overhand throw, as hard as you can. Do you understand?"

"Yes, but then what must I do?"

"The crowd will surge forward, then retreat, and there will be much upset. That is why, Liliana, you must stay fixed at the far edge of the crowd—here." Again, he pointed. "At the edge of Rue Peletier, at the corner by the wine shop where Celeste and Odéon can find you. You must not waver. Understand?"

"But what about Odéon? Where will he be?" She burst into tears. "I am afraid—what if you get killed, brother?"

Odéon said, "Wipe your tears, child. After I throw a bomb, I will return to your side. Carlo has already given me my orders. You only need to know yours." He passed her a well-worn gray handkerchief, one that Celeste had seen around his neck at times.

Celeste said, "You must be strong, Liliana. Carlo is brave; you must be, too. Odéon will come back to you. This is no time for tears but for ridding France of the one who has crowned himself emperor despite the people's will. This joker who gives lavish hunting parties and flaunts his mistresses deserves his end. I do this for my mother just as you do it for your brother. That is why we must act. Why you must have courage."

"Well, there you have it. The girl has spoken." Odéon brushed a crumb from his coat sleeve. Celeste admired his bearing and the way he stayed so relaxed in the face of such a dangerous mission.

Carlo swept the back of his hand across his lips. "I will make a compromise with you—all of you. Liliana, you will go now with Celeste and stay at Madame Faucon's. When you go to the square, you are to stay next to Celeste at all times."

"But where do we get the bombs? Will you give them to us now?" An imaginary crow tiptoed across Celeste's fingers and sat there, angling its head, this way and that. She shuddered.

"No, Odéon will have them. The helpers will wrap each one in a black silk pouch. You will throw them while they stay inside the bag. That way, at night, the dark color will be hard to spot."

Felice's voice rose above the murmuring group. "We must go now. We will not return here. Odéon, Carlo, to our next meeting point. The rest of you know the place and the details."

Carlo and Odéon rose and moved their chairs back to the table.

Liliana sucked in her lower lip. "I fear I shall not be brave enough." Her eyes brimmed with tears.

Celeste shook off the imaginary crow. She no longer saw it sitting on her hand, but its dark, pointy feathers had scraped at her courage, too. If only she had let Odéon make the turn to Le Havre. By now, she would be well on her way to San Francisco. If only she could summon the strength to see this through.

"You have more muscle inside you than the strongest bull ox." Carlo reached out and gathered Liliana into his arms. He kissed the top of her head while her shoulders shook.

Of course, she would be sobbing, too—Celeste knew the familiar pain of loss exceptionally well. And Carlo was slipping away from her life, causing another pinprick. "I promise I will take care of her as best I can." Celeste reached out her hand and clasped Liliana's.

Liliana slipped her hand from Celeste's grasp. Carlo drew both women toward him, and he kissed Liliana's head, then Celeste's cheek.

Carlo chewed his lower lip. "I swear I would kill myself if anything were to happen to you, my darling sister, and you, dear Celeste."

"But I want to be with you at the opera." Liliana wiped her palm on her skirt.

Carlo frowned. "That cannot be. I will be in danger, and I will not be able to take you along when I leave there."

"I would have been alone anyway? *Merde!* You never told me this—have you been hiding this secret from me?"

Odéon broke in. "We do not know how this venture will turn out, Liliana. You must trust that Celeste will do her best to keep you safe."

Liliana hunched over, cradling her hands, resting her elbows on her knees. Celeste reached out and put her arm around her shoulders. The girl shook her off, and Celeste retreated a few steps. She could not blame the girl; she had faced abandonment that way herself. Suddenly. No warning. Then the dark yawning well.

An errant puff of chimney smoke blurred her eyes, and she wiped them with her sleeve. "Dust to dust, ashes to ashes," the priest would say in the annual Lenten Mass as he made the sign of the cross in ash on her forehead. They might all end up as dust sometime soon.

Thirty

THE EARTH'S HALF ROTATION

14 January 1858

After spending a tense evening and following day under Faucon's watchful eye, Celeste watched the dusk cast its specter upon the streets of Montmartre. Lamplighters crossed the lanes illuminating the ice-encrusted lamps. Liliana clung to Celeste's elbow in the cart as Odéon headed down from Montmartre to the Boulevard des Italiens. Celeste checked her apron pocket—good, the pocket watch was there. She took a glance at it—6:45 p.m. Right on time—a chance to observe the street from the wine shop in front of the theater before crowds buried it underfoot.

In front of a livery stable, Odéon drew the horse to a complete stop. A boy ran out from the stable yard and clutched the reins. Odéon slipped coins into the boy's hand and turned to aid Liliana and Celeste, but they had already leaped down of their own accord.

Liliana grabbed Celeste's arm and held it so tight Celeste feared her circulation would be cut off. "Liliana! You must be strong—upright—

no grabbing me, *bien*? Otherwise, I will leave you here with the stable boy. Is that what you want?"

The girl drew back, seeming startled. "I am sorry—I will do better."

"Ahhh. You are wearing it." A smile flitted across Odéon's face the way a small bird flits from branch to branch on a summer's day.

Celeste drew the black mantilla about her and pulled it more tightly, shrouding her back and shoulders. "A special occasion, *n'est-ce pas*? Besides, I hoped that the black lace would prevent anyone from noticing me."

Odéon's mouth opened halfway. "Your loveliness is hard to ignore for anyone, but at least this covers your hair, and if you—" he pulled the edges of the mantilla closer around her face and forehead, "do this, you will be well concealed. And above all, eyes down when someone—such as the imperial guards or the police—stares at you." He brushed his lips across hers, and she savored the sweet tobacco that clung like perfume on his mouth.

No more time for idle chatter. Odéon pointed in the direction of the opera house, and they walked in silence along the three wide blocks. Boulevard des Italiens seemed to extend for miles, cutting a wide swath into the city. Along the way, cafés filled with patrons lining up for dinner; bars flickered with silhouettes of men raising glasses and women wearing gigantic peacock-feathered hats. When they passed gaps between buildings, shafts of icy air permeated her wool scarf and seeped into her gloved hands, making them numb.

Odéon's voice rang out. "Almost there. See?"

They rounded the corner from Boulevard des Italiens onto Rue le Peletier, and on both sides rose a series of four-story buildings, topped by small chimneys. She expected a grand square like the palace at Compiègne, but the street widened at a spot she guessed to be the theater's entrance where horses and carriages drew up to release their passengers.

Carlo's drawing had not been to scale. Her mouth went dry. This space supplied little room for their operation. Harder to navigate; easier to be spotted. Like a closet. She could not imagine how Carlo and Felice would maneuver through the cramped street, throw their hand bombs, and get away.

Odéon's hand tapped her shoulder. "Take a good look at the theater. C'est magnifique, n'est-ce pas?"

She nodded. Though smaller in scale than the American Theater in San Francisco, the opera house had an appealing grandeur. A red awning sheltered the porte-cochère where the horses and buggies drew up, letting off men in top hats and ladies in sumptuous capes over lacy skirts. For a moment, she lost herself—if only she were one of them with Odéon on her arm. Indeed, her mother had lost her chance. If Faucon had told the truth, Maman had thrown her happiness away when she planned the death of the prostitute they fished out of the Seine like a dripping sturgeon.

Lights illuminated the foyer behind the port-cochère, and the second floor sported high arched windows between a series of columns. Was this what they had all come to destroy?

She checked her pocket watch, which read 7:10 p.m. She followed Odéon into the wine shop, Liliana trailing behind them. The server brought them a carafe of house red, and they sat sipping at a window table. She noticed her hands shook when she lifted the goblet to her lips. *Not too long now.*

Crowds had already begun to gather outside. No doubt they had seen the posters advertising the performance of *William Tell*, which they would have ordinarily ignored. Still, tonight's grand imperial show brought them away from home and hearth into the bitter wintry night. Most of them sported working-class attire: tattered jackets, women's skirts with permanent mud stains on the hem. They would do anything to see the imperial couple on the news sheets: tales of their robes, their finery, any bit of jewelry would remain on their tongues for months and feed the gossip rags.

A series of well-dressed single men wound their way from left to right through the crowd. She suspected the worst: imperial agents. She remembered Pietro Fargella's words at the palace of Compiègne—spies were everywhere. She moved away from them, but parents towing children surrounded her. Days-old purple jams and red jellies decorated the little ones' mouths.

Celeste gazed at them. Since they could no more afford the theater than a slice of Easter ham, they lingered at the edge of spectacles such as this one, made even more stellar with the appearance of the emperor and his wife, Eugénie. One minute the square lay relatively empty, pickpockets and swindlers lurking at the edges awaiting their prey. The next moment the gentry packed the square in such tight formation, she wondered if any air could circulate among the people.

A troop of imperial guardsmen clattered up, their horses parting the crowd, and they assumed parallel lines separating the public from the opera's carriageway. That is where the imperial coach would stop, according to Carlo's directions. Not long after, a troop of guards on horseback escorted an advance carriage that inched from Boulevard des Italiens toward the opera house. The entourage whipped its horses through the pressing mob, seeming not to care that its stinging lashes might catch a child or a mother who stood in the way.

She caught her breath. Neither Felice nor Carlo had mentioned an advance carriage. But it would make sense. In that carriage would ride the emperor's entourage: his assistants along with the empress's ladies-in-waiting. But then—the timing was thrown off since their plans had not included this delay.

A cry followed—*les voilà!—there they are!* Celeste struggled to catch her breath. Where were they pointing? A round-bellied gent in a top hat blocked her view down Rue le Peletier in the direction of Boulevard des Italiens. Though she eased forward between him and a spidery woman with long arms, she could only see the gleaming breastplates, red-feathered helmets, and imperial flag the standard-bearers carried.

Celeste stood on tiptoe, and something brushed her hand. She looked up at Odéon's expression, his lips parted. "What is it?" she asked.

"I see the emperor's carriage," he shouted.

A sudden pulse surged through her veins, and she lost her bearings. The crowd blurred. The pressure of all the bodies pushed her relentlessly forward, their rank odors and stale clothing making it even harder to breathe. The earth did a half-rotation—oh no, she could not faint now. She would be swept underfoot.

Someone's arm thrust around her shoulders and yanked her close to a body. A familiar tobacco scent rose from a jacket. Thank God it was Odéon and not someone else capturing her in the net-like embrace. He swept kisses across her face, and his mouth lingered on hers. "I love you."

"Your secret is safe with me." She pulled him in, closing her eyes against his chest. "I will love you forever," she said.

"No matter what happens, we are one," he said.

His hand grasped hers, and he passed the round silk-covered hand bomb into her right palm.

"But wait. Where is Carlo? Felice? I do not see them. Besides, Carlo is supposed to signal for us to throw." She rasped the words above the crowd's growing roar.

The mob kept its forward trajectory, and though they were supposed to stay back by the periphery, an invisible wave propelled them toward the theater's entrance, exactly where they should not be. Suffocatingly close not only to the point where the coach would arrive but also to the gendarmes whose eyes glared at everyone beneath their blue and red hats.

Celeste reached out her other hand—good—Liliana worked to stay balanced next to her, appearing lost, her mouth half-opened. She would never forgive herself if Carlo's sister came to harm, but her next move was a mystery. When Celeste clutched the silk scarf, she felt the weight of the hand bomb against her skirts. If only she could save herself and Liliana.

The crowd undulated, and the front of the mob turned into the back. Felice's plan was going topsy turvy. She clung to Odéon's elbow, and from what she could tell, they stood again in the middle of the crowd. Cheers, shouts, and roars reverberated all around them. She trembled, entrapped in the middle. She could not leave Liliana—their plan would not work—everywhere she looked, throngs pressed one way or the other. Liliana yanked on her elbow, her sobs rising. Celeste had no idea where they were going.

A flash, a bright object—the emperor's coach made its way down Rue le Peletier, the guard forcing the crowd forward and whipping those unfortunates who came too close. As the coach turned into the theater's carriageway, a cheer went up. A crash came from the right-hand corner of the façade, followed by three other earsplitting sounds, igniting the jockey box of the coach, ejecting the driver, and upending the horses hit by shrapnel.

Celeste strained to see the door of the coach but in front of her lay a mélange of bodies: imperial guards lying prone on the ground, horses moaning as they struggled on their sides, police appearing dazed, missing their arms, wandering around the coach, and then—through the isinglass coach windows—the wide-eyed faces of Emperor Napoléon III and Empress Eugénie.

The mob around her swung in all directions, like giant arms avoiding a swarm of bees. Something jostled her with such force, her hand opened, and no matter how hard she tried to keep hold of it, the silk scarf holding the bomb slipped from her grasp, hit the ground beneath her, and the bomb rolled, wobbling through the crowd toward the imperial coach.

She had no chance of retrieving it. If she bent down to grasp it, even a little, she was in danger of being pushed to the ground, and within the fulminating chaos around her, the fires burning, horses screaming, the guards slicing through the crowd—somebody would kill her. She looked back—she could not see Liliana. Or Odéon. Then, to compound the horror, there she was alone, sprayed by blood pulsing from a dying horse's neck.

And even worse, she had failed to throw the bomb.

She lingered watching, almost paralyzed. Blood dripped from her right sleeve. Around her, the crowd drew back, a numbing sense seeming to return to the mesmerized throngs. Small groups turned, some running, some limping, and by some strange intelligence, the mob thinned. She knew no one wanted to be close to the scene; someone could face accusation. Madame la Guillotine sharpened her blades, if only in Parisians' minds, but that was enough knowledge to send the crowds home.

Only the twisted few savored the desperation and horror lingering at the edges of this torn imperial postcard. Despite the devastation, the emperor continued with his plans. Two guards appeared from within the melee fronting the imperial couple: they jerked open the now-crooked door of the coach, which miraculously stayed upright, and the emperor stepped out, his, the only uniform in range without blood on it. Following him was the caped and hatted figure of Empress Eugénie, the sparkle of her emerald and diamond necklace a bizarre counterpoint to the entangled body parts and gore on the path. Bits of brain and patches of horsehair clung to her skirts. Several guards surrounded them and hustled them away and into the theater.

Someone grabbed Celeste's shoulder—hard. Carlo yanked her arm with such force she nearly lost her footing. "What?" She was in no mood for someone to tell her that she had failed. "Carlo," she breathed.

"Shhh! Do not say my name. Odéon and Liliana are over there by the wine shop. Come! Stay with me."

She snapped her arm away from his grasp. "This is not wise. You told me yourself you must get away. To stay with us would increase suspicion. Those agents who survived will be gathering, no doubt already looking for suspects. Is yours a kind of death wish?"

"I love you, and no matter what happens, I will find you one day. You must believe in our love." He pulled her toward him and engulfed her in kisses.

Though Celeste doubted the truth of his words, she let him have his kisses; his final words surrounded them in a fine mist. Her eyes closed, and she savored the warmth of his lips. A click reverberated.

Somebody pressed a gun barrel against her ear. The guard spat. *"Putain!* Get lost!"

She reeled, wiping the spit off her mantilla. The guard's saliva mixed with tobacco juice, so it clung to the silky lace. He had called her "whore,"—though it might be true, how dare he say it.

The guard swiveled toward Carlo and pressed the pistol between his eyes. "You, my friend, are an assassin! I saw you throw a hand bomb!"

She backed away, then nearly lost her footing as a swarm of police officers surrounded Carlo. He called out. "Remember me always."

"I will," she answered, but now her first thought was to find Liliana and Odéon. She could not spot them. The crowd dispersed as on a battlefield, gendarmes flooded the square, whistles blowing, sabers raised. And her vision blurred as she stumbled back to the street corner she knew as the meeting place, only to see soldiers storm the wine shop and in minutes drag out Felice. To her horror, someone had bloodied his face.

Odéon was nowhere, and the crowd swallowed Liliana. Celeste sagged weakly against the wall of the corner building; she had lost them all.

Thirty-One

It Will Cost You, Mademoiselle

After several minutes' wait at the corner, she dared not linger any further. Plainclothes police, accompanied by secret agents, carpeted the square like flies on a dead cow. She ran several blocks, pushing her way through oncoming traffic until she reached an unfamiliar square. A line of carriages waited next to a well-lit restaurant where diners in evening dress ate at various tables. She prayed no one would see her bloody clothes and summon a gendarme.

Through sputtering breaths, she spoke to a driver. "Can you take me to Rue de L'Abreuvoir?"

"Which arrondissement?"

"Eighteenth. Montmartre."

"*Et voilà.* It will cost you, mademoiselle."

"I will make it worth your while." She opened the carriage door and flung herself inside. At least she was the only traveler; she could not deal with another passenger under these circumstances. Through gauzy curtains, she watched the streets of Paris flash by like printed scenes on stereoscopes. After a series of left turns, right angles, and crossings, the carriage made the ascent, growing ever steeper, toward the hill of martyrs, Montmartre, and Madam Faucon's brothel.

She had to leave the country. Her fingers worried the tobacco plug stuck on the lace of her mantilla. Spies would have spotted her among the fray in the square. Once the authorities shared their intelligence, local police would put all the terrorists on a watch list. The gendarmes would put up roadblocks, and communes would plaster signs on public buildings. Sketches would populate bulletin boards in town halls.

ASSASSIN! Wanted for attempts on the emperor's life!

There would be no chance for her in France. The courts would not pity a former daughter of France, now American, who had come back to destroy the empire. Her destination reached, she handed a fistful of francs to the driver and sidestepped a young couple arm in arm on the street. Montmartre was for lovers, obviously undeterred by the freezing weather and slippery roads.

She rapped on the brass lion doorknocker and waited. If only they would hurry. She questioned whatever she had done. All she wanted was to doff these bloody garments and dive into the covers of her bed where she could pretend this never happened.

Hortense's heavy eyebrows bristled around the open door, and she grunted. The cigar smoke and strong scent of brandy and opium lent a smoky sweetness to the air Celeste inhaled. An enraptured crowd of men, dizzy with lust, watched two girls stripping and making love to one another in the center couchette of the drawing room. Writhing nudes and frothy-mouthed men turned her stomach. How often she had seen these scenes, both in her mother's brothel and in New Orleans. Not tonight. Certainly not tonight.

After tracing her way up the stairs and through a labyrinthine corridor, Celeste found her room, where she flung open the door, then closed and locked it behind her. She took the key from the lock, turned, and saw the slightest movement—there—in the corner—near the bed-stand. She breathed in a lungful of heavy musk perfume. Someone was in here. With shaky hands, she lit a candle, held it high, its sputtering light casting rays around the room.

A cat would not have been quieter.

Tante Faucon sat tucked in a corner, crouched in the dark, a giant spider awaiting her prey. Celeste put her hand to her mouth. She would not scream to draw attention, but she could not fathom what Faucon wanted. "What are you doing here—in my room?" She set the candle on the dressing table. If only she could keep her hands from trembling.

Faucon put her finger to her lips. "*Shhhh.* Tonight's guests include the emperor's agents. I did not expect them, but they are downstairs, and soon they will be here on this floor with the girls. You are not safe here. One of my girls lives near the opera. She serviced one of the officers who said the gendarmes are rounding up suspects. Imperial agents have been questioning the Englishman who may have been an instigator."

Celeste shook her head. "Thomas Allsop? No—they could not know all about the affair—who was involved in the plot. It is too soon. Unless—" She swept a trembling hand across her forehead. "They have Carlo, and I fear for him."

Faucon's eyes glittered. "If they already arrested people, they could have coerced or tortured them into giving up names. It does not take long."

"Well, I can simply stay in this locked room while the girls and men go about their business."

Faucon's spidery arms fluttered. "For all your worldly experience, ma chérie, you are incredibly naïve. Any whore will talk under knife-point. You know that as well as I do. The men will wonder who is in this locked room. They will ask, "Is it a *putain* with special privileges? A private whore to a wealthy man? Which man? Describe him.

"They will be drunk, out of control. The girls will stammer. The men will say, 'Ah—there is no man, is there?' The girls will look guilty.

An empty room—a single whore. The johns will act loose. Curious. To shut them up, the girls will tell them about you. Just to finish up with one man and collect the bag of francs."

"But Tante, you must take pity on me. Let me hide within these walls."

She waved a hand as though brushing a fly from her web. "You must leave—now—by the servant's entrance. Take all your belongings with you in case the gendarmes raid my house."

"I can't believe you are casting me out. Where will I go? And what about Liliana and Odéon?" She dug her thumbnail into the underside of her index finger.

"What about those two? If they come here, Hortense will not open the door."

"I have no choice but to return to Brianna and Edward in the Marais. You will tell Odéon—or at least tell Hortense to let them know, right?"

"I do not know the address of this Brianna." She sniffed. "At least you might be willing to write it down."

"Here," Celeste opened a drawer where she had previously tucked a pencil.

31 Rue du Roi de Sicile

Madame pulled an eyeglass from her pocket and read it by candle-light. "Which arrondissement?"

"Fourth—only a couple of blocks from the Seine. Not far from Notre Dame."

"My memory is faulty, you know." Faucon's long fingernails scratched against the paper's surface. "But it can become better with a bit of—you know." She held out her palm.

"Oh, of course, and I nearly forgot to pay you for letting me stay here." Celeste's fingers fumbled inside her reticule—her gold coins dwindled in number. Thank the stars she had her ticket for the *North*

Star. She would need the rest of her money to get to the ship. But then she considered her passe-port and knew she would have to show her papers through checkpoints northward to Le Havre. She was an accessory to an assassination attempt—in a matter of time, she would be spotted and arrested.

As she dropped the coins in Faucon's hand, a sudden urgency rose inside her. "Odéon is reliable and loyal. He knows to bring Liliana here. They may be late to join me, but they will come."

Faucon canted her head toward her shoulder. "You have much trust in a man. I cannot say the same for myself. Men are pigs who root about in bed and then flee the house without paying. That is how I view men."

"Odéon is not like that."

"Look. You got yourself into this situation. I trust you will figure out the rest. I do not want to know your plans from this point on."

Celeste swam in the dark muddy pools of Faucon's beady eyes where the candlelight played hide and seek. Somewhere in those murky waters lay the truth, drowning along with her mother's love and desire for swift justice.

A coal-sized lump formed in Celeste's throat. "I need your help."

Faucon sprang from her corner nest and set a bony index finger on Celeste's lips. She pushed her lips into her teeth so hard that Celeste slapped her hand away.

Faucon spat. "Shut your mouth. Allsop will squeal about Mont St. Michel. About your mother. About Felice. About the shipments of bomb parts. Within minutes, not hours, you will be under arrest. Look at you, covered in blood. If you stay here, I am ruined, and the livelihood I built upon years of struggle will be, *poof!*" She threw a hand into the air. "Gone forever."

"I have no one but you." Celeste faltered, her knees giving way. She reached out and held onto the bedpost for support.

"*C'est ridicule*! What a ridiculous notion. You look like a strong, healthy woman to me. Pull yourself up." Faucon's tone softened a bit. "You talked about the people in the Marais."

"I do not want to seek help from them. Edward is in poor health, and Brianna has enough worries."

Faucon lifted Celeste's valise from where it sat against the far corner, and she plunked it open on the bed. "Change your clothes and pack, my girl. Now. The program downstairs will soon be over; you have little time to gather your things and go out the back door. *Vite!* Hurry up."

After she changed out of her bloody day dress and into a fresh one, Celeste set her jaw, opened the leather buckles of the valise, and emptied her drawers into the traveling case—chemise, nightgown, day dress, stockings. In they went, along with her comb, brush, tooth powder, and Madame Le Brun's calling card. She stuffed them into her traveling case; she locked up the contents. From behind her, Faucon's heavy breath tickled the hairs on the back of her neck.

She shrugged into her spare coat. "What should I do with this bloody thing?"

Faucon's eyes glittered. "Give it to me. I will burn it in my bedroom fireplace. No one will suspect anything."

"Where might I find a carriage to Paris?"

"Place du Tertre."

Voices emanated from the hallway—first two, then other murmurs—slurring words, giggling comments, shuffling feet, slamming doors. Faucon went to the door, opened it a crack, then more expansively. "There are voices down below on the landing. Stay back."

Celeste lifted her valise and reticule from the bed; she set the mantilla on her head. Hell, the plug of tobacco continued to stick to the fold. She placed her cloak around her shoulders.

Madame glanced back. "You are one foolish girl. Take off that mantilla! Here—wear this." She pulled a shawl from around Celeste's shoulders, set it over her hair, and then tucked the fringe under her lapel.

Celeste opened her valise and folded the mantilla into the traveling case.

More voices. Footsteps rose from the stairwell.

"Come with me." Faucon wrapped a bony hand around Celeste's wrist.

She pulled back.

"Stupid girl." She dug her fingernails into Celeste's arm and drew her into the corridor, where she pointed to the end of the hallway. "Go through that door where you will find an outside staircase leading down to the street, Rue de l'Abreuvoir. Go left outside the house, then take the first right up the hill to Le Consulat Café. Turn left at the cross street and go over to Place du Tertre. The carriages wait there."

Celeste faced Madame Faucon. She pulled her close; the woman's heartbeat pounded against her chest. She kissed one hollow cheek, then another. "Au revoir, merci." To her surprise, rather than flinch, Faucon held her lightly, much as one would tender a fallen sparrow.

The evening breeze rustled the thatch of leafless vines across the street from the brothel. Celeste scurried toward Place du Tertre, following Faucon's sharp, clear directions. She passed the shuttered shops and glanced at the frosty windows of Le Consulat Café, its patrons hunched deep in conversation amidst their usual community. She could see herself—them—that day at the far table at the back; she had sat deep in observation of Felice, Carlo, her source of immediate attraction, and Odéon, whom she had not even thought about at the time. All had plotted today's failed events.

If only she had sat at a different table that day. Things would have turned out differently. And then, other choices would not have led her to Carlo, Liliana, Odéon, the marquis—and Maman. But mainly to Odéon. If only she had recognized him, had paid more attention to him, the man who with each passing day had gained such importance in her life. She missed him—she longed to know where he was. He might be safe or under arrest. And she yearned for Liliana. If Faucon did not relay the message with Brianna and Edward's address, her two precious people would be forever lost.

She turned left at the corner past Le Consulat Café. Midway down the block on the left, a crowd gathered around a broadsheet filled with giant letters and exclamation marks plastered on the building's wall. She pressed into the midst of the gathering.

The paper bore the headline

ASSASSINS!

Below in smaller print,

Arrested—Thomas Allsop, Felice Orsini, Carlo di Rudio!

She did not have to read much further than

Reward for Information!

In coordination with the imperial guard, the gendarmes seek the whereabouts of one Celeste Bazin, described as a young blond woman in a black mantilla seen throwing a bomb toward the carriage.

They also seek a man known only as "Odéon," named by Orsini as part of the bomb-throwing team. Anyone who sees either one is to report their whereabouts to the local gendarmerie.

Celeste returned to the street, elbowing her way out of the news-seeking crowd. She banged her suitcase against a pregnant woman of considerable girth. *This hellish valise.* She should have traveled more lightly. Maybe she should dump its contents; perhaps she should, but wait a moment. Its contents. The calling card. Geneviève. She never thought of her before. A voice whispered in her head. "My husband is a retired magistrate. He knows many influential people in Paris. If you are ever in need of help, please get in touch with me, dear girl. Promise me that."

Celeste took quick steps toward Place du Tertre. Crowds of men, women, and children strolled arm-in-arm, blowing frost breath into the air and skirting patches of snowdrifts. The rising steam from the roasted walnut vendor mingled with the occasional whiffs of garlic and thyme from the cafés situated around the square. Parisians relished their evenings outdoors, and barring stormy conditions, their laughter and joy were hard to suppress. She could drink wine and listen to a guitar's strumming or an accordion's happy-go-lucky tune.

She ducked into the entrance of a closed hat shop and unlatched her valise. After fingering the contents, she reached the bottom of the bag. The calling card. She lifted it out, patted the rest of the contents back into place, and latched the traveling bag, which she set on her foot for a moment. She leaned the card toward the light from the square.

48 Place du Tertre

Celeste looked for number 48. Jostled by the passing flow of walkers, she found the ceramic number on the building in front of her. Upon its blue tile, the number 24. Aha! Across the square should be the number 48.

She valise-bumped her way across the square, tracing her steps around steaming food vendors, piles of horse manure, and ice-encrusted patches of gray snow. She gained the doorway and knocked. *Blast that damn traveling bag.* Geneviève must have a better answer. Or else the earth might open its slimy jaws and swallow her whole.

After several minutes of waiting, then pressing her finger on the bell so often her fingertip lost sensation, she turned away and sat down on the stoop. Maybe they had gone away. Perhaps they were out among these frostbitten crowds on the streets, seeking a bit of air rather than their stuffy firesides. *Mon Dieu*, maybe they were away on a trip.

The darkness deepened, and the nut vendor packed up his belongings, setting his boxes and coinbox in a hand cart, then quashing his coals with splashes of water. The hiss of the water hitting the fire reached her and her ridiculous, self-inflicted situation. Where earlier tears fell, her cheeks numbed to the touch. The crowds thinned, and laughter drifting out of the cafés took on a harsher note.

She tightened Faucon's shawl around her head. Her fingers grew stiff when she tried to move them. Perhaps she had gloves in her valise—that is, if she remembered to pack them. An hour passed, followed by another. A gendarme patrolled the street, crossing the square. He might be advancing toward her.

She rose to her feet—one more attempt to ring the bell. If not, the gendarme might book her for vagrancy. She had seen many scenes on Paris streets. A woman alone, abandoned, without a destination, forced into the workhouse. She alternated fingers, pressing the bell in one continuous note. Someone must come—they must!

Heavy footsteps crunched the ice and snow on the surface of the square behind her. Though she kept her finger on the bell, her thoughts darkened. The gendarme would arrest her on the spot. Or ask her what she was doing. Or shake his head, pity shadowing his face. He would whistle for his fellow gendarmes to put her with the other whores on their way to the lockup.

"Mademoiselle!"

A muffled male voice behind her—then a young girl's voice. "Celeste, we are here."

She dared not turn around. It would be a trick. Something to entrap her. The girl's voice would be from a whore they had already caught. Oh no, they already knew her name, her identity, had a cell cot waiting for her. She closed her eyes, gathering strength, and then she pounded even harder on the door.

Thirty-Two

Forever and a Day

The door creaked. Celeste's waiting lasted so long, and her attention was so fixed, she might have imagined the faint sound. She lifted her knuckles. Much like leaves rustling underfoot in autumn, a hand swished inside against the doorframe. Then a *snap!* Somebody drew back a bolt, and a crack appeared, letting out a beam of light.

"Who is it?" A woman's muffled voice penetrated the darkness.

"*C'est moi.* Celeste. Your friend from Place de L'Abbaye."

A child's voice. A widened crack in the door. A small nose at knee height. "Grand-mère! It is the lady who bought me meats!"

"Yes, your grand-mère brought me to Rue de L'Abbaye to the abandoned brothel, do you recall? Back in November?"

"Ah, I remember my mother told me about that—about you."

The door swung open. Nancy and small Jacques peered out—Nancy in a long nightrobe, her hair spilling over one shoulder. Jacques in footed pajamas, a red-striped nightcap on his head.

Nancy said, "My mother is in the sitting room—go ahead."

Celeste strode into the drawing room, her valise banging her thighs. Geneviève lounged in a fireside chair. She had wrapped herself in a long brocade nightrobe, her white hair gathered like a crown atop her head.

Rather than go to Geneviève and plant the customary kisses on her cheeks, Celeste collapsed like a spent balloon on the fainting couch.

Geneviève regarded her. "I do not know you, do I? Why did you insist on all that knocking? We meant to ignore you—we are preparing for bed—sitting here with a small glass of port. I was about to read a story to small Jacques. You can thank him for making us answer the door because you drove us crazy."

"I am sorry to disturb you, madame." Celeste pulled the shawl away from her face and allowed her hair to stream about her shoulders.

"Oh, yes. Now I know you—the young woman searching for your mother. Give me your name again."

"Celeste."

"And have you found her?"

As the moments passed, Celeste revealed the episodes leading her to her mother in Mont Saint Michel, her entanglement in the assassination plot, and the events leading to this moment. She had gotten as far as telling of her recent "wanted" description on the news sheet when Nancy's voice rose in the corridor.

Celeste's heartbeat quickened. For God's sake, it must be the gendarme—the one who tailed her across the square. Just when she had found safety and help. She squeezed her eyes shut.

La! It was not the gendarmes as she had suspected. Instead, she peeked through one eye as Odéon paced into the room. Following closely behind him slid the lithe, cloaked figure of a young girl.

As though no time passed, as if they were together all along, as though no assassination attempt occurred, first Odéon, then Liliana, swept onto the couch, surrounded her on both sides, clutched her, and brushed kisses on her face.

"How did you know to come here—to Place du Tertre? I told Madame Faucon to tell you to go to Le Marais."

Odéon grasped her hand and kissed it. "We had to come here to get a carriage from Montmartre to Le Marais. And it was Liliana—"

"I was the one who spotted you, though at first I hardly recognized you without your black mantilla." The young girl wrapped her arms around Celeste's shoulders and held her tight.

Geneviève's voice rose above the crackle and whizz of the burning fire logs. "I trust you know these people?"

"They are like diamonds to me, madame."

Odéon said, "Celeste, we must leave Paris—now."

Nancy said, "Perhaps you should stay here. It is dangerous to travel at night. We have extra rooms in Grand-mère's big house now that Grand-père—." Her voice faltered. She walked to the side table, poured three glasses of a ruby-colored liquid, and set them on a small tray.

After carrying them to Celeste, she leaned over, her brown, gray-streaked hair spilling over her shoulder. "Please, this Spanish port will warm you."

They each took a glass.

Celeste let the port slide down her throat, its sweet taste carrying the promise of summer's glory, of raspberries, blackberries, blueberries, waiting for field-picking, waiting to pop into her mouth.

Geneviève broke the momentary silence. "My husband, the magistrate, had a heart attack last month, and he is in heaven now."

Little Jacques said, "He is with the angels next to Papa." He bit his lower lip.

Celeste saw the ribbon of loss entwined in his features and those of his grand-mère. Geneviève's eyes, once blue and vibrant, had recessed into gray-black shadows, the specter of death enshrouding her. "I do not know what to say—my greatest sympathies to you, Nancy, and small Jacques."

Odéon said, "We are not safe here. And what is worse, our staying would put you and your family in danger."

Celeste leaned forward. "I must return to my mother in Mont St. Michel—to tell her my final goodbye. Then I am bound to the *North Star* in Le Havre, a ship to take us to L'Amérique. I have booked a cabin for February 1, and I can accommodate Odéon and Liliana, but every imperial agent, each patrolling gendarme, will hunger for our whereabouts."

"I see. It is a matter of your identity. You have done well to come to me. I will be back in a few moments." She grasped the cane resting against her knee and leaned on it while she pulled herself out of her chair. After a series of grimaces, she made her way out of the room.

"Where are you going, Grand-mère?"

Nancy patted small Jacques' head. "She is doing something for these friends of ours."

He turned to Celeste. "Are you going to stay with us tonight—will you read me a bedtime story?"

"Ah—I do not know, *mon petit.* I must talk to my friends."

Odéon squeezed her right forearm, and Liliana rested her head on Celeste's left shoulder.

Nancy rose. "Come, Jacques. Let us prepare a small repast for them. I believe we have a bit of cold quiche left from luncheon."

He aimed a glance at them, the tail of his nightcap curling over his shoulder. "Are they starving, Maman?"

Celeste said, "Small Jacques, I have a lion roaring in my stomach."

"Does your lion like Quiche Lorraine?"

"Bien sûr. Of course!"

After Nancy grasped small Jacques' hand, they headed out of the room, presumably toward the kitchen.

Celeste relished the comfortable silence with her beloved Odéon and young Liliana. If only she could rest here, to let time capture them within the warm firelight's caresses.

Not long afterward, Celeste heard the tapping of Geneviève's cane. She held leaflets in her hand. "These will serve you well. My husband bore a long, simmering hatred toward the emperor and the repression of free speech. He helped many friends escape Paris over the years. I knew he had some of these passes on his desk. At first, I thought I would find at least ten, but he must have given many away before he—" Rather than finish the sentence, she handed the papers to Celeste. "I found two in his bottom desk drawer, and I almost gave up the search when I found one between pages of a book of essays by La Montaigne, one of his favorite authors."

"Passe-port?" Celeste scrutinized the official signature, the imperial stamp, the place for her name and date.

"Indeed," Geneviève moistened her lips. "It is the least I can do to help you who have endured so much. Just when you have found your mother, you now must escape this mad country of ours. I love France—its soil is part of my soul—yet I fear this dictator who calls himself a monarch. We are at risk of losing everything we fought for in the French Revolution."

She laid the documents on a side table, along with a pen and a bottle of ink. "Come, sign your names, and take your papers. And we must make a new name for you, Celeste, for you cannot travel with your Christian name."

Liliana signed her document, and Geneviève rolled a blotter over the wet ink. "Please put it in your reticule lest you leave it under a cushion somewhere."

Liliana nodded and returned to her seat on the fainting couch.

"Now you, Monsieur."

Odéon signed his name and held the paper up, examining its contents against the firelight.

Celeste followed. "And so, what should my name be?"

Odéon's husky voice moved the air behind her. "Take my name."

A breath caught in her throat. "Delamare—well, I suppose . . .."

Geneviève frowned. "Not a good idea. The authorities will be after you, Odéon, and once they figure out your connection, they will arrest you. For now, take my name, ma chérie. You are Celeste Le Brun. Your middle name?"

"Marie."

"*Alors, c'est simple.* Celeste Marie Le Brun, daughter of the magistrate—that is, until you arrive in L'Amérique when it is safe to take back your surname."

A rattling of China cups on a tray, followed by footsteps, announced Nancy and small Jacques who carried in their supper. After pouring chamomile tea and serving the China plates and linen napkins, Nancy said, "I couldn't help but think about your need to go and see your mother again."

After taking a sip of tea, Geneviève said, "I believe going there is most unwise."

Nancy said, "I agree."

"How so?" Her voice grated against her throat. The first bite of garlic-spiced quiche bumped down her throat like a rough pebble.

Geneviève said, "Dear girl, isn't it obvious? The gendarmes are slapping your identity on communal walls all over France—soon people will spot women like you behind every wine barrel, every wagon wheel, every cellar door."

Odéon put down his fork, bits of egg lingering on his beard. "I agree, mademoiselle. The imperial guards live on Mont St. Michel—seasoned warriors, many of whom served as spies and agents in our past wars. They have sharp eyes and torturous claws. No secrets stay hidden for long. The moment you set foot again on the island, you are bound for the prison."

She sensed a hollowness in the pit of her stomach. "But Maman—what about her? Thomas Allsop would have told them about her signals."

Odéon brushed his fingers through his beard; bits of egg fell onto his plate. "They can do nothing more to her. She is already theirs. The emperor is leaking money—so many wars, so many plans for remodeling our cities. The state would not retry her—they would simply discount her as a madwoman and leave her in her cell."

Nancy said, "I think if you go visit your mother in Mont St. Michel, you will put her in greater jeopardy. The guards might become rough with her. If she is as weak as Grand-mère, it will not take much to eliminate her."

"But I did not give her a proper goodbye."

Geneviève pulled her chair toward Celeste and sat knee-to-knee with her. "A simple fact is this. There is no proper goodbye. Any leaving is unfinished: words left unsaid; memories unshared; that last utterance; the one shared breath remaining; the lingering doubt that we could have done more, made them happier, consoled them more fully, comforted them."

Celeste's empty plate tipped against Geneviève's knee. "I am sorry." She passed the plate and fork to Liliana, who set them on the side table. Then she took both of Geneviève's hands in hers. "Would Maman forgive me if she knew I had to leave without seeing her one last time? I need to apologize for failing her."

"Your mother knows in her heart that you fulfilled the mission on her behalf. Failure is relative, ma chérie. You tried to end a major source of evil in our world, and you showed all of France that not everyone is willing to live under a tyrant's heel. You enacted your mother's heart's desire—something she yearned for. But now, you must live your life, make your happiness with your companions. Go to l'Amérique; build your future."

Small Jacques' voice echoed. "L'Amérique. Where is that, Maman?"

Nancy hushed her son. "I'll tell you later."

Geneviève continued. "When your mother sent you away to New Orleans, she had a purpose. She wanted freedom for you. Now you must return and enact the life she dreamed of for you."

"But she abandoned me."

"Consider that when she sent you away, it hurt her more than it did you. A daughter is part of her mother; she shares her beating heart, thoughts, and desires. To send you away meant sacrificing part of her own body. Can you think of how it hurt her every morning when she no longer heard your laughter? Saw you grow? Missed your wedding day or the baptisms of children? Think, child. She gave you life. Now you must embrace it and let go of the past."

"And at this hour, you all should rest." Nancy pointed to small Jacques, who had fallen asleep at her feet. She hoisted the boy over her shoulder and rose. "I must put him to bed, but I also think you must sleep. Grand-mère, where shall we put our guests for the night?"

"I have a bedroom upstairs for you, Celeste, and your young friend Liliana."

Nancy said, "Odéon, you may sleep on the fainting couch. I shall bring down a quilt and a pillow for you. The fireside will keep you warm all night."

He pointed toward his pipe. "I also have this, my little personal fire."

After settling into their upstairs room and seeing Liliana safely into the other side of the bed, Celeste lay down, turned on her side, fluffed her pillow, and blew out the candle. Odéon called his pipe his little personal fire. He was that and more to her—much more. She snuggled under the comforter and closed her eyes to meet the dark unknown.

The following morning's breakfast of *pain ordinaire*, plum jam, fresh pears, and café au lait awakened Celeste. She drew the identity papers from her valise that she had left in the kitchen corner.

"What time is the first carriage operating?"

Nancy glanced at the clock above the sideboard. "It is seven o'clock. The drivers begin to gather around 7:30. You should be able to find an early cab to the coaching station in central Paris. From there, you will find coaches that will take you to Le Havre, providing you lodge at roadside inns along the way." She unfolded a news sheet—I bought this from the newsboy in Place du Tertre this morning. Celeste, I thought you would want to see this headline."

Odéon joined her at the sideboard. He reached over and held her shoulder as they both looked at the article.

ASSASSIN ARRESTED!
Raoul Gomez! More suspects arraigned!
Swift trials to come.

Odéon frowned. "Carlo will meet his fate—he looks forward to life imprisonment or Madame la Guillotine. Will Felice give him up, or will he protect him so Carlo will face lesser charges? We may never know until the empire holds the trial."

Liliana elbowed her way in between them. "What did you say about Carlo?" She scanned the headlines, let out a sob, and sagged against the sideboard. "Where will they imprison my poor brother?"

Odéon took a puff of his pipe, then breathed out his smoky words. "They house the traitors of the empire at Devil's Island."

"Where on earth is that? It sounds ghastly." A series of *what-ifs* crowded Celeste's mind. If only she had been kinder to Carlo. More accepting. More loving. Once she had thought she loved him; it was her fault the guards caught him. Like a rose thorn caught in her skin, prickly thoughts festered. She might love him still.

Odéon said, "It is on French Guiana. A small island. I once talked to a man who had survived the penal colony there. He was the only one who lived out of 100 prisoners incarcerated at the same time. He was the lucky one to return to France after serving his sentence. The rest died on the island of malnutrition, fevers, insect bites, beatings, torture.

"Some men also contracted leprosy and were bound on the island for the rest of their lives. Prisoners who survived the *Île du Diable* call it The Dry Guillotine. They say the quick and easy death of the blade would be preferable to the slow agony of Devil's Island."

Celeste gasped. She wondered how any government could dream up such horrid practices. The light scratch of Geneviève's cane announced her arrival. She crossed the kitchen to the sideboard, where she took Celeste's hand and laced it under her elbow. "Ma chérie, I fret that if you do not leave now in the early hours, someone will have spotted you at Place du Tertre last night, and if you go later, you have a strong chance of being recognized."

Celeste gazed into the light blue eyes of her friend. They were clear like those painted on images of the Madonna, reminding her of the medal around her neck. "I cannot thank you enough for these." She patted the identity papers clutched in her hand. "And for letting us stay the night. What would I have done if you hadn't opened the door?"

Nancy's voice broke through their sweet moment. "I must insist you leave now. People are gathering at the carriage stop. You are in greater danger every moment. But this—," she gathered a large clump of Celeste's freefalling blond curls, "must be well hidden from sight on your journey."

She opened the sideboard drawer and drew out a box. "Let me pin your hair into a chignon. Then wear the shawl over it. And do not rouge your lips until you are back in L'Amérique. My father-in-law used to say that the emperor's spies traveled on the ships, and they might extradite you from your first port of call on American shores."

She pressed Celeste down into a chair and swept her hair away from her face. "Here, I am pinning your hair into a central swirl, but be sure to catch stray hairs along the way. You may have these extra pins. And do not smile. Try to look severe. Do not make eye contact with anyone. They are sure to notice your sapphire eyes."

Celeste held her head straight and pulled her mouth down into a half-moon. "What do you think, Odéon?"

Small Jacques skipped into the room, holding a ball and some jacks. "You look funny, mademoiselle."

Odéon spoke through his laughter. "You do look a bit ridiculous, but maybe relax your face a bit more—there you go. You want to be dowdy, ordinary."

Liliana said, "Let us put the shawl over her head and see—there. She looks plain as long as she pulls the shawl close about her face, *n'est-ce pas*?"

Not long after, Celeste, Odéon, and Liliana mounted the carriage steps. Celeste leaned out the open window and said, "I will write to you from San Francisco. Please come for a visit someday."

Geneviève stepped close to the carriage and grasped Celeste's hand. "I may not weather such a journey, but small Jacques—well, he shall see the world—won't you, *mon petit*?"

"Oui, Grand-mère! I will come to visit you, mademoiselle Celeste! Will you come too, Maman?"

"Of course." Nancy nodded, patting his shoulder.

The carriage jerked, the horse's reins jingled, and the vehicle rolled across the stone square. Celeste leaned out of the window. "You will always be welcome at my house. *Au revoir, à bientôt!*"

"We hope to see you again someday." Nancy waved, then picked up small Jacques, who fit neatly onto her hip.

Celeste leaned against the hard carriage seat. Carlo's life hung in the balance. An uneasy silence lurked among them. Liliana wiped her damp cheeks with a handkerchief while Odéon tamped tobacco into his pipe. As the carriage took the twisting road from the hill of martyrs into Paris, she remembered her first day returning to Montmartre—the organ grinder, his monkey, Le Consulat Café, Felice, Carlo, Odéon, then later their camp under the willow tree. Everything had happened so fast, so intensely, she could hardly breathe.

She gave Odéon a sideways glance. "Have I properly asked you to join me in San Francisco?"

"What?" His hand jerked, and bits of tobacco sprinkled on his great-coat lapel.

After edging closer to him on the seat, she whispered, "Well, monsieur, I am not sure I ever formally proposed such a journey and a future life together."

"Do you mean that? Or are you saying that to get rid of me? Maybe you would like me to jump off the carriage and leave you and Liliana on your journey? There are plenty of places where I can hide in Paris."

Liliana cleared her throat. "You need your privacy, and I'll leave you to it. I must pull out my drawing paper and finish a sketch." She busied herself applying a black pencil to a river scene, by all accounts.

Celeste struggled to make sense of all the black streaks upside down; then, she snuck her arm under Odéon's elbow. "All right. How about this? Would you care to join me on the *North Star* voyage to San Francisco by way of Panama?"

"I would be happy to join a lovely lady such as yourself on the voyage you suggest." His eyes crinkled, and he gave a deep, gratifying sigh.

"And would you come and live with me on DuPont Street in San Francisco?"

"Only on one condition, mademoiselle."

"And what would that be?"

"That you be my wife and vow to love me forever and a day."

"I think we could manage forever—but a day? Well, we must give that some thought. Liliana, do you think we should vow to love forever and a day or just forever?"

Tears sprang to Liliana's eyes, and her olive cheeks deepened to a rose color. Her nose swelled from weeping. "Since I would give one more day to see my brother Carlo alive, I think you should vow that extra day." She searched her skirt pocket, eased out a handkerchief, then wiped her nose.

Celeste said, "Then forever and a day it shall be, my Odéon." For a moment, she heard the familiar rustle of Maman's starched skirt against the empty seat across from her.

Thirty-Three

THE MARVEL

Le Havre
1 February 1858

A low-slung clipper ship called HMS *North Star* tugged at the waterline, her rope lines straining against the quay. Hazy clouds floated over the channel, and gusts of wind ruffled the fringes of the French flag at the customs office. Any moment they would be boarding, and up to this time, Celeste suffered suspended, then pounding, heartbeats. Tucked within the refuge of their large coach, sheltered within the confines of five other passengers, she, Odéon, and Liliana had passed through their frequent road stops and coaching inns without notice.

The ticket agent at Le Havre had questioned her cabin booking since it was under the name Celeste Bazin, but she slid a hundred francs toward him, and his disapproval changed to cordial greetings. She looked at the bright, freshly painted starboard side of the vessel, sailors busy swabbing decks, polishing brass quadrants, wrapping lines against masts.

Celeste and Liliana stood side by side, touching elbows. The ticket agent promised boarding at five o'clock with sailing at 6. "I hope Odéon found the teacart. I could use a warm drink—these breezes are turning my ears to blocks of ice," Liliana said.

"You have a way with words. My ears are buried inside this warm shawl, so I barely feel anything."

"It is true—all I see of your face is your nose and mouth. I think your disguise has worked well up to now."

"Shhh," Celeste pressed her finger to her lips. "The less said, the better."

Odéon approached, balancing three steaming teacups, and he passed one to each of them, saving one for himself.

"Merci," Celeste mumbled. "I will show you later how grateful I am."

He reddened under his beard. "I look forward to your gratitude, mademoiselle."

Two men in top hats made quick steps out of the ticket office toward the quay and strolled from one tiny group to another, some passengers waiting to board the ship or hugging relatives gathering to see them off. At first, Celeste paid them no mind, but she caught Odéon staring at them.

Celeste took a sip of tea. The hot liquid burned her tongue, yet she had to swallow it. To spit it out would draw too much attention. She wondered who those two top hats were and chafed that their good luck had run out. The men reached a group closest to theirs, and by the lilt of their sentences, she knew they were asking questions.

With her free gloved hand, she tugged the shawl even closer around her face. If only she could be as invisible as one of the Daughters of Charity in their nun's habits. She stared into her tea, the steam warming her face.

Footsteps smacked the boards of the quay, coming ever nearer. The pair continued going from group to group. Nausea rose from the pit of her stomach. A familiar voice rang out, but she could not hear the words; since she was buried so deeply in the shawl, she heard only muffling. She pressed the woven material back on one side to hear more plainly.

Odéon said, "I know you."

It took a moment for the steam to clear from her vision, but she recognized the hook nose, the expensive topcoat, the rolling cadence of a nobleman. There was no mistaking the marquis.

He appeared breathless; in fact, he clapped a hand on Odéon's shoulder and bent the brim of his top hat. "I am not used to all this fuss; my poor lungs do not work well."

A man in a roman collar stood next to the marquis. He took off his curé's hat and bowed toward her and Liliana. "Welcome, Father," said Odéon.

She could not figure out what Father Jean was doing here. Maybe the marquis came to embroil them in yet another conspiracy. Odéon asked, "*Mes Seigneurs*, have you booked passage on the *North Star*? What do you wish?"

The priest said, "I deliver news—how much time until you board?"

Odéon searched his breast pocket and peered down at his pocket watch. "Five o'clock. It is half-past four." Luggage carts trundled past them, followed by well-dressed passengers. A lady in a fur coat carried a cage holding a squawking cockatiel. Two scruffy lads rested on the dock, sharing swigs from a cider bottle.

"It is noisy here. Can we speak over there?" The marquis pointed to an isolated area of the quay. "What I am about to say is not for other ears to hear. I will not say your name, but would you please follow me?"

She turned to Liliana. "Please stay here and wave to us if they make the boarding announcement."

The girl nodded and directed her gaze toward the ship.

The marquis grasped her arm, and she followed him and Father Jean to a secluded area that held the ship's material. Boxes of folded canvas sails rested between piles of boards and drums of tar. They stepped over coils of rope into a shelter formed by fishnets set up to dry.

She perched on a large box marked "dry goods" while the marquis and Father Jean sat on waist-high coils of rope. "We shall keep our voices low," the marquis said.

"How did you know I would be here? Did someone—Felice—or Raoul—or even Carlo—reveal my secret? If so, I am afraid, for that means others will be in pursuit."

"At the château, you told me the date you sailed on the *North Star,* and I marked my calendar. February the first. Things happened with your mother, so I told Father Jean that we would know where to find you—that is, if you had not been—" he grimaced.

"Arrested?"

"You must know there are wanted posters with your name on them all over France. The Palace of Justice is already scheduling a court date for a speedy trial. Any day it will begin. Who knows what will happen to Felice and Carlo? Surely they will suffer the most severe punishment."

"The posters say they also have Raoul." Her stomach clenched.

Father Jean cleared his throat, perhaps a signal.

"Are you here to give me a blessing, Father? In case I am also arrested?" Her lower lip trembled involuntarily.

"No, but we are not here to discuss that. Instead, we deliver news of your mother."

"Maman? Has she been re-arrested? Put into a harsher cell? Tell me. I would not leave France without knowing."

The clergyman leaned forward. "Your mother has gone to heaven. She died three days ago."

Maybe she had not heard correctly. She tugged the shawl away from her face and forced it behind her ears. For a moment, she hovered, daring not to breathe. "Please say that again."

"She has been dying for some time, even before your visit, Celeste.

Surely you saw something when you visited her. She was so weak—scarcely a shadow of herself."

"What was wrong? They were cupping and bleeding her. Surely she could have recovered." She fought the scream rising in her throat. "Don't tell me they executed her? What is it you are not telling me? So many people lie, father; it is as common as daily bread. Are you serving me half-truths with the communion host?"

He flushed and shook his head. "Blood poisoning. Two weeks ago, she cut her foot on an iron rod sticking up through a tile on the floor of her cell. The prison doctor treated her. At first, it seemed like nothing, but gradually, she grew weaker, and one by one, her organs refused to work."

The marquis said, "She went peacefully, my child. I was at her bedside, along with our Father Jean and Marcelle Le Pont. Even the warden visited her."

The chaplain touched her fingertips lightly. "There is something else, my child. Your mother made a full confession and conversion during her years in prison. Though she was too old to become a nun, she spent her final years in service. By aiding the rebels, she decided to act on behalf of humanity. She fought for France against a tyrant who harmed the poor and innocent, so she fulfilled the mission of Saint Vincent de Paul and the Daughters of Charity."

Celeste sensed the holy medal tingle against the bare skin of her chest.

The marquis said, "I loved your mother so much, and she refused my ring for years, saying she wanted to be the bride of Christ, even though she was too old to take the veil. It took me a long time before she agreed to marry me."

"But wouldn't the Catholic Church excommunicate Maman for her acts against the emperor?"

Father Jean nodded, "It is true—her rebellious acts toward the emperor did not align with the values of the Catholic Church, but I believe her motives were pure and well-intentioned, bolstered by her own life of passion and suffering. Thus, she died in forgiveness and love."

The ship's bell clanged. "I must board the ship." The words grated in her throat.

The marquis pulled out a handkerchief and swept it across his eyes. "Indeed, you must. Go, child, and start your life anew. There is nothing more for you here in France."

"I wanted to bring Maman back to San Francisco with me—I shall always regret failing. Am I an utter disaster, Father?"

"No—no." The chaplain helped her to her feet. "You enacted your mother's wishes. You moved against a tyrant who is nothing but a devil to his people. Women cleaning their cupboards, bathing their children, and milking their cows are raising a silent cheer. Do you not see the results of your heroism?"

"I only hope that one day he will be removed from power."

The marquis said, "Forces greater than us will ensure that happens, but when and how is not up to us. When a tall building falls, the earth thunders for miles around. When the emperor falls—and believe me, he will— France will breathe the air of freedom. But only God knows when that will happen. And our country will suffer greatly."

Darkness crept over the land, and the clouds and sky merged into one gray mass. Try as she might, she could not get her hair to stay fixed under the shawl. The channel's fierce winds filled the sails, and the splashing water on deck formed slippery puddles rimmed with ice. But above decks, she would catch her final glimpse of the Normandy coastline as she passed.

Odéon stood behind her, his arms snug around her waist. "I do not want to risk losing you overboard."

She clung to the portside railing. "This may be the last time I see France, the country of my birth."

"The same for me, *mon amour.*" His voice faltered.

"We made it this far—then New York—the trip through Panama—and I cannot wait for you to meet Mei Li and let me show you all around San Francisco. I think Liliana will enjoy living there, though we will have to find work for her—and you."

"I can work as a blacksmith or stable hand. A growing city will need those services."

"I wish Liliana would come up and see the coastline." Liliana advanced toward them, mincing her steps like a binge drunkard, one step forward, another back, then to the side.

"What are you doing, youngster? And you do not have your coat on?" Odéon asked.

"I woke up from my nap." She pointed. "There it is! I did not want to miss it!"

A sailor barked. "Just there!"

Off the *North Star's* port side, the ship crept past Mont St. Michel, the towering Marvel, the statue of Saint Michel atop the church, the gray storm walls holding fast against the tides, the abbey prison fortress housing the doomed. Against a dark sky, the island rode the shimmering waves like a mysterious misshapen vessel. Set firmly on the mount, the church spire on the tower's highest point reached up into the heavens, a symbol of man's eternal search for God's presence, forgiveness, and love.

Celeste might have failed Maman. After stepping out of Odéon's arms, she leaned over the railing. She bent her face into the wind, letting it prick her face. "Even though I have lost you, I have gained Odéon and Liliana. I will carry on your work in service to humanity." Some waves splashed onto the deck, drenching her legs.

"Look there!" Odéon tapped her shoulder.

A strand of hair crossed her face, obscuring her view. She swept it away and followed his hand toward the east-facing windows of the prison fortress.

A lone light flickered in the darkness.

Author's Notes

Madam in Lace reflects the spirit and verve of Paris, Mont St. Michel, and Normandy as I found them on my visit in 2019. My various walking tour guides and companions took me to places that would feature strongly in the novel, such as a former brothel, Place Pigalle, Place du Tertre, Le Consulat Café. As I climbed the hilly places in Montmartre and looked down on Paris, it was easy to imagine Celeste and her friends as they lived in 1850s France.

At the palace of Compiègne, I visited the royal apartments where Louis Napoléon held his autumn court, and the interior and exterior sites mentioned were on my palace walking tour. Once again, it was not difficult to conjure up the bustle and furor as the servants prepared the court for their emperor's hunting festivities. Indeed, I located a daguerreotype that showed a royal party and guests arranged on the palace grounds, attired in buoyant white dresses as depicted in the novel.

The château in the novel is modeled after Château de Bouceel, where I stayed in Vergoncey. The structure dates from 1763, and it does belong to a marquis who regaled us of his family's stories and their ancestry. The building's interiors and grounds inspired references to the settings at the château as I found them.

Montmartre needs no introduction since it is one of the most visited tourist sites in the world. I spent a day hiking its battlements, examining its interiors, and sitting in the abbey cathedral on the mount at Mass. At the same time, the noonday sun brightened the clerestory windows amidst the chants of monks and nuns during the religious service. I could picture Madeleine in that spot at the moment when Celeste recognized her. Based on historical research, I learned what Madeleine's life would be like in prison, which inspired me to write her scenes.

Though the theater on Rue Peletier no longer exists, maps of Paris from that period assisted me in authenticating the route Celeste and her revolutionaries would have taken in preparation for the assassination attempt which occurred. The revolutionaries involved, Felice Orsini, Carlo di Rudio, and Thomas Allsop, did exist. After the assassination attempt, Felice faced trial and was executed by guillotine on March 13, 1858. Carlo di Rudio was sentenced to death, but his sentence was commuted. He went to Devil's Island prison, escaped, and later served in America's 7th Cavalry in the Civil War and survived Custer's Last Stand. He died in Pasadena, California in 1910. Thomas Allsop escaped imprisonment and fled to America, then returned to England, where he died in 1880.

Historical Works Consulted

Conflicts in French Society, Theodore Zeldin, ed. London: George Allen and Unwin, Ltd., 1970.

De Vazzani, Griscelli, *Memoirs of the Baron de Rimini, Secret Agent*, London: Remington & Co. Publishers, 1888.

Maneglier, Hervé. *Paris Imperial: La Vie Quotdienne sous le Second Empire.* Paris: Armand Colin Editeur, 1990.

Orsini, Felice. *Memoirs and Adventures of Felice Orsini*, Edinburgh: Thomas Constable & Co., 1857.

Richardson, Joanna. *La Vie Parisienne. 1852-1870.* New York: Viking Press, Inc., 1971.

Ravelle, Francoise. *Fastes et Rayonnement du Second Empire.* Paris: Editions Parigramme, 2016.

Straus-Schom, Alan. *The Shadow Emperor: A Biography of Napoleon III. New York: St. Martin's Press, 2018.*

Acknowledgments

My developmental editor in New York, Michael Mohr, provided apt comments and suggestions that helped me shape the story. My Elk Grove Writers and Artists writing class gave me the initial feedback and gentle encouragement that strengthened my novel. Members included Kathleen Torian Taylor, Bethany King, Liz Abess, Lisa Dornback, Evangeline Freathy, Carolyn Radmanovich, Loy Holder, Lorna Norisse, Sandra Heaton, and Judy Vaughan. My EGWA manuscript critique group parsed the pages and gave their most honest impressions that helped guide my revisions. Members included Mary Ann Bernard, Susan Wiedner, Emily Boyd, Sande Heaton, Sharon Darrow, and Carolyn Radmanovich.

I would also like to acknowledge my stalwart and patient traveling companions to France in 2019. Shannon Post and Judy Vaughan provided guidance and suggestions as we investigated the settings you will find in *Madam in Lace*. I owe them many thanks.

About the Author

Novelist and historian Gini Grossenbacher is one of California's respected and sought-after creative writing coaches and educators. She is a prominent literacy activist and developed an award-winning and innovative curriculum for the teaching of literature and the language arts in school districts and private academies across Northern California. Gini is a sought-after speaker and literary critic who has appeared in print and broadcast media on the subject of great authors and the joys of historical fiction.

Gini is a liberal arts graduate of Lewis & Clark College, one of the oldest institutions of higher education in the American West, has done postgraduate work in European history and Italian literature in ancient Perugia, and has a master's degree in educational governance from one of the nation's most important and prolific postgraduate campuses for school and university leadership.

Gini is also a lifelong forensic historian with a special hands-on interest in the recovery of women's narratives too often neglected in the stories nations and great cities tell about their origins. She has done in-place literary and historical research across five continents and wandered back alleys and elegant high streets from Bangkok and Kyoto to Singapore, from Mexico City and Martinique to Caracas, from London and Paris to Rome and the medieval hills and historic towns where Francis and Clare of Assisi reinvented European monasticism.

Madam of My Heart is Gini's debut novel, the first in *The American Madams* series. To learn more or request Gini as a speaker, go to *www.ginigrossenbacher.com.*

Made in USA - North Chelmsford, MA
1330483_9781735842769
09.06.2022 1708